YOU'VE GOT

Plaid

ELIZA KNIGHT

sourcebooks
casablanca

For my Disney princess crew.
You lassies mean the world to me.

Published by Sourcebooks Casablanca, an imprint of Sourcebooks
P.O. Box 4410, Naperville, Illinois 60567-4410
(630) 961-3900
sourcebooks.com

Printed and bound in the United States of America.
SB 10 9 8 7 6 5 4 3 2 1

Dear Reader,

When I first imagined the concept behind this series, I knew I wanted to create a cast of incredibly brave female heroines who would have to risk nearly everything for the good of their country and their future king. The Jacobite era of Great Britain's history is the last civil war fought on the united soils of Scotland and England, ultimately coming to rest in a rather tragic ending for many. Throughout the tumultuous years were born many heroes—dozens of which were women.

I wanted to incorporate their bravery, tenacity, and enthusiasm for their cause and their loyalty to a prince they wanted to be king, so I used many of their stories when creating those within this series. In *You've Got Plaid*, you will find Fiona's story to have a flavor of the lives of Flora Macdonald, Barbara Strachan, Anne Leith, and the countless unnamed women who risked their lives to deliver messages to their male Jacobite counterparts, mixed in with a generous helping of my imagination.

There is also a fun rumor that the Christmas carol "O Come, All Ye Faithful" was in fact a Jacobite call to arms, and that the line "come and behold Him, born the king of angels" was code for "come and behold him, born the king of the English"—who just so happened to be Bonnie Prince Charlie. Allegedly the Latin verse was actually a celebration of the prince's birth rather than of Jesus's, all connotation of which was lost when it was translated in the nineteenth century. Learning that his people were nicknamed angels, it seemed a fun theme to incorporate into the series: Prince Charlie's Angels.

I do hope you enjoy reading this book and the rest of the series as much as I have enjoyed writing it!

Best wishes,
Eliza

Prologue

MacBean Lands
Highlands, Scotland
Summer 1725

"What are ye doing?"

Fiona MacBean, second of four children born to Chief MacBean and his stronghearted bride, turned around to see her three siblings standing obstinately in a line, hands on hips, feet tapping.

Her elder brother had a knowing smirk on his face, as though he'd caught her red-handed. Her younger brother, Ian, was emulating Gus to a T, and sweet Leanna, the youngest of the brood, waggled her brows at Fiona in a way that meant she had a secret and was having a hard time keeping it in.

Fiona pulled her hands away from the gap in the tree and tried to clear her expression of anything other than annoyance.

"I'm just looking for eggs in a quail's nest."

"Nay, ye were no'. Just tell us what ye found." Gus narrowed his eyes, the same way their father often did.

"I told ye, the squirrel ran up the tree. He was running in a circle just here." Fiona zigzagged in front of the tree, and then hurried behind it before coming around the front and pretending to scurry up the bark.

"We know what ye do when ye come out to the woods," Ian said, looking up at Gus for approval.

"Aye, we know," Leanna added, not wanting to be left out.

Fiona crossed her arms and scowled. "The lot of ye are a bunch of storytellers."

"Och, who's telling stories now?" Gus said, taking a step forward.

Fiona clenched her hands, forgetting she held the slip of paper that had been folded neatly and shoved into the nook in the tree.

"Who's it from?" Ian asked.

"Read it to us," Leanna added.

"Hand it over. If ye dinna, we'll only be forced to take it from ye." Gus held out his hand.

At twelve years old herself, Fiona didn't often take orders from her brother, born just shy of eleven months before her. But if he were threatening to tackle her to the ground, that was something entirely different. Gus was bigger than her, having just shot up another four inches in the past summer. But she was faster...

Fiona took off at a run.

As a little girl, she'd spent a great deal of time running through the forest, her feet slipping on leaves, boots catching on roots. She'd hidden in the hollows of trees, leapt over fallen oaks, slid down embankments. There was no nook or cranny in the forest she'd not claimed as her own. And as much as her siblings tried to find her in every single one, they were not always successful.

Her father didn't like her traipsing off alone in the forest, especially not with the uprising. The damned loyalists, who she assumed were the English when he said it, had been a nuisance to all their hides for as long as she could remember.

Fiona had been born just a couple of years before the first Jacobite rising in 1715, and in fact, on her second birthday, her da had been away meeting with a war council along with other prominent Scots and titled men from England. Had fought beside old King James, and proudly showed his battle scars whenever he was a bit too deep in his cups. He'd been a sprite man of about twenty-five back then. There'd been a few more battles since, but none won, as yet. That didn't mean they were going to give up.

Every year, Fiona went with her father to a secret meeting of the lairds and earls and other warriors to discuss their latest plans. They thought she was off gallivanting with her friends and siblings, not paying attention. Which she mostly was, but she was also very good at spying, and so the children often had her listen in on the talks, then bring back the news of what she'd learned.

There was one particular lad who seemed keen on her skills. His name was Aeneas but he asked her to call him Aes, and he had a smile that could melt the heart of even a lass who spent more time than not irritated with lads, namely her brothers.

He'd caught her one of the days listening in on an important conversation.

She didn't see him in the hall with any of the other children, nor did she see him accompany any of the lairds. Aes was just as much a mystery to her as anyone else.

When she talked with her friends Jenny and Annie about him, they couldn't figure out who Aes was, either, so they spent their days and evenings searching out the boy with the soot-colored hair and a mischievous grin. But he only seemed to show up when Fiona least expected it, and when her friends weren't around, to prove he wasn't a ghost.

Every year she saw Aes, and their fondness for each other grew. Just this past spring, he'd told her he didn't want to wait until next year to see her again. Fiona suggested he write to her instead, to which he wrinkled his nose. If he was writing her letters, her father would want to know who he was, and he'd want to read them.

Fiona had asked what was wrong with her da knowing who Aes was, but he said it was best no one knew, so they'd sketched a map of the wood surrounding her family's small lands, and she'd drawn an X on the spot where there was a tree with a secret nook that she often hid pretty rocks in. If Aes could find it and leave her letters there, their friendship was meant to be.

She'd been checking that tree for months, and today was the

first time she'd found anything—a piece of folded paper, and she'd be damned if she was going to let one of her sticky-fingered siblings get their hands on it.

The calls of her siblings sounded behind her, and she laughed as she ran, dodging this way and that. They would be lucky to catch even the barest hint of her. She slid down an embankment, putting her heel out in just the right spot to stop herself on a root, and then launched onto her feet once more.

Fiona ran fast, her feet barely touching the ground, until she could no longer hear Gus, Ian, and Leanna behind her. And still she ran, until she felt certain she was alone.

She sat on the ground, a tree at her back, knees tucked up to her chest, and carefully unfolded the letter. It was short, the script scratchy, reminding her quite a bit of the way her brothers put chalk to tablet during lessons with their tutor.

She and Leanna were very lucky their father insisted they learn to read and write. Many young ladies she met at various feasts and festivals were not so lucky. In fact, her friend Jenny had to sneak lessons, and Annie was told by her da that if he agreed to let her learn, she couldn't tell anyone for fear it would make her less marriageable. Fiona thought that sounded awfully ridiculous. But what did she know? She was only twelve and didn't think much about marrying anyway.

Biting her lip, Fiona read what Aes had written in three crooked lines.

Dear F,

Have I found the right tree? For I've left a note in thirty-three.

                              Your devoted friend, A

Thirty-three? Oh, what a fun game it would be to find all thirty-three trees!

Fiona rounded the tree only to jerk back behind it. On the other side, only a few paces away, were three dragoons on foot who didn't seem aware yet of her presence. How had she not heard their approach? She must have been so engrossed in the letter.

Her breath caught. They'd looked to be grimy from weeks without bathing, their cheeks a bit hollowed from lack of food. They traversed the roads south of here, but never had she seen them in her wood.

Every cautionary word her father had given her tunneled back into her mind, and every argument she'd made to herself about how she would be fine mocked her.

I'm no' alone. She straightened her shoulders, willing her siblings *not* to find her. Four children wouldn't stand a chance against grown soldiers any more than she would, no matter how used up the men appeared.

Fiona chanced a glance. The men surveyed their surroundings, and the one in the center grinned, the cool blue of his eyes deadly. But it wasn't a happy grin, or one she ever wanted to see on anyone's face. The crimp of his mouth was vile, predatory, showing teeth that looked too big. He took a threatening step forward and she jerked back.

"You don't need to hide from us."

Fiona bit down hard on her tongue. They'd seen her. Every inch of her skin crawled to run, to hide, to fight.

"Ye're no' supposed to be here."

Goodness, nay! It was Gus, his proud voice calling out over the trees as if in warning to his siblings.

"Haven't you got a smart mouth," said one of the dragoons. "Do you know what we do with lads like you?"

A hand on her arm stopped Fiona from whirling out of her hiding place to protect her brother.

Ian stood in front of her, finger to his lips. Fiona searched behind him for Leanna but he mouthed the word *home.*

"I've an idea," Gus was saying. "But I'll no' be your sheep this night."

The dragoons sputtered with outrage, and from her hiding place Fiona heard a scuffle, Gus's cry of pain, and a guttural groan from one of the dragoons.

Ian pulled his slingshot from his belt and whipped a rock around the tree, hitting his mark by the sound of it. The distraction was enough to give Gus the extra seconds he needed to escape. The three of them took off like a shot, the dragoons shouting obscenities behind them as they gave chase.

In her peripheral vision, Fiona made out blood dripping from Gus's nose, but other than that, he appeared no worse for the encounter. They ran as fast as they could, leaping over fallen logs, scuttling under low-hanging branches, until the sounds of the ruffians in hot pursuit were nothing more than a fleeting memory.

Still, they didn't stop until they'd nearly reached home, met on the road by half a dozen of their father's men and Da himself, fully armed and expecting a fight.

"Where are they?" Da demanded.

Gus hooked his thumb behind him. "Back in the woods."

"How many?"

"Three."

"What have I told ye about being so far from home?" Though the question was asked of all three of them, his gaze centered on Fiona, and she knew that he meant it for her.

Fiona raised her chin but didn't argue.

"Get back to the castle with ye," their da ordered.

One of the guards peeled off from the contingent to follow them home as they ran, fearing the wrath of their father, but also praying he'd use that ire to eradicate the dragoons who'd dare to trespass.

In the courtyard of Dòchas Keep, their ancestral home, rumors flew back and forth about an attack on two of the clanswomen

who'd been doing laundry just that morning. A trio of dragoons—
and one with stone-cold blue eyes that reminded them of the dead.
How close had she come to suffering the same fate?

One

Dòchas Keep
Scottish Highlands
April 1746

"DINNA LEAVE THE CASTLE," IAN MACBEAN, INTERIM CHIEF OF the clan, demanded from the bailey, armed to the teeth for battle.

Fiona MacBean stared hard at her brother, taking in the way his lips were pressed so tight they were nearly white. His red hair, the same fiery color as her own, was tucked beneath his feathered cap which was set at a jaunty angle, softening the hard lines of his face and the determined furrow of his brow.

Fiona tossed her hair back with a slight shake of her head. There was no way in hell she was staying in the castle when there was vital information to be gathered and intelligence to be shared. Hell, the reason Ian was even headed off to war was because of her, which made her feel doubly guilty.

Ian's departure and subsequent insistence she stay home were rooted in a message she'd delivered several months prior to her brother Gus. It'd informed them that their baby sister Leanna's betrothed had hightailed it to the eastern shores of America with the dowry Gus had so graciously imparted on him early. A hefty amount of coin they couldn't afford to lose. *Bastard.*

The news was so mortifying to their clan that they'd kept it mostly secret, telling those who needed to know that Gus had escorted Leanna at the summons of her betrothed so the two of them might settle somewhere in Maryland, rather than that she and Gus were chasing him down. Which meant that Ian was now in charge of everyone in their clan—including her.

"Fiona, I mean it. Gus entrusted your safety and that of the clan to me while he's gone."

Ian didn't understand. He never had. And he'd spent entirely too much time looking up to Gus for answers rather than forming any of his own. Her work as a spy courier was as integral to their support of Prince Charlie as his work on the battlefield.

A shiver of fear raced down her spine. Her only consolation about Ian going to war was that he'd be with Jenny Mackintosh, Laird of Clan Mackintosh and charmingly named the Colonel by Bonnie Prince Charlie after she'd raised arms and her men succeeded in warding off the redcoats who wanted to take the prince's head.

It wasn't that Ian wasn't skilled at fighting. If anything, he was a damned beast on the field, but Fiona would feel better knowing he was with people she trusted, not some fools that might turn tail and run when the going got tough.

"Fiona?" Ian let go of his horse's reins and marched toward her. Too late, she realized how much she'd been in her own head rather than paying attention to her brother.

He reached her, pressing his hands to her shoulders, his deep-green eyes piercing into hers. "Please, for the love of all things holy, bloody well stay here. I canna have ye running about the countryside when I'm preoccupied with war."

"I've already *been* running about the countryside, and ye know it."

Fiona knew how to protect herself. Had made it her business to learn to fight against men bigger than her, so she'd not be made a victim. She was well versed in the use of daggers and knew which spots to hit to fell a man. The pins in her hair were also sturdy and sharp enough to inflict damage. More often than not, she could be found with daggers hidden horizontally in the layered leather of her belt, as well as in her boots. One could never be too prepared.

"Aye, but at least then I could come to your aid if ye need me."

He pressed his lips together, and the recollection of how close they'd come to being attacked by dragoons over the years sat heavy between them. "I canna save ye if I'm in a bloody battle."

She didn't need saving, but she wasn't about to make him worry about her while he had dragoon pistols pointed at him. Better to placate her brother now and apologize later.

"Aye, fine, Ian. I'll stay put. But ye better come back, else I'll be angrier than a stuck pig that ye made me rot in this keep while ye went away to have all the fun."

Ian sighed with great relief and rolled his eyes. "I'll come back, I promise."

"Good. Because if ye die, I swear I'll kill ye all over again."

Ian laughed at the line the four siblings had been repeating to one another since their first encounter with dragoons in the woods so long ago.

"Until we meet again, wee sister."

"I'm older than ye." Fiona slugged him in the chest, not hard enough to hurt.

Ian grinned. "But ye're still smaller." He danced backward away from her, out of reach of her swinging hands.

"I'll spare ye the energy now, because we both know the Colonel is going to run ye ragged, but when ye return, Brother, we're going to spar."

Ian pointed at her and nodded. "Ye can count on it." He leapt up onto his horse and issued orders to their men.

The summons to join Jenny's army had directed them not too far from MacBean lands. Prince Charles Stuart—the regent for his exiled father, and rightful heir to the Scottish throne which had been usurped by Hanoverians—had set up camp at Culloden House. This had forced Duncan Forbes, owner of the house, to either rally with the Jacobites or run. Fiona couldn't understand why a Scot *wouldn't* want their natural king to take his place.

Having grown up surrounded by men focused on the return

of the Stuart line, it came naturally to her. So unsurprisingly, she'd kept up a childhood pact with her two dearest friends to do everything in their power to make certain the prince regained his rightful place.

Jenny was a natural leader and soldier, Annie a healer. And Fiona, well, she'd learned subterfuge early on, and she had an excellent memory. Relaying messages from one Jacobite camp to another had been a skill honed as a girl and now had earned her the nickname of the Phantom because of it. She was proud of the work she'd done for the prince. Proud that he'd taken note of it as well.

"Be well!" Fiona called out to the men as they crossed under the gate, waving her arm and watching until the very last of them had disappeared down the road.

She waited an hour.

That seemed a sufficient amount of time to allow to pass before she changed out of her day gown and into her sturdier traveling wool.

"Going, my lady?" Beitris had been her lady's maid since they were both fifteen years old. There was an eager look about her eyes, as she'd begged on more than one occasion to go with Fiona, but the risk was too great. Traveling through the woods alone was dangerous enough. Taking a maid along would slow her down. There was also the fact that even the sight of a wee mouse had Beitris screaming and running for the nearest chair.

"Aye. The duty of a postmistress calls." Of course, being a postmistress was the perfect position in which to conduct business in a more clandestine fashion. The dragoons tended to leave her be if they saw her delivering mail, as she was officially appointed by the royal government. It allowed her to roam freely, but it wasn't always a safeguard either—especially since she used it as a cover to deliver rebel messages.

"What of your brother's order?"

Fiona raised a brow. "The prince himself named me one of his most loyal messengers." And he'd given her a ring to prove it. She glanced down at the simple round cabochon emerald on her right middle finger. Any message delivered from the prince clearly could not contain his signature or seal, but a simple presentation of this ring denoted that she carried his official business.

Which was why she had to get herself to Culloden House and the battlefield.

"Stay safe, my lady. Ye've told your brother much the same, but as ye oft leave in secret, no one has been able to tell ye as much."

"I will." Fiona pulled Beitris in for a hug. "I've kept myself alive this long, have I no'?"

"This is true."

Like everyone else in their clan, Beitris worried what ill could befall Fiona while on the road. The royal postmistress badge could only take her so far and wasn't a guaranteed free pass from a ruffian, be he an outlaw, a dragoon, or a drunkard.

Fiona didn't fear the repercussions for herself, but rather for the men in her life because of what they might do to protect her honor. Her father—God rest his soul—had been horrified when she first took the position and had passed his fears on to her brothers. Any of them would have gone to battle and died for her, and their deaths would be forever on her head, which was why she was damn careful whenever she left the house.

She didn't want men to die for her. She wanted them to fight for the *cause*. And so she'd bid her father and her siblings to allow her to keep her postmistress position for the sake of their country. They'd agreed on one condition, and that was if she ever found herself at the end of a dragoon's pistol, she would quit. Fiona agreed, and she didn't regret that decision. Nor did she regret not telling them when such occasions occurred. They all had to do their part, and this was hers.

Remaining quiet allowed her father to fight many a battle,

keeping their family safe, until he'd finally fallen on a beach in the north when a government ship fired a cannon at the gathered warriors.

Destroyed by the loss of her husband, Fiona's mother had withdrawn even from her own children, and several summers past went to live with her sister in Orkney. She didn't even write, not wanting a memory of her life at Dòchas, which Fiona tried not to take personally, though in truth she felt quite abandoned. The loss of both of her parents so quickly put her into a melancholy from which she couldn't seem to pull herself out.

It was actually a missive that Gus brought her from her old friend Aes that caused her to rise up and believe in herself once more.

Over the mountain of fear is your dream attained.

Aes would never know how that simple phrase changed her life. How she lived every day with it racing through her brain. Because though she was brave and though she risked much, she was not without fear. Not reckless as some might accuse her. She was crossing the *mountain of fear* and reaching for her dream—a better, safer Scotland, ruled by the Stuart line as it should have been since before she was born.

So although she understood fear, she wasn't going to be ruled by it. Fiona was going to be the conqueror of all the things that terrified her. The conqueror of everything that stood in the way of what she wanted and cared about.

She'd made a pact with her friends, with herself, to stand up to the blasted dragoons and wouldn't let a little thing like fear stand in the way. And so she'd traveled to the secret meetings of the lairds, though her da was no longer present. She offered her services as a courier to them, and with the help of Aes, and out of respect for her departed da, had made it happen. Though most of the men at first thought to send her on fool's errands, she quickly proved she was not the wee idiot many believed her to be.

With a thick cloak, gloves, and an extra pair of hose covering her feet in sturdy boots, Fiona slipped out of the castle unnoticed. The air was frigid and the sky gray. Soon it would either snow or pelt frozen ice onto their heads. She was guessing the latter. She slinked around the guard's blind spots until she crossed the forest edge.

Normally, she would have taken a horse, but given she didn't want anyone to know she'd left right after her brother's very public proclamation that she should stay, and her destination was only a few hours' walk away, she chose to take the path on foot.

To some, a forest was a vast and haunting place, dark and shadowed, littered with two- and four-legged creatures that could just as easily do harm as ignore a body's presence. Within the wood there were spaces to hide, places to leap out from. There were nooks to curl up inside and high-altitude places from which to observe the world. The forest was at once peaceful as it was chilling.

Fiona felt at home in the forest, even when the green of the pines had turned into glistening gray icicles. The place housed her greatest triumphs and had the potential to harbor her worst nightmares.

Having grown up with a wood surrounding her clan, she'd become quite intimate with the way roots looped from the ground, and which trees would give her hives, and which would give her shelter. She knew paths to get to the surrounding clans and could peer through the leaves at the top even in the height of summer to see the sky, and then would know which direction to take.

Since she was a girl, she'd expanded her forest knowledge, recognizing landmarks and remembering events that had taken place. For example, the route from Dòchas Keep to Cnàmhan Broch, the castle of her dear friend Jenny, held a path she'd not traversed since she was twelve years old, the day they'd run into the dragoons.

And she hadn't let running the forest end when she'd become a woman. If anything, she considered herself an expert in forestry. An expert in people too.

When danger was afoot, Fiona either made herself invisible, or she made the ones who messed with her disappear. Sometimes, just from her own memory.

There was a reason she'd been gifted with the name Phantom.

Fiona liked to think she was the most well-versed at keeping herself hidden. Even when in plain sight. She was a master at her trade and had dozens of costumes that she could don, voices that she could use, and various personas that she plucked out of her basket. But when she wasn't dressed in costume, she was aware of how she turned heads. It was one of the reasons she kept her fiery hair in a cap. The flaming-red color often garnered notice, as did her unusual eyes. They were a color of blue that was nearly violet.

Men and women alike called her beautiful. She wanted to be flattered by that, but in the end, she also didn't want anyone to remember her.

Thinking of that, Fiona shoved her red hair farther into her cap. Powder smeared on her face paled the natural flush to her skin and hid the smattering of freckles over her nose that everyone thought was adorable. She'd smeared coal beneath her eyes to give her a more tired look, not that it was truly needed. She sported exhausted circles any time of day or night, for she only slept in short snatches. When this war was over, when Prince Charles was back on the throne, she'd sleep for days.

Until that time, she had to keep moving forward.

Never stop.

Tonight, she was dressed as a healer. Her frock torn in a few places, stains on the front apron to look as though she'd been elbows deep in a man's guts, and a basket looped over her arm filled with herbs and vials, she continued on. Inside the tiny bottles were various tinctures that she had mixed herself—poisons, if truth be told. If she were to administer these tinctures to anyone, they would find themselves feeling a bit ill. Or dead.

Fiona wasn't a violent type, despite the knives and poisons. She would much prefer to avoid any sort of conflict or confrontation whatsoever.

If she were stopped by a dragoon along her postmistress route, she typically pled her duty to the mail, batted her lashes, and went on her way. But that was by day. During the night, things were a bit different, hence the costume. If caught now, they'd question why she was traveling alone at night, and she'd say because the ill did not wait for sunup, and she couldn't wait for an escort when someone could be dying.

But being that it was night, the darkness helped to keep her hidden. Not that they'd have any easier time finding her during the day. Fiona's costumes were always muted browns and greens to help her blend in with the foliage of the forest or hedges lining a road, and the moors if she were lying in the thick grasses.

As a child, she'd been an expert at playing seek and find. In fact, her siblings could not get her to come out even when their mother was demanding their return. One of her favorite games was to sneak out of her hiding spot while they were in a panic, rush home, and be seated at the table having a bite to eat when one of them finally reappeared. This used to drive them all crazy, and she rather liked doing that—well, at least driving her brothers into a rage. More often than not, she tried to spare Leanna.

Wasn't that the job of every younger child? To make one's older sibling go a bit mad?

She smiled thinking about it now as Culloden House finally came into view.

Straightening her shoulders, she prepared to present herself to Prince Charles. The men recognized her as she walked through the courtyard and into the house, nodding with respect, and she in turn greeted them the same.

The prince was at the dining room table, which was spread out with maps, scouring the area.

"This ground here." He pointed to a spot on the map.

"'Tis surrounded by bogs," his advisor Murray responded.

The prince grinned, showing off a bonnie dimple in his cheek. "All the better for the dragoons to get stuck in."

Murray, it appeared, was immune to the smile that made many women swoon. "But it may end up hindering our men as well."

The prince looked up then, his blue eyes alighting on Fiona. He truly was a bonnie fellow, almost too soft-looking to be planning a battle. The prince straightened, and Fiona curtsied.

"You've returned, mistress. Good. I've a stack of messages awaiting your dispatch."

"Your Highness," she said.

"MacDougall, give her the coin pouch."

One of the prince's men approached with a heavy purse, her payment for services rendered.

"Any news?" the prince asked.

"Cumberland's men are on the move. They've been sighted near the Grampians."

The prince nodded. "Good. Then he brings his men to their death." He came forward and presented her with his hand, and Fiona bent to kiss his ring.

When she rose, he was grinning at her, a dazzling smile that would no doubt win over many a woman, but not her. Fiona was about one thing—the mission. Falling for a man, especially one as unattainable as the prince, would be disastrous.

"You have been instrumental in all of this, Mistress MacBean. We could not be where we are without you. Do not forget that. Your loyalty has been noted and you will be rewarded."

The heavy coin pouch in her hand and knowing she was helping to thwart dragoons were payment enough. But if the prince wanted to give her more, perhaps offer her and her brothers a place at his court when he was finally sitting on the throne in Edinburgh and London, she would not dissuade him.

Three days later…

Fiona hopped over a fallen log, slick with ice, and then stilled at a movement some distance to her left. Gingerly she eased toward the sound, peering through thick lines of pine. A troop of men, but not dragoons, rather Highlanders. They thought themselves silent, and they mostly were to anyone of normal aptitude for spying and hiding, but not to Fiona.

She crouched down, closed her eyes, and turned her face toward the sky.

Men were on the move, slowly but deliberately, heading back toward Culloden if she were to hazard a guess. But they shouldn't be. That was not the plan. Why were they headed that way?

She'd been given a missive from the prince to deliver to the men at Nairn, that reinforcements were catching up but had been waylaid. From the sounds of it, the army from Nairn was returning before she'd had a chance to deliver the news. She'd not been dallying either. Something must have happened.

"Blast it all," she muttered under her breath.

Fiona darted to her left, ducking beneath tree limbs, dodging roots and fallen branches, and yanking her skirts from clawing brambles, pausing every so often to listen to the sounds of the men. She finally spied them, moving shadows mixed with the other obscurities of the night.

She searched their chests for glints of moonlight on brass buttons that would indicate she'd come across a troop of dragoons instead of the Highlanders she'd assumed to be there. But there was no glint, and the shape of their caps had her believing for certain now that they were Jacobites, solidifying her fear that they'd turned around from Nairn.

Still, she remained careful as she orchestrated a path to collide with theirs in a way that seemed completely natural, so as to avoid being fired upon or in case she was wrong about who they were. And believing them to be rebels, she plucked the Royal Postmistress pin from her jacket so as not to confuse them be they strangers to her.

Fiona met the soldiers at the front, standing in the center of the road like an apparition. The lot of them drew up at the sight of her there, a few gasping. Most wore kilts and boots, and even in the night, she could make out the shape of caps on their heads. Definitely Highlanders. Most likely Jacobites.

"Is it a sprite?" one man asked, followed by jeers and a few whispered confirmations.

Fiona rolled her eyes, knowing that in the dark they'd not be able to see quite that well.

When no other men stepped forward, Fiona opened her mouth to speak, only to see a tall Highlander shift from a few men back and come to stand before the group.

"What are ye doing in the road?" His voice was low, gravelly. Tired and irritated.

Was he the leader of this pack?

"I could ask ye the same thing." This was not the response the man would be expecting, and that was all right. She didn't often do what people were expecting, and she still stood strong.

"Move aside, we've no business with a woman roaming in the middle of the night. Ye could only be up to one thing—and we're no' interested."

Fiona suppressed a derisive snort. It would not be the first time someone had accused her of being a whore, or tried to make her into one. Rather than take offense to it, she pitied the man lobbing the accusation, for truly was that the only thing he could come up with for a woman roaming the roads? Sad.

"'Tis a good thing my house is no' on fire, or my entire family massacred, for ye'd be of no help." She tossed her head gently, feigning affront.

The man's stance shifted, a sign of guilt, but he said nothing. Lord, he was big. A head taller than most of the other men, and easily twice as broad as herself.

Though it was hard to see just where he was looking or the expression on his face, the way the hair on the back of her nape prickled she instinctively knew he was staring her down. Examining her as hard as she was examining him.

"Did they send ye?" he asked.

This was a tough question, because he could mean the men who had actually sent her or the dragoons she'd just alluded to.

"Who would send me to ye? Do I know ye, sir?"

The man grunted, a sound that was an answer at the same time it wasn't.

"We've no' met afore," he said. "I dinna know of any women who roam the forest at night."

She would have brought up the healer disguise, except that doing so might lead to him asking for help and any help she gave would be more detrimental to his men than not. Though she'd watched Annie work on men any number of times, Fiona had never quite picked up the skills for healing. And she didn't really care to. She could sew a stitch if needed, but the lines would be jagged, and she'd have nothing to ease the pain, nor any salves to make sure infection didn't set in.

Well, they'd wasted enough time with unpleasantries. She had about thirty seconds or less to establish trust with this stranger in order to relay her message.

"It is no' without purpose that we meet upon the road, though I expected it to be closer to Nairn," she started.

A few men drew their swords, immediately jumping to the wrong conclusion.

"That is no' necessary." She set her basket down and held out her hands. "I am unarmed." She eyed their alleged leader and said the one line that would prove who they were. "God Bless the King."

"And his bonnie son," the soldier replied.

Good. She didn't smile, though she might have under different circumstances. Instead, she reached for her sleeve, and now the large man put his hand to the hilt of his sword. She pulled out the silver coin she carried with her, tucked into a secret pocket of her leather bracer, a token that every Jacobite would recognize. On one side was the royal arms of Scotland and on the other was the face of Prince Charles. Jacobite coins in one's possession could get the bearer killed. But they were also a currency that those loyal to the prince understood well. Not until she was certain who these men were would she dare to flash the emerald, which was now secured on a chain around her neck and tucked into the bodice of her gown.

"Catch," she said smoothly, tossing the coin in his direction, not that surprised when he caught it in the dark.

"I canna see it."

"Ye know what it is."

"Aye."

"Then ye know we are no' enemies."

He grumbled something inaudible in response and there were a few gasps among the men. He tossed the coin back, and she returned it to the slit in the leather bracer up her sleeve. Then he held out his hand.

"The message."

"I've got nothing to hand to ye, sir," Fiona said. "Ye need to listen."

This was something she'd learned a long time ago. If the package to be delivered by and for rebels was something she could memorize, then she did so. It was less risky for all parties involved that way, especially her. However, there were plenty of other, more conspicuous deliveries she had to make which required incredible caution, especially when they were potentially mixed with the Royal Mail.

The group seemed to be holding their collective breath, waiting.

When he didn't step away from his men, she said, "Are ye in charge of this regiment?"

He turned and eyed the men behind him, who nodded. Why in the world did he need their affirmation?

"Aye," he grumbled.

"Then if ye would, please be so kind as to step away so I might make good on my delivery, for I will only whisper it in your ear."

"And what if your delivery is a knife through my heart?"

Fiona laughed, the sound tinkling and innocent, one of her other weapons. She'd learned long ago, surrounded by her father's men in the great hall, that her laugh not only brought smiles to others but also acted as a siren's call of sorts.

"Sir, I've no weapon in my hands as I've shown ye, and given your size…" She moved her hands in front of her indicating the distance from his feet all the way up to his head—showing him both her empty hands as well as complimenting his physique, though she could barely see it. "I canna imagine that ye have much to fear from me."

"Perhaps it is those ye travel with."

"I am alone." She kept her voice steady, devoid of any fear or inflection that might cause him to worry. "I come with a missive from Himself."

"God?"

She rolled her eyes. "I canna decide if ye're toying with me, sir, or if perhaps ye were no' meant to have the position that has been bestowed upon ye."

He snickered quietly, but she could hear it all the same, and then he stepped away from his men, and she took several steps backwards, with him following.

"What if I'm no' a part of the regiment ye think I am?" The low rumble of his voice, edged with something akin to teasing, skated over her spine in a way she dared not identify as pleasant.

"Are ye no'?"

"Nay, but I am curious how ye'd get out of it."

"A lass never divulges her secrets."

"Except the ones she's duty bound to reveal."

"Aye, but those are no' secrets to keep to myself, but wish to be disclosed to the right ear."

"Hmm." He stared at her silently for a moment and then demanded, "Tell me."

They were two dozen or so paces away from the men now. "I must first know your name."

"Why?" He sounded irritated.

"It is a requirement."

"Whose?" He crossed his arms over his chest, showing her, even in the dark, just how broad and strong he was.

Fiona wasn't intimidated. Even the biggest men could be bested if put to her test. "Mine."

"And if I dinna wish to give it?"

She shrugged. "Then I canna perform my duty and we've wasted enough time already."

"I am wasting your time?" It came out as an exasperated question, and also somehow a statement. The man was perplexing.

"Aye."

"Hmm."

Fiona was done playing games. "Name."

"Brogan Grant."

"Thank ye for that. Now lean close."

He did as she instructed, bending until his head was close to hers, and she was all too aware of how close his lips were to her mouth. Fiona drew in a silent breath, holding it, then with her finger on his chin, turned his face away.

She leaned in closer until her lips were a mere whisper from his ear, and she breathed in his woodsy, masculine scent, again feeling that strange tingling along her spine.

Get on with it, Fiona.

"The chevalier's army is lagging behind, but shall be with ye shortly." Rather than calling him the prince, she used his nickname.

"Whose army?" He turned toward her as he spoke, his breath on her face, and she lurched back both shocked at how close his mouth had been to her skin and that he was daft enough to question who she spoke of.

"Your prince."

"We were told to turn back."

"I can only give ye the message I received. He was no' aware of your orders to return, only that he was to meet ye there and was delayed."

"I have to follow orders."

Fiona sighed. Why did men have to argue so much? "I understand."

"Will ye give him a message for me?"

"Aye," she said wearily.

"Tell him that we've been told to turn back. No sense in meeting us in a place we will no' be."

"Done."

"And what is your name, lass?"

"Why?"

"Because it is a requirement," he said, brandishing her own words back at her.

Fiona smiled. "Alas, it is no' a requirement of mine, and better for ye no' to know." Fiona started to back away. "Good luck, sir."

"How will I know ye gave him the message?"

"Because his regiment will no' be far behind ye when ye're back at Culloden."

"How do ye know that's where we're headed?" He had the temerity to sound suspicious.

"'Tis my business to know the whereabouts of men."

"Hmm," he grunted again, a sound that was seemingly synonymous with his personality, and sent a curious frisson through her brain. She didn't like that.

The man had moved her in a way that no one had before, and she didn't even know him. Couldn't trust that he wouldn't do wrong by her, by anyone. He could have even lied about his name. What did she know?

Needing to put distance between them, Fiona hurried backward into the foliage at the side of the road, concealed herself, and then watched him. He stood there for several breaths, staring at where she'd just been before turning back to his men.

Fiona raced back the way she'd come, her muscles aching only when she was nearly upon the prince and his men some miles away. She was used to running great lengths and doing it quickly, but that did not mean she didn't suffer from time to time.

She relayed Grant's message to the prince, and climbed upon the horse they offered to give herself a moment's reprieve. There was a plummeting feeling in her gut, accompanied by the very air seeming to swell and contract, as though the earth itself experienced the dread she did. A warning, perhaps, of terrible things to come.

The men had been on their way to Nairn to mount a surprise attack on Cumberland's army, but with multiple regiments being recalled to Culloden, the surprise attack that would have given them an advantage did not seem to be the way things would be going. All the needless walking was bound to tire the men out, and to be tossed from one battleground to the next had to be hard on their morale.

A tired and downtrodden army would have a hard time beating a legion of bloodthirsty maniacs.

The Jacobites had won several battles before, facing off against the royalist army's retinue of dragoons. At this point, Cumberland simply wanted to annihilate them all. To murder them in their sleep.

She'd listened to Cumberland speak to his men one night, disguised as a loyalist wench in a tavern of secret Jacobites, serving ale and letting them pinch her bottom before disappearing with a stolen pouch full of their coin. Cumberland was an arsehole. And violent beyond anything she'd ever seen. There was a deep-seated anger in the man and a hatred for Scots that went beyond the normal animosity most English had for her people. It was like staring the devil in the face when she'd looked at him. And the way he'd stared back at her so blankly with beady eyes, as though she were nothing, not even the shite on the heel of his boot, had sent a bone-chilling fear racing through her.

Rumors whispered across the moors that Cumberland swore he was not going to lose again, no matter what it took for him to wave his victory flag. A sight that an overactive imagination brought careening to the front of her mind. It was enough to make her knees go weak.

Was it wishful thinking to pray that her dear friend Jenny would go home and leave the fighting to others? That her brother Ian could just return to Dòchas Keep and everyone would go about their lives as usual? It was hypocritical for Fiona to even think it, for she would never do the same. She buried her hands in the fur blanket one of the prince's men draped over her lap, some of the ice in her bones starting to melt.

Fiona knew the answer. Jenny wasn't a quitter. Ian wouldn't turn tail and run. And *life as usual* was a battle to the death. Jenny had spent years raising an army, weapons, and funds for the prince. She wasn't going to give up because Fiona told her it was too dangerous. Fiona could hear Jenny now, saying something like *"The reason I'm doing this is because of the danger. We need to recover our rightful king and our lands."*

The stakes were rising. The danger was closer to home. Already so many she loved had suffered and lost. There was no telling how much more they were going to be made to give. Or how much longer they could go on fighting.

Fear and worry were making Fiona question everything.

Two

THE AIR WAS ACRID AND SOUR WITH THE SCENT OF BURNING flesh and gunpowder. Men were screaming, clawing their way along ground slick with blood and icy rain as they searched for a way to escape the horror.

Brogan Grant, bastard son of Chief Grant, tried to give as many of his men as he could that very thing—an escape. Slicing and cutting. Bashing his body when necessary against dragoons so Grant men could stumble away from the swords and bayonets and guns. Cannon fire detonated all around them, the massive missiles exploding into the ground from every angle, tearing limbs from men and horses alike.

He wasn't officially a military leader, didn't hold a title. Nay, Brogan Grant was just another bastard born of a powerful man, with a will as unbending as steel. That unwavering grit had gotten him to where he was now. Men respected him, expected him to take the lead. Just like in the predawn hours of this morning when they'd run into that wench in the forest. Brogan wasn't the leader of the regiment, but he'd been the only man to respond. Their own leader had been growing restless, angry, and irritated. Refusing to take the lead as he should, and just expecting Brogan to pick up the slack because he was their laird's son.

Government troops were getting closer, breaking through the line of Highlanders. The Colonel—Jenny Mackintosh—fought with her men nearby, and shouted to a lad, "MacBean! Take 'em out."

She expected one man to take out a dozen or more government troops? And a MacBean at that? The bloody bastards had been the enemy of his clan for generations it felt like.

Brogan watched as the warrior peeled away from the men and filled the gap between Highlanders and government troops in a whirlwind of hacking, taking out one after another as they flew at him like wasps. Rivalry or not, they were in this fight together. Brogan joined the MacBean warrior, giving the Highlanders enough time to regain momentum as they fought. Within a breath, the other men in the regiment joined the fray, pushing back the government troops.

"Go!" Brogan shouted to a man at his feet who'd stumbled. He leapt over his back, thrusting his sword into the dragoon about to skewer him with the end of his bayonet.

The dragoon fell, and Brogan rounded on the dead man's friend, thrusting his blade deep. The time for reflection ended as he made his way through a batch of whoresons. But there were too many. The Highlanders were weakened from months of campaigning with little food and even less rest.

"Fight!" Brogan shouted. "Dinna surrender!"

But no matter how loudly he shouted, his fellow Jacobites continued to fall around him like the droplets of icy rain pelting against their faces.

Another cannon fired, and the earth sprayed up around his shoulders. *Bloody hell!* That was close.

Highlanders fell.

They ran.

The number of men around him in red coats increased, as did the stains of red at their feet. He found himself further separated from the fighting men he knew until he was surrounded by only men in red.

Those who weren't being murdered were being hauled away. Prisoners? The number of Highlanders around him dwindled as they succumbed to one of those two fates, or they retreated.

There would come a point when he couldn't take them all on his own. Brogan cursed under his breath, his feet retreating before he could even think to back away, his body going into self-preservation.

Where was the prince?

He turned around and around, fighting off redcoats as he searched the field, not seeing the prince or his white horse. Had he fallen? Where was Captain Shea, commander of the prince's bodyguard?

*Dammit…where was *he*?*

Brogan Grant had joined the fight for two reasons. One, he loved Scotland and he didn't want to see it destroyed by a bunch of red-coat-wearing bastards. Two, he truly believed that Prince Charles Stuart was the rightful heir to the throne.

This was as much about Protestant king versus Catholic king as it was Scots versus English, an age-old fight that should have been resolved when Queen Elizabeth handed over the English throne to her Scottish nephew. But here they were again, fighting a battle that had begun before Brogan was even born.

"Die, Scot scum!"

Brogan whirled to find a pistol pointed right at his forehead, and behind that, the sneer of a pale face flecked with droplets of blood.

There was no time to respond with any number of insults he could pluck from his head, because the dragoon was pulling the trigger.

Fuck.

Nothing happened. Brogan blinked, and so did the man, surprised that his pistol had not just blown a hole through Brogan's head.

"God has other plans, I see," Brogan said, and thrust his sword through the man's gut, twisting and then pulling it out.

The dragoon fell, his pistol firing toward another dragoon who fell from the impact.

Holy shite. Brogan had been spared. He stared skeptically up at the sky, questioning the move of a God he wasn't sure he believed in, but didn't waste time retreating from the advancing dragoons.

As he ran, something caught his line of vision, a targe, the prince's shield he'd been presented with before the battle by the Duke of Perth. The head of Medusa in its center was what drew his attention, for it was a unique piece. Worse, however, was that jutting from beside one of her slithering snakes was an arrow. Brogan stopped short, eyes scanning the surrounding bodies, but seeing none so bonnie as their prince. He scooped up the targe, breaking off the arrow.

Targe in hand, Brogan charged toward the woods from whence they'd emerged before battle, searching for any men he could find that were from his own regiment or clan or a Jacobite. With several Grants in tow and a few newcomers, he ended up gathering six as he went, each of them unwilling to leave the battlefield despite the overwhelming color of scarlet flowing in the trampled grass—the blood of their fellow men and the living, breathing redcoats.

They ran until they were all out of breath, cramps filling their sides, and then he stopped, staring at the men and realizing he was only familiar with a few of them.

"I'm Brogan," he said, through gasps of air, patting his chest. Saints but his sides were burning. When was the last time he'd slept? "We need to get to the prince."

One of his clan's men spoke next. "Dugall Grant. Aye, we should check Culloden House." Scrawniest among the Grants, yet somehow he'd escaped the dragoons' blades. Brogan guessed that must have been because Dugall was quick, though he was sporting a swollen eye, and flecks of blood on his face indicated where shrapnel had sprayed into his skin.

"Sorley MacLeod." A man raised his hand, showing up bloodied knuckles. MacLeod eyed him the same way Brogan did most, with an air of arrogance and suspicion. Brogan liked him already. "I dinna think the prince would go back there."

"Keith Grant." A distant cousin of Brogan's, the man had a deep gash in his shoulder, the blood having soaked his shirt. "This bloody hurts. But I agree, we should check the house first, just in case any of his men might know where the prince would head next."

Brogan nodded to Dugall. "Tie up that wound on him to stop the bleeding. We dinna need a man to fall while we're running."

"James Stuart." The man to Keith's left spoke, coloring a bit red as they all swiveled their heads toward him. "My mother used to work in the castle for the Stuarts. A relation. Anyway, I agree, go to the house."

"Are ye saying…ye're a bastard?" Brogan couldn't finish the thought, not wanting to ask outright if the man was related to the prince.

"I'm a bastard," James offered but said nothing further. He didn't look much like Prince Charles or the king, but that didn't mean anything. He could take after his mother.

"Fin O'Malley. Not a bastard, not a Scot, though there's nothing wrong with that. I, too, say we go to the house. And," he indicated his shoulder, "I could use some help putting this bastard back in its socket."

"We welcome the Irish among us. Gladly." Brogan stepped forward and gripped Fin by the elbow of his healthy arm and helped him to the ground. "This is going to hurt. Are ye ready?"

"Ready as ever."

Brogan made quick work of bringing Fin's arm forward and then up over his head, the loud popping noise nearly drowned out by Fin's growl of pain.

"Better?" Brogan asked.

"Aye, thank ye."

Brogan helped him up. "Hold the arm close. We'll make ye a sling when we get to the house."

Brogan nodded to the last of them. "And ye? What's your name?"

"Charles Stuart." He winced. "My mother prayed I'd be as bonnie as our prince, but she didna rut with the king, if anyone is interested in knowing that. James is my cousin. I say the prince is likely no' there, but we may be able to gather information, at the verra least a horse or two." The top of his ear was bleeding, where he'd been nicked by a bullet from the look of it.

"All right, to the house then. I agree he's likely no' there, but we may be able to find out where he is. We need to find him and protect him. As far as I can tell, he didna fall on the field." He relayed how he'd found the targe with the arrow protruding from it, displaying it for them to see, and explained that there was no body attached.

"I saw him head this way with his guard," James said. "'Tis why Charles and I ran, so we could protect him. But we lost sight of him in the fray."

"We'll go search Culloden House first."

Without horses, their travel was going to be difficult. But perhaps they'd find a few spares at the prince's headquarters that they could borrow. Hell, steal was a better way of putting it because they certainly weren't going to be returning them anytime soon.

Without another word, the men set off, running without pausing despite the cramps in their muscles, the icy rain freezing their blood, the minor injuries they'd suffered, and the burning ache in their lungs.

As they drew closer to the prince's headquarters, muffled shouts sounded from the inner courtyard. Bloody hell, were they too late? Had the dragoons beaten them here?

Brogan let out a curse and picked up his pace, the men following suit.

Expecting to see the place swarming with redcoats, he was surprised to see that despite the shouts from behind the low curtain wall, it looked deserted. The ostentatious stone building was perched on a hill, looking rather grand for what used to be a military fortress. Its windows were black and splattered with rain, the gates wide open as if expecting its occupants' imminent return, or as though someone had simply thrown them wide—or forced themselves inside.

A woman's scream rent the air, followed by a man's guttural bellow.

"Shite!" Brogan burst through the gate with his men behind him to discover not a woman, but a lad, in loose breeches and a worn, thin shirt and frock coat. The youth's overly long red hair was fisted in the hand of a bastard dragoon in what looked to be a struggle to the death for the both of them.

Poor house servant had likely been accosted by the dragoon while trying to escape. There did not appear to be any other redcoats around, but Brogan wouldn't put it past them to fall from the sky like rain, sneaky bastards.

Neither the lad nor the dragoon seemed to notice the seven warriors who'd entered the courtyard, and though Brogan only paused for a brief moment, it was enough to assess that the lad could likely handle his own. He opened his mouth to scream again in a sound that could perforate a man's eardrums, and then reached back to grab at the dragoon's hand where it yanked mercilessly in his hair. The dragoon's other hand tore at the front of the lad's frock coat.

As Brogan ran forward to free the boy from the clutches of the devil, metal glinted from the lad's hand as he swung it from his hair toward the dragoon's neck, slamming it hard. Rivulets of red spilled over the lad's rain-soaked fingers, and everyone stilled. The dragoon's eyes widened in pain and shock, and the lad—who looked a hell of a lot more like a lass—stilled, staring in horror at the man's face as the life seeped from his eyes.

Brogan sprang forward then, his hands around the imp's waist, pulling him—or *her*—away from the dragoon's body as it slumped all the way forward, falling face-first into the mud.

The sprite whirled on him, but thankfully, the weapon that had been miraculously pulled from his or her locks was not stabbing toward him. Brogan frowned, hands around a waist that felt most assuredly feminine.

"Hush, now," Brogan tried to soothe. "I've got ye now."

"Get off me, ye fecking bruiser."

Brogan was stunned by the lass's language, and an odd sense of familiarity struck him regarding the mud-smeared face. Too busy studying the vibrant blue eyes, he didn't notice the fist aimed at his head until she slugged him in the face.

Brogan let go of the imp and touched his cheek.

To her credit, the blow did sting, though it wasn't anything that could have warned him off if he were her enemy.

"Dinna hit me, I'm trying to help ye."

The lass dressed as a lad snorted. "I dinna need your help." She shoved away from him with long, slim, feminine fingers.

"I know ye're no' a lad," Brogan said.

Fury filled the face of the sprite. "Tell that to my cock."

Brogan's lip twitched, barely a smile before it was gone. "Show me." He couldn't help teasing even in this moment of life and death, for he was more certain than ever that the little imp standing in front of him was in fact a woman.

"Sir, that is…" She swallowed. "Are ye some kind of…lad… buggerer?"

One of Brogan's men behind him coughed, trying to suppress a laugh. "Grant, let the lad go. I definitely do no' want to see his cock." The other men in their party snickered.

"He's no' got a cock." Brogan grinned, though it lacked any humor. "He's too bonnie to be a lad, dirt and all." His eyes skimmed down to where her chest was bound beneath a loose-fitting shirt. "My sister used to do the same thing," he said as if he could read her thoughts. "Are ye a spy, then?"

"A spy? This is ballocks." She shoved against his chest with enough power to make a lesser man wobble. A frown marred her dirt-smeared brow when he didn't budge.

"I'll no' tell anyone your secret. But ye're no' safe running around the countryside. A lass is always safest at home."

She narrowed her eyes at him. "Ye're an idiot."

Brogan choked in shock. "Ye're a bit full of yourself."

Her chin jutted up a notch.

"Are there any other dragoons in the house?"

"No' that I saw."

Brogan frowned, trying to decide if he should believe her or not. If she was a spy, she had no reason to tell him the truth. There was every possibility that the man she'd killed had been her partner and they'd gotten into a dispute.

"Who is he?" He nodded his head toward the fallen dragoon.

"How the hell should I know?"

"Does your mother know ye speak like that?"

"Awfully presumptuous of ye to think she's still alive."

"Ye're right, after witnessing ye easily kill a man," he mocked.

Her eye twitched, and she bared her teeth, making a hissing sound that he certainly wanted to step away from, but refused to back down in front of his men. This lass was utterly addled and full of fury, it would seem.

"I'll ask ye again, what is your business here?" Then he softened his voice, adding, "Ye've nothing to fear from us."

Fiona narrowed her eyes but tried not to feign too much interest so as not to draw their unwanted attention. "Allow me to pass. I want no trouble."

"Answer the question."

She studied the man in front of her and the warriors who formed a line blocking her means of exit.

Though they all wore Highland caps, frock coats and kilts, there were subtle differences in the quality of the wool, the wear in the tips of their boots. The man immediately blocking her exit seemed to be the best dressed of the lot and wielded the most authority. Standing before her, he made it abundantly clear with his body that he was not going to allow her to pass. Had he not seen what she'd just been forced to do to the last man thwarting her escape?

She gritted her teeth, trying to push back the tiny niggle of fear at being alone in the courtyard with seven large men who were all armed to the teeth.

The warrior's blue eyes pierced into hers as though he planned to read every thought that didn't pass her lips. Lord, but he was trying her patience, and there was something extremely familiar about his voice and the lines of his face. Where did she know him from?

Something tickled the back of her brain like an annoying midge flying about her temples.

Sweat trickled down her spine, but still she kept up the insolence of an adolescent lad despite him already calling her out for the female she actually was. "What business is that of yours?"

"There's a battle right now," he said as if she were stupid. "No' too far from here."

"Everyone knows that," she interrupted with a bit too much insolence. "And from the looks of ye, the lot of ye were there. Congratulations on living when so many others didna."

This time the crack in her voice was real. The men all winced, examining their own minor injuries.

To have seen so many of her beloved countrymen butchered on the field of battle had been the single most devastating thing Fiona had ever witnessed. She'd seen battles before, but none so catastrophic. With Ian having been among the guards who'd swept the prince from the battlefield, she prayed he remained with the prince, well away from danger.

She needed to find General Murray. He'd taken the other surviving Jacobites who'd escaped the fray to Ruthven House, along with Jenny and her men. The prince wanted them to disband. To run and to hide until they were called up for service once more.

Highlanders would be hard pressed to hide... Still, she had a duty to the prince to convey the message. She'd hurried back to Culloden House, only a mile or two from the battlefield, to change into this getup. No need for the postmistress here. Dressed as a lad seemed to be the safest bet with a war going on, as no woman could consider herself safe from men who needed to slake their battle lust on a body willing or not—not that being dressed as a lad had seemed to help her much. She'd been about to set out from Culloden House while the prince and his entourage headed to Invergarry when she'd run into the dragoon staring through the windows.

Poor bastard. If only he'd left her alone.

She'd been told that on the morrow, the prince and his retinue would likely try to make their way to the Hebrides.

Fiona blinked away the rapidly gathering tears. Now was not the time. She had to push the images, the heartbreak away. Focus.

She straightened to her full height, which still only brought her chin to midchest with this mammoth, and she started to skirt around him.

"Where are ye going?" This time when the large warrior spoke, his tone had subtly shifted. Colder somehow. He didn't need to stop her with his hand, because the tone of his voice was enough.

"Home, as ye pointed out, is the safest place for me."

"Ye were at the battle." It was not a question.

"Nay," she lied. Well, it wasn't a full lie. She'd been there, watching, though she'd not taken part, though there had been plenty of times she'd wished to interfere.

He grunted, and she found that sound to be so irritating. And *again*, striking a familiar chord.

She narrowed her eyes, trying to place him, this time actually taking all of him in. He was tall, broad, and wickedly handsome— the latter of which she tried to ignore. His hair, though matted from battle, was dark and full of curls. His skin, beneath the specks and smears of blood, was tan despite having just come out of winter, and his eyes were a shockingly brilliant blue. His jaw was pronounced and covered in a shadow of black whiskers. He'd not shaved today, and perhaps not the day before either. His blue gaze pierced her with the intensity of his stare.

He wore his Jacobite cap at an angle, the white cockade looking defeated. The frock coat he wore fit him in a way that pronounced the broadness of his chest and the trimness of his waist. The muscles of his arms bulged from the fabric, except for where there was a perfect slice and the fabric darkened perhaps with blood. His boots were not new, but neither were they as worn as others, indicating he had some money to his name. But he was not adorned with any jewels or anything else that would mark him as of noble blood. Nothing except the haughty angle of his jaw.

He was not a man she would forget if she'd laid eyes on him before.

"I'll ask ye one more time, where are ye headed?"

Throat suddenly dry, heart pounding, she worked hard to keep her body from tensing. "What the devil, man?" Fiona said, bringing out her insolent lad. "I told ye I'm going home. My ma will be worried, and I intend to ease her burden."

His eyes narrowed as he studied her face, trying to catch her in a lie, she supposed, since he'd already accused her of being a spy.

She frowned, trying to look as tough as she should feel, as angry as she was for being waylaid. Every moment she wasted with this arrogant Highlander would make it longer before Murray and the rest of the Jacobite army at Ruthven got the message from the prince to disband.

The men were in mortal danger if they remained at Ruthven

House, and it would be this man's fault if she didn't deliver the message in time.

The prince was on the run now. There was an air among him and his guards that a revival in the cause was hopeless. From what she could tell, the Jacobite mission to restore the prince to the throne seemed to have shifted to an abandonment of ship. But it couldn't be the end. Fiona didn't believe that. There had to be hope. She had to keep that hope alive.

"Where does your ma live?"

"With me da," she answered, specifically avoiding the information he was looking for and trying not to snicker at the flash of annoyance that crossed his face.

"And where is that?"

"In the very cottage I was born."

"Ye're avoiding the question."

Fiona shrugged, working hard to hide her smirk. "I've answered ye two times now."

He came closer, the clomp of his boots on the ground slow and deliberate, and that grunt falling again from his throat. And suddenly she knew who he was. Fiona's eyes widened slightly, recalling a very similar battle of wills just this morning.

There was no way in Hades that she'd happened to run into the same irritating Highlander who had tried now to thwart her missions twice in so short a span of time.

Fiona worked hard to keep her eyes steady on his, refusing to retreat or give in to what he wanted.

"Ye're a bit cocky for a wee lass."

"My da would be proud of me." And that was the truth. Her da would be exceedingly proud of all she'd accomplished and sacrificed for Scotland. And so would her brothers, even though Ian was bound to be furious with her for disobeying a direct order.

She'd watched him escape the battlefield from afar, him none the wiser to her being there, and she prayed he'd stayed on the road with the royal entourage rather than head back toward their family's holding. He'd not been badly injured from what she'd witnessed. In fact he'd fought like a bloody madman.

"What is your da's name?"

"Da."

The man cursed under his breath. "Ye're trying my patience."

"And ye're trying mine."

"I ought to whip ye for your insolence."

She straightened, seething. "Ye ought to let me pass."

The Highlander sucked his teeth against his lips as he leaned closer, his gaze raking over her.

She gritted her teeth. "If ye dinna let me go, people will die." She started to march around him again, but the skin of his palm branded her knuckles, and she stopped moving.

His eyes widened as he stared into hers, as if he'd just discovered some secret.

"Why do I know ye?" he growled.

"Because we've met before, Brogan Grant."

"The messenger."

"Ye've a quicker wit than I would have granted ye."

"Hmm… What are ye doing here?"

"The same thing I was doing early this morning."

"And this time dressed differently."

"I like change."

He made that disgruntled noise again and she wanted to punch him in the throat. "Let me go."

"I canna. Ye're too reckless. I'm taking ye home."

"Ye dinna know where I live, and besides, I'd refuse to go."

"Did ye no' see the carnage, lass? Cumberland and his army willna hesitate to tear ye apart. Another Scot no' so chivalrous as myself would do the same. Ye'll no' have a choice about going home. 'Tis for your own safety."

"I dare say I will. Ye know nothing about me."

They glared at each other for an interminably long time, both of them breathing hard, trying to wait out the other. She wasn't giving in to him this easily. No way in hell. She'd worked too hard to just give up and go home.

"I suppose ye think by glaring at me I'll simply cower and give ye the whereabouts of my domicile and allow ye to escort me back all proper-like? Well, ye're delusional should ye think it would go anything like that."

"A woman's place *is* at home."

A bitter laugh escaped her then. "And where is a man's place? Because I should think it was the field of battle and no' running away like a coward."

"I killed as many of the bastards as tried to take me out. I watched my clansmen die. I'm no' running away."

"Oh really? Then where are ye going?"

"None of your business. And ye're trying to distract me. Ye need to go home afore some danger befalls ye. The bastards will no' be kind if they find ye."

"Ye said as much already and still I'm no' convinced. Perhaps ye turned tail and ye're no longer a Jacobite. Are ye rushing down to the border where ye can swear your allegiance to King George? Why are ye no' with Murray, serving at his command?"

Anger simmered in his eyes, and perhaps a more cautious lass might have been scared by it, but she wasn't. She was equally as angry. Already she knew he wasn't a traitor, but he'd insulted her, and she was just pushing that platter right back.

"How dare ye say such to me? I am more loyal than most of the men on that field."

Fiona was still suspicious of who these seven were. Why had they come to the house? Were they here to raid? Instinct told her no, but still she had to question him. "Then what are ye doing here?"

"We're trying to find the prince."

She raised her brows. "Good luck with that."

"Ye know where he is." It wasn't a question, and he wasn't exactly stupid. He was a soldier and it was his duty to fight for the prince.

It was her duty to rally his troops. And she wanted to help him, she did.

"I make it my business to know where everyone is." An idea struck her then, how she could use these men to her own advantage. But she didn't want to ask. "Let me go."

"Tell me where he is. And I'm no' letting ye go."

Perhaps instead of asking, she could negotiate with him. "Ye've never been in a negotiation, have ye? Normally there is a give-and-take."

"I dinna need to negotiate. Tell me where he is. It is our duty to protect him."

Fiona jutted her chin forward. "As it is mine."

He narrowed his eyes more, and she felt the urge to hit him so strongly that her fist actually clenched beneath his hand, and it took every effort she had not to break free of his hold and raise her fist to his godlike jaw.

As if sensing her indecision, he glanced down at his hand over hers and gave a gentle squeeze. "I will make ye a deal, lass."

Fiona released a laugh, but not with humor; it was a frustrated sound that burbled from her throat. "I'm no' in the mood for making deals. I'm in the mood for completing my mission. And ye're getting in my way."

Three

BROGAN HAD NEVER FELT THE DESIRE TO STRANGLE A WOMAN before. And it wasn't as if he wanted her to die, or even to hurt her. Nay, he just wanted to...throttle her. To shake some sense into her. It was the oddest sensation.

He gritted his teeth.

Why was Fate putting this woman in front of him two times in the span of less than a day? And both times with her being less than honest?

The hour in which he had patience had long passed. He was tired, hungry, angry as hell over the way the battle had played out, and on top of that he wasn't entirely certain what was going to happen next, which was bound to make him snap at any moment.

Brogan didn't like the feeling of unease when plans weren't met. When plans weren't made. Chaos was not an environment in which he thrived.

Having been abandoned by his mother at such a young age, simply dropped on the castle steps of his father when he was barely out of leading strings, it was a difficult thing for him not to have every moment of his day, week, month planned out.

Perhaps this was also why men often looked to him for advice, because Brogan knew what was going to happen. Or at least he mapped out how things were going to go. There were always several scenarios completely played out in his mind. He made himself aware of battle plans, inserted himself when necessary, and moved on. Probably why the six men behind him had followed him here. Brogan exuded authority. Funny, since it was stability that he craved, not that he'd admit that to anyone. And today that stability had been shattered.

Which made this meeting with the mysterious woman kind of ironic. The same woman out delivering messages… As if Fate were taunting him with his need for permanency.

Brogan frowned fiercely into her eyes, so deep a blue they were nearly violet. There was a smattering of freckles across her nose and cheeks that were mostly covered in dirt, giving her the look of a playful sprite, which he knew her to be anything but. Despite the mess she tried to make of herself, she was very beautiful, and he'd be hard pressed to find himself thinking her a lad on any day. What other idiots had actually fallen for the ruse? He doubted the dragoon she'd felled had. In retrospect, the bastard had been tugging at the front of her frock coat in quite a lascivious manner.

Who are ye?

She'd had the Jacobite coin. She had knowledge. She had costumes.

There were many women who traded messages via a secret route in order to get them to their loved ones, to share information. Hell, nearly every Jacobite woman did. But they did not all traverse the roads. They did not all risk their lives. Except for one.

A phantom messenger. Brogan had always believed she was a rumor, a story for the men to gain hope at night. Or perhaps like most rumors, the tale was steeped in some truth. The Phantom as a series of women passing gossip had somehow morphed into one beautiful, seductive lass. Her lips were full, red, even when pinched with anger.

Bloody hell. *Was* she the Phantom?

Could an *ordinary* woman stab a man in the neck as expertly as this one had?

Brogan didn't have much patience when it came to women. Often found them shrill, diabolical even in their machinations. A fair number of women had wanted to bed him, hoping he accidentally got them with child so they could benefit from the coin in the Grant coffers, for it was well known that his da had given him a yearly stipend, not that it meant anything now that he was fighting on the opposite side. Before his father's turn to treachery changed things, Brogan had been careful. He often chose to have his bed partners when pretending to be someone else—and he never allowed his seed to penetrate a woman's body. He still felt the same way now, coin or no.

This bastard wasn't going to father more bastards.

That was something he had in common with this lass, pretending to be someone they weren't. Why was she hiding from her true self?

Why did he care?

He didn't.

Finally, he spoke. "We've both a mission to complete, lass. I need to find the prince, and I've a feeling ye know where he is. Ye've a need to get on the road and go back to where ye belong— *home*. Behind a locked door. Preferably with your da giving ye a good whipping for putting yourself in such danger. Ye know ye could have died just now? That bastard"—he pointed at the body—"could have killed ye."

"I'm well aware of the dangers. More so than ye, even. And what an intelligent melon ye've got on your shoulders. Ye've nailed my mission on the head. Let me go, and I'll head home right now." The sarcasm in her voice dripped like sap from a tree.

"I dinna trust ye, if truth were to be told."

"Well, ye just did tell the truth, and since we're being honest, I dinna trust ye either." She glanced behind him at the rest of the men, her gaze settling on Sorley. "Him, however, I trust just fine. And perhaps the rest of them, too, silent as they may be."

Brogan growled in irritation. "Why?"

She smiled. "Instinct."

Cheeky wench. "Fine. Tell Sorley where the prince is then, and I'll escort ye back home."

"I've a better idea."

"What?"

"Ye can go bugger yourself."

Brogan reared his head back, a bit stunned once more by her crude language. "Ye've a waspish tongue."

"I'm no' ashamed. Just because I'm a woman doesna mean I canna speak my mind."

Brogan ran his tongue over his teeth, curbing his own retort when he wanted to give her a lashing that would blister her ears.

"Ye know I'm a Jacobite, lass. Ye know we just fought in the battle. Why are ye being so difficult? I delivered the last message ye gave me to the men who needed to hear it, and we waited for the return of the regiments afore we went to battle."

"I'm being difficult because ye're no' listening to me. While ye may believe it is my place to be sent back into my family's home, ye dinna seem to understand that I've spent more time on the road likely than ye have. I'm no' some fancy-dancy lady that swoons at the slightest mention of a sword. I just killed a man. Do ye no' bloody understand it yet, mate? I'm no' who ye think I am."

He gritted his teeth as she leaned up toward him as though she were upbraiding one of her servants.

"Here's the thing, princess. Neither of us can remain here arguing in plain sight. This jackanapes is only the first of many dragoons who are going to come here looking for the prince or any other Jacobites they've not killed or rounded up. What's it going to take to get ye to leave?" And why did he bloody care?

He could just leave her. Walk into the house as he had planned, take the horses, and not think about her for the rest of his life. Except he couldn't. Somehow, she'd put her claws in him.

Both of them stilled at the sound of a horn in the distance.

"If ye want to help me so much, why do ye no' just come with me? I'll take ye to the prince myself when we're done."

The men behind him were growing antsy. Brogan turned to face his men, who waited anxiously for what he would decide.

"Fine. Let's get some supplies and saddle up the horses."

With a nod to the men, they slunk across the grass to the back entrance of the house, in case any more surprise visitors came in through the front. To be safe, they closed the gates and barred them tight. In the back of the house, they found the door bolted. At least someone had taken precaution there.

"It wasna locked before," the woman grumbled.

Brogan peered through the glass windows beside the door, catching movement. Determining it was not a redcoat within, he tapped on the glass, and the movement ceased. Whoever it was took stock of who he was from their own hiding place behind an archway wall.

Brogan tapped again, and the person popped out from behind the wall, then cautiously approached. Upon seeing the way they were dressed through the glass, the man opened the door and ushered them in.

The entire house was permeated with the scent of fresh-baked bread. Who the hell had been baking while a battle ensued not two miles away?

The man eyed him suspiciously. "How can I help ye, soldier?" He glanced from Brogan to the lass, then back again.

"What are ye doing here?" Brogan looked beyond the man. Had they interrupted him stealing something, or was he a defector? "Give us your name."

"I'm Joseph, and I was ordered by the prince to return and gather the valuables." There was a tremor to his voice, and a slight shake to his hands that he hid by grasping them behind him. Again, he glanced at the lass.

"Who is baking bread?"

"The servants."

Brogan frowned, feeling more and more like he'd arrived to interrupt something nefarious. "Why would he ask ye to do that instead of fighting alongside him?"

The man shook his head. "The prince doesna expect to win. Cumberland will come to the house to try and steal whatever he can. The prince asked me to secure the items. He escaped the field with his guard and said they'd make a circle and come here, but he has no' yet arrived."

The men all looked at each other, each of them with narrowed eyes. Something wasn't altogether right about the soldier's story. And yet the lass seemed completely unfazed.

"I can vouch for him," she said with a shrug. "The prince did ask."

Brogan narrowed his eyes. Was it she who'd delivered the order?

"We need horses," Brogan said. "We'll catch up to the prince and his guard in case they ran into trouble on the road."

The soldier nodded, looking behind him nervously.

"Is there anyone else in the house?" Brogan asked.

"The servants."

"And?"

"A handful of soldiers." As he said it, several Jacobites faded from the shadows, their heads hung in shame.

"We were tired," one of them said, before covering his face in shame.

"So the lot of ye cowered here while the rest of us fought?"

Silence was his answer.

"No' everyone can kill so easily," the lass said. "They are to be admired for protecting the prince's belongings."

Brogan did not agree in the slightest.

"We're taking the horses," he said. "The rest of ye cowards stay here in case the prince returns. 'Tis the least ye can do after deserting him on the field." Brogan had to work to keep his fury inside when what he wanted to do was pummel these fools into the oiled wooden floors. "Cumberland is no' going to let him live, should he find him, no' if it will cause an uprising again.

Cumberland is in line for the throne, and he'll no' let the prince stand in his way."

The men all regarded one another grimly. If Brogan didn't find the prince soon, there was no telling what would happen to him. The royal heir was certainly adept with a sword, but having been raised in France well away from any strife, his skill was more attuned to that of a chivalrous parlay with friends or a duel. The roughness of the Highlands and the butchering of Cumberland's army had been a shock to the prince when he'd arrived the summer before. And while he'd gotten better at the guerilla tactics that had helped the Highlanders win countless battles, he'd not fared well on his own, or with the few men he had in his contingent.

Brogan would find him. He had to.

"Are the horses in the stable?"

"Aye." The man looked sideways. "But we'll need them to make our escape too."

Brogan narrowed his eyes. "We'll no' leave the stable empty, but I'm certain as a man in the prince's service, ye'd no' deny us the use of the prince's own horses in finding him and bringing him to safety. Especially after ye deserted him on the field."

The man nodded and looked down at his worn boots in shame.

A twinge of guilt tugged at Brogan's heart. "Dinna let fear make your mind a muddle, nor cause ye to forget who ye serve."

The soldier's throat bobbed in answer, and surprisingly Fiona gave a small gasp. He glanced down at her, her cheeks coloring. Why such a reaction?

Brogan frowned all the harder before nodding to his men. "Gather supplies and meet me in the stable."

"I'll help ye with the horses," Sorley said, then spoke to the men left at the house. "There is a vault in the cellar. Ye can keep hidden there if the redcoats come."

Brogan wanted to ask Sorley to explain how he knew that, but that would have to wait.

"Ye too," Brogan said to the lass. He wasn't leaving her inside where she might easily escape out the back.

While the rest of their seven gathered a few supplies from the kitchens, Brogan, Sorley, and Fiona cautiously made their way to the stable. The hair on the back of Brogan's neck prickled the entire time. Was the lass about to put one of her hairpins through his neck? Or were the dragoons getting closer?

"I dinna like this," Sorley said.

"We need to get the hell out of here."

"I couldna agree more." The lass shuddered, looking over her shoulder, and Brogan believed the clear alarm in her manner.

Inside the stables were at least a dozen horses, two still saddled. While they worked to saddle five more, Brogan asked, "How did ye know about the vault?"

"Had to hide in there myself a couple of years back."

"Oh?" Could Brogan trust him? Why would he need to hide?

"Aye. Old Man Forbes was hosting some dragoons. I snuck in to steal a bride."

"That was ye?" the lass asked, a slight chuckle.

Brogan spied a small grin on Sorley's face, and a touch of nostalgia that was foreign to him in the man's expression.

"Did ye win?"

"Aye." Sorley grinned. "She's waiting for me back home. Likely going to chew my head off when I finally make it back."

"Sounds like a good woman."

"She is."

They finished saddling the horses and brought them to the courtyard as the men approached with satchels of supplies and skins of water.

From the darkened windows of the manor house, shadowed faces appeared, almost as if floating above bodies that couldn't be seen. The men moved out in silence, taking their time in the woods and checking for any hints of movement and all the tracks they could find. The sounds of the battle had ebbed, which wasn't a good sign. It meant the redcoats would soon be scanning the surrounding areas looking for survivors they could murder or take prisoner.

"Prince Charles would be smart never to return to Culloden House," Sorley offered as they went down the road, riding beside Brogan at the head of their pack, the lass centered between them.

"Aye," Brogan said.

"Where do ye think he's gone?"

"My bet is on where he landed. Ship's still there." Brogan slid his glance toward the lass to see if she reacted, but she kept silent. She wasn't going to spill a word until he'd helped her deliver her message to the men at Ruthven.

"Ye think he'll flee the country?"

"Nay, but he'll seek refuge in a place he knows Cumberland will have a harder time finding him."

"Then do ye no' think that Cumberland would look there first, at his ships?"

Brogan didn't answer, hoping to gain some clue from the lass between them. The sound of approaching riders had them all on alert.

They edged off the road, taking refuge in a copse just a few feet away and not as well hidden as Brogan would have liked. Hell, it was damn near impossible to hide seven men, a woman, and eight horses, but they did the best they could.

Six redcoats barreled past them as if their lives depended on it. Coats flapped against the flanks of their horses, making them all a windswept blur as they went.

"Messengers," Sorley said.

"How do ye know?"

He shrugged. "I can just tell."

Brogan narrowed his gaze. "Who are ye?"

"I'm really no one, trust me. Though I've been called the Retriever before."

Brogan snorted.

Sorley rolled his eyes. "Ye're lucky to have me with ye. I've retrieved any number of people from where they've tried to hide."

"Might ye retrieve King George and send him back to Hanover?"

"I'd have loved to do that, man, trust me."

Brogan grunted, and they all moved back out onto the road.

"But I'm willing now to put my skills to use in finding our prince."

"And so ye think he's gone to his ship?"

"I wager he's headed there."

"Ye're the retriever, after ye."

"I've a feeling I'll regret telling ye that."

"Ye might."

Behind them, the men snickered, not to be outdone by the derisive snort of the imp between them. And just as suddenly, all of them stopped. Carried on the wind was the unmistakable sound of men…marching. Only one troop of men would be marching so loudly through these woods—dragoons.

The lass's head whipped backward, staring down the road in the opposite direction, at the same time Sorley let out a low whistle.

"Come," Brogan muttered under his breath, hurrying his mount up the incline and into the trees where they could easily watch the road below but not be seen. Sorley and the men followed.

The imp didn't argue, surprisingly.

As the troop of dragoons passed, the eight of them remained utterly silent, their horses complying to the silent command as well.

About two dozen redcoats marched, their uniforms mucked from battle, faces smeared with soot and blood. Not a single one of them was clean, each of them having participated in the slaughter of the Jacobite army. It took every ounce of willpower that Brogan had not to leap from his position and tear into them. Slice them into ribbons and stomp on their still-beating hearts.

But he remained where he was, stiff as a board, angry as a bear.

The dragoons slowed as they reached the bend in the road, staring at the tracks in the dirt. Tracks that led north, south, and up the rise into the woods, where Brogan and the others stood. Debris had been dislodged from the embankment, scattering onto the side of the road.

The dragoons looked as tired as Brogan felt. But that didn't mean they'd simply pass up the opportunity to fight.

Two men conferred, pointing at the tracks, both of them avoiding looking up. The leader whistled, and a man from the back of the pack of mongrels hurried forward, given orders that Brogan couldn't make out.

The man bent and touched the loosened dirt, sniffed.

"Jacobites?" the leader asked. "Every rebel is to be killed on sight, per the duke's orders."

Killed on sight? So now they were simply to be murdered. Rain started to pelt once more, icy and stinging in its force. Would they never get a rest from it on today of all days?

"Deer," the dragoon determined, glancing up the embankment to where they were hidden.

He was lying. Had to be. Curious. Why the hell would he lie? Unless he didn't like the odds of a band of Jacobite rebels hiding above them where they'd have the clear advantage.

Brogan grinned. *Come on… Call out the order to investigate. Let us smash in a few more dragoon heads…*

But the leader of the regiment called for them to move forward, and the man who'd declared Brogan and his men to be a bunch of deer watched their hiding spot surreptitiously through the rain as he marched back to his place in line and they continued on. Brogan committed the man's face to memory. If he ever came across him, he'd thank him. Maybe even let him live.

None of them moved as the line of dragoons continued to pass. Even as the last of them faded into the distance, only leaving their footprints in the road, Brogan and the others remained still, just in case the troops were inclined to circle back. All of them knew this game, and Brogan found himself particularly impressed at how well the woman knew it too.

Given he'd met her under suspicious circumstances twice now and she seemed to hold fairly important information, she wasn't just some silly maid. He was pretty certain of that. How deep into the well of spying had she fallen?

"What is your name?" he asked in a low whisper, eyes still on the road.

"I told ye once afore it was best ye no' know."

"That was before we were hiding out together in the woods. Before I found ye being attacked at the prince's headquarters."

"Dinna make it sound like we're comrades." She swiped at the water dripping into her eyes, which didn't hide the fact that she was rolling them.

"Och, lass, trust me, I know well what we are to each other."

"And what is that?"

He frowned, unable to answer, for he wasn't exactly sure what to say. They weren't exactly enemies since they were both fighting for the same cause, and they weren't friends because of it either. He didn't trust her, thought her to be a spy. They'd already caught one Scots lass spying for Cumberland in their midst some months before.

"Two people who dinna trust each other, though we're on the same side," he replied.

She snorted. "That's all ye could come up with?"

He shrugged.

"Listen, Grant, I need to be on my way and so do ye, so I say we just part ways here. I'll tell ye how to find the prince, and ye can pretend I'm headed straight home to lock myself up in my bed-chamber until a white knight comes to rescue me."

It was on the tip of his tongue to argue with her, but why? She was giving him what he wanted, and though he did believe she should go home, he had to come to terms with the fact that it wasn't really any of his business.

Brogan held out his hand to her, prepared to shake on the agreement.

She stared down at his palm and fingers smeared with blood, and he started to pull away, but she placed hers in his, equally dirty, and squeezed. "I hope ye take no offense when I say I hope never to see ye again."

And then he changed his mind. "I take none, for the feeling is mutual, lass. But unfortunately, I canna agree to your proposal."

She frowned. "Why no'?"

"I made ye a promise I'd help ye in exchange for the prince's whereabouts, and I'm a man of my word." Even as he cursed himself for being that way.

"I'm ever so grateful for your sacrifice, sir, but it is entirely unnecessary. And though I'm quite certain that until now I miraculously made it through life without your wise and sage advice, I must summon the courage to go on without ye."

Brogan grunted, hardly able to keep himself from baring his teeth at her. What a stubborn and mocking wench.

"The prince is—"

Brogan reached for her, placing his hand over her mouth as she mumbled the rest. "Dinna say it. I refuse to hear it."

She grumbled against his hand, and it was only when he felt her teeth sinking into his palm that he yanked it away.

"Good God, mate, ye're more stubborn than I am." She stared at him, incredulous. "Shall I tell your men, then?"

"Nay. We go as one," one of the warriors, perhaps Sorley, said behind them.

The lass stared at him, challenge in her gaze. "Dinna make me regret agreeing to this madness."

"Or what?"

"I'll be forced to inflict bodily harm."

There was no hint of humor in her voice, which made it difficult to distinguish if she were jesting or not. Certainly she must be. "I'd like to see ye try." There was a teasing edge to his voice that was slightly foreign. Was he...*flirting* with her? *Ballocks!*

"I'm always up for a challenge." She rolled her striking eyes and turned away from him as if he were of no more interest to her, and she steered her horse out onto the road.

He had to stop himself from reaching for her, pulling her back, and telling her to be careful. That she really should go home...that all of this was stupid and not worth it. But she had a message to deliver, men's lives were on the line, and he wasn't going to be the one that got them killed by waylaying her any longer.

A piece of her flame-red hair came loose from her cap. She shoved it back where it belonged, as if it were something she was quite used to doing. Given how he'd met her running around the woods as though she owned them, he wasn't surprised.

Brogan watched her for a few moments heading down the road, his limbs itching unreasonably to chase after her.

"What do ye make of her?" Sorley asked, brows screwed up. The rest of the men grumbled their own curiosity as they followed her down the road.

"Of who?" Brogan cleared his throat.

"The woman," James offered as if Brogan truly might not understand the question.

Brogan shrugged. "The prince trusts her. If we're fighting for him, I suppose we ought to trust her too. She's no' lied to me yet."

Sorley waggled his brows. "In what capacity did ye meet her afore?"

Brogan snorted. "No' in an assignation, if that's what ye're referring to. She's more likely to rob me than anything else." Especially of information. The way she posed questions, the way she watched him, had him thinking that she was indeed very adept at her specific skill set.

"Are ye coming?" she asked from ahead, staring behind her as though trying to urge a bunch of bairns to follow.

What the bloody hell had he agreed to? If anything, maybe on this journey he could prove to her that he was right, that the place for her was not out here alone on the roads with dragoons but tucked safely behind a wall.

Four

FIONA SLID HER HAND DOWN THE NECK OF THE SLEEK HORSE she'd taken from the prince's stable and contemplated Brogan Grant. How was she going to get rid of this giant lug and his entourage? Running through the forest, hiding in hollowed-out trees was a lot easier when it was just her, but this man was the size of a tree and those with him weren't much smaller.

When the eight of them had shimmied up the hillside and watched the devils in red round the corner, stop short, and sift through the loosened debris of their horses' hooves, she'd been certain there would be a battle right then and there.

The man who proclaimed them to be deer was certainly lying, and the other redcoats had to know it. Was it a trap? Or were they giving themselves permission not to kill any more Scots?

She frowned, not believing the latter to be true. Rare had it been for her to witness one kind redcoat, let alone half a dozen in one place. And yet they'd been let go when an issue for their outright murder had been ordered by the Butcher. *Bastard.*

Fiona bristled all over again. Loved ones, friends, companions, so many people that she cared about had been lost to this fight. There was not one person with Scots blood running through their veins that had not been touched by this tragedy.

She had to warn as many people as possible of Cumberland's new order. No one was safe. There could be no more acting, no more pretending. If there was even an inkling, or a feeling, or a dragoon needing an excuse to slake his bloodlust, life would be taken.

Fiona slowed her mount, bile rising in her throat, her stomach squeezing and rebelling even when she had nothing inside it. She coughed as her body fought to expel everything, including all the thoughts tormenting her mind. Pulling back on the reins, she leaned over the side of the horse gagging, unable to stop her throat from working, the clenching inside. She spat onto the ground.

Something warm brushed her ankle. Brogan was there. He let out a low sound under his breath but said nothing, and when she sat back up, he held out a flask.

"Drink."

Fiona wiped her mouth with her sleeve and took the proffered flask. As she swished the whisky around her mouth to rinse, then spat it out, Brogan watched her. Handing it back, their gloved fingers brushed and she couldn't help but wish that their skin touched. Suddenly needing to feel that contact with another human. So long had she been running, so long had she been without affection. Just the warm brush of his leg and gloved fingers soothed some of the nervous energy that was catapulting through her veins.

"My name is Fiona," she blurted out. Och, why had she so freely told him that? One kind gesture and she was spilling secrets?

She looked away, not wanting him to see those thoughts running rampant through her mind. Not wanting him to see her regret in sharing, and then for him to ask questions as a consequence.

"Hmm," Brogan mused, the low gravel tone growing on her. "I'd no' have pictured ye as a Fiona."

She whipped her head back around, frowning, slightly offended. "And what would ye have thought?"

"Jezebel." The man said it so seriously, she almost allowed the shock of it to show on her face, but then noted the twinkle of humor in his eyes. The bastard was making a joke. At a time like this.

Fiona rolled her eyes. "Ye can call me Mistress."

He snorted.

Fiona straightened her shoulders. "We are going to my family's home first. 'Tis on the way to the Ruthven Barracks."

He nodded, his brow furrowed.

"I'm no' staying there," she warned. "I simply want to tell them what we just heard. It is my duty to make sure my clan is safe."

"Do ye no' have a brother or a male cousin who could do that?"

Fiona bit the tip of her tongue to keep from issuing a tart retort. The man knew nothing of her family and yet he made assumptions. She supposed most people would, but still it irritated her.

"Every person has a duty to their family. *Every* person, Brogan Grant. One day ye'll understand that, and I pity any sister of yours, or a future wife or daughter, who must feel inferior to ye." She drew in a breath, holding his gaze, challenging him to put her down.

Brogan cocked his head but said nothing. Did he have family that he wanted to warn?

"We should warn as many as we can," Fiona said. "Do ye want to warn your clan?"

"I will, after meeting with the prince." He eyed her with an expression she couldn't make out.

She glanced at the men behind them, the six of them staring at her with unreadable expressions. *I'm no' weak*, she wanted to shout, but they'd all seen her bent over a horse gagging, so they'd already formed their opinions about her.

"Onward," she said in a voice as strong as she could manage, mustering some of that authority she'd tried to wield when they'd first met.

"After ye," Brogan said. He didn't strike her as a man who often followed others, and yet he was allowing her the lead. Curious.

Granted, he didn't know exactly where her family home was. She'd not been forthcoming with that information.

Fiona focused straight ahead, urging her mount into a trot and then a gallop, feeling the need to move, to have the sting of the icy air and rain on her skin.

The sounds of battle had ceased completely as they made their way back toward the field, but the acrid scents of gunpowder and cannon fire were still strong, and mixed with it was the metallic scent of blood. Despite the rain, the scents clung heavily to the air. She feared it would be that way for a long time to come.

Even when they were far away from this place, she was certain to still recall the scent. Visions of the battle, of the carnage would haunt her forever.

How many men had lost their lives today? Her stomach clenched and she feared being sick once more but managed to hold it in.

Then her blood ran cold as an anguished cry reached them. They stopped, staring in the distance at the battlefield as a cloaked woman bent over the body of a dying man. Several warriors comforted the cloaked figure. But Fiona knew there could be no soothing touch that would heal the heart from death. When the woman stood, the warriors lifted the body of the fallen man and loaded him onto a wagon.

Fiona narrowed her eyes, uncertain if she could believe what she was seeing. What tricks her mind tried to play on her. Of all the thousands of men on the field, of all the thousands of lives lost, what were the odds that one of them would be known to her?

"Nay..." she murmured, her heart clenching and all of her going cold at once.

"What is it?" Brogan asked.

The figures grew smaller and smaller, but Fiona's heart continued to pound. "My... I think that was my friend Annie. I pray it was no'. For if it was, then she mourns the loss of a loved one."

With her heart and head in contradiction, Fiona turned her horse in the direction of the caravan that had disappeared down a rise.

She needed to know.

The men followed her without question. By the time Fiona got to where she'd last seen Annie, there was no one in sight.

Brogan rode up beside her, the concern on his face evident. She hoped this was not going to be another opportunity in which he'd seize on her womanly emotions and inability to continue with the mission.

"Ye saw them before, aye?" she asked, wearily avoiding his gaze.

"Aye." He said nothing more, no arguments, no veiled insults, but a quiet agreement.

That was all she needed to keep going forward. She had to find Annie. They searched the surrounding area but came up completely empty. Annie, if it was indeed her, had disappeared with the mist.

When an hour had passed and the men stared at her with question, she knew what needed to be done before Brogan spoke. She cut him off as he opened his mouth. "I will look for her when we have delivered our message."

He nodded, though the expression on his face said he didn't believe that would happen. A shadow of pity crossed over his gaze before he flicked it toward his men and back. Thankfully, the sympathy was replaced by his typical disgruntled affect.

She opened her mouth, about to admit that Annie was her dear friend, and that what she'd witnessed on the battlefield had nearly crushed her as much as if it were her own blood. That someone close to Annie must have died, and she prayed it wasn't sweet Graham.

But Fiona snapped her mouth closed, concerned that the simple glance from Brogan had made her want to admit too much. To a virtual stranger.

What was this war doing to her? She was giving away all of her secrets, all of her inner thoughts. Doing such made her vulnerable. And even if Brogan didn't seem an immediate threat to her now, there was no telling what he could use against her in the future.

"Let us go to Dòchas Keep," she said, her voice low because she feared using her normal tone would reflect the depth of emotions racing through her mind.

"Ye're a MacBean?" His voice was flat, but there was a sharp alertness in his gaze.

"Aye."

"I fought with a man today you might be related to. Ian MacBean."

"My brother. Were ye wounded?"

"Nay."

"Was my brother?"

"Nay."

She cocked her head, waiting for him to say more, but he didn't so she simply nodded and pushed her horse back into a gallop.

But even the few hours of hard riding over the moors to Dòchas did not dissipate the heaviness in her heart.

The towering keep of her family's seat came into view nestled in a valley between Loch Dochfour, Loch Ashie, and Loch Duntelchaig.

Loch Dochfour led in from the North Sea via the Moray Firth and drained into Loch Ness in the south. Their lands were coveted and often attacked for where they were located and how fertile they were. But for generations they'd protected the water crossings all the way up to their enemies the Grants at Urquhart Castle. When her grandfather was young, he was among an army of five hundred Jacobites that laid siege to the castle and lost. The Grants blew up their own castle after that to avoid another attack, which seemed backwards in Fiona's mind unless they thought they'd lose another fight.

She glanced at Brogan. Was he a Grant of *those* Grants? If so, that would explain why he'd not expounded on his talk of her brother during the battle. A chill swept down her spine as she calculated the chances he would enact a generations old revenge on her and her clan.

With that question in mind, Fiona pulled on the reins, coming to a sudden halt, and turned in the saddle to pin Brogan with her stare.

"Our clans have no' always seen eye to eye," she said.

He grunted, his expression unreadable.

"Before I allow ye to go another step with me, I need to know that my clan has nothing to fear from ye."

Brogan knitted his dark-brown brows and had the temerity to look offended. "I didna come with ye to hurt anyone. I came with ye to help and to protect our rightful king. What my grandfather and your grandfather did matters no'."

"Ye'd be a rare Highlander to think so."

He shrugged, and a shadow passed over his eyes. What she wouldn't give to know what thoughts were going through his mind just then. Did he not see himself as a regular Highlander? Perhaps he was lying.

When she was certain he wasn't going to speak and she'd started to push her horse again, he mumbled under his breath in a tone clearly not meant for her ears, "Dinna know why anyone would think blowing up their own castle was a good idea anyway."

Fiona grinned. She lowered herself down over the saddle and urged her horse into a full gallop toward the castle. Already, she'd wasted enough time on the road.

When she was close enough, she removed her cap so the warriors manning the gate would see her flame-red hair and know she'd returned. Without her having to shout a single greeting from a distance, the gate started to open.

She rode through with the bedraggled Highlanders, greeted by several worried members of the clan.

"Where is Master Ian?" Her elderly uncle, Tam, approached, worry pinching his white bushy eyebrows.

Fiona felt his concern all the way down deep in her gut, and she prayed the prince's entourage were already at Invergarry.

"I believe he is with the prince. Safe."

"They are on the run," Brogan corrected her, pulling no punches and causing her to bristle.

Oh, the nerve of him to interrupt her and worry her clan unnecessarily.

"So they are no' safe?" Tam stared at Brogan.

"As safe as a rebel can be just now with—"

Fiona cut him off. "We have lost this battle but we are no' beaten, Uncle." She flashed Brogan a glower.

"Ye left without a word," Tam accused her.

She blamed Tam's turn of conversation on Brogan. Aye, this was his fault. She'd come to relay a message, to stock up on supplies, not to be lectured or have to assuage her clan about Ian. Alas, she was now going to have to do all of it.

"I'm so sorry, Uncle." She leapt from the horse, wrapping her frozen arms around his frail body. "I couldna risk the lot of ye knowing where I went, just in case..." Thoughts of what happened to her friend Annie's home sent horrifying flashes through her mind. How Cumberland had destroyed everything.

Uncle Tam nodded. "Come inside. Ye're making me cold."

"We're no' staying long," Fiona said. "We're needed elsewhere."

Tam waved them in, a thousand questions coming at them from various people in her clan. Brogan and his men dismounted, handing their horses off to stable lads and following her into the castle. The familiar scents of rosemary and lemons greeted her, the same herbs and fruits her mother had the servants use to clean, a tradition they'd all kept.

Inside the great hall, servants and clanswomen gathered, the men consisting only of the very old, ill, or young. A long trestle table sat in the middle of the room with benches down the side and massive chairs at the ends. The great hall of Dòchas Keep was smaller than most, as they were a smaller clan. Those who were invited to dine with the laird were honored guests at the table only large enough to seat eight on either side and one at each end.

In the spring and summer, when the weather cooperated, they set up tables in the bailey for the clan to all eat together.

Fiona's parents had wanted the clan to be close, for everyone to feel as though they played a part, so they ate together often, and she'd looked forward to hearing all the different stories and ideas that were shared over a communal meal. Even when both of her parents were gone, it was a tradition she and her brothers and sister kept.

The castle felt oddly empty now. She was so used to hearing the boisterous sounds of lads and the tittering of the females watching the men. But it was quiet. The majority of the fighting men had gone with Ian, and the silence of their absence echoed. Fiona's heart skipped a beat at the worried looks on the lasses' faces.

Without the youngest of their men to defend the castle, they were left in the care of older warriors and young lads who'd been forbidden to go to Culloden. Being so close to the battlefield, she was surprised to find the castle had not yet been infiltrated.

"Have any of Cumberland's men demanded entry?" Fiona asked.

"No' as yet. Hoping they think we're too small. But in case they do, we've hidden away anything that might name us as Jacobite supporters."

Fiona slid a glance toward Brogan, who was assessing the men in attendance; he nodded at Uncle Tam's statement. The rest of the men gathered around them in a half circle, making her feel equal parts safe and closed in.

"Good." Fiona gravitated toward the heat from the hearth, tearing off her gloves, dropping them on the warm stones, and holding out her frigid fingers to the warmth in an effort to get away from everyone and to get warm. She'd forgotten how it felt to not be cold. For a split second she considered stripping off her boots and hose and holding her feet up to the flames, but she refrained. The older gentlemen in the clan would likely be horrified. It was bad enough she traipsed around the countryside unescorted, but to start stripping in the great hall… She didn't want to give anyone a fit of apoplexy, especially her uncle whom she knew felt a massive amount of responsibility for her.

Fiona glanced behind her at the seven men, all of them looking exhausted and battle weary. "The lot of ye should burn your clothes. We'll give ye something less...rebel-like to wear."

"I'm no' burning my clothes." Brogan spoke in a way that brooked no argument, and she completely understood why he'd not want to. Fabric and clothes were expensive commodities. Likely he didn't have any to spare. But his were covered in blood and ripped in places. And the men all wore plaids, which was tantamount to telling the dragoons that they were in fact rebels.

"Would ye consider wearing breeches instead of your kilts? The plaids are bound to get us noticed on the road."

Brogan frowned, staring down at his kilt and then at his men, then noticing that those within Dòchas were all wearing breeches. "Breeches then."

"Good. And we'll get the rest cleaned."

"Have we the time?"

She nodded. "We will ride harder tomorrow."

As of now, they were only a few hours behind the men on the way to Ruthven, and they had horses. Most of the infantry were on foot and would have to stop from exhaustion soon.

Fiona and the seven soldiers could probably afford to stay the night, and in fact they should. The last thing they needed was worn-out horses and to make mistakes because they were tired. They'd just fought in one of the most horrific battles to date. The fact that they were still standing there alive was a miracle in itself. They deserved a month of rest or more.

"We'll head out before first light," Fiona said. "Tonight we rest." *And let the ice melt from our bones.*

The warriors' shoulders visibly sagged with relief, except for Brogan who stood tall, stoic. Almost like a statue. He showed no emotion, no weakness.

Uncle Tam ordered water warmed for the eight of them to bathe, and the clanswomen volunteered to clean the men's clothes, as well as offered up plain breeches and coats to the seven soldiers.

Other women volunteered to mend their hose, their shirts, and anything else that needed fixing. Mugs of warm cider were pressed into their hands, and Fiona allowed herself to be led up the stairs by Beitris, who clucked her tongue about the state of her mistress's hair and the dark purple smudges of exhaustion beneath her eyes.

As they waited for the bath to be filled, Beitris scooped bites of stew into Fiona's mouth as if she were a bairn, complete with wiping her lips with a linen napkin.

"I can feed myself." Fiona grabbed unsuccessfully for the spoon.

"Well I know it," Beitris said as she shoved another bite into Fiona's mouth. Sometimes it was nice to let someone care for her, though she was only going to allow it a few more moments before she physically wrested the spoon from her maid's hands.

At last the bath was filled, and Fiona sank into the heated depths, worried that the cold ice in her bones would turn the water frigid, and blissful when the opposite happened. Beitris washed her hair in silence, giving Fiona needed time to reflect on all that had happened so far and to formulate plans. Of course, with the heat of the water, relaxation set in and none of the planning she'd intended to undertake took place.

She fell asleep more than once during the bath. Lord, she needed a good night's sleep. She would be helpful to no one if she was too tired when it came time to depart. That was exactly why they hadn't left already. The men needed to rest. And yet she didn't treat herself the same way. Somehow she expected herself to be superhuman in strength. Ridiculous. That was one of her faults. Never realizing just how tired she was. Never quitting even when she was on the verge of collapsing.

Out of the bath, Beitris brushed her hair before the fire as Fiona shivered in her night rail, wrapped in a fur blanket. Her nails were turning purple on her prune-like fingertips and toes. The water had only done so much to warm the permanent chill that seemed to have seeped into her body all the way to the marrow. She prayed the fur blanket and the fire would be able to do the rest.

"Let me come with ye," Beitris was saying. "'Tis no' safe for ye to be alone with seven men traipsing the countryside."

"Ye do remember that I've been traveling alone for years? That I've traveled with the prince and his entourage? As a postmistress, I have often encountered our enemies."

Beitris frowned. "Somehow this seems different."

Fiona chewed her lip, imagining her maid's horror when she'd seen her arrive with seven large and muscular strangers. "I know what ye're thinking, Beitris, but I trust them."

But maybe she shouldn't.

Perhaps trusting them was merely because her only other choice was to face the dangerous roads alone. And though she'd done it a million times on her own, something in her gut told her *now* was different from *before*. Hell, her eyes and ears were telling her that much. Cumberland had issued orders for every Jacobite rebel to be executed on sight. She stood a much better chance of survival with seven large warriors by her side than she did alone.

They'd lost the battle. But they weren't going to lose hope. Not on her watch.

"But we are no' giving up," she whispered. "We will keep fighting. Praying. Scotland will be our country again."

"I ought to advise your uncle to lock ye up." Beitris wove Fiona's long hair into a braid.

Fiona sat forward, turning around to give Beitris a suspicious glare. "Ye wouldna."

Beitris nodded perfunctorily, in a no-nonsense way. "I would."

"No' if ye value your life." Fiona stole the brush and brandished it like a weapon.

Beitris stole back the brush. "'Tis your life I value, my lady. And seeing as how I'm the only one in the room who does…"

"I value my life. I value the lives of all our people, of our country. That is why I must go. This is no' an argument I care to visit again," she snapped.

Fiona turned back around, staring at the fire, wishing everyone would just understand how much her part in all of this mattered. She was the prince's bloody personal messenger, had the ring to prove it. If the prince trusted her, shouldn't the rest of her clan?

Beitris was quiet for a moment. Then with a great resigned sigh, she said, "One of your hairpins is missing."

Fiona thought back to Culloden House and the crazed fool who'd been trying to assault her. How she'd had to sink that hairpin through his flesh. How his life had ebbed right there before her.

"Aye." Her voice cracked with emotion.

"Ye used it? On a man?"

"Aye."

Beitris mumbled a soft prayer. "I beg ye, my lady, one more time, please stay."

Fiona turned around and faced her maid, her friend, then pulled her into her arms and listened as Beitris sobbed against her shoulder. "I will be all right."

"Where are our men?" Beitris sobbed. "Why have they no' returned with ye from the battlefield?"

"I dinna know." Fiona bit back tears. "I hope to find them with Ian," she said, though she had a feeling that what she would find was not something any of them wanted to bear witness to.

Her eyes dipped closed, a tear streaming down her cheek. She feared for her brother. Devastation at what she'd witnessed, the stress of feeling like murderers lurked around every corner, ready to run her through with their bloody traitorous weapons, made her weary. She clung to her friend and let herself cry for the first time in months.

The ale was good but had nothing on the whisky Uncle Tam poured into Brogan's cup. The men drank heartily of the smoky spirits, and Brogan went from being quite cold to glorious warmth, like that of a seal laid out on a rock beneath a summer sun.

He sat in a chair, legs spread out. Skin finally warmed.

The fact that he and his men had scrubbed down in the great hall didn't bother him at all. Though he did keep glancing toward the arched doorway where Fiona had disappeared for her own bath.

He took a long pull of his whisky, dressed now in a clean *léine* shirt and a short waistcoat in the same faded brown as his breeches. He was quite nondescript.

However unseemly going barefoot among women may be, his boots were before the hearth with the rest of the men's. The leather had grown quite soaked, and he hoped that they'd be dry by morning, but he doubted it. In fact, he had doubts about the woolen plaids being dried too.

Brogan ran a hand over his face. He was grateful for the warmth, the bowls of stew that were coming out of the kitchen, the dry clothes, and a break from imminent danger, but at the same time he distinctly felt as though he didn't belong here. He was a bastard, a soldier, relegated to the barracks, stables, and war camps. Not dining in the great hall as though he meant something.

"What are your intentions with my niece?" Uncle Tam stood beside him, arms crossed as he stared into the fire, his white, bushy brows pushed down into his eyes as he made to study the flames.

"We made a deal. I'd accompany her in making a delivery, and she'd lead me to the prince or at least give me directions."

Uncle Tam glanced up at him. "So ye know about her antics?"

"Antics?"

"Running around the Highlands like a damned messenger."

Like a messenger. The lass *was* a messenger, and clearly her uncle didn't support it. Interesting.

"Aye."

The old man shook his head and sighed heavily. "She's been doing it for years. I think even since she was a lass."

"Truly?"

"Aye."

"Why has no one put a stop to it?"

"They've tried. Does no good. Besides, now she's got the ear of the prince. If His Highness thinks she should…" Tam shook his head. "Hell, she's the verra reason everyone met at Glenfinnan. 'Twas she who spread the word of the gathering and the prince's pronouncement of his intentions. Nobody had laid eyes on him until that moment…"

Brogan was stunned by that news. She'd played an integral part in getting the revolution started, and her uncle wanted her to quit. Wasn't he proud of her accomplishment? Nay, it wasn't that, it was fear. Fear that she would die doing her duty like any brave soldier.

"She's a brave lass," Brogan said, concerned for the little pique of irritation he felt in his chest at her being admonished.

"Aye," the old man said grudgingly. "I blame her da."

Brogan sipped his whisky, trying to understand exactly what the hell the old man meant. He was either proud of her or he wasn't. "Where is he?"

"Dead."

Brogan nodded, feeling the pain of loss, though for an entirely different reason.

"In any case, we may be a small clan here, but if any harm comes to her while she's under your watch, I'll have my men come after ye with swords drawn. Your ballocks will hang from our gates until they rot away."

"Understood." Brogan took another long pull of whisky, irritated. The man wouldn't stop his niece from running off into danger, but instead put the entire weight of responsibility on Brogan's shoulders. That hardly seemed fair.

Besides, he'd not known the wench long, but from what he did know of her, it wouldn't matter what he did or said; she would do what she desired.

Fiona MacBean wasn't a team player.

And yet she *was*. Because if she wasn't, she wouldn't be risking her life helping the prince or the rebellion. If anything, she was the head of the team. And that thought was rather disturbing.

In any case, Brogan needed to be rid of her soon. Because though he wasn't afraid of Uncle Tam or Clan MacBean, he was in favor of keeping his ballocks exactly where they belonged.

At that moment, there was a rustling of skirts from the alcove and he whipped his head toward it, his chest doing strange things in anticipation of seeing Fiona's fierce and beautiful face.

But it was only her maid, looking harried as she rushed toward the kitchen with an armload of fabric.

When Fiona didn't appear behind her, disappointment flared within Brogan, which in turn only irritated him even more. He took another pull of whisky, then grabbed one of the extra blankets that had been left for them and found a place on the floor to wrap himself up and go to sleep.

Though he closed his eyes, sleep didn't come easy. Nay, instead he was haunted by the haughty, floating face of a daring and foul-mouthed phantom—Fiona.

Five

As planned, they left Dòchas before the sun rose, heading southeast toward Ruthven. Fortunately, the rain had ceased for the interim, giving them a reprieve from the wet and their clothes a chance to keep them warm. Though the miles between them and the battlefield grew, the fear at being on the road surrounded by the enemy did not diminish.

Fiona could smell blood in the air, the smoke of burned-out cottages, and despair. Surprisingly to her, she was relieved for the company of Brogan and his men. They gave her a sense of security, and when things grew too quiet, one of them rattled off a bawdy jest that had them all, including her, in stitches.

Every so often, she found her gaze sliding toward Brogan, where she studied his profile and wondered at his thoughts. But inevitably, her mind would ping its way back to the reason why they were together.

Her heart was never going to stop racing. The duty to the rebellion that she'd fully embraced for years had always been dangerous, but things had changed overnight. And now the danger was more imminent. Eight Jacobites traveling on the road were bound to be noticed.

Despite her enjoying their company more and more, it was better that she part ways with them as soon as they arrived at Ruthven, for their sake as well as her own.

The first light of morning hit the icy moors, and their party woke, stretching out the stiffness a night of sleeping on the cold ground brought. They'd been on the road no more than a quarter hour when bloodcurdling screams had them all stopping short, their veins freezing on the spot. Wails of devastation.

Someone needed help. Fiona turned in her saddle one way and then another, trying to determine the exact location. The men seemed frantic to find the source of the cries too. Another scream rent the air, coming from the left, and Fiona swiveled in that direction, urging her mount to veer off the road and into a field.

"Fiona," Brogan called after her, but she ignored him.

If he wanted to remain complacent to those who suffered, that was his choice, but she would not.

Thick black smoke curled above the trees lining the road as she led her horse into the dimness of the forest, following the sounds of anguish and the ever-increasing scent of burning. Before she'd reached the location, a series of pops cracked the air. Gunfire. And just as suddenly as the cries had pierced the wind, they were silenced.

Fiona's heart ceased its pounding against her breast. Her eyes widened impossibly, and her breath held painfully in her lungs.

There was only one reason for those cries for help, screams of pain to be silenced—death.

She forced her horse forward, one step at a time, until she could see in full view what had happened. Redcoats burning out a small cottage, poised with their pistols over prone bodies. Several Jacobite soldiers and a woman lay facedown in wet grass thick with their blood. Shot dead. Silenced.

This was what the dragoons had inadvertently warned them about on the road. Cumberland's plan to eradicate the opposition.

Fiona swallowed the scream rising in her throat, biting her palm to make sure it didn't escape. Through the miasma of her emotions, she felt rather than heard Brogan's approach. He stopped beside her, watching the carnage taking place just a short distance away.

She looked up at him, tears blurring her vision, and he raised his finger to his lips, indicating she should remain silent.

Though she nodded, she didn't trust herself. Tremors racked

her body, and she kept her hand to her mouth, biting her fingers as tears flowed down her cheeks.

Those nameless faces could be any one of them. Could be Annie with the men she'd seen rushing from the battlefield, could be Jenny hiding out in a cave or running in the woods with her rebel soldiers. Could be her brother Ian, or any of the MacBean clan. Could be Gus and Leanna if they somehow returned to Scotland at the wrong time. Could be every single person at Dòchas.

They stood silent for several more minutes, and then Brogan's fingers brushed her elbow as he reached and tugged at the reins of her horse with a cock of his head back toward the way they'd come.

Warmth tingled and prickled her skin from that slight touch, and she wanted to lean into it. To crawl onto his lap and curl up. To feel safe for once, totally and completely sheltered.

But to feel that protected again she'd have to return to a state of naivete she never wanted to revisit. To feel completely secure would mean becoming ignorant to everything in the world.

And there was no going back. Not with everything she'd seen and done.

They should leave, run the horses as hard as they could before they were discovered, and yet she couldn't turn away from the carnage displayed before her. The bodies bleeding into the ground. The way their deaths mirrored a possible fate in store for her and the seven men she traveled with. If the dragoons turned, if they caught their scent on the wind or happened to hear the tinkling of a bridle, all they would have to do was look. And they'd see Fiona and Brogan hiding in the woods. They, too, would be shot dead on the ground.

Silenced.

And still she wouldn't go. Whether it was shock or bravery or downright stubbornness, she shook off Brogan's hold.

Should she honor them in death, or flee and save herself?

Tearing her eyes from the brutal scene, Fiona nodded to Brogan. She was no good dead. And neither was he. She turned her horse back in the direction of the road, trembling and fighting back tears, while in the distance the dragoons celebrated the lives they'd taken.

It took everything within Brogan not to gather Fiona in his arms. He'd never experienced such raw emotion before, watching her suffer. It punched him repeatedly in the gut. Tears gushed down her face, horror written in every angle of her features.

It made him wonder what horrors she had witnessed before now.

When did seeing such horrific things over and over again finally make one numb? And when did the horror end?

The men waited back on the road, as he'd instructed, having guessed what they would come upon in the glen. They all took one look at her tearstained face, glanced at Brogan as he shook his head, and knew instantly what they had witnessed.

They hung their heads, all of them riding mournfully on in silence. Hurrying away from the destruction, the danger.

Fiona raced off at breakneck speed, taking turns too fast, urging her horse to leap over boulders when it was easier to go around them. Each option she took was more dangerous than the last, until finally Brogan grabbed her reins and pulled her horse to a stop. Sweat glistened on her features, mingled with tears, and the look on her face was enough to stop him cold.

"Why did ye do that?" she screamed.

Brogan jumped down from his horse and walked around toward her. "If ye want to beat someone up, come off that horse and beat me. But I'll no' let ye hurt your mount or yourself."

Red flamed in her cheeks and she jumped off her horse. Teeth bared, body tight. She was itching for a fight, it was obvious, and he'd let her take all of her rage and pain out on him. She needed it. Needed to get it out so they could continue on smartly. To run in a blind rage would only put them all in more danger, and they couldn't risk that. Not with dragoons scouring the countryside looking for someone to kill.

"Ye think me so incapable? So reckless?" she shouted. A tiny fist flew at him, hitting him square in the chest.

There was a slight sting with the blow, and he nodded in appreciation. "Aye. Ye're a reckless wee fool. Hit me again."

She flew at him, pummeling his chest with her fists, letting all the anger and despair, the anguish and grief out on him. Brogan, not caring about the pain she inflicted on him, knowing later his chest would likely be covered in bruises, held his arms out to the side and let her beat him until he feared she'd split her knuckles. Then he wrapped his arms around her and hauled her against him. She fought against him, calling him every blasphemous word in her vocabulary until she finally went limp.

He held her close, her breaths heavy, heart pounding against his, and he whispered, "Shh…" in her ear. "I've got ye."

Within a breath, she started to fight against him again, but not as hard as she had before, and he murmured against her cheek, his lips brushing her hair, her tears, "Hush, sweet lass, ye're safe with me…" until she finally stilled, until she clung to him and great sobs racked her body.

Taking note of her emotional destruction, the men turned their backs to afford Fiona and Brogan privacy in the middle of a moor where there was none to be found.

Brogan swallowed the emotion tapping into him. He was a soldier. Soldiers didn't get emotional. And yet he felt her pain.

When she calmed, Fiona shoved away from him with a frown, and as she glared up at him, face flaming, eyes red-rimmed and swollen, looking like a self-righteous warrior queen, she grumbled,

"I'm sorry for… Thank ye…for…" She cleared her throat, her hands on his chest as she pushed away.

"Ye need no' thank me, lass."

She swiped at her face, frowning. "I'm no' a coward."

"Quite the opposite." She was incredibly brave.

"I'm no' going home." Her shoulders were rigid, and despite that, he could see that she wasn't as pent up as she'd been before. That she wouldn't drive her horse into the ground and the lot of them into an early grave.

"I didna expect ye to."

That wasn't entirely true.

When he'd first met her, Brogan had one hundred percent expected her to go home, but the more time he spent with her, the more he understood the importance of her position within the rebellion. Only now he knew home was the last place she needed to be.

That very revelation wreaked havoc on his mind.

Women had no place in war. Women were to be protected, not the other way around. And yet in the past few days, he'd seen a woman leading a regiment of men and a woman risking her life to deliver important information—that very same woman's spying and delivering messages sanctioned by his leader.

The idea that women were just as much a part of this revolution as the men had never occurred to him before, and it still sat uneasily with him. How many other women were a part of the rebellion that he didn't know about?

Were any of them sisters?

Och, he hoped not.

He'd seen what this war could do to women. Hell, they'd witnessed the execution minutes ago of a woman right alongside the rebels she supported. It made him want to grab Fiona into his arms and carry her all the way back to Dòchas Castle where she'd be safe.

The conflict within him was real, and a damned pain in the arse too.

"What are ye waiting for?" Fiona called down from where she sat, back ramrod straight, atop her horse. He'd barely noticed her climbing up. "We've a lot more miles to cover."

Gone were the tears, gone was the raw emotion that had cut through the attitude on her face. The Jacobite messenger, the rebel spy, was back.

By sundown, they crossed over the arched stone Bridge of Carr spanning the snaking river Dulnain into a nearby village. Brogan stared down at the cobbles of the packhorse bridge. His great-uncle had been the one to commission it, as the river afforded no place to easily cross. So much history in one place. He was proud of it and yet felt infinitely severed. He was a bastard at odds with his father who hadn't sided with the Jacobites. It was hard to be proud of his heritage when he found himself struggling with so much inner conflict.

The village was quiet. Were they aware of what had happened on Drumossie Moor? Were they fearful of being subjected to the impending cruelties of Cumberland's army? Culloden was a hard loss for them all.

Ahead, in the waning light, Brogan spotted several men huddled together. He slowed his horse, the rest of his men and Fiona doing the same. While not wearing redcoats, neither were the villagers wearing traditional Highland dress. It was too hard at this vantage point to see if they were enemies or not. But since Fiona had insisted Brogan and his men change before they left her family's castle, they were not dressed as rebels either, for which he was glad.

The men ahead of them came to stand in the center of the road. One had his hand out to stop them; the others had their hands behind their backs, possibly grappling for weapons. Brogan tensed, prepared for a standoff in the middle of the road. They should have circled the town, not bothered to try to find shelter and food. Every village would be hostile ground now that they'd woken the devil.

"Good evening," Fiona said, her voice calm and even, a kind smile on her face. If he'd not seen her kill a man a few days ago, he might have thought she was docile. "Might we appeal for your hospitality? Is there a place for us to rest our horses and bed down for the night? Perhaps have a warm meal? We are willing to pay."

The men frowned and said not a word, their gazes cutting hard across the lot of them. Seeking silent answers to unasked questions.

Brogan gave them the same treatment, staring at their hidden hands, wondering when the weapons were going to come out. As he studied them, their eyes drifted over Fiona. Hunger and lust and something a little more sinister.

"Is that your woman?" the man in the center asked.

"Nay. But she rides with our party under our protection."

The man's brow furrowed even further, the derisive curl to his lip giving way to exactly what he thought Fiona's part in their caravan was. Brogan's fist clenched and he forced himself not to punch the man in the face. He also prayed that Fiona's inner wolf stayed caged. Best they leave this town.

The man started to shake his head, and Brogan opened his mouth to try to convince him to agree, when Fiona did the same thing as she'd done when she first met him, which was flip a coin through the air. The man in the center caught it and tossed it back without even looking to see what she'd given him.

"We've got no place for ye here, but ye'll no' be bothered if ye make camp outside the village."

In other words, they didn't want any trouble. They thought Fiona and the soldiers to be rubbish, did not want to even consider who they might be. Or worse, they thought them traitors or dangerous. Perhaps they were only giving them shelter outside the village with promise of no trouble and then they'd send dragoons to gather them up in the middle of the night.

"Our thanks," Fiona said, her tone slightly tighter than when she'd first spoken to them, but perhaps only noticeable by Brogan.

Had anyone else ever tossed the coin back at her without a second glance?

Fiona, Brogan, and his men crossed through the town, the hair on the back of Brogan's neck prickling as the villagers followed their retreat. Once on the opposite edge of town, Brogan subtly increased his mount's pace, the others following suit. Just outside the makeshift wooden walls, they found they were not the only ones to have been tossed from the village center.

Several small campfires crackled. Figures huddled close together, trying to gain warmth in the quickly chilling evening.

There was safety in numbers, but not with Cumberland's army on the loose. And not with the men in the village so suspicious. The dragoons would see any gathering of men outside a village as a sign of rebellion. Brogan and his men needed to get the hell out of there. His gut tightened, instinct bidding them run.

Fiona dismounted before he could tell her to stop and approached the first campfire. She pushed her hands toward the flames and then whispered to the people there, who shook their heads.

She went to the next one, doing the same, until she'd visited all three fires. When she returned to him, she said, "We should move on a little longer, though 'tis dark. I've warned them of what we heard, what we witnessed, and they understand the danger. There is nothing more we can do but leave."

One group was already putting out their fire and disbanding.

"Without walls or the cover of trees, they are sitting ducks," Brogan agreed.

"Aye. I told them as much." In the flickering firelight from the remaining campfires, he could see the worry lines creasing her brow.

Fiona urged her horse forward, taking them farther from the village and toward the forest.

They found a spot within the trees and dismounted. Brogan followed Fiona's stare up at the sky, through the trees now a hazy purplish-gray dotted with stars. She closed her eyes and drew in a deep breath. He felt that inhalation all the way to his toes. Concerned in the same sort of way. There was an ever-present tension in his shoulders, hell, his whole body. Even in the middle of the forest with no apparent danger in sight, they could be set upon at any moment.

"We should be safe here for now." Brogan wiped his hand down his horse's mane.

"Aye," Sorley added.

"We'll take shifts," Brogan said. "I'll go first."

The men divided up who would take watch, and when she wasn't chosen, Fiona said, "I'll also take first watch."

"Ye need no', lass." Brogan thought of the deep-purple smudges beneath her eyes, the fact that she seemed to be perpetually awake. The lass needed rest.

Instead of agreeing—and why would he have ever thought she would—she rounded on him, her voice crisp with irritation. "Because 'tis a man's place?"

"Nay, because I know how exhausted ye are."

"I'm no more exhausted than anyone else."

"And I'm too tired to argue." He shrugged. "Stay up if ye like."

They rubbed down their horses, saw that they had plenty to graze upon. None of them dared build a fire, though they all could have used the warmth. Instead, they ate their rations in silence, and half of them wrapped up in their plaids to sleep while the other half listened.

All the while Brogan watched Fiona, trying to decipher just what he was going to do with her.

Sorley plopped down next to him, picking his teeth with the end of a thin stick. "What do ye make of her?"

"She's a stubborn chit."

Sorley chuckled. "Aye."

And the more time Brogan spent with her, the more he absurdly liked her.

———

Fiona woke to the sound of rustling, scurrying. Eyes wide, she searched in the dark, certain they were about to be set upon either by dragoons or, equally disturbing, a horde of rats.

One and the same really.

"There's a hound that's followed us." Brogan's voice broke through the darkness as though he'd read her mind.

"Followed us?" Fiona frowned, her heart aching for the loss of her own beloved hound the year before.

"Aye."

"For how long?"

"Since we crossed the Bridge of Carr."

A mile or so. Fiona sat up, rubbing the sleep from her eyes and stretching out the kinks from her bones. She made a clucking sound with her tongue and riffled in her satchel for a piece of jerky.

"Dinna feed it," Brogan said. "It'll only keep following us."

"I'm no' going to let the poor thing starve." Though she ought not waste their resources either. Och, what could one tiny piece of meat harm?

"He doesna look starved." Was that sarcasm she detected in his tone?

Fiona lifted her chin, though he could hardly see it. "A treat then for no' tearing out our throats."

"He doesna look vicious either." Definitely sarcasm.

"That's because I've given him an olive branch." She raised a brow toward Brogan and tossed a piece his way, chuckling at his surprise.

Brogan grunted. "I'm no' vicious."

Fiona laughed softly and held out her hand. A cold, wet nose snuffled at her palm, gently taking the dried meat before the scuffling sound of paws hurried away. She'd not even had a chance to pet the poor thing.

Brogan tsked. "He's stolen your treat and willna give ye anything in return."

"No' all gifts require anything in return," she retorted.

Again, he grunted.

Fiona rolled her eyes and stood. The man was either full of opinions or grunted his judgments. There didn't seem to be an in-between.

"Where are ye going?" he asked.

"To seek a moment of privacy. We should get going before the sun comes up. Have ye slept at all?"

"Aye. The hound woke me."

"Me as well," one of the other men said, followed by a chorus of agreements.

"I promise no' to be vicious if ye toss me a hunk of meat," Sorley teased.

A round of chuckles filled the camp at that.

"Well, good, if we're all awake, we might as well continue on." Fiona stretched her arms up over her head. Then chucked pieces of jerky at each of them, laughing herself when they jumped with surprise. "'Haps we'll reach Ruthven well before night falls once more."

Fiona was grateful for the warmth of her horse's girth on her legs when she mounted. The few hours of sleep she'd garnered had left her mostly frozen. When this war was over, she'd be grateful to finally let warmth seep back into her bones. That was if she made it through.

They stuck to the woods when they could, avoiding the roads at all costs in order to move safely, though not necessarily faster.

One thing Fiona required, however, when they passed by a village was to ride through and warn them of Cumberland's orders of execution. The people needed to know of the increased danger. Though she insisted on riding alone, Brogan asserted his need to go with her each time, leaving the rest of the men outside the walls.

Like a band of brothers, Brogan's men were not willing to sit idle, and instead patrolled the perimeter and reported back. The very act made her smile. They'd become tightly knit while on this jaunt, and it all started with a bit of teasing.

By late afternoon, they crossed over the River Spey, the towering fortress of Ruthven Barracks coming into view seated atop a hill, its strong, imposing stone walls cutting against the afternoon sky. Ravens cawed over the structure, swooping and landing before being shooed away by the guards.

The road to the fortress followed a narrow, shallow burn and then cut across a field, putting them in view of those within, but also in plain sight of any hidden enemy forces watching the barracks.

"We made it," Fiona muttered, more to herself than to anyone else. The journey here had been easy compared to some, and harder in so many other ways.

"Let us no' wait," Brogan said in reply.

At the gate, Fiona pulled the emerald ring from her bodice, brandishing it for all to see.

The doors were opened almost immediately, and a loud squeal from within had Fiona's attention jerking to her dear friend Jenny running, her long blond locks streaming behind her like a cape.

Fiona tossed herself from the horse, landing with her feet already in a run as she embraced her friend in a fierce hug.

"Ye're no' dead," Fiona breathed out, emotion pummeling her chest and tears scratching at her eyes.

"Neither are ye."

"Thank God."

They squeezed and squeezed until it hurt, the relief raw and powerful. Fiona hadn't realized until she saw Jenny how very much she worried that death had come to claim her at the hands of a red-dressed bastard.

After several heart-seizing moments, they pulled apart, smiles cracking their faces and tears on their cheeks. They laughed at each other, swiping at their tears.

Fiona turned to Brogan and his men. "This is my dear friend Jenny. Chief of Clan Mackintosh. Known by some as Colonel Jenny, or Mistress J. Jenny, these are my brothers in arms, Brogan, Sorley, Keith, James, Charles, Fin, and Dugall."

The men dismounted and Jenny greeted Sorley with familiarity, which sparked Fiona's curiosity. She'd have to ask her about that later, but right now she was distracted by Brogan, who came forward to grip Jenny's proffered arm.

"Colonel, 'tis an honor. Brogan Grant. Ye handled yourself well on the battlefield."

Jenny appraised Brogan for a moment. "And ye came to the aid of Ian MacBean."

Fiona flashed her gaze at Brogan. She knew they'd fought together but not that he'd aided her brother. A little tug on the inside of her chest had her trying to swallow hard against a lump in her throat.

"Aye. I couldna let him have all the fun," Brogan jested.

"Och, nay," Fiona said. "Ian would be more than happy to share, I'm certain."

Brogan grinned down at her, and her stomach did a little flip. He really was incredibly handsome. If only she'd met him under different circumstances, the minor flirtations, the witty banter, the teases might have led to... What? A kiss. And judging from the confident air that surrounded him, Brogan would be good at it.

Clearing her throat and attempting to force herself away from these thoughts, Fiona said, "I came to relay a message from the prince."

Jenny nodded. "Good. Murray is inside."

Fiona linked her arm with Jenny's as they headed toward the door, leaving the men to take care of the horses. Inside, she found Murray gathered with several of his men around a table covered with maps. There was a fire in the hearth, and candles lit about the room. It smelled stale, like sweat and ale, and panic if it were to have a scent.

"They plan the next steps." Fiona was not asking the question, rather stating the obvious, perhaps because she was a bit surprised they would do so without the prince's orders. Then again, Murray had been doing a lot of things on his own without the prince's direct say-so.

Part of her was irritated by that knowledge on behalf of her benefactor, but the other part understood. After all, most of the prince's army was here, but without him to command them.

"Aye." Jenny nodded at Murray, the prince's right-hand general, who glanced up from what he was doing. "A message from the prince."

Murray straightened and approached Fiona. The man's features were pinched with frustration. "Where is he?"

Saints, but it was times like these she hated to be the one presenting the bad news.

"He is no' coming here," Fiona said. "He was headed to Invergarry Castle, where they hoped to set up a camp. If it becomes dangerous, he will make his way to the Hebrides. But he bid me give ye and the men a message. Ye are to disband."

"Disband?" Murray exclaimed, incredulous.

There was grumbling from the men at the table behind him. She'd known this news would not be welcome, for it wasn't welcome to her either. All of them had put their hearts and souls into the cause. Being told to disband was just a bootheel to the precious organ.

"Aye, for now," she continued. "He says that he will raise his standard once more when we've had a chance to recover from the loss at Culloden. For now, all are to disband and hide in plain sight. There is something else we learned on our way here. Cumberland has ordered his men to execute without mercy anyone they suspect to be a Jacobite." Her throat tightened and she cleared it, trying to bid away the emotion that kicked at her gut. "We witnessed his order in action on the road."

"How could he have given up on his people so easily?" Murray growled.

"He's no' given up," Fiona tried to reassure the men assembled, even while inside she was starting to doubt the reassurance. "He merely wants everyone to lie low until we have had a chance to regroup. The loss at Culloden was devastating for our cause, for Scotland. Prince Charles needs more time. We need more time."

The men all lowered their heads, nodding, each of their thoughts on those they'd lost.

"We will rise up. We have to. This is what we do. Our lawful king, our country, must be put to rights," Fiona said. "And the prince will no' give up on his people."

Murray nodded, though his frown was fierce. "We will no' give up on Scotland."

"Never," Fiona agreed.

A chorus of agreement rang out through the barracks, the men pronouncing their allegiance to the Jacobite cause. Was it just Fiona, or did it sound like the men were less inclined to praise their prince by name? And did it really matter? For the Jacobite cause *was* to bring Prince Charles to the throne.

Jenny gently squeezed Fiona's arm. "Ye look exhausted. Let me get ye a chamber. We've no' got much in the way of sustenance, but I gather there's enough porridge for the lot of ye."

"We're grateful for anything ye can provide." Fiona turned to the men, resolute in her decision. "This is where we part."

Brogan frowned, took a step closer. "No' yet."

Fiona straightened her spine. She had to remain strong. "I'll be leaving at first light. I need to return to Inverness and locate my friend Annie. There are other messages that need to be relayed, lest suspicion fall on my head." She bit her lip. "I am a royal postmistress. I suppose I should have told ye that before."

Brogan's eyes widened, and he let out a short curse under his breath. "I said no' yet." His voice sounded strangled, as though he was trying to hold back words or his reaction at the very least.

Fiona bristled and opened her mouth to respond, but he gave a short nod and turned on his heel, the rest of the six men following behind him, effectively cutting off her reply and her argument. The stubborn man…

"Ye're no' in charge of me, Brogan Grant," Fiona called after him, then grumbled to herself before noticing Jenny wide-eyed beside her. But he didn't even turn around, inciting an intense need inside her to chase after him and make sure he understood exactly where they stood.

"What was that all about?"

"I made a deal." Fiona sighed. "He was to come with me here, and then I'd lead him to the prince. I've just told everyone where the prince was, and where he may head. My duty is done."

"Apparently he doesna see it that way." Jenny stared after Brogan's retreating figure. Then smiled wryly. "He is a handsome brute."

"Who is handsome?" Jenny's husband, Toran Fraser, joined them, a jovial smile on his face. "Should I be worried?"

Jenny laughed and wrapped her arm around her husband's middle. "Nay, love. I have eyes for no one but ye."

Fiona stared after Brogan, frustrated at his dismissiveness but also intrigued by his stubborn response. *No' yet.* What did that even mean? The man was simply not accepting that she planned to leave.

"Jenny, I…" Fiona bit her lip.

"Go," her friend said with a laugh. "I know that look."

"'Tis no' what ye think."

Jenny glanced at Toran, sharing a smile with him that Fiona found irritating.

"'Tis no'," Fiona said petulantly. "And if ye say so again, I'll have to call ye out, battle-hardened soldier or no'."

Jenny just laughed. "If ye say 'tis so, then it is."

Fiona growled, finding it even more irritating that she sounded so much like Brogan. This—their relationship, nay, their acquaintance—was nothing like whatever Jenny might say it was. They were nothing. Could be nothing. Would be nothing.

And to prove it, she *wouldn't* go after him. Nay. She'd made up her mind, and she'd leave when she damn well pleased.

"We are departing, my friend," Jenny said, interrupting the internal argument. "When ye arrived, we were just heading out. I'm gathering rebels to break out our soldiers who've been taken by the redcoats."

"I wish ye well, my friend." Fiona tugged Jenny in for another hug. "I will see ye soon."

Jenny pulled away, holding on to Fiona's shoulders and locking eyes. "Aye, ye will. Be well. Stay safe. Dinna be afraid to let anyone in here." Her friend tapped her on the chest.

Before Fiona could respond, Jenny jogged after her husband, leaving Fiona speechless.

Six

Fiona slept through the evening meal.

At first Brogan had been concerned that she'd ignored him and run off, but after insisting a servant check on her, he was informed she was indeed asleep. The lass had to be exhausted. As tough as she pretended to be, even the hardiest people still needed rest sometimes. Truth be told, he was worried about her.

When dawn lit the sky the following morning, Brogan was already in the courtyard of the barracks—all eight horses saddled, supplies restocked—and shaking the arm of Murray to whom he'd made a pledge regarding the prince.

Fiona had been late, making Brogan uneasy that she'd snuck off without them again. After a short discussion, the men had agreed to stay on with him per Murray's orders. They would accompany the lass on the mission she insisted upon before completing their own. No one wanted to see her traipsing the blasted dragoon-infested countryside alone. And Murray worried that the prince's private messenger would fetch a pretty coin for any dragoon, especially if they found out that she'd been playing both sides.

All they had to do was see the ring she carried, for even the best held secrets could be leaked. A few added days to their mission would make little difference since the prince was in hiding and not planning to retaliate against Cumberland's army anytime soon. Fiona was the best person to lead them to the prince, or at least that's what he'd insist, when in fact he'd pledged to Murray to protect her.

Part of Brogan really wanted her to go home. Hoped that if they just so happened to see Dòchas, they could make a stop and her clan elders would insist she remain. He'd tell her uncle about

Murray's request and dust his hands of her. The other part knew there was no way she'd abandon the cause now, and that latter part of him nonsensically agreed with her. Likely if her brother wanted her to remain, he would have locked her in the tower before he'd gone off to battle.

At last Fiona appeared, her gaze defiant as she approached him, no doubt to repeat what she'd declared the night before. But Brogan spoke before she could.

"As I said last night, we're no' to part yet. We'll go with ye, and then ye can take us to the prince."

She looked ready to argue with him, but then nodded, saying nothing as she brushed past him and mounted her horse in one well-practiced and graceful move. Brogan swallowed hard, trying to calm the way his heart pounded when he watched her, and decided to take that as her agreement. They bid the men at Ruthven farewell and headed down the road after Fiona. Hours passed, and when they stopped to stretch and rest the horses, still they didn't speak.

When they bypassed the road that led to Dòchas, Brogan stopped her with his hands on her reins, his fingers brushing hers. "Where are ye leading us?"

Fiona frowned down at his hands, her face coloring slightly. "I need to find my friend."

"What of your messages?" He pulled his hand away.

"I can deliver them along the way. And Annie…" She shook her head, swiped at a stray lock of hair that came over her eyes. "She's got no walls to protect her and a heart that willna allow her to abandon anyone in need. She needs to know about the dragoons' plans, as well."

Annie sounded a whole lot like Fiona.

"I need to make certain she's safe." She bit her lip, drawing his attention to her mouth. "If she was taking the wounded from the battlefield, then my guess is she's hiding them while they heal. She'll no' be far from there, right in the center of the dragoons."

Brogan's blood ran cold as ice, all thoughts of her lips gone in that sobering moment. "Why would she do that?"

"She's a healer. She'd no' leave a man in need."

"She could be dead already." Brogan instantly regretted saying that.

"Dinna say such," Fiona exploded, her gaze full of fire. If she'd had a pistol in her hand, he was certain a bullet would have pierced his heart. "Dinna ever say such again."

Brogan nodded, holding his hands up, truly regretting letting his thoughts slip so easily past his tongue. Normally he wasn't one to speak much, but around her, he seemed to be losing some of his inhibitions. "My apologies."

"Where is your hope?"

His frown deepened. "I've seen enough to know hope helps no one."

"Without hope, ye'd no' be standing where ye are, Grant. I warrant ye'll want to change that line of thinking before this war is through. Hope is what gets us from point A to point B, arriving alive."

He gave a swift shake of his head. "That is called strategy."

"And dinna all soldiers *hope* their strategy works?"

The lass had a point there.

"I fulfilled my duty to ye," she continued, a distant coldness coming into her voice that made him uneasy. "Ye know where the prince may be. Go. Leave me to what I have to do. I dinna need a nursemaid."

"Are ye insinuating that I am a nursemaid?"

Her chin notched up, but she said nothing. Didn't matter, the expression on her face said it all, and he wished to walk back time.

"Ye are," he mused.

The men snickered, and Brogan turned to glower at them all. "I go with ye because ye need a protector."

"And what makes ye think it is ye who should take up the

mantle? Go." She waved at him. "I release ye from whatever sense of duty and honor plagues ye. And I assure ye that I've been at this a lot longer than ye have."

Brogan grunted his frustration and decided to be honest with her, again disregarding his own judgment. "I made a promise to Murray."

"What promise?" Suspicion flashed in her eyes.

"Ye're the prince's messenger. Ye hold the ring. Ye may be the only one left."

"And so Murray has ordered ye to be my guardian?"

"He has asked me to make certain ye get to the prince alive. And if that means we have to traipse after ye, then so be it."

Agitation came off the lass in waves. Her teeth were bared, and at any minute he expected to bear the brunt of her ire.

When she said nothing, he fanned out his arm. "If that means I have to follow ye around as ye deliver messages afore we go to the prince together, so be it. Lead the way to your friend."

"Dinna speak to me, then. At all." She seethed. "I dinna want to know ye're there."

"Dinna be cross," Brogan said. "'Tis for the best."

But perhaps that was not the right thing to say, for he was fairly certain he saw smoke coming out of her ears.

"Ye dinna get to tell me what is best for *me*." She turned and urged her mount into a gallop.

Brogan stared, incredulous, at his men who all looked as though the woman had taken their sweets and crumpled them on the ground.

"Good luck with that," Sorley said with a long drawn-out sigh as if he'd dealt with something similar before.

Brogan was fairly certain he was going to need a lot more than luck.

Brogan had lost her.

And this time it was real.

He turned in a heart-pounding circle, regretting ever having trusted a MacBean. It would seem even a war where they were on the same side wouldn't be enough to keep them fighting together.

At some point when they'd stopped to rest, the lass had managed to mount her horse and ride off without any of them noticing. How in the bloody hell was that possible? He'd been keeping his eye on her like a hawk, and in an instant, perhaps when he blinked, she'd disappeared.

Anger sliced through him, disappointment too. Fiona had abandoned not only him, but the men and their mission of returning to the prince. Was this a sign she wasn't true to the rebel cause?

"Where the hell did she go?" he growled.

The men stared at him with similar shock and disbelief. All he knew was she wanted to go back to the battlefield and find her friend. A place he'd agreed to accompany her. The stubborn fool could be anywhere, and the likelihood of her being captured was extremely high. Especially alone. Dragoons were like hungry wolves on the hunt for anything or anyone they could maim.

Frustration gave way to something akin to dread, but he didn't want to call it that, for to do so would be to admit he was actually worried about her. Which he shouldn't be. Couldn't be. They were together on this mission and not by choice but by obligation. Which was why he needed to pummel any notions of disappointment back into oblivion.

Except that he had made a choice in the beginning.

Damnation!

"Perhaps the hound knows," Sorley suggested.

Brogan looked to where Sorley indicated. Hiding in the brush, the tip of his snout the only thing visible, was the same hound that had been following them for days. A wee thing with long, thin snout and red-gold hair, its legs were short and its body long. The one Fiona secretly tossed food to when no one was looking. She hadn't even taken the hound? Oh, that did it. Brogan let out a roar of frustration, which sent the poor creature to cowering and himself to feeling like a major cad.

Approaching the dog with his hand held out, Brogan cooed. "Come here, lad. Do ye know where the lass has gone?"

The hound snapped at his outstretched fingers, and Brogan leaped back before the dog could bite them off. He supposed it was just payback for having bellowed at the poor thing. "Wee bastard is no' going to be any help."

"'Haps if ye offer him a treat as the lass has done," Sorley suggested.

"I'm no' giving him a damn thing," Brogan said even as he reached into his sporran to pull out a bannock and tossed it to the beast, who eagerly goggled it up, melting Brogan's furious heart a fraction of an inch.

Sorley chuckled. "Right, sir, no' a thing."

"In Ireland we call that giving in," Fin teased.

"'Tis how I was conceived," James snorted, and Charles elbowed him in the ribs.

Keith and Dugall shared a look, then Keith said, "Let's no' waste time seeing if the hound will lead us on a merry chase and instead search for the wench ourselves."

Brogan shot his cousin a glower. "She's no' a wench."

Keith held up his hands in surrender. "Apologies, sir, but—" He cut himself off, and Brogan turned to face him squarely.

"Have ye something to say?"

"Aye. 'Tis only that days ago we were given a second chance at life, a purpose. And that purpose was to aid Prince Charles. Now here we are far from the prince's side, chasing a woman who's told us where he is and that she wants no part of us. I'm just wondering when we're actually going to do what we were meant to?"

Brogan ground his teeth. "Murray—" He cut himself off,

though, realizing he was only making an excuse, because somehow his entanglement with Fiona had become personal.

Aye, Murray had ordered him to protect her, but if she'd run off once she was likely to do so again, and by chasing her he was doing exactly as Keith said, which was straying from their mission. Though the main mission, supporting the prince, could theoretically supersede the latter.

And yet, she was the prince's messenger. So, in a way, they were doing their duty to the prince by protecting her. If she were to be caught, the phrase *Dinna kill the messenger* would become very real in their eyes.

The argument even sounded weak to his own ears. He stared at each man, trying to gauge how they felt about the situation, but none of them were very forthcoming.

With any luck, finding her friend would convince her to stay home, wouldn't it? Brogan scoffed at the entire situation. Living in a castle with a brother who was chief and fought for the Jacobites wouldn't serve her well. Especially if the dragoons came calling.

He'd agreed to help her deliver a couple of messages, not traipse all over Scotland searching for a headstrong lass and getting them into more dangerous situations. Why did he feel such loyalty to her? These men were soldiers of the prince, some related to him by blood. They'd willingly followed him as he'd been blinded by... what? Desire?

Aye... He did desire the lass, and it hit with a shocking thud in the gut. Bloody hell, he also admired her.

That was not a feeling he often had for women. His mother had abandoned him. His father's wives had shunned him, and every other woman he'd encountered wanted him for one thing. Before now, he'd thought women were good for nothing but tending to a household, marriage, and breeding.

But now... He'd seen so much more. Knew so much more.

And it was changing him.

Fiona was changing him.

The question was, did he want that change?

Brogan quite liked who he'd been before, but now he felt as though his eyes were being opened in an entirely different way.

And she'd left him. He cursed under his breath. Once more, a woman he had allowed to get under his skin had proven he was expendable. Not even worthy of a goodbye.

Well, enough was enough. He wouldn't put his men in danger searching for a lass who didn't want to be found. "We'll go to Invergarry Castle where the prince is hopefully still housed."

The men all nodded their agreement. Brogan looked down at the hound who'd crawled from beneath the brush and was staring up at him in hopes of another treat.

"Ye can come, too, if ye want, lad."

─────────────

Guilt riddled Fiona at having left in the dead of night. But there was nothing to be done about it. She had to leave. The men had places to go, and she was holding them back. She could see it in their eyes when they thought she didn't notice.

And Brogan, with his misplaced sense of responsibility. He was better off without her.

Why, then, did she feel a particular pang of regret when she thought of him?

That was a sensation that needed to be quickly wiped away.

Leaving had been easier than she'd thought. The men all went to sleep, save for her and Fin, who were on watch. When he wasn't paying attention, she saddled her horse piece by piece, subtle about it. After all, they'd taken two different sides of camp, and she'd volunteered eagerly for the side with the horses.

When Brogan took over Fin's watch, she waved Keith away, telling him she was not yet tired. At some point, when Brogan had gone off to seek a tree for a private moment, she'd taken the opportunity to mount her horse, toss the hound a thick bit of meat she'd been saving to keep him from following, and then slip away.

In the dark, it would have been hard to see if she'd gone missing, and she guessed, since they didn't speak, that she would have at least a half hour before anyone took notice.

That had been hours before, and she'd not seen nor heard from them.

Cullidunloch Castle, the once grand home of her dear friend Annie, loomed on the moors. Even from this distance she could see the blackened, burned-out walls and the missing roof.

Just before the Battle of Culloden, she'd heard what happened here. And it pained her to know that her friend had been through such a trying ordeal. She was lucky to have made it out alive.

Having not known the extent of the damage to the keep, Fiona had half hoped to find Annie here. But now she doubted such would be the case. With no protection from the elements, remaining in the castle would be just as dangerous as a horde of dragoons making camp on the lawn.

Except… Were those riders?

Fiona squinted, trying to get a better look at the riders leaving the castle, cloaked mostly in muted colors. If she had to hazard a guess, she'd say they were not dragoons. There wasn't a single speck of red.

A lone rider peeled off toward the west, and the band of four went east. Fiona's gut told her to follow the single rider, smaller than most male soldiers. Could it be Annie?

She was at too far a distance to call out, but not too far to follow. Down the rise she rode, in the direction of who she hoped was her friend, for she was fairly certain it was Annie.

Annie did not stick entirely to the road, which made following her a bit difficult, but Fiona was always up for a challenge.

At last, she watched from a discreet distance as Annie unlatched a gate and led her horse onto a crofter's property, only to be greeted by a squealing woman who Fiona recognized as Annie's maid, Eppy.

They both went into the house. Fiona circled the property to make sure they weren't being watched, and then she too unlatched the gate. Urging her horse through, she was greeted by a large black hound with bared teeth that looked ready to start barking his head off.

"Hello, my friend," Fiona said. "I mean no harm, lad." She reached into the saddle bag and pulled out a strip of jerky, hoping it worked as well for this hound as it had for the one in the forest. "I'm friends with Annie."

The dog cautiously approached, tail wagging slightly. He sniffed the meat, looking up into her eyes, asking her silently if she was serious. Fiona smiled. "Take it."

He was quick to snatch the jerky and ran several yards away just to make sure she couldn't take it back. With one last cautious look, Fiona made her way to the door of the croft and gave it two short raps.

"Who is it?" Annie's voice rang out through the door, and Fiona sighed with momentary relief, having been afraid this entire time that perhaps her mind had been playing tricks on her.

"Annie, 'tis me, Fiona."

The door was yanked wide, revealing Annie MacPherson. Her dark hair looked to have been swept up in a bun at some point but hung in loose tendrils around her face, and her amber eyes flashed disbelief.

"Come in, quick." Annie peered over Fiona's shoulder as she ushered her inside. "How did ye find me?" Annie closed the door.

Eppy set down the fire poker she'd been brandishing, revealing an older woman who stood behind her. Both looked relieved to see it was only Fiona.

"I followed ye back from Cullidunloch this morning, but I

promise that I wasna followed." Fiona studied the croft, taking in the sight of more than a dozen recovering soldiers. Some in worse shape than others. So it *had* been Annie she'd seen on the battlefield.

Fiona was going to have her work cut out for her in getting Annie and these men to safety. But one thing was for sure: they couldn't stay here. Not with what she'd witnessed on the road. That croft with Jacobite soldiers and the lone woman who'd been executed could have easily been these inhabitants here. After they'd had some time to catch up, Fiona finally broached the topic.

"I came to relay a message. The redcoats are searching the countryside for any remaining Jacobites. They've received orders from the Butcher to slaughter anyone with allegiance to the prince."

"Nay…" Annie's hand pressed to her chest and she looked ready to collapse at the news, eyes darting to every man in the room, in particular one who couldn't take his eyes off her. Beneath the bruises and beard, he looked to be handsome in a rugged sort of way.

"Aye," Fiona said. "They went through the field and killed those who'd yet to be rescued, and a neighboring cottage which housed many of the injured, they…" Emotion welled in Fiona's chest.

"Ye need say no more, I understand."

"Ye're no' safe here. I want ye to come with me. I'll give ye a few moments to pack up your things." Fiona prayed that Annie would leave with her now, but seeing the men who lay helpless, she knew it would be a feat to get her friend to agree.

As predicted, Annie argued, "I canna leave the wounded at the mercy of the Butcher's men, and I canna leave Mrs. Sullivan. I brought the soldiers here, and I put her in danger. They are all my responsibility."

There were at least seven injured men that Fiona could see. Some who lay beneath blankets, and a couple upright, leaning against the walls for support. The latter group were still healing, but those who lay asleep... There would be nothing moving them for now save death.

"How?" Fiona practically choked on the question, the woman she'd seen shot at the last croft suddenly evolving into Annie.

Annie rubbed at her head with fingers that were red and raw. "I dinna know. But we canna leave yet. No' until everyone is able to walk out of here."

"Please, Annie. Ye must leave afore then. Some of these men willna be able to stand for weeks." She took her friend's hand in hers, hoping to persuade her, knowing all the while it would be futile.

Annie squeezed her hand back, then dropped her hold. "I canna leave without them, Fiona. I willna. I know the risk of remaining behind."

Something inside Fiona's chest felt like it was shattering. God, if Annie weren't so honorable... If only she were a little bit more selfish.

There was only one thing she could do—make certain her friend remained safe and warn her of any redcoats in the area. The danger would be worse for her, because if the men were to get close then Fiona would distract them, risking her own life in the process. "I will be your eyes and ears, then. I'll make certain ye're the first to know if they are coming closer."

Annie shook her head. "Nay, ye've got to get your messages out. I canna take ye away from your duty. We'll be fine. Eppy and I can manage."

One of the men in the corner pushed himself to standing and volunteered to help. Annie tried to argue with him, making an example of the bearded man who stared at her with an intensity even Fiona could feel.

And then another man stood, volunteering. And another.

After denying the handsome wounded soldier who she addressed as Lieutenant, Annie faced Fiona, a frown marring her features as she offered her food and a place to rest.

"I am hungry and in need of a few minutes' rest, but truly, Annie, I would like nothing more than for all of us to leave right now. However"—she glanced at the seriously wounded—"I can see that would be impossible at the moment. Perhaps I can take at least the men who can move and deliver them to a safer location?"

Annie agreed, and Fiona had to take it as a win. At least for now she'd be helping her friend out of a dangerous situation.

Seven

Two weeks later

ANNIE IS SAFE. ANNIE IS LEAVING THE COTTAGE.

Fiona repeated these lines to herself as she made her way through the forest toward a place she was just as familiar with as she was Dòchas Keep—the secret conduit to the prince and the rebellion.

Droplets of water left over from the rain dripped from the freshly budded leaves. Everything smelled alive and awake, for spring had finally decided to gift them with her presence.

April was behind them, and the worst of the massacres, Fiona hoped, too. Though the redcoats seemed to have doubled in number as they continued their search for Jacobite rebels. Even now, she was bone-weary going through the forest.

She'd managed to help Annie as best she could, but the rest was up to her friend. Between managing to keep Annie informed of the goings-on around the cottage filled with healing Jacobite soldiers, she'd also had to keep up with her own messages and made a trip to her family's castle to update them on the situation. They'd also had word from Ian, who was still in the prince's service.

Fiona neared her destination, not yet spying the tree that housed the tiny box Aes had made for her all those years ago, hidden in the alcove of a tree that she hoped was never felled.

Aes, or *A.M.* as he preferred to go by these days, had kept up his messages to her throughout the years. And while she'd stopped writing for a time when he informed her he was to wed and she'd been harboring feelings about the two of them for so long, she had finally picked up her quill and scratched out a hasty congratulations.

Funny, though the messages continued to come, she'd not actually laid eyes on her childhood friend for at least a decade. Sad, truly, for in her heart of hearts, she'd always thought they'd end up together.

An image of Brogan flashed before her mind's eye, so vivid she had to blink for fear he was actually standing in front of her. The infernal grunt. The maddening smirk. The looks of admiration from his men, and the swirl in her belly when his eyes met hers. The way his arms had felt when they wrapped around her. When she'd been in his company she'd worked hard not to notice any of it, not to think about it.

Och, but she could practically see him right now, frowning down at her with disappointment for having run away. Aye, that was what she needed to remember. Not the parts of him that seemed to abduct the sense from her brain, but the irritating parts. So she pretended he was there in front of her, about to admonish her.

Thank goodness he wasn't...

She frowned. Why in Hades was he coming into her thoughts anyway? The blasted man. She'd not seen him since she'd snuck away two weeks ago, nor had she heard through any of her contacts about him, and good riddance.

Although she knew it wouldn't be good riddance for long.

She'd been delivering messages between Jacobite rebels in hiding since they'd parted, and she'd made one drop between government garrisons, which allowed her to keep tabs on the dragoons marching about. But at some point she was bound to be summoned by the prince to return, and then she'd have to abandon her postmistress duties, else possibly risk the prince being caught. Prince Charles would want an update on his men, and she would need to spread the word about regathering the forces. And Brogan Grant would be there, smirk and all.

Her tree came into view. A wide oak that could be a thousand years old for all she knew. Its expanse seemed big enough to fit a family inside, a small family anyway. Fiona dismounted and stilled, listening to the sounds of the forest.

When it seemed like all was clear, she edged closer to the tree and reached inside the alcove just at the right height above her head that no one could see the tiny box inside. She used the key she kept tied around her neck to open the box, half expecting for it to be empty.

Inside, however, was thick folded parchment. She pulled out the packet and stuffed it into her bodice, then relocked the box and returned it to its place. She would not read the message here. That was something she'd learned as a child when her siblings would come upon her so engrossed in whatever she was reading that she wouldn't hear their approach. The box needed to remain a secret, or else it would need to be destroyed.

Tucked deeper in the woods, and again certain that nothing seemed out of place, no one lurking about, she unfolded the packet of parchment.

Two pieces—one map and one missive with a familiar scrawl.

Dear F,

It is time. Go to him.

A.M.

Fiona stared at the map, deciphering easily where the tree was because Aes had drawn a small X there, and then following the waterway of the River Ness, she trailed the line to Skye.

If the prince had already made it that far, this was a good sign. Spirits renewed, she remounted her horse and headed west. And damn if she didn't get a rush of heat imagining Brogan being there when she arrived.

Brogan stood at the mouth of the River Moriston, where Loch Ness waterfalled into the winding waterway. The river glen was in the heart of Grant lands, which meant that he knew exactly where they were. But they weren't any closer to finding the prince.

He picked up a stick and whipped it as hard as he could out into the river. Some of the anger relinquished as the hound he'd named Milo charged after the bounty. They'd been riding for weeks, always just a few days behind the prince or in the completely wrong direction. Whoever the prince had with him was doing a fantastic job of keeping not only the redcoats at bay but everyone else too. And not once had Brogan run into Fiona or even caught the slightest hint of her being nearby.

At this rate, Brogan and his team were better off just staying put and waiting for the prince to traipse by.

"Ye think I'd be used to meeting ye on the road like this."

Brogan's heart thumped in his chest, and he had a momentary sense of being breathless. He whipped around at the sound of Fiona's voice to find her seated on a horse and staring down at where he stood with a smirk on her too-beautiful face. The sun shone down on her, as though she'd just appeared from thin air, brought to life by the golden rays.

Brogan glanced back toward the river where his men watched her, unsurprised at her presence. They had to have seen her approach and said nothing. The bastards. They'd been dealing with his brooding over her being missing for weeks now. He supposed he should be grateful they were all still with him.

"My lady," Sorley murmured, and the rest of the men managed to get in their greetings to her as well, not a face without mirth present. In fact, Fin teased her about appearing just as quickly as she'd disappeared, and she gave him a good ribbing back about it being his stench that had caused her to flee. Joshing each other as though they'd all been chums for years.

Brogan tried to hide his surprise at seeing her. The lass truly was a specter. He'd figured she would already be with the prince—a thought that had plagued him for nigh on the entire time they'd been apart, for he'd feared greatly for her and thought he'd made the wrong decision in not chasing after her. Every time they'd come across a burned-out cottage or misfortune in a town, he'd been afraid to find Fiona's lifeless body.

But there she was in the flesh, looking as exhausted as he remembered. Purple smudges beneath her eyes, a bit dirtier, and just as damned beautiful. He swallowed hard, feeling desire slam into his body in a way it hadn't done in…well, ever. She was supposed to be the thorn in his arse, the weevil he couldn't get rid of, and yet…a sense of pleasure at seeing her made his chest swell, and his skin tingled like he was a bloody imbecile.

"Ye look like hell, Brogan Grant." The words didn't sting, laced with humor and accompanied by that petulant curl to her lips.

Why did she have to be so damn enticing? He ripped his gaze away from her lips and up toward her eyes sparking with merriment. "I reckon I look better than ye, lass."

She laughed, the sound volleying from her throat to punch him in the ballocks.

Fiona glanced toward the men who'd drawn a little closer, issuing a small wave. "Good to see ye again, gentlemen." And then she added in a tone that could only be deciphered as taunting, "Glad to see the lot of ye kept your big bad leader alive."

A few of them chuckled until Brogan shot them a warning glare and growl.

"How did ye find us?" Sorley asked, rubbing his chin in contemplation, but Brogan assumed it was more to stifle his laughter.

"Quite by accident. Seems we are headed in the same direction." She gestured toward the water with a wave of her long, slender fingers.

"Which direction is that?" Sorley asked when Brogan couldn't seem to find his voice.

"Skye." Fiona slid her glance from Sorley back to Brogan, and if he wasn't mistaken, there was a flash of something more than mere curiosity in her gaze.

"I knew it," Brogan said, irritated. They'd been about to cross over to Skye a sennight before and been persuaded to turn around.

"We never should have believed that damn boatman." Sorley picked up a stick and threw it into the water for Milo.

Fiona winged a brow at their conversation. "What boatman?"

"We were going to cross over to Skye a week ago," Sorley said.

"Was the prince no' at Invergarry?" Her expression was shuttered.

"He'd just left." Brogan turned away, crouching to dip his hands in the loch and splash his face. The cool water wasn't enough of a jolt to his senses, even when he repeated the move several times. At last, he ran his hands over his wet hair and stood, using the bottom of his shirt to wipe his face. When he finished, he spied Fiona watching him, her eyes on his movements, on the small bit of skin that he'd just let show.

Good God… All the cold water in the world wasn't going to help him. Maybe not even if it had been frozen over.

"Ah." She ran her tongue over her lower lip and then turned away from him, watching the men who were in various stages of wiping down their horses and washing themselves from their ride. "He doesna stay in one place long, I imagine, with the dragoons searching for him. No one should."

"Agree," Brogan said, deciding he needed a swig of whisky to take the edge off.

"Is that…?" She cocked her head, studying the soaked hound beside Brogan who'd just come up for another toss of the stick into the water.

Brogan grunted. "Aye, the wee lad ye abandoned in the wood."

"I was talking about the hound," she teased.

The men laughed, but Brogan only imagined tearing her off that horse and silencing her with a kiss. "If ye were a man—" He wouldn't desire her so much.

"Ye've told me many a time I'm no', so I'm certainly no' going to start worrying if I were."

Her wit was too much for him.

Brogan nodded toward Milo. "Dinna concern yourself with him, the hound has found his place." *With me. And I willna abandon him.*

"Him?" Her eyes twinkled with some jest he did not know the meaning of. "That's a female hound."

"What?" Brogan jerked his head down to look at the wee beastie holding the stick proudly between sharp teeth.

Fiona was clearly trying to keep herself from laughing as she bit her lips. "Aye, she came with ye?"

"*He* did." Brogan crossed his arms over his chest. Where did she get off trying to say his hound was a lass?

"She."

"He," Brogan insisted.

Fiona cocked her head to the side. "What happened to his ballocks, then?"

Several of the men snorted, and as if to prove the point, the dog flopped onto its back and started pawing the air as if scratching the clouds.

Fin let out a guffaw. "Shite, she's right."

Brogan frowned. "I'm no' one to judge a man by the size of his ballocks."

"Ye didna look?" she asked with a tinkling laugh. "Because she's no' got any ballocks. No more than I have."

"I didna need to look," Brogan insisted. "He lifts his leg like a male when he pisses."

"There is no' anything there, my friend," Fin said with a laugh.

Fiona chuckled. "I rubbed her belly, and she was certainly missing the requisite male...equipment."

The men snorted.

"'Haps she likes disguising her sex, as I have in the company of brutes." Fiona shrugged. "I wouldna blame her for it."

Brogan grunted. "'Haps I should leave the two of ye alone to discuss brutes then."

"Milla," she crooned, ignoring him and reaching into her satchel to pull out a piece of jerky, then tossing it to the ginger hound who was quick to leap up and snatch the meat.

Surreptitiously he spied the back of the hound, noticing a distinct lack of anything there. Bloody hell, he couldn't even tell a female dog from a male. How was he supposed to lead men?

Fiona climbed down from her horse, this time to rub Milla behind the ears and croon at her. The wee beastie acted as though being reunited with its long-lost mother. Was it bad that he felt jealous?

He'd been the one to take the animal in, feed it, care for it over the last two weeks after Fiona had left them both. He'd even gotten used to the feel of Milo—*Milla*—curling up beside him at night, found himself petting her while he contemplated their next strategy. And Fiona... Well, he didn't want to go there.

Women...they were always at the root of his problems, and that didn't appear to be changing anytime soon. This was his fate.

"Mind if I join ye and your men? I am on my way to the prince now." She stood from petting the dog and walked to the water's edge.

Brogan watched her bend down, dipping hands into the water, scrubbing away the muck from her arms, and then splashing water on her face and wiping it around the back of her neck. She closed her eyes for a moment, face toward the sun, and water dripped slowly from her nose to her lips, down the sides of her temple to her jawline and the long column of her neck. Brogan found himself growing inordinately thirsty. He imagined lifting her up from where she crouched, running his tongue along the wet rivulets.

Holy hell... Where had that thought come from? He needed a cold dip in the loch. Fiona was off-limits, for rational reasons. And reasons she'd proven, like her ability to up and disappear without thinking about anyone she'd left behind. Or the recklessness with which she ruled her life. To him, Fiona had only proven herself to be unreliable. And since when did he like to surround himself with unreliable people?

Stiffening, he worked a frown onto his face and hoped none of the men noticed him practically panting after her. He shifted his stance, his breeches growing tight right in the damn center. "Are ye going to run away in the middle of the night again?"

"Were ye bothered that I did?" She stood facing him, her shirt wet and clinging to her breasts.

Brogan forced his eyes up. *Dinna look, ye weaselly bastard.* Keeping his tone irritated, and not for the right reasons, he said, "It does bother me that ye did. Ye could have had the common courtesy to let someone know ye were leaving."

"I told ye many times I didna want to travel with ye." She marched back to her horse, her hips swaying gently and making it hard for him to swallow.

Brogan grunted. She had a point, and it didn't sit well with him. Neither did the way the rest of the men were watching her.

"My men and I are a unit. Everyone works better together with communication. If ye want to be in a man's world, then ye need to follow the rule of men."

"Huh. All right. Then I'll be on my way." Foot in the stirrup, she mounted as easily as if she were climbing stairs and nudged her horse forward, prepared to depart.

Blast if that tiny increment of movement didn't give Brogan a moment of panic. He didn't want her to leave. And not because he wanted to strip her bare and toss her into the loch for a swim... and a kiss. And to slide his body over hers.

The lass wasn't one to play by the rules, and he should have known that already. He was a fool to threaten her, for she simply didn't care enough to change for him, for anyone.

"Wait," he said, and she paused, looking down at him as though he were a petulant child and she was waiting to hear whatever excuse he might have for his bad behavior. "Ye can stay with us. But communication is essential."

"I am no' adverse to communication, Grant. Communication is my mission in this rebellion, ye of all people know that."

"Then ye'll tell me next time before ye run off."

She pressed her lips together and nodded. "Aye. And I should also tell ye that there was a troop of at least a dozen redcoats following me."

Brogan let out a small expletive. "Ye couldna have said as much when ye first got here?"

"I was...distracted." She eyed him, implying it was his fault.

Lord, did he know the feeling. Brogan tore his gaze from her and faced his men. "Mount up. We'll go to my caves."

"Your caves?"

"Aye. My caves."

They crossed the water at a shallow point, picking up the pace on the other side.

"How far were the dragoons when ye reached us?"

"I'd no' seen them in at least a half hour."

"So close."

"Aye. I've been avoiding them for nearly two nights."

Brogan gritted his teeth, not wanting to shout at her, but goddammit, he wanted to shout at her. The lass was watching him, a look on her face that was unreadable. Was she baiting him, or trying to gauge his reaction?

How did she know he was going to be there? He couldn't help but think it was too much of a coincidence that she just happened to see him upon the road.

Aye, she was the prince's messenger, but there was a lot more to the lass than she let on. She was too good at what she did, which meant she was likely the spy he'd suspected all along.

A spot behind his ribs gave a thump. He was glad she was back, an admission he wouldn't make aloud. Seeing her alive, knowing that no burned-out cottage he'd come across had held her body seemed to lift a weight from his shoulders that he hadn't realized had settled there.

"Did ye find your friend?" he asked, genuinely concerned.

"Aye." She flashed him a smile, but didn't expound on that.

"Is she safe?"

"She should be now."

"But she wasna?"

Fiona shook her head. "Things could have ended verra badly for her if she'd no' left when she did. Things could still. But I trust she'll get where she needs to go."

Was that a silent dig at him, that he should trust she would get to where she needed to go too?

"Where is she headed?"

"East. To her brother and cousin in Aberdeen." She turned to look at him, a challenge in her gaze. "And nay, I dinna also have a brother and cousin in Aberdeen to go to."

Brogan held up a hand in surrender. "I said nothing."

"But ye thought it, Brogan Grant. Ye're thinking a lot of things."

"How do ye know what I'm thinking?"

"I can feel it."

She could feel it… Just the way he could feel the heat of her ire, and it made him think of other hot things. The way her body felt when he'd held her against him, consoling her after seeing so much death.

Bloody hell… He'd been too long without a woman if he didn't think this termagant would drive him to the brink of sanity.

Och, but how very satisfying it would be… All that pent-up anger and frustration inside her, that rage just begging to be let loose as he set her to flame and vanquished her troubles in a molten vat of screaming pleasure.

Brogan cleared his throat. Where the hell were these thoughts coming from?

He needed to focus on their journey. Make certain they went in the right direction before he got turned around because all he could think to follow were the hills and valleys of her figure. Brogan tracked a familiar path in his mind from the winding river, over the moors, and up into the craggy mountains. There was a cave that he'd visited often as a lad. His own hiding spot where he could go to think, to escape the clan, to escape everything.

Not many people had ever been there with him. In fact the number was less than the fingers on his left hand, and now he was going to bring an entire group there.

Brogan circled back behind the men, telling them to keep moving forward, to be certain they weren't being followed by the dragoons that Fiona had been avoiding.

Hell, she took so many risks. It was almost as if she thought herself invincible. A feeling he himself had on more than one occasion. Feeling it even now since he'd not died on the field of battle that had claimed the lives of so many, and since he'd not been killed running from Cumberland's men for weeks.

He was cheating death. All of them were. But it only made the sense of rightness stronger. If they were not to be smitten, perhaps that was because their cause was just. They would prevail. They would find the prince, and the army would rise up again to defeat the bloody bastards who would try to put them down.

At last they came to the rise, and Brogan could make out the cave ahead, distinct to him because of the mountain ash tree that grew at its peak.

"That's it ahead," he said to Fiona, who nodded. "Ye all settle in and I'll circle back again to make sure we've no' been followed."

They did as he instructed. The cave was big enough to house

the horses inside too. Despite them all being out of view, watches would have to be taken.

When he returned to the cave, the men had built a small fire at the front and were roasting a few squirrels they'd caught while he was gone.

Fiona sat closer to the back of the cave, her back to the wall, legs stretched out long in front of her, ankles crossed. Her arms were crossed over her chest, and her eyes were closed as if she was sleeping. She was so beautiful like that, so peaceful looking. Even the wrinkled furrow between her brows had smoothed. Milla was curled up at her feet looking completely comfortable.

"Dinna just stand there staring, Grant. 'Tis rude."

She might look peaceful but her acerbic tongue was still in place. He couldn't help but grin, finding her refreshing.

"I've missed your wittiness," he teased.

One eye popped open. "I've no' been called witty before."

"Is that so?"

"Dinna sound so surprised."

The eye closed and he came closer, sliding down the wall to sit beside her. Milla stretched so that her paws brushed his boots.

"How did ye know about this cave?" she asked.

"I came here often as a lad."

"I have a place like that," she said sleepily.

"Oh?" Brogan imagined a smaller version of Fiona discovering a hiding place the way he had.

"Aye. In the woods near Dòchas." Her mouth grew tight for a second and then relaxed.

"Do ye still go there?"

"Aye." She blew out a long breath. "Though my brothers, I'm certain, wish I didna."

Brogan felt the same way and found momentary camaraderie with her kin. "Why's that?"

"Similar reasons to why ye say I shouldna go there." There was a definite eyeroll with that line, but he couldn't see it.

Still, Brogan grinned, finding some satisfaction in the fact that she recognized his inclination. "Dangerous."

Fiona nodded. "I can take care of myself."

"Ye've proven that." Just because he didn't like her methods didn't mean she wasn't sitting there beside him, visibly unharmed. But there was no telling what went on inside her tough exterior. He'd seen her break once when they witnessed the execution. She was not without some fragility.

"I've had to."

There was something in her tone that said she'd had to deal with things far scarier than what he'd witnessed her going through, perhaps more than once.

"Ye're a brave lass, Fiona, but even brave lasses have weaknesses."

She opened one eye again, her head rolling toward his. Lips curled down in a frown. "What's your weakness?"

"I shall tell ye mine if ye tell me yours."

"Deal." Both of her beautiful violet eyes opened then, staring at him intently. This close, he could make out the freckles that covered the bridge of her nose.

"I'm no' a patient man," he admitted, "and I can be a bit cynical."

She snorted. "I could have told ye that. Tell me something that nobody knows."

"Why would I do that?"

"Because, Brogan Grant, the two of us keep running into each other. I think we were meant to be…friends." There was a softness in her voice just then that stretched through the small distance between them and touched him.

"Friends?"

"A foreign concept to a man like ye, I gather?" She chuckled softly. *Friends…*

It wasn't that the notion was foreign, though he didn't count many people as friends. He'd not had the luxury. It was that to be her friend…

Brogan swallowed hard, smiling, and gave a little grunt. He wanted to be her friend, but he wanted more than that too—which made his smile disappear. Friends didn't think about each other naked, did they?

"A warrior doesna have friends." He crossed his arms over his chest, telling himself it was to be more comfortable and not because he was closing himself off to her.

Fiona laughed. "Even evil villains have friends."

"Nay." He wagged his finger. "They have minions. There's a difference."

"Is that so?" She sat up a little straighter, running her hand over Milla's belly. "So what is the equivalent of friends for a hero?"

"Ye think I'm a hero?" He puffed his chest out and rested his hands behind his head.

Fiona made a noncommittal sound and shrugged. "Ye're on the right side."

The lass loved to deflate him, didn't she? And yet he didn't feel deflated. He wanted to laugh, because she was only teasing. "True." He thought about it for several moments and then said, "Do camp followers count?"

Fiona made a gasp of mock outrage at his insinuation that the women who often followed war camps and offered the warmth of their bodies at night to the soldiers could be friends.

"Am I wrong, though?" he teased.

She shoved at his chest, and his arms dropped from above his head as he laughed.

"Ye're incorrigible, Grant. Another of your weaknesses."

Brogan's grin widened. "Ye may be right, so why dinna ye tell me yours?" He tweaked her nose.

"I might back out of this deal," she said with mock petulance, "for I dinna feel ye truly put in any effort."

"I beg to differ. I bared my soul." He clasped both his hands at his chest.

Fiona scoffed. "Fine. I dinna like being told what to do. Satisfied?"

Brogan laughed, the sound loud and booming in the tiny cave, and drawing the attention of the men who sat around the fire.

"If ye're telling jokes, we want to hear," Sorley called.

"I've got a joke for ye," Fin said. "Three men walk into a tavern. One's a Scot, one's an Irishman, and one's an arsehole. The barkeep says, 'I'll get the first two of ye a drink, but we dinna serve *Sassenachs* here.'"

The men roared with laughter, Sorley offering up another joke.

"I'll be back. I need some air." Fiona stood suddenly and exited the cave.

Brogan let her go for a minute, giving her privacy, and then he followed her, waiting by the mouth of the cave for a moment, Milla by his side.

The sun was starting to make its descent, painting the forest in interesting colors of pink and orange. The mountain ash tree outside the cave had started to bud with pretty pink flowering petals. Soon there'd be red berries on it, drawing birds and bees. He'd watched them for hours as a child and found himself wishing for those times again.

Fiona's movement caught his eye. Milla trotted over to join her.

"There's a nice vantage point of the moors over here," Fiona called from where she leaned against a tree.

Brogan sauntered over, the two of them leaning together and watching the gentle wave of evening air brush against the grass in the distance. He glanced down at her, noticing the way the waning light played on the flames of her hair and colored her skin golden. Good Lord, she really was the most beautiful woman he'd ever seen.

Fiona's eyes caught his and they stared at each other, locked in silence. There was an intensity between them that had flared before they'd parted, and now that they were back together again only seemed to have grown molten.

His gaze drifted toward her lips, full and pink. What would it be like to kiss them? To brush his mouth over hers and just forget for a moment all of the past two weeks, two months, two years? Forget the word *friends*...and be something more?

"This is a nice vantage point too," he said, but he wasn't looking at the moors. His gaze skated over her face, and pink blossomed on her cheeks.

She licked her lips, a nervous move, but one that made his gut clench at the sight of that tiny pink tip, and when his gaze went back to hers, Brogan saw hunger there. Fiona leaned forward, lips parted, and then she backed away again, hesitating. Had she been about to kiss him?

Brogan leaned down, coming close, his nose a mere half an inch from hers. He stilled, waiting for her to pull away. When she didn't, he tilted his head and brushed his mouth over hers, drawing in a deep inhale. Lord, but he loved the scent of her.

Fiona sucked in a breath, not one that was shocked, but as if she too were trying to breathe him in. His hand came to rest on her hip, gently tapping, not wanting to possess too much and scare her away when he truly wanted to wrap his arms around her and haul her up against him.

Fingers curled into his shirt, and she pressed her mouth harder to his—hungry, needy, giving him permission to tug her closer. Arms around her waist, he brought their bodies together, turning his back to the tree with her leaning against him, giving her the control for the moment to step away if she wanted to.

But she didn't.

Fiona's hands slid over his chest to his shoulders, a hand to the back of his neck and then threading in his hair.

Her touch sent fervent shivers coursing through his body. Everything seemed magnified. His heart pounding against hers, the thrum of blood in his veins, the heat of his body, the sense of her curves pressed against him. Her scent, her taste, her touch, the little soft sighs escaping her. Brogan had never felt a kiss more deeply than he did at that moment. No other kiss had meant more.

He deepened the kiss, slanting his mouth over hers, dipping his tongue into the crevice between her lips and coaxing her open for him. Which he didn't have to work overly hard to do.

Fiona's kiss was ardent and full of fire. As intense as he'd thought she'd be. The lass never did anything in half measure. And the passion coming off her in waves threatened to undo him.

Eight

FIONA WAS DROWNING IN A SEA OF SENSATION.

Brogan's body was hard against hers. His arms around her were solid and strong. His mouth soft, yielding, and demanding all at the same time. He tasted of sin and smelled like desire. Every second her mouth was on his, every moment she dragged her fingers in his hair and kneaded her palms into his taut muscles, it chipped away at the wall she'd built around herself.

The man was taking down her defenses one brush of his lips, tongue, and hands at a time. She was powerless to stop it.

Nay, that wasn't exactly accurate. He'd given her all of the power in this instance. Pausing to let her walk away, skimming his mouth on hers, testing her, and then tugging her against him. She'd thought about pulling away for the briefest moment.

But curiosity and desire got the better of her.

Fiona had met many men, thousands of men, in her line of work, and in her own clan at the festivals and meetings of the rebels when she was younger. She'd developed a good sense of people by traveling so much and delivering messages. Knew when she was in danger and when she wasn't.

The only thing she was in danger of now, with her lips slanted against Brogan's, her tongue sliding deliciously over his, was losing herself. Losing sight of her mission.

The latter would be bad, but the former… Wouldn't it be nice for once to relax and let pleasure take over? Let someone else take care of her?

Aye, it was all too easy to fall into that chain of thought.

Having seen her dear friend Jenny fall in love, Fiona knew it was possible to have a relationship with a man and still see a mission through. But Toran wasn't like Brogan. Brogan wanted her to go home. Didn't he?

Palms flat to his chest, she pushed away gently, staring into his hazy blue eyes and wishing she could just crash back into him.

"I'm no' going home," she said for good measure.

"I know."

Keeping her voice strong, she added, "I willna be persuaded."

"I know." A soft grin played at the corners of his mouth, and his voice was whisper soft.

"I aim…" She swallowed hard, working to make her voice sound stronger. "This doesna make me your woman."

"I would never seek to own ye."

The words melted Fiona's heart. How did he know just the right thing to say? She leaned in again, brushing her lips on his.

"I'm no' a toy to be played with whenever ye want, Brogan Grant."

"I'm a man, Fiona. I dinna play with toys."

Why did the words, spoken so gruffly and deeply, send a shiver of want skating over her limbs? Why did he have to say all the right things?

Saints, but she wanted to kiss him some more. To melt against him. To let him touch her. To feel…

She pushed away instead. "Good." Fiona licked her lips, cleared her throat, and started to back away. With a nod, she said, "Good," again.

"Good." He eyed her, his expression guarded. What was he thinking?

"We canna do this. We just canna. I need to…see to my horse." She whirled around then, too afraid to keep staring at him because she'd either run away or leap into his arms. Both of which would not be good. She'd already run once, and to do so now would be to defeat the purpose of her mission. To fall for Brogan Grant… That would defeat her promise to herself.

Fiona was not a blushing virgin. That bartering chip had long since been lost to her friend Aes when she'd thought they'd be together forever. One kiss when they were barely more than seventeen, and she'd been ready to sign her life over to him. It had been her choice and she didn't regret it. It had been only once; they'd never had the opportunity again, and then he'd betrayed her heart by marrying another. Fiona never slept with another man again, too afraid to open her heart up like she had before. To allow someone else to see her vulnerable side.

Not until now.

Brogan made her want to strip out of her clothes and lay herself bare to him. To let him show her what it was like to be loved by a grown man.

She shivered, lips still burning at the memory of his mouth on hers. Skin still tingling from the way he'd stroked her back and hips. The hardness of his body beneath hers. The firmness of the bulge in his breeches that had pressed against her stomach.

Fiona quickened her pace until she was alone with her horse. Milla caught up, sniffing her leg and staring up at her with what could only be discerned as an *I know what ye were doing, ye naughty lass* look.

"Ye would have, too, old lass," Fiona said with a sniff, bending down and rubbing the hound's soft ears. "And I dinna regret it one bit."

She looked up then to see Brogan standing a few feet away, witnessing the exchange. Heat suffused her cheeks and she buried her head in the dog's neck.

Dawn came quicker than Fiona would have liked. She'd slept well with Milla curled up beside her, and the men surrounding her in the cave. It was the first time in weeks that she'd felt safe enough to let herself fall into a deep sleep. They were quick to pack up their things and head out.

She and Brogan barely talked, both of them in an unspoken agreement to stay clear of each other—mostly on her part because she was afraid she'd kiss him again. Though she made small talk with the men, it was clear they thought something was going on by the looks they passed back and forth.

They made a stop in Glenmoriston village to gather supplies, but the regard from those inside the village was not the warm welcome Brogan seemed to expect. Everyone appeared worried. They eyed them with suspicion. Judging gazes fell on Fiona, and she could only guess what they'd say about a woman traveling alone with men. She'd heard it before and chose to ignore it.

"Glenmoriston was occupied by Jacobites before Culloden," Brogan said. "Rumor has it that my da is planning a coup. 'Tis why everyone is acting so strange."

"And your da," Sorley said, "he is no' a Jacobite?"

Brogan gave a quick shake of his head. "He's a spiteful bastard. Split the clan, with those in Glenmoriston honoring the cause, and his faction, well… We'd do best no' to tarry."

Fiona was surprised to hear this. So Brogan was going against his own father? The people didn't trust him because of it, that was clear. But she found it brave he was willing to do so.

No one in their party argued as they quickly packed their satchels with goods they'd received in exchange for a few coins and headed out of the village. Fiona had sought out a few women who mentioned hearing the prince had passed by some days before, but they'd not seen him themselves.

Fiona and Brogan avoided villages—and each other—as much as they could over the next several days. Speaking little, which seemed to suit everyone. Every time Fiona and Brogan were alone, she opened her mouth to say something, to bring up the kiss, but then her throat went dry and she backed down. He looked much the same, and she ran away from the heat rising in her cheeks. The men seemed to notice there was a subtle shift in their midst, but they said nothing either.

Exhausted and feeling like they were chasing a ghost, the men were losing steam, and their horses needed a break.

They set up camp in the woods near a trickling burn. A few of the men went to hunt while Fiona sought out some privacy to wash in the shallow water. Spring was finally yielding to less frigid temperatures in the evening, and while it wouldn't be pleasant to wash in the cold burn, it would be better than nothing. Being clean rather than covered in the dust and grime of travel seemed a great prize for a few moments of torment.

She sat on the embankment, Milla by her side, and stripped out of her boots and hose, her toes sinking into the grass. Milla edged toward the water, drinking, while Fiona unstrapped the knives under her sleeves, tucking them into her boots. She rubbed at her wrists, which were damp and raw from wearing the straps for so many days with no breaks.

She leaned back in the grass, taking just the barest break to appreciate the peace of the moment. With her eyes closed, she drew in a deep breath and let it out slowly, relishing the scent of the forest. The water trickled in the burn, and a light breeze rustled the trees. Overhead, the sky had not yet given way to dusk, and a few grouse flew from branch to branch, chirping in lively conversation.

The sounds lulled her into a trancelike state of being half-awake, half-asleep. Her body relaxed, the aches of riding easing out of her muscles.

And then she startled awake, not even realizing she'd fallen asleep. Beside her, Milla made a low growl in her throat, hackles raised. Fiona started to sit up, then stilled. She wasn't alone. The air felt charged with menace. Not daring to sit up too quickly, she sent her fingers edging toward her boots and her knives.

Fingers curled around the hilt of one, she lay low, circling her head until her view settled on boots—several pairs of boots. Gaze sliding up, she encountered red—the color of her nightmares—and her mouth fell open, a silent scream on the edge of her throat.

"Do not even consider making a sound," said the familiar voice of a man she wished long since dead. The very man who'd assaulted her brother in the woods all those years ago. The very man who'd tormented so many Scotswomen, including her friends. As he continued to speak, ice slid into her veins and she started to tremble. "Or we'll be forced to kill that precious hound." He made a threatening noise at Milla who was crouched and growling now, her teeth bared.

Fiona sat up straight, turning on her knees to see the men behind her. There were at least a dozen of them, all surrounding Captain Boyd, the bastard who saw no problem in violating any being whether human or animal, but most especially women. The monster who was the reason she'd learned her skill with knives, the reason she always had one on her.

Fiona willed her trembling to cease.

Willed her mind to think, to plan.

Willed her stomach to stop its twisting before she vomited and showed him just how much he terrified her.

"What do ye want?" Fiona asked, slowly rising to her feet.

"Drop the knife."

"Nay." She shook her head, her grip tightening on the weapon.

He grinned. "I said drop the knife."

She shook her head again, sweat beading beneath her arms.

"When I issue an order, it is to be obeyed," Captain Boyd snapped.

"I'm no' one of your men, and I'll no' drop a means of protecting myself." She was surprised at how strong her voice sounded, given her insides felt like they were turning into mush.

"Then I'll have to disarm you." He stepped forward, and Milla snapped at him, which earned her a boot to the face.

Milla yelped in pain, and Fiona cried out, dropping to the dog instinctively, which only gave Boyd the upper hand. He was quick to take it, yanking her up by her hair. Fiona shrieked in anger as pain wrenched through her scalp.

"Why are you alone out here?" he demanded.

So he hadn't found the camp yet? They must have come from the opposite direction. Well, she wasn't going to tell him about it. Her life was only one; telling them of the men could mean eight lives lost, for they were outnumbered and Boyd was cruel. He'd not fight with honor, that much she knew to be true.

Sweat trickled down her spine, and she forced herself not to give in to fear.

Boyd, he could go to hell.

She stomped her heel down, landing on leather with a satisfying growl. But without her own boots on, the damage to his foot was minimal.

He laughed, pulling tighter on her hair as he sniffed her neck. "I'm going to have fun with you."

"Nay, ye're no," she said through gritted teeth, trying hard to ignore the pain. To be strong. To *think*.

She had to get out of this.

She had to keep the men safe.

"And then I'm going to let my men have fun with you too."

"Never," she hissed, kicking again. This time her heel landed against his shin. She jabbed with her elbow, catching his ribs, and despite the pain wrenched from his grasp in an effort to get away, but he only held tighter, his arm going around her neck.

"Lieutenant," he said to one of his men, who came forward.

"Aye, Captain?"

"Show her what we do to fighting bitches."

The lieutenant drew back his arm and punched her hard in the stomach.

Fiona cried out, but there was no sound, all the air gone from her lungs as pain filled her middle and she gasped for breath. Her knees buckled, but Boyd caught her by the hips, grinding his groin into her rear as she doubled over.

"Is this the way you like it, you naughty gal?" His voice was sugar and daggers, and she gagged, bile rising in her throat.

"Just…kill…me…" she managed to get out.

"Oh, no, no, no, we would not do that, not without having some fun first."

———

Brogan stiffened where he'd been crouched, stacking wood into a makeshift fire. At first he'd heard growling, then a piercing howl of a dog in pain followed by the cry of a woman.

Fuck!

Fiona.

He leapt to his feet, Sorley and Fin cursing and joining him. The other men were still hunting. No telling where they were, or who they'd be facing or how many. They had to be careful not to let whoever was attacking Fiona hear them approach.

Weapons drawn, they hurried as silently as they could through the woods. He never should have let her go to the burn alone. Had argued with her against it. Bloody should have followed his own advice.

Heart pounding, blood rushing in his ears, they ran, but every step forward felt like another one back, and finally he saw a sea of red in the forest. At least a dozen dragoons, and at their feet, Fiona doubled over in the arms of their leader.

On the other side of the burn he caught movement—his men who'd gone hunting. They raised their bows, the dragoons not at all aware of what was happening. Milla glanced his way, her tail thumping from where she lay.

Dinna give us away. He willed the dog to hear his order.

Milla didn't move. Thank the saints.

Brogan nodded to Sorley and Fin, and then stepped out of hiding. "If ye value your life, ye'll take your bloody hands off her."

The dragoon leader looked up sharply, the rest of his men who stood between them turning around, hands to their weapons.

"Oh, would ye look at that. A Highlander husband has come for ye." The man laughed. "You're sadly outnumbered, lad, but it was a valiant effort."

Brogan whistled, and arrows sang toward them, felling four of the dragoons. "Another two rounds and your men will all be dead."

The dragoons shouted in surprise and drew their swords, turning in a circle looking for the unseen enemy. Three of the men were dead instantly, and the fourth clutched at the arrow in his chest and let out garbled, pain-filled sounds.

The leader glared down in surprise at the men who'd been felled, his face blotched and purple. The bastard yanked Fiona up, holding her back tight to his chest. Pain was etched on her face, but anger too.

"Captain Boyd," Sorley growled, giving a name to the vile dragoon captain.

Boyd yelled, "Attack," and those remaining swung their broadswords and yanked their pistols from their holsters.

A volley of arrows sank into four more dragoons, but Brogan didn't wait for the rest. He cut his way forward, dispatching two men, while Sorley and Fin took two more, one of whom had an arrow in his chest that didn't seem to bother him at all.

Trudging through the bodies of the men their arrows had felled, Brogan reached the bastard who held Fiona in his grasp. He had a knife at her throat now, and while he mostly looked full of rage, there was also fear in his eyes.

"Did ye think we'd let ye get away so easy?" Brogan asked. "We dinna take kindly to ye butchers hurting our women."

"You will be found and you will be gutted," Boyd spat out.

"Maybe, but ye're already found and about to be gutted, which is a sure thing." Brogan grinned menacingly, his fingers flexing on the hilt of his sword. Oh, how badly he wanted to run this man through.

"Come any closer and I'll slice her head right off." Boyd tightened his grip, the edge of the blade making a dent in Fiona's precious neck. "And then your show of aggression will be for naught."

Brogan shrugged. "Ye'll still be dead, and no' able to harm another."

The man paused as if not expecting Brogan to be so nonchalant about Fiona's life.

Brogan stabbed his sword into the ground, not allowing his hand to leave the hilt. "Tell ye what, step away from the lass and I'll give ye a running head start."

Boyd's eyebrows lifted with interest, his beady gaze shifting to take in all of the Highlanders standing before him.

"I'll be taking her with me."

"No' part of the deal." Brogan's voice was lethal. "Run or die."

Run and *die too.*

Out of his periphery, he watched Fiona fiddle with her belt. The man didn't seem to notice as she flicked a piece of the leather open and pulled out a small blade. Perhaps Brogan wouldn't have to wait for the man to make his choice after all. If she wanted to run him through, Brogan would gladly stand back and allow it to happen.

He scanned her face, their gazes locking. "Ye're a brave lass," he said with a nod.

Tears shone in her eyes, but so did determination.

"She's hardly brave," Boyd started to say, but she moved at the same time, blade gripped in her left hand, and stabbed backwards behind her into his ribs. There was a moment of astonishment and pain on the man's face. The bastard loosened his grip, but not long enough for her to get away, and his surprise was replaced with anger.

He was going to cut her throat.

Brogan didn't hesitate, letting his own dagger fly. It landed deep in Boyd's right eye, stopping the bastard right in his tracks.

Brogan dove forward to grab Fiona as all life left the man's body, his arms falling to his sides, and for a moment he teetered on his feet, before tumbling backward into the water.

Brogan caught Fiona in his arms, and she wrapped herself around him, trembling. From behind her back, he watched Milla approach the man's body, lift her leg, and piss all over him.

Keith, Dugall, James, and Charles splashed through the water from the other side to get to them, all visibly shaken by what had just taken place.

"Are ye all right?" Sorley asked.

Fiona, still trembling, managed to turn around to face them. Her skin was pale, eyes wide, but she nodded.

"He was…" She pressed her lips together. "He is…" Her throat bobbed as she swallowed and stared down at the body. "I knew him before."

Her gaze met Brogan's, steady, resolute.

"How?" he asked softly.

She righted herself and walked over to Boyd, bent and pulled her knife from his ribs. "He is the reason I learned to use a knife."

A chill ran down Brogan's spine. She had a history with this man, one that was dark and full of fear. He regretted that he'd not forced Boyd to die a more gruesome, painful death.

"And we are all glad he's dead," Brogan said.

She nodded. "There will be a lot of people rejoicing in his passing. But there will be a lot of people hunting for his killers too. Captain Boyd… He's…he was in charge of the garrison at Inverness."

"Shite," Brogan said, followed by similar curses from his men.

"Aye, my Kenna and I had a run-in with him some years back too," Sorley said. "He's the devil in disguise."

"We'll bury them," Fin said. "No one will find them here."

"We dinna have any shovels, and doing so will take forever," Keith said. "Let's burn them."

"The smoke will bring attention to everyone within miles."

"Dump them in the burn then. Let them float."

Brogan walked forward and pulled his knife from Boyd's skull. "We'll bury this bastard and send the rest floating."

He looked to Fiona for confirmation. "Burying the past," she murmured. "Burying the devil."

"We could burn just him if ye want," Brogan offered.

She gave him a small smile and shook her head. "Thank ye for the offer, but we just dispatched him to an eternity of fire already."

He bowed to her, his hand over his heart. "I dinna know what happened in the past, but I'd kill him all over again if ye needed me to."

"There would be no more fitting fate for him than to die a thousand times over and over," she whispered.

Fiona crouched low, finally unable to stand, he assumed, and Milla came up beside her, nudging her until she could lie on her lap. The poor beast had a swollen eye, from however Boyd must have hurt her.

Fucking bastard, harming women and animals. He deserved what he'd gotten. There was no telling how many Scots the man had killed on the battlefield or tortured in the garrison.

Brogan found a thick branch and stabbed it into the earth, using it to dislodge dirt and dig a grave for the man who'd tormented so many.

Fiona slid her trembling fingers into Milla's fur. The warmth of the hound and her soothing licks on Fiona's chin were a comfort, but still she trembled. How close she had just come to being one of Boyd's victims.

With every toss of dirt from Brogan's efforts, she came closer to burying that fear. The man had hurt so many. Gus. Jenny. Had come close to hurting Annie. Sounded like he might have hurt Sorley's woman too. He'd harassed her on more than one occasion when she'd delivered messages at the garrison. She was lucky he'd not recognized her in the woods. So many women he'd shattered, so many men he'd brutally murdered.

And he was no more. Fiona stared at his body. Lifeless, limp, and all the danger he represented had simply disappeared into the ether with a few fatal blows.

Her damage to his body had been lethal, though the wound would have been a slow bleed, and he would have had a chance to slice her neck from ear to ear before death came. If not for Brogan, she'd be dead.

It was the second time he'd come across her battling a dragoon, and she knew what that meant.

After he buried Boyd, he would not suggest they go find the prince; he would insist they return to Dòchas. That she remain at home, safely behind walls and protected by warriors.

A large part of her was ready to give up. Ready to toss aside all the things she'd worked for and let the men handle the rest. To climb between her soft sheets, beneath her thick coverlet, and allow herself to be spoiled by Beitris and anyone else willing to do so.

The other part of her, the one that spoke with more authority, said she wasn't allowed to give up. That to give up now would be tantamount to treason, and she wasn't a treasonous sort.

With the men floating slowly away in the burn, all hands helped Brogan dispose of the body. The final bit of dirt was placed on the pile and a heavy stone over the center, so if the wolves came digging they'd not be able to pull his body completely away.

Brogan turned to face Fiona, and she was thankful the trembling had ceased. She stood slowly, prepared to argue her case for going forward.

"I dinna think we should camp here tonight," he said.

The men all nodded in agreement.

"It grows dark, we should find somewhere else soon," Sorley added.

Fiona opened her mouth, surprised he'd not insisted they turn around. She closed it again and nodded, not trusting the sound of her own voice to come out strong.

An hour later, in complete darkness, several miles away from the scene of her nightmares, they made camp. In the dark, she leaned against a tree, and Brogan joined her.

He took her hand in his and brought it to his mouth, softly brushing his lips over her knuckles.

"I'm here if ye need to talk," he said.

Words she'd have expected from her friends Jenny and Annie, but not words she'd ever heard uttered from a man's lips before. Fiona leaned into him, resting her head on his shoulder, the solidness beneath her cheek a comfort.

"Thank ye."

"I mean it."

"I know."

He passed her a small flask, and she eagerly accepted it, taking a longer than usual sip of whisky and relishing the burn in her throat.

"I was twelve when I first met Boyd," Fiona said.

Brogan stiffened, but only for an instant. His fingers threaded through hers, holding her hand against his chest as she retold the story in a near whisper of what happened in the woods all those years before. Reinforcing that a monster had been put down.

"If not for Gus…I might not even be here today to have witnessed his death." The breath left her and she felt weak once more.

Brogan stroked his thumb over her knuckles, holding her hand tighter and giving her the sense he wasn't going to let go.

"After that, I learned how to protect myself in case I ever found myself alone with him again."

Brogan passed her back the flask, and she took another long, heady gulp, the spirits burning a path down her throat.

"As I said, lass, ye're verra brave." There was a tightness in Brogan's voice, filled with emotion.

"Thank ye for saving me. Another moment and he'd have... ruined me." She'd have begged for death then.

Brogan tipped her chin toward him. "Even devils canna ruin angels."

Then he brushed his lips over hers, and the tension started to melt away. He called her brave. He called her an angel.

Fiona kissed him back, her hand on his bristly cheek. Brogan didn't realize how much his words, his tenderness meant to her.

"Also," he said against her mouth, "I think I'm in need of a belt like this." His fingers toyed with the belt housing the small dagger.

"It comes in handy."

"Ye're a soldier, lass. Dinna let anyone tell ye different."

"I'm one of Prince Charlie's angels. There is a difference." She laughed softly.

Brogan stroked his thumb over her cheek, and it felt so good. Fiona leaned into his touch, wishing they never had to part.

"Ye're Scotland's angel," he said.

And she wanted to be his... Boyd's words, spoken as a taunt, about Brogan being her Highlander husband came back to haunt her. What if he were?

Milla took that moment to worm her way between them, snuffling along Fiona's neck. Fiona smiled and leaned her head back against the tree. It might have been dark, but they were still at camp and the men surrounded them, privy to their conversation, even if whispered, and certainly discerning the sound of their kisses.

"Good lass, Milla," Brogan said, his voice gravelly with laughter as he patted the hound.

"The best darn dog eight people never asked for," Fiona said, "and could never do without."

Nine

"Brogan, if I may have a word." Fin approached him as they readied their horses for another long day of travel.

"Aye." They stepped out of earshot of everyone else, curious gazes following them.

"The thing is, Grant, that the lass is no' entirely safe."

Brogan crossed his arms over his chest. "I'm listening."

"I think if ye are no' going to make her your wife, then I will."

Brogan blanched, this entire conversation catching him completely off guard. "My wife? Ye do realize we're in the middle of a war, aye?" This was not the time for such frivolities. And yet he could still hear Boyd's words, calling him her husband, how his heart had lurched at the thought before he'd thrust it aside in order to concentrate on the danger.

"And she was nearly... Well, ye know what happened yesterday as well as anyone else here."

"Being my wife wouldna have changed what happened." In fact, believing she was his wife seemed only to spur Boyd on. The man wanted to see them both in pain by his actions.

"'Tis true, but having your name would give her an added measure of protection, along with the backing of your clan. There is also the fact that the two of ye have become quite... close."

"Are ye accusing me of being dishonorable?" Brogan loomed forward in challenge, jutting his jaw.

Fin didn't back down, and Brogan had to respect him for it. "I'm no' accusing ye of anything, Grant, but someone has to look out for the lass's well-being if it is no' going to be ye."

Brogan grunted, grinding his teeth.

Fin held up his hands in surrender, shaking his head. "Just an idea, man. Just an idea."

Brogan nodded, and Fin walked away. But he was not yet ready to leave his thoughts.

What Fin said had merit. If he married her, she'd have his name and be protected by all the Grant clan. Even those on the opposite side would respect that he'd wed.

But would she agree?

Fiona was too much of a free spirit. She'd laugh in his face. But he supposed he ought to offer. Brogan had certainly been taking liberties in kissing her. And marriage wasn't exactly something that seemed entirely horrid when he looked at Fiona. Which was why he'd ignored the tremor up his spine at the thought of being tied to anyone.

For years, the MacBeans and Grants had been at each other's throats. Perhaps an alliance between the two of them would help assuage some of that. If clans would even still come back together after the Butcher was done destroying their country.

With his decision made to propose, Brogan frowned and turned around to head back to camp, running right into the lass who stood behind him.

"I didna hear ye approach," he said, trying to hide his surprise.

"I'm sorry." She smiled softly. "Is everything all right?"

"Fin was just pointing out to me how incredibly unsafe it is for ye to be on the road with us."

Fiona's brows drew together, and while she remained silent, he preferred her to rage at him. This was an argument they'd put to rest and he was bringing it up again.

"And ye agree with him?" she asked haughtily.

"Ye know my thoughts."

Now she crossed her arms over her chest and tapped her foot. "Ye want me to go back to my castle, which is equally dangerous given the redcoats traipsing through Inverness as though it were their own personal playground."

"We killed the worst of them yesterday," he offered.

Fiona scoffed. "I thought ye understood. I thought ye knew me better." The words launched from her mouth like an arrow, lodging in his gut.

"I'm trying to protect ye, lass."

"By locking me away?"

He shook his head. "Nay."

"What, then?"

Brogan started to doubt his plan. Maybe it wasn't such a good idea to propose to her. Not, at least, when she was shouting at him. "I dinna know."

"This entire conversation is frustrating."

Fiona pursed her lips, hands on her hips as she looked to the side, studying a tree, while he could practically hear the thoughts churning in her mind. One volatile line after another. At last, she turned back to him, a fierceness in her violet eyes that he'd only seen a couple of times since they'd met, and both times it had been when she was under attack.

"I asked if ye minded if I joined ye on this journey, and ye agreed. Now ye're changing your mind. The only thing making me feel unsafe, Brogan Grant, is no' knowing whether or no' ye have my back. Ye're either with me or ye're against me, and right now it feels an awful lot like ye and I are no' on the same side. Ye need to make a choice and make it fast, because I'm getting tired of the games."

There really wasn't a choice to make. As much as their two families had not seen eye to eye, he had no doubts now. "I am with ye."

"Promise ye'll never demand I return home. Promise that ye understand my need to continue on this mission."

"I want to protect ye, lass."

"Ye're under no obligation to do so."

No obligation, which he would be if he made her his wife.

Damn Fin for putting the thought into his mind.

Because if she were his wife, he could do more than protect her. He could kiss her whenever he wanted. Spread out his kilt right now and make love to her on the forest floor. The thought had the blood in his veins pumping hard. There was no doubting his desire for her.

His mind whirled with all the positives that would come from a union with her, and all that could go wrong. Was he ready to make that commitment? A moment ago, he had been. All this waffling back and forth was giving him a chance to back away, and he didn't want to back away.

"What if I were under obligation?" He edged closer.

"What?" She sounded exasperated. "Are ye talking about Murray again?" Fiona touched her fingertips to her temples. "Just stop."

"I was no' talking about Murray."

"What, then?" She spread her arms out, the frustration coming off her in waves.

"What if we…" The words died on his tongue, and he couldn't seem to make his mouth work.

"What if we *what*?" Her eyes searched his, curiosity mixed with her irritation.

Anger started to spark inside him at the thought of something violent and vicious happening to her. "I canna let ye come so close to death again."

She let out a loud groan, arms thrown up in the air. "We are both under threat of death, Brogan. No' just me. We are in this together."

"I canna risk another bastard thinking ye're fair game to torment. I canna risk your safety. All I've done since we've met is try to save ye."

The glower that turned full force toward him was enough to make him want to stand back. He watched her hands, expecting her to flick open the pocket in her belt and skewer him. "I'm no' in need of saving. I can take care of myself."

"I know ye can, lass, but sometimes even the strongest of women needs someone to lean on."

"I've my family. Why would I need to lean on ye?"

The words stung, and even from the distance between them, he could see that she regretted saying them.

She let out a long sigh, as if trying to let go of some of the rage.

"Ye dinna need to lean on me, Fiona MacBean, but ye have, since the day of the battle—before that, if ye want to count me passing on your message. I have been there for ye. For no good reason, either. I could have left ye to your own devices, told ye to go off on your way. Trussed ye up and dumped ye on Dòchas's doorstep, but I didna. I believed in ye, because I think ye play an important part in this shite fest we find ourselves in. Now, I'm proposing a different sort of alliance."

"What are ye saying?"

"I'm saying that ye should… We should wed."

"What?" The word was a bellow that sent several birds flying overhead. "Ye canna be serious. War is no reason to wed. Neither of us are the ones to make such important decisions based on clan alliances—especially given our clan history."

Brogan gritted his teeth. She didn't need to throw his bastardization in his face. "Fine then, no' a real marriage. No need to get your drawers in a twist. I can see that look on your face."

"A fake marriage?" Her eyes narrowed, incredulous.

"Aye. Everyone, even my men, will think we've wed. And when the prince is safe and ye're back at home with your brother, I'll release ye from any obligation to me."

"What is the advantage of that? I can see none other than placing a label on me."

"If ye canna see that being aligned to me is to your advantage, then there is no point in continuing this conversation."

"'Tis more than that, and ye must realize it, Grant. I'd be giving up quite a lot by tying myself to ye. Independence, for one."

"I'd no' take away your independence."

"But everyone else would expect it. They will look to ye when I speak, instead of looking at me."

"And I'll look right back at ye, lass." And he meant it. If the bastards wanted to take away her voice, he'd give it right back.

She was silent for several long moments, her lips pursed, her eyes scanning his face. "A fake marriage?"

"Aye."

"With a priest, though? It will make it real."

"No' if we hold our fingers crossed behind our backs," he teased.

"No' if we dinna consummate it."

Brogan grunted. Not consummating a union with her would be damned difficult, but she was right, it was the only way in which they could annul their union. "Aye."

"What if I wanted to…lie with ye without the obligation of being tied to ye for the rest of my life?"

No lady had ever uttered those words before, Brogan was fairly certain. Or at least none in his experience. But hearing the words from Fiona's lips was enough to make his mind go numb with need.

He cleared his throat. "I'd no' make ye into the thing I'm trying to save ye from being."

"Ye're trying to save me from being what, exactly?" Her fingers toyed with the latch on her belt, all of her ire returned, focused back on him.

Those were the wrong words to say, clearly, for he'd basically just called her a whore, which was not at all his meaning. Lord, he was making a bungle of this. "I'm no' good with this." He waved his hand, dismissing his previous words.

"What is 'this'?" She waved her hand, mocking him.

"All of it."

"Clearly." She harrumphed, lips pursed, flicking the button on her belt that held the small dagger in place. The threat was evident.

Brogan was about to walk away to clear his head when she said, "I'll consider a fake wedding with ye."

Stunned into silence for a moment, he wavered on his feet. Had he heard her? But the look on her face said it all—this was not a game.

"All right," he said in a slow drawl.

"On two conditions." Her tone made it clear she would not budge on this. "I get to keep my dowry. And I get to continue with my duties."

"Done." There was no hesitation on his part.

"What's in it for ye, Grant? Ye've yet to tell."

"I did. It'll be less of a headache." That was as much as he was willing to divulge to her or himself.

―――――――――――

What the bloody hell was going on?

Fiona had never been more confused in her life. Brogan was sending out conflicting signals and saying things that made no sense. Didn't he think her presence was annoying? Wasn't that why he was always subtly and not so subtly telling her to go home?

And now he wanted to introduce a fake marriage into it?

Brogan rubbed a hand through his hair, a frown marring his mouth, lips she enjoyed kissing. A wife would get to kiss those lips every day, any time she wanted.

And yet she'd not be a true wife to him. This was to be a fake marriage. Which was irritating, too, considering the night before she'd been thinking about giving herself to him. Making love.

If they were to be fake wed, that was the last thing they should *ever* do if they wanted to get out of their marriage. Wedding in the eyes of God meant a marriage that was consummated.

What exactly had Fin said that put him in this state of mind and going down the path of a fake marriage?

Hell, she herself had been thinking about marriage last night.

Och...but it was all so ridiculous, and a complication neither of them needed. They had one goal—find the prince.

Adding a marriage to the mix would only muddle that mission.

A *fake* marriage, she had to remind herself.

Maybe he did have a point. If they were married, there would be less question in the villages about her riding with so many men and no escort. People might respect her messages more.

Which was a horrible realization.

They should respect her messages for who she carried them from and what she'd been able to do for this country, not for who she was attached to.

And yet when they'd sought shelter in a village two nights past, the men had judged her to be a whore.

This was about preservation. Brogan was right. She'd gotten herself out of trouble hundreds of times, but the stakes were rising, and he had been there for her a lot over the last weeks.

Sometimes even the strongest of women needs someone to lean on.

Why did he have to make so much sense?

"I think we could both use less headache," Fiona said, mimicking his words. Let him have his way. She already knew he felt more for her than he was letting on. Just like she was hiding so much.

Brogan put out his hand, and she stared down at the offered appendage for several breaths before putting her own hand in his. He drew her closer, eyes locked on hers.

"We might be getting fake married, but I'll no' be fake kissing ye." His voice was low.

"As long as that's as far as it goes." She regretted saying the words as soon as they were out, because she very much wanted it to go farther, if only for that one time to look back on.

"Aye."

He brushed his lips over hers. It wasn't a sensual kiss, not like what they'd shared before, but a perfunctory one. One that sealed a deal.

"What is the dowry that ye want to keep so badly?"

"Probably a stable full of Millas," she teased. In truth, she wasn't certain what it was anymore. It used to be a chest of coin, a parcel of land, and other goods, but since the war had waged on in Scotland, coin had to be used. Land had to be sold or rented. Knowing that Brogan didn't care for any of it was a comfort, because she would have disappointed him had it mattered.

He chuckled and led her back to his men. "I'll make the announcement," he said.

A shudder passed through her. They were really going through with this farce.

As soon as they reached the men, he cleared his throat. "We are to be married."

The men nodded, Fin let out a cheer, and Keith stared at them as though they'd gone mad. Perhaps they had.

"But the MacBeans," Keith said, drawing to attention their decades old clan rivalry.

"An alliance is being formed, and past transgressions will be forgiven," Brogan said.

Past transgressions? She winged a brow at her fake betrothed, and he winked back.

"Mount up." He let her arm drop and went to his horse, climbing into the saddle.

How deeply did his feelings about past transgressions go? Did it matter? She supposed it really didn't.

But as Fiona put her foot in the stirrup and rose up onto her own horse's back, snapping her fingers at Milla to follow, she realized she didn't know all that much about the man she'd just agreed to pledge her life to except that he was a bastard and at odds with the chief of his clan, his father. Even if their marriage was supposed to be fake, he could change his mind. Seduce her and then they'd lie together and there'd be no turning back.

Would that bother her?

Fiona bit her lip, refusing to think about it again until she was standing before the priest giving her vows. This was nothing more than a business transaction. A way to make her safer and to give their party more allowances in villages. It would make them *all* safer, and that was definitely something she could get on board with.

Ten

THE HIGHER THEY CLIMBED INTO THE MOUNTAINS, THE MORE arduous the journey became.

The rain fell in torrential droves, slanting down sideways, spiking hard against their skin, and making it difficult to see. The craggy ground grew slick with mud, and more than one horse slipped, so they all climbed down to make walking easier. Rivers of mud ran over their boots, and the rain pelting down soaked the horses, their clothes, their supplies.

The wind picked up, pushing trees they could have used for shelter sideways.

"We need to go into town," Fiona said. "We need to seek shelter for us and the horses. We'll get nowhere like this."

"Ye're my wife," Brogan said, and she nodded her agreement, though they'd yet to find a priest. "She's my wife," he said to his men.

"And he's my husband." Saying so in front of witnesses would be good enough for now. Still, it made the entire idea of dissolving their union a lot easier in the end. She was both relieved and disappointed.

The men nodded and sounded off a cheer, offering their congratulations through the pelting rain.

Down a valley and perhaps a mile or so away was a small village. They had no way of knowing who lived there and where their loyalties lay, but they had to take a chance. The rain was showing no sign of slowing, and even as she thought that, a round of thunder hollered from above and lightning struck not too far away.

One of the horses whinnied and reared up, making the other animals skittish. Even Milla darted away, afraid of what was to come.

They made their way down a slick, winding path that looked to have been trod upon many times, and after what felt like an hour but was in reality perhaps only twenty minutes, they arrived at the small crofters' village. As expected, there was no one outside.

Light came from the windows of a building, where a sign near the door waved rapidly in the wind, in danger of coming loose. Fiona was able to make out the name as it blew: *Cluanie Thistles Tavern.*

Brogan tried the handle, but it was locked, so he rapped on the door while the rest of them huddled in a circle.

An older gentleman opened a square in the door to peek out at them.

"What do ye want?"

"We're in need of a warm meal and shelter," Brogan said. "My wife and I along with our brothers."

"Large family." The man shut the little door without another word, and the lot of them exchanged glances, wondering if he'd open it back up again.

Brogan was raising his hand to knock again when the door whipped open. "Ye can come in. Horses around back."

Brogan tugged Fiona forward while the rest of the men took the horses.

"I've one room upstairs for the two of ye, and your men can sleep either in the stables or in here somewhere. Most men seem to find a spot on the floor." He nodded toward the tavern with tables and a hearth, then stated the price.

Brogan nodded, handing the man some coin. The innkeeper counted the payment in his palm, then nodded toward the dining area.

"Food and drink in there. I'll have the missus make up your bed."

Your bed.

They were to share a single bed. They were, after all, pretending to be husband and wife. A warm shiver raced over her spine. Nay, nay, nay. She would take the floor.

With Brogan's hand on the small of her back, she walked into the main dining area where two long tables and benches dominated the center of the room, and several smaller tables were shoved against the far wall. There were only a few people inside, drinking ale and slurping stew.

They eyed her and Brogan with curiosity. Brogan nodded and then directed Fiona toward one of the tables in the back with only two chairs. Once they were seated, he looked across at her, his blue eyes hooded, and held out his hands. She stared down at his extended palms, studying the lines and calluses.

"Hold out your hands," he said.

She did so, placing her hands into his. "Is this what married couples do?" she asked, teasing.

"Aye." He chuckled, his thumbs rubbing over her knuckles. "We need to set a good example."

"Hmm," she said, thinking about what kind of example she could set; say, leaning over the table and kissing him. Heat crept up her neck and cheeks at the thought and she looked away, trying to hide her reaction.

Their six companions came boisterously into the room, each of them halting and practically running into one another when they spotted Fiona and Brogan, hands clasped. Sorley was the first to shutter his stunned expression, followed by Fin who shouted, "Drinks on me for my brother and his new bride."

Keith observed them suspiciously, but as soon as Fiona locked eyes with him, he looked away. What was he thinking?

The men had taken over a long table, and a serving wench brought out a jug of ale, passing them cups before bringing cups over to her and Brogan.

"Stew and bread all right, sir? 'Tis all we have."

Fiona's mouth watered. "Perfect."

The wench nodded and headed off to fetch their dinner.

Fiona picked up the jug and poured them each a cup of ale. She tentatively took a sip. It was warmer than usual and not very good, but Fiona was thirsty so she managed to choke it down.

"This is shite," Brogan murmured, watching his men slug back their cups as though it were liquid gold.

A moment later, the same wench returned with a blanket. "For your wife. Ye look a bit chilly in that wet gown."

Fiona took the blanket, only too happy to drape it around herself. "I hope the stew comes quickly so I can go upstairs and sit before a fire," she murmured to Brogan when the woman had left them alone again. The hearth was quite far from where they'd sat to eat.

"Ye'll catch your death if it is not served soon," Brogan said. "Let's change tables."

Fiona shook her head. "Nay, I've been wet before and for longer."

He raised a brow. "Is that so?"

"Think about how icy and cold it was at Culloden."

"True enough. At least now the weather is milder."

She stared out the closest window, watching the wind whip the rain against the panes.

"To Mrs. Grant!" Fin shouted, and she turned to see him holding his cup into the air.

Fiona laughed at the jubilation in the men's voices, their hair plastered to the sides of their faces and even now water still dripping off their noses, and yet they were truly happy. Or else it was the ale they were guzzling.

She raised her glass and took a sip, and when she glanced back at Brogan, he had the oddest expression on his face.

The wench brought their steaming stew, placing it on the table. Fiona's belly growled, and she bit the inside of her cheek in embarrassment. How long had it been since she'd had a warm meal? She didn't hesitate to dig in, glorying at the warmth on her tongue even though the stew itself was decidedly lacking in flavor. She dipped stale bread into the broth and ate heartily.

Their conversation was light during the meal, mostly appreciative grunts over having something warm to eat. The men had quieted too.

Fiona was scraping the last remnants of onion and broth from her bowl when a shadow darkened their table.

She glanced up into the face of one of the other patrons who stared down at them, consternation knitting his brows.

"She's your wife?" the stranger asked.

Brogan set down his bowl and spoon slowly and stared up at the man. He rested his hands casually on the table. "Aye."

"Ye're newlyweds?"

"Aye."

The man nodded, hooking his thumb behind him toward Fin, Sorley, and the lot of them. "The lads seem awfully proud of the two of ye."

"They are." Brogan leaned back in his chair, his full attention focused on the stranger.

"Huh. Ye said the lot of ye were brothers, but one of 'em's Irish."

Brogan didn't take his eyes off the man. "He is."

"How's that possible?"

"He's my brother," Fiona said in a perfect Irish brogue.

Brogan, not missing a beat, didn't even blink as he said, "My wife's Irish."

The man nodded and held up his cup. "Cheers to the two of ye then."

"Thank ye."

The man backed away, eyeing them some more as he sat down with his mates.

"That was a good impression," Brogan murmured.

"He is after something," Fiona replied in equally low tones.

"Looking for a reason to turn us over to the authorities."

A shiver passed through Fiona, and images of Boyd and his men came crashing back. She gripped the edge of the table to still her trembling hands. "Best tell the men to be careful tonight."

"I think they'd be safest sleeping in the stables with the horses if those men camp out in here."

Fiona nodded.

Brogan stood and approached the men, giving his orders softly. The men all broke out into laughter as if he'd told them a joke, and then he nodded to Fiona to join him. She stood, the cold, wet folds of her gown slapping against her calves and making her wince.

They headed toward the stairs. The tavern owner gave Brogan a key.

"After ye, wife," Brogan said with a smirk.

Fiona lifted her heavier than normal skirts away from her boots and made her way up the tiny, narrow stairs, each step groaning beneath her and Brogan's clomping boots.

There were only four doors at the top of the stairs, and one stood ajar.

"That must be for us." Fiona made her way into the small but cozy chamber. A bed was shoved against the wall, and the wooden floor had a threadbare but clean rug on it. A small hearth was blazing. A very tiny circular table flanked by two wooden stools held a glass carafe of watered red wine and two pretty wineglasses.

"The honeymoon suite," Brogan teased.

Fiona made her way to the blaze, small though it was, and held out her chilled hands. Brogan came up beside her doing the same.

"I'll sleep on the floor," he said.

"I dinna want ye to be uncomfortable. I'm happy to sleep on the floor. I've done it many times."

"So have I, lass." He winked slowly, taking her breath.

"We'll take turns. I'll wake ye in the middle of the night to switch places." She used her no-nonsense tone so he wouldn't argue, and so she didn't ask him to join her on the bed.

Brogan stared, using the same tone as he said, "I'll tell ye to go back to bed."

"This is no' a true marriage, Brogan. Ye dinna need to be chivalrous." She rolled her eyes.

"I'd be chivalrous even if we were no' married, in case ye had no' noticed."

Fiona pursed her lips, keeping her gaze on the flames.

"Ye need get out of those wet clothes and allow them time to dry." He searched through his satchel and pulled out a clean shirt. "Put this on."

"What about ye?"

"I can wrap a sheet around me." He tugged back the coverlet and pulled off the top sheet. "See? A perfect substitute."

He was right, and yet the idea of stripping nude, even with his back turned, had her belly flopping. "Turn around then."

He did as she asked, giving her his back as he stripped out of his clothes one article at a time. Fiona found herself staring as he unbuttoned his jacket, revealing a soaked linen shirt that clung to muscles that rippled with each movement. Then came his boots and hose, his breeches, until he was just in the clingy wet shirt, and she could see his bare legs up to midthigh.

She swallowed hard when he lifted the shirt, revealing his bare arse, before she whirled around.

Dear God, the man was incredibly built. Even his behind was full of muscle.

She tugged off her wet garments with trembling fingers and turned around to make sure he wasn't looking before she peeled off the last layer and stood naked before the hearth. The fire warmed her skin, which felt soggy from the rain. She closed her eyes a moment, letting the warmth of the flames soak into her body.

There was a hiss of breath, and her eyes flew open. Brogan still faced away, but that didn't mean that he hadn't seen her.

"Were ye looking?" she asked.

"Nay," he said too quickly.

She grabbed the shirt and tugged it over her head. "Liar. I'm dressed now."

He turned around slowly, his eyes heavy-lidded with the same intense look on his face she'd seen when he wanted to kiss her. The sheet was draped around his hips and tied at the side, leaving his entire torso bare. Taut muscles on his belly broadened into his chest and wide shoulders. A light sprinkling of dark hair covered his chest and tapered as it drew into the sheet. A noticeable bulge from between his hips had her biting the inside of her cheek.

The man was beautifully built. Unfairly so. Staring at him, taking him in, Fiona wanted to touch every part. And the last thing she was allowed to do was just that.

She sat down heavily on the bed, knees up, tucking the shirt around her legs so that the only things showing were her hands and toes. The move was more for her than for him, to stop herself from walking forward and pressing the flats of her palms to his chest, running fingers over the muscles of his broad shoulders, pulling away the sheet that hid the hard part of him she wanted so much to conquer her.

"Dinna pretend that ye were no' looking either, lass."

She'd watched him undress and blatantly ogled his naked chest. There was no use in denying it. Fiona shrugged but said nothing, and he chuckled.

"Good night," she said, slipping beneath the covers.

"Night, lass." Brogan blew out the candle, though the fire still emitted some light.

Fiona watched him from the bed as he settled onto the floor, shifting so she could see him better. They'd slept near each other for countless nights, and yet the intimacy of being in a bedchamber together was incredibly different. There was no one else in the room. No one to stop them from doing whatever they wanted. No one except for themselves.

This being their "wedding night," the men likely expected them to be sleeping in the same bed. Kissing. Touching.

Heat suffused her face, and a tingle of desire raced over her skin. Would she mind if Brogan climbed into bed with her?

"Here," she said, tossing him a pillow, which hit him on the shoulder. Giving him that took away any excuse to invite him to bed so he could have a pillow.

Brogan chuckled. "Thanks."

He adjusted the pillow beneath his head and let out a loud yawn, stretching an arm out and then flopping it over his eyes in exhaustion. His yawn was contagious and soon Fiona was also drawing in breath, eyes watering at the strength of it.

"Go to sleep," he said. "I can hear ye moving around."

She smiled into the dim light, rolling over so she could no longer see him and hoping that helped to take away any distractions so she could succumb to sleep.

Falling into unconsciousness wasn't hard, but her dreams were vivid and disturbing, waking her throughout the night and causing her to feel as though she'd hardly slept at all. More than once she'd found herself sitting up, considering sliding down onto the floor with Brogan if only to have his nearness to soothe her worries.

Her dreams were plagued with visions from the battlefield, of seeing her friends hacked down by demons dressed in red coats. Then she was running, being chased by a horde of the undead who brandished their swords at her. When she finally reached safety, the door burst open to reveal Annie and the soldiers she'd been healing, slaughtered in a terrifying pile of bodies.

At last Fiona could take the nightmares no more, waking in a cold sweat and shivering from terror. If Brogan offered her the whisky flask right now, she was certain she'd drain it. She swiped at a tear rolling from the corner of her eye, sending up a prayer that her friends were safe.

She stared at the small window, watching as the darkness faded to gray. Milla shuffled over and started to bop her cold, wet nose against Fiona's.

"I got her," Brogan said.

Fiona turned over to see him stand up and start to get dressed near the door.

"Are your clothes dry?" she asked.

"Mostly. Take your time. The rain is still pelting down. I've a feeling we may be here another night."

Another night in this room. It had taken an effort for her not to reach for him this night. How was she going to control herself a second?

Eleven

THE RAIN POUNDED THE EARTH IN THICK DROVES, MAKING it hard to see beyond five feet. There'd not been a moment's break from it. Outside, the ground was so soggy that when Fiona stepped into the grass, her entire boot was swallowed by mud. These were no conditions in which to travel, and if the prince was smart, he and his entourage were likely hunkered down too.

The men bided their time taking care of the horses and playing games of cards between mugs of ale and napping. Fiona joined them, even taking in and dishing out the ribbing that had come with being a part of their brotherhood. They spent an exceptional amount of time on her accent, pitting her and Fin against each other if only to see them argue in loud Irish brogues.

Perhaps this was Mother Nature's way of making certain they all got the rest they needed, as well as the companionship. The horses certainly appreciated the break, Fiona was sure.

She stepped back inside, stomping her feet and shaking the rain from her cloak. She'd need to set it before the fire again to dry.

The tavern was still filled with men who'd been there when they arrived, along with a few new guests who'd sought shelter from the storm. Fiona tried to join the men in a game of cards, but they were so bloody competitive, she gave up.

Alone in her chamber, she read letters from friends she kept hidden in the lining of her skirts.

Hours later, a knock sounded at the door and, bleary-eyed from having fallen asleep, she blinked, trying to process the sound. A few letters lay open on her chest. Setting them aside, she threw her legs over the edge of the bed and opened the door to find Brogan standing in the corridor with Milla, who was wagging her tail in excitement.

Brogan grinned. "Are ye hungry, lass?"

Her stomach rumbled since she'd not yet eaten a thing, and Brogan looked down toward her belly with a humorous grin.

"Aye." Fiona rubbed at her belly in hopes it would silence.

"They are serving soup downstairs." He eyed her face, which she was sure gave away her sleepiness. "Were ye asleep?"

She shook her head. "A little. Also reading."

Brogan raised a brow. "Anything good?"

She shrugged. "Just some things that reminded me of home."

Brogan offered his arm. "As your husband, I'd be happy to escort ye to the dining room."

She smiled and slid her hand over his taut arm. "Thank ye, husband." Just saying the word made her feel as though they shared a secret.

"Was your sleep peaceful?" he inquired.

"Aye."

"Good." He patted her hand. "Last night I was worried ye were being chased by demons."

Fiona looked up in surprise. "I was. How did ye know?"

"Ye were talking in your sleep, lass. I almost woke ye."

"Next time, please do." She shuddered at the terrifying images.

"Want to talk about it?"

Fiona started to shake her head but then stopped, because the truth was she did want to talk about it. Very much so.

They descended the stairs, her in front and him behind.

"I was on the battlefield and dragoons were everywhere, hacking away, but they did not have human heads."

"Demon heads?" At the base of the stairs, his warm hand touched the small of her back as they walked into the dining room. Men lounged at the long tables, and all but one of the tables for two were filled.

Even in the daylight, it smelled just as strongly of ale.

"Aye. Demons." She glanced around at the strangers. "They've a full house now, do they no'?"

"The rain is bringing everyone in off the roads. I've a feeling the soup will be thin."

"Thin or no', as long as it's hot."

"Agreed." They took their seats at the table. The wall beside her arm was damp and cold, giving Fiona a chill. She glanced around the room, eyeing the new people, wondering if any of them were spies for Cumberland's men. A woman sat with a man not too far away, her eyes vacant as they locked on Fiona's. The man across from her was drinking his ale and glaring. Just looking at them had her on high alert. Something about them caused the hair on the back of her neck to rise. And Milla let out a low growl before Brogan silenced her with a snap of his fingers.

Should they be suspicious of the strangers?

Fiona offered the woman a warm smile, but the woman did not smile back. Instead, she frowned and stared down at her own cup of ale before taking a hearty sip. The man belched and called the wench for another round.

At one long table were the men in their party, and at the other were the men who still eyed them with suspicion. Was that the way the world worked now? Where everyone suspected everyone else of being bad in some way?

Fiona picked at one of her nails that was hanging loose.

Brogan drummed his fingers on the table in a slow rhythm. "Are ye all right?" he asked.

Fiona glanced up at him, trying to smile, but the way her lips curled felt false. "Something feels off."

He nodded. "This whole place feels off."

She watched him surreptitiously look about the room while he said, "Tell me the rest of your dream."

Fiona smiled, pretending to be telling him a jovial story in low tones. "Besides being chased by demons and fearing they'd hack my body into a million pieces, I was also witnessing the deaths of the people I care about."

Brogan shot her a look and reached over the table to squeeze her shoulder. "Bloody hell, lass, that sounds like a terrible dream."

"Bloody terrible."

"Ye should wake me next time."

"What could ye do?" she asked with a shrug.

"Distract ye."

Before she had a chance to ask just what he meant by that, the server brought over two steaming bowls of soup and planted them on the table. "Assuming ye'll want bread?" she asked.

"Please," Fiona replied, making certain to keep up the Irish accent.

The serving wench returned a moment later with two crusty slices, placing them on a plate between them.

"Bottoms up," Brogan said, dipping his spoon into his bowl.

"A mug of ale?" the wench asked.

"Aye," Fiona answered as Brogan had a mouth full of soup.

The wench returned a moment later with a jug and two cups, placing them on the table none too carefully, liquid sloshing over the side. She reached to pour, but Brogan stopped her. "We've got it, thanks," he said.

They watched the serving wench go off in a huff and raised their brows at each other, wondering just what in the world was wrong with the woman.

After their meal, they took Milla for a walk about the property, having to make a run for the inn as the sky opened up on them once more. They rushed into the building, heading for the stairs, him taking them two at a time and Fiona trying to keep up. By the time they made it to their room, they were laughing like children.

"Shall we impose the same rules as last night?"

"Aye." Fiona turned her back on him, tugging out of her clothes and pulling on the oversized shirt she'd worn the night before. Oh, how she'd wanted to peek behind her, but already caught doing so once, she didn't want to push it.

"Are ye done, lass?"

"Aye," she said breathlessly, taking his question as a cue to turn around.

Again he was draped in the sheet, and there was something so very intimate in the way they stood there together like this, barely dressed. Everything prickled and she hoped he didn't see that her nipples had tightened beneath the shirt. She crossed her arms, trying to hide the evidence of her desire for him, but the mischievous rogue raised an eyebrow and said, "Cold?"

Fiona nodded, not trusting her own voice.

"A glass of wine, then? Mayhap that will help to warm ye. Come stand by the fire too." Heat edged his words, enough to warm her without getting closer to the flames.

Was he feeling the spark of desire as much as she was?

Fiona sat on the floor before the hearth, watching his movements, marveling at the way his muscles rippled as he shifted. He poured them each a cup of wine and then handed her one as he sat beside her.

The heat of his body seeped into hers, and she started to feel warm. What would it be like if she leaned into his naked skin, felt the brush of that chest on her?

"Have ye been fake married before?" she asked, bringing the cup to her lips and taking a small sip.

Brogan chuckled. "I've never let a woman get that close to claiming me."

"So ye're a virgin, then?" This she said with a little snort.

He nearly spat out his wine as he whipped his head toward her. "Nay. Why would ye suggest that?"

"A woman allowing ye entry into her body is a bit close to claiming, would ye no' say?"

"They were no' entering mine, lass. There's a difference."

"Ah, so a man canna be claimed by making love?" She licked a droplet of wine from the rim of her glass, noticing too late how his eyes were riveted on her tongue.

"I would no' say what I've done with women afore was making love."

"What would ye call it, then?" She took a sip of wine, grinning at the challenge and looking forward to whatever answer he might give her.

"Rutting. Mowing. Swiving."

Her face grew hot at the vulgar words, and yet at the same time a frisson of hunger plunged somewhere between her thighs to hear him speaking so. Brogan took a sip of his wine and then turned to stare down at her, a slow wink dipping his eyelid closed and causing her to blush all the more.

"What about ye?" he asked.

For half a second, she thought that Brogan meant for her to tell him what she would call the act of lying with a man. Fortunately, she realized rather quickly that was not to what he was referring. It took Fiona a moment to find her voice, and even when she did, she sounded breathy. "I've never been fake married before. Unless ye count a lass's daydreams."

He grinned. "And who did ye daydream of being wed to?"

"An old friend." She sighed. "But he is wed to someone else."

"'Tis hard to think that any sane man would choose another woman over ye." Brogan's bare shoulder touched hers, and though she wore a shirt, that thin barrier did not keep out the heat of his touch.

She laughed softly. "Believe it or no', Brogan, I am somewhat difficult to get along with."

"Och, I dinna think so. Else your two friends, Jenny and Annie, would no' have stuck by your side. And even as much as I find ye to be a pain in the arse, I was willing to fake marry ye." His tone held a teasing lilt, and she shoulder-bumped him back.

"Your intelligence is coming into question, sir," she teased.

"I think it already was. But alas." He held up his glass of wine. "Cheers."

Fiona clinked glasses with him and then sipped the wine, already feeling warm and dry. Cocooned in a false sense of safety here with Brogan. They could have been the only two people in the world. No matter what happened in the end, these moments with him would be forever burned in her memory.

Fake marriage or not, she would never be able to forget sitting here in a thin shirt, and him bare-chested and wrapped in a sheet. There'd only been a few people in her entire life that she'd sat on the floor before a hearth with. Her brothers and sister, and her friends Annie and Jenny. Not even Aes. Unless one were to count a campfire, but sitting round a campfire didn't bring up such intimate thoughts as being in a bedchamber only half-clothed.

"Tell me more about your family," Brogan said.

"Ye mean besides what ye know of us already, being old enemies?"

He chuckled. "I want to hear the good parts."

"I'd love to share them, put a salve on some of the bad ye might have been taught. Ye met my brother Ian on the field."

"Aye, one hell of a fighter." Brogan actually looked impressed, and she wasn't sure why that surprised her. Maybe because she knew him to be a skilled fighter, and most fighters had an ego bigger than the sky.

"My brother Gus took my sister Leanna to America," she said, feeling a sudden pang at their absence. It had been so long since she'd seen them.

"That's a long trip. Have ye heard from them?" Brogan shifted off the floor to get the carafe of wine from the table and bring it back to refill both of their glasses.

Fiona shook her head. "They only left a few months ago. The journey there is nearly six weeks, and I suspect not to hear back for some time. Especially no' now." Wherever they were, she prayed they were safe and that Gus had been able to find Leanna's wayward betrothed, a story that she shared with Brogan now. "I hope he finds the bastard."

"Ye're all verra close."

"Aye. Before my da was killed, and Mama felt compelled to leave, we all were. The loss of our parents only drew us closer."

"And what of your duties to the prince and as a government postmistress? Does your family know?"

She was quiet for a long time. "Aye." Fiona glanced up at him, realizing how much she trusted this man. "I must confess something ye may have already guessed."

"What's that?"

"I am the Phantom."

A slow grin curled his lip. "I had guessed. And I'm glad ye felt comfortable enough to tell me. Trusted me with it."

"We're in this together, are we no'? If I didna trust ye, none of this would work."

"Aye."

"What about ye? Have ye any brothers and sisters?"

"I have many." He chuckled. "My da was no' exactly the type of man who cared where his seed was planted."

Fiona bit her lip, having forgotten that Brogan was born to one of Chief Grant's lovers.

"Are ye close with any of them?"

He shrugged. "We played as children, but there is always a distance put between those born legitimately and those no'. My da provided for us, but that was about it. We had a roof over our heads, food in our bellies. The lads were trained as soldiers, and the lasses were trained to work in the house."

"How many are ye?"

"A dozen."

Fiona's eyes widened. "'Tis a lot."

"Aye." He took a long sip of wine and turned to grin at her. "We had a secret handshake, the bastards. Do ye want to learn?"

"Aye."

"All right, stand up." Brogan stood and held out his hand,

pulling her to her feet, and she was faced once more with his bare skin but tried her hardest to look up into his face instead. "Hold out your left hand."

He extended his hand in front of her, and she did the same, finding it endearing that he still remembered something so meaningful from his childhood that gave him a sense of belonging, and even more so that he was about to teach it to her.

Grasping her hand in his, he slid his palm up to grip her arm, and then let it go, slapping her hand. "That is the first part. Now, we turn to the side and tap our ankles to each other, first one and then the other."

Fiona stared down at their bare feet. They were going to touch bare feet, bare ankles. Flesh to flesh. Even if just a tap. She followed his lead, a shiver of awareness coursing through her at the shocking connection, however brief.

"Now your right hand. We'll do the same as we did with the left." Their hands clasped and warmth traveled from where he touched her to lodge right in the very center of her body. "And then we embrace, but no' for long, just a quick embrace." He leaned close, his hand on her back, pressing her chest to his, and she lost all breath.

Her nipples puckered as her unconfined breasts, covered in barely a whisper of fabric, brushed the heat of his skin. *Goodness*…

Gone too soon, he pulled back.

"Think ye can do it again, but quickly?" he said with a waggle of his brows.

Fiona grinned at his delight. "Aye," she said, very much indeed wanting to do this again and surprised at how sensual she found the simple act of a childish handshake. Then again, Brogan could make anything sensual. He was so large, so strong, so…*him*.

He grasped her left hand, then they turned and tapped ankles before embracing once more, and then clasping their right hands.

"Ye picked up on it rather quickly," he said.

She nodded, wanting to lean into his body, to press her lips to his skin. To make up a secret handshake of their own.

The smile faded from Brogan's face as he watched her, replaced by a look of desire, mirroring exactly how she felt from head to toe.

"Dinna look at me like that," he said. "It makes me think of kissing ye, and I canna think of kissing ye. Not when we both promised this would be a fake marriage."

Fiona nodded. "Completely fake." Except they were here alone in this room, no imminent danger, both half naked.

A frisson of heat caressed her skin, and she found herself staring at his mouth. Not caring about what was fake and what was not. All she knew was that she very much wanted to kiss him right then and there.

She took a step forward, and Brogan met her halfway. They reached for each other, her hands sliding up over his chest to his shoulders, the heat of his skin singeing her fingertips so much she expected to see smoke. Large hands spanned her waist, and then their bodies were colliding at the same time as their mouths.

Fiona kissed him with all she had, sliding her tongue against his and tasting wine and desire.

Zounds, but he was massive.

Her nipples tingled as she pressed them to his chest. Her toes touched the tip of his, and behind the sheet his arousal grew, pressing against her belly. Fiona moaned against him, and he kissed her deeper, a hand tangling in her hair. He walked her backward until her back hit the wall beside the small window, and he pressed her there, caging her in.

She liked the way that felt, his body surrounding her with heat, and desire thrumming through her veins. This was…delicious. Intoxicating. Brogan's palm slid over her ribs to just beneath her breast, stopped, and she ached for him to touch her. Arching her back in silent invitation for him to go on, she muttered, "Please."

Brogan groaned against her mouth, sending chills all over her body at that gruff sound filled with desire and passion.

His mouth slanted over hers again and again, and she felt possessed, claimed, and was all too willing to give in to him. The heat of his palm covered her breast and she gasped, her nipples hardening even more. A simple brush of his thumb over her nipple sent incredible heat and delicious wanting racing through her. She needed more. All of him…

Fiona clung to his body, wanting to be closer and not knowing just how to get there. She lifted her right leg, sliding her bare foot over his calf, and the way he pressed against her, his body tucking farther between her legs, made her shiver and moan at the intimate, heated touch.

"I want ye to touch me," she said.

"We canna go further than this." Brogan's voice was tight, rough.

He was right…but… "I dinna want to stop."

"We must," he groaned, and then swept his arms around her back and beneath her legs. Lifting her into the air, he carried her to the bed where he laid her down, following her with his body. "We canna be man and wife," he said.

She shook her head. "Nay, but we can… Can we…?" She didn't know exactly what she was asking.

"I can give ye pleasure," he murmured against her neck, his body covering hers and pinning her blissfully to the bed with his hard weight.

"I want to give ye pleasure too."

"Ye have no idea how much this is killing me," he said.

"I have a verra good idea." Fiona laughed. "For I feel the same."

Brogan pressed his lips to hers, his body rocking overtop of her, and she instinctively spread her thighs, her knees coming up on either side of him. God, the weight of him pressed to the apex of her thighs set her blood to boiling. She moaned against his mouth as he rotated his hips, grinding them into hers.

Pleasure coiled inside her, intense and full of fire. He held up his weight on one elbow, his other hand massaging her breast. With tender kisses, he made his way down her neck to her chest, his mouth on the fabric covering her nipple, teasing her skin with his teeth.

Fiona bucked at the sensual touch, and then he was sliding her shirt out of the way, up over her thighs. Air hit her exposed sex, and Brogan kissed his way from her belly to between her thighs.

He paused, staring up at her. "I'm going to taste ye."

"This does no' mean we're wed, does it?"

"Nay," he drawled.

Oh, sweet relief… And then he did taste her, with long, languid strokes of his tongue.

Fiona gripped the sheets, her back arched, mouth open, gasping with pleasure. This was…this was… He quickened the pace, his tongue circling a nub of flesh that seemed to be sending flames of rapture coursing through her.

"That's it, lass," he crooned against her heated flesh. "Moan for me."

And oh, did she moan, crying out in pleasure as wave after delicious wave coursed through her. A strange and wicked sensation whipped through her that she'd never experienced before and left her breathless and full of questions. Was this normal? Was this something that happened whenever a man put his mouth on her? Would it happen to him if she were to put her mouth on him?

Fiona sat upright, Brogan still planted between her thighs.

"Lie back down," she said, shoving at his shoulders, and he rolled over, obeying her command.

Fiona tugged at the knotted sheet until she revealed the hard, solid length of him. Running her fingers along the satiny skin, Brogan shuddered.

"What are ye going to do?" he asked.

"The same thing ye did to me."

He started to shake his head, but she ignored him, leaning

down until her hair tickled his thighs and belly, and then she slid her tongue along the length of his arousal. His skin was hot velvet.

With trembling fingers, she gripped his shaft, holding him steady while she familiarized herself with his very hot, throbbing appendage. She'd never kissed a man's cock before…and the very act of doing it left her drunk with power and full of longing.

Brogan let out a curse under his breath, his muscles tightening, a hand running through her hair.

She licked again, circling her tongue around the tip, and he groaned.

"Take me into your mouth," he begged.

And she was quick to deliver, wrapping her lips around him and sliding him deep inside. Brogan let out another curse, and she grinned as she slid back up. He liked this a lot. As much as she'd liked it when he did it to her. She sucked him in, then slowly released until his hips bucked upward and he begged her to go faster.

One hand gripped around his shaft, she increased her pace until he was muttering a string of curses and practically bucking off the bed in his enthusiasm to finish in that same earth-shattering way she had. He stiffened, crying out, and attempted to pull away, but she held tight until he'd spilled his warm seed on her tongue.

"Good God," he groaned. "That was…" He let out a long sigh.

"Incredible?" she asked.

"Aye."

"But we are still no' married?" she asked, needing to be reassured.

"Nay."

She collapsed against him, and he used part of the sheet to wipe at the mess on his belly.

"I think I'm going to like being fake married," she teased, her hand on his chest, her head on his shoulder.

Brogan wrapped his arm around her and pulled her close, sharing his warmth.

"I could get used to this," he murmured against her head.

Fiona nodded, not saying anything. His words and all they'd just shared collided in her mind.

Though they were fake married, she still wasn't dumb enough to think sharing such intimacies wasn't exactly that—*intimate*. They were two consenting adults, and the bliss she'd felt in his arms had been enough to temporarily take away all of the worry and fear.

Even now, it was starting to creep back in around the edges. She closed her eyes tight, trying to force it back. Brogan trailed a hand down her back, and she shivered.

"Are ye cold?" He lifted the coverlet up over them both.

Nay, she'd not been cold at all. In fact, she was a lot further away from cold than she'd ever been before. Still she nodded, not wanting to share her feelings with him completely.

Fiona snuggled closer, feeling safe and comfortable in his arms. This couldn't happen again. And it probably wouldn't, because after tonight they'd be on the road again, the men surrounding them when they camped at night. When they finally did meet up with the prince's entourage, there would be no privacy or shared rooms—and Ian wouldn't stand for it, might even restart the decades-old clan feud in retaliation. They could drop the facade of being wed, and then they'd have to answer for lying.

But for now, right now, they had this moment. This one night.

She snuggled closer, one leg tossed over his, the hair on his calf tickling her foot. Milla scratched on the door to leave the room, and Fiona gingerly crawled around Brogan who was already softly snoring, deep into sleep.

Wrapping an extra blanket around her, she opened the door to their room and let Milla out into the hall. The sounds from belowstairs were quiet. So Fiona crept down the stairs, following Milla who padded toward the door at the rear of the tavern. Bodies curled up over tables in the tavern itself didn't stir as she passed.

She let the dog outside and watched Milla take off toward the barn in the moonlight. Shadows bounced off the ground, and she half expected some brigand to leap out at her. The bliss of the night spent in bed with Brogan was like a dream, shattered only by her fear of what would happen next.

Fiona shivered, hugging the blanket tighter, wishing she'd stopped to put on her boots. Her feet were freezing, and the cold from outside seeped over her bare toes and inched its way up her legs.

Fiona watched for a few minutes in case Milla came back, but she didn't. The hound would find the men in the barn, sleep with the horses. And so Fiona crept back up the stairs to the chamber she shared with Brogan.

As quietly as she could, she shut the door and crawled back into bed, curling her body around his in an effort to regain some warmth.

Brogan mumbled something in his sleep and then pulled her into his arms, tucking her against him. If only this were a moment she could experience every day for the rest of her life.

Twelve

BROGAN LAY ON THE BED BESIDE FIONA, WATCHING IN THE DIM light of the fire as her chest rose and fell, her beautiful face peaceful. Gone was the pinched look between her brows. The slight frown had disappeared. Her features relaxed, a phenomenon he didn't think happened very often.

Something had changed between them tonight that shook him to the core, irreversibly transforming him in a way that left him feeling unsteady. The sparked tension that had been increasing since the moment he'd first laid eyes on her had finally exploded in passion. And rather than leaving him sated and with the ability to walk away, his desire for her had only grown. He wanted, *needed* more. Things between them would never be the same. And that was damn scary.

It wasn't just that they'd shared physical intimacy. As he'd pointed out to her earlier in the evening, he'd shared that with dozens of women. Per his usual, he'd tried to pull away at the last minute, choosing not to spend anywhere near her—even if it was her mouth. A reflex he'd honed for years and years. But Fiona hadn't let him, and he'd not had the power to resist her.

There had been one other major difference in tonight's dalliance besides the fact that they'd opened up so deeply to each other that he'd allowed himself to lose control, and it was that he'd pleasured her with his mouth.

Brogan didn't do that with other women. His fingers, aye, his cock, always, but his mouth? Nay. To him, that had always been an act one step too close to intimacy. But the moment he'd pressed Fiona up against the wall, all he could think about was how she'd taste, what she'd sound like when she climaxed, and how much he wanted to be between her thighs.

Even now, he thought about waking her for another go of it, but they both needed their rest. And he needed his mind to calm down enough to let him do so. If he were to give himself an accurate assessment, he would say that so far, he was failing miserably at this fake marriage. Because all he wanted to do was be with her. Know her, touch her.

That was not what this fake marriage was about. He was supposed to be offering her protection. Not fawning over her, drooling like a hungry lad starved for affection. This was becoming too much. She was too much.

Brogan let out a soft groan and rolled away from her to stare up at the ceiling. Then flopped his arm over his eyes, trying to force himself to sleep. To not think about her. To not think about how much she was changing him, or the subtle shifts he'd made in just one night. The fire had gone down low, but the room was warm. Too warm. He tossed the sheet aside, allowing the air in the chamber to touch all of his skin, and still he was hot. Mayhap it would be best to just get up, go outside, and cool off. But then if she woke from a nightmare and was looking for him to comfort her, he wouldn't be there.

Och, why did he even care about that?

Days ago this woman had been out of his life. She'd abandoned him weeks prior, and now he was ignoring his own physical comfort in preference to a wife that wasn't really his wife.

Ridiculous.

Sham marriage... He had to remember that.

Just when he was finally starting to drift off, a sharp, rapid knock sounded on the door, startling him.

Brogan's eyes sprang open and he jumped to his feet, a rush of blood pumping through his veins. They were being attacked. They'd been found out. Behind him, Fiona bolted upright in bed, and when he glanced at her, he could see concern in her eyes bordering on fear.

Sorley's voice came through the door. "Brogan, wake! They've taken to the forest with two of our horses."

Brogan opened the door, realizing too late that he was completely naked. Sorley eyed him up and down, though somehow the lad managed to keep the judgment from his face.

"My clothes are drying, dinna look at me like that."

With an eyebrow raised, Sorley nodded, a smirk on his lips.

Brogan ignored him. "Which two horses?"

"Yours and Fiona's."

"Do ye know who it was?" Brogan immediately thought of the man who'd questioned them two days ago, how he and his friends had continued to size them up. *Bastards!*

"Aye, we think some men from the tavern." Sorley narrowed his eyes. "Can ye at least put on a sheet while we're talking?"

A sheet landed on Brogan's head, tossed from Fiona behind him, and he was quick to wrap it around his waist.

"I woke to the sound of the barn door closing. I got up to investigate, only to see them riding hell-for-leather. At first, I didna realize they'd taken our horses, but the way they rode so fast made me suspicious. We slept right through it, Brogan. All of us." Sorley grimaced, punching his hands together in frustration.

"Damn," Brogan muttered, anger surging through his limbs. How dare those jackanapes steal their horses right out from under their noses! And to think if he'd just gone outside to cool off like he wanted to, he might have been able to put a stop to it. Or they might have jumped him from behind. Either way, he'd have cracked a few noses and likely prevented the theft. Nay, he couldn't think like that. Nothing good came from trying to place blame, even if the blame was on one's self. Problems had to be solved, not ruminated over. "Let me dress and I'll meet ye downstairs."

Brogan made hasty work of tugging on his breeches, shirt, hose, and boots.

"I'm coming with ye," Fiona said.

"Nay. Stay here where 'tis safe. We dinna know who they left behind and what plans they've made. I'll no' have another knife at your throat."

"I'm no' going to stay here while ye rush off to find our horses God knows where."

Brogan straightened. "Aye, ye will, *wife*." He said the latter in a reminder of why they'd pretended to wed to begin with. "Because the whole reason ye're in my bed is so I can protect ye. If I dinna make it, ye still must."

She pressed her lips together defiantly, and he wondered if she was going to listen to him or not. But at last she gave a sharp nod, and he left the chamber. Down in the tavern, several men still slept with their heads on the tables as if they'd simply fallen over during conversation. He touched one louse on the shoulder, shaking him slightly until the man stared up at him with his red and bleary eyes.

"What are ye waking me up for?" the man slurred, rubbing furiously at his eyes.

"Where are your friends?" Brogan asked, but the man only glowered. And so Brogan helped him up from the table by the scruff of his neck. "Where are they going with our horses?"

The man's scowl deepened, and he shrugged, trying to escape Brogan's hold and doing a little arm swing that did nothing to loosen himself.

"I dinna know what ye're talking about. I have no friends here, and I certainly dinna know anything about any horses gone missing. Ye've got the wrong man."

"Somebody knows something," Brogan growled. "Which one of ye is going to talk?" He shook the man's head by the hair. "I think the world could do with one less scoundrel."

The bastard yelped, the defiance in him evaporating as he whined, "All I know is they thought ye were a good mark."

Brogan muttered an expletive and resisted the urge to toss the worm into the wall. "Where did they go?"

"I dinna know. They didna tell me. I just overheard them talking about it. They waited till all the sounds from above grew quiet and then stole your horses."

Brogan growled, staring hard into the man's eyes, trying to decide if he wanted to snap his neck or toss him into the mud outside. The bloody whoresons had been listening to him and Fiona in their bed play. That made him want to commit murder.

He glanced at his remaining men who'd come in from the barn. "Sorley and Keith have already gone after the thieves. Saddle me a horse. I'm chasing them down, and hopefully our men have already located the bastards and taken back the horses."

Footsteps sounded on the stairs, and then Fiona appeared wide-eyed at the door's opening. "What's going on?"

Brogan somehow managed to keep his mouth from falling open. The wee wench had completely disregarded his orders to remain abovestairs. He vacillated between carrying her back upstairs after tossing her over his shoulder and telling her everything. Tossing her in the chamber seemed like a really good idea. He might even give her a smack to the bottom. Then again, why should he be surprised? She'd gone out of her way to let him know she was in charge of herself from the moment they'd first met.

"Brogan," she said, snapping him out of his head.

Instead, he tried intimidating her with a glare and hoped she'd take the hint and march back upstairs. Which she did not. She'd heard what Sorley said upstairs, and to brush her off would be to ignore the large fact that she was a part of this group. That she'd seen more and done more than most men in this country. He wanted to protect her, for her not to know about thieves in the dark, but she already knew, and keeping anything from her would just be offensive. Besides, they had to trust each other. He wasn't about to start lying to her now.

"This bastard's friends are the ones who stole our horses."

Fiona cocked her head to the side, studying the man Brogan still held up by his hair. "Why only two?"

That was a damn good question, and one he'd not thought of before.

Narrowing his eyes, Brogan thrust the man onto the bench and backed up a step, arms crossed, hoping that if he let go, the bloke would be more open to talking.

"Answer the lady," Brogan demanded.

But before the man said a damn thing, with dawning dread Brogan understood exactly why. The hair on the back of his neck stood on end and prickles covered his skin. This was a trap.

Fiona seemed to sense the same thing at the exact moment.

She whirled around as a man came up behind her. The lass was quick to grab the dagger from her sleeve, but her attacker's knife was longer, reaching to her belly, while she could not extend far enough. The tip of the arse's blade brushed the fabric of her gown, but quick-thinking Fiona held her dagger at the man's thumb. She'd cut off a finger if he tried to run her through. The odds didn't seem to scare her, though, and she glowered at the man, as fierce as any warrior.

Brogan was making ready to jump the bastard when two men at the table with the whoreson he'd roughed up leapt from their places and immediately attacked, punching Fin in the gut and attempting to do the same to Brogan.

Rounding on the man, Brogan kicked him in the groin. The bloke fell to his knees, but he wasn't done yet. Brandishing a knife toward Brogan, he tried to slice Brogan's legs. Brogan grabbed an empty mug from the table and hit him over the head, knocking him out. Fin dispatched the second man at the same time. The rest of those in the traitor's camp had backed up toward the walls, their hands held up in surrender.

Brogan faced the only man who still had a death wish, for he continued holding his knife at Fiona's belly, eyes skittering around the room.

"Get away from my wife," Brogan warned.

Fiona backed away slowly, but the man followed, confident that his weapon could do more damage. But then Fiona did something the outlaw had not expected. She tapped her dagger's blade against the traitor's, shoving it aside. The man narrowed his eyes, obviously having assumed she would just allow him his control. That was a laugh. If the man had known Fiona even a fraction better, he wouldn't even have attempted that.

The man licked his lips nervously. "Ye think to sword fight with that puny dagger?"

"I think ye're a fool," Fiona said nonchalantly. "For ye do realize ye're outmatched, aye? Even if ye were to dispatch me, the rest of my family would leap onto ye with their blades sinking into your flesh. This is a losing battle for ye no matter what. So I might as well have a wee bit of fun before ye kill me."

"Ye're no' afraid to die," the man said with a strange cock to his head as if surprised.

"I am no' afraid of ye." And she didn't look it anymore either. Her face was placid, bored even, and she didn't tremble a bit as she flicked his blade away again.

The man brandishing the knife finally figured out that he had little recourse but to drop his weapon and hold his hands up in the air, else he would die, there was no question.

As he did that, the dagger clattering to the floor, Fiona kicked it away. The door to the tavern flung open, and Keith and Sorley burst through, red-faced from exertion.

"We got them. We got the horses back."

"Where are my friends?" asked the original traitor Brogan had fought with from his place on the floor, waking.

"Ye'll no' be seeing them for a long time," said Sorley. "The lot of ye should've known better than to steal our horses. We dinna take kindly to thieves and especially no' thieves of our dearly beloved horses."

The man who'd held his knife to Fiona's belly started to quake, his knees buckling as he fell and then turned, searching out Brogan as the leader of the pack.

"I swear 'twas no' my idea. 'Twas his." He pointed to the man still lying on the floor. "We were stealing the horses as a distraction, and then going to rob ye. Saw your coin purse looked mighty full. We're hungry, and there's nowhere for us to go. Our houses have all been burned out by dragoons. My fields destroyed. We have nothing left." The poor sod sounded sincere, his eyes pleading for mercy.

As convincing as the man seemed, if Brogan thought he could trust this person to tell the truth when he had plotted to steal their horses and rob them of their coin purses, he'd be a fool. If they were so desperate, they could have asked for help, and considering how much the men had been imbibing in ale for days without being thrown out by the innkeeper, Brogan had his doubts about just how needy they were. Not to mention the bastard had threatened to kill Fiona.

How was Brogan to know whether to trust anyone with the entire country turning on its ear? Hell, his own father had turned against the Jacobites. If blood couldn't instill trust, no one could.

He wished that Fiona would go upstairs, disappear like the phantom she was, but deep down he knew she wouldn't. The lass was as invested in this fight as he was. Brogan scanned the rest of the tavern, taking in the owner, his wife, and the rest of the patrons. Which one of them was going to turn on them next? Was it cynical that he believed someone would?

So many in Scotland were going through hard times. Many had turned to crime and violence in order to survive. Brogan wasn't naive enough to believe that wasn't happening.

Which was also why he was looking at those left and wondering which one of them would try to make them victims again.

"Tie them up," Brogan instructed his men, and his gaze fell on the tavern owner who was quietly seething in the corner. "Were ye in on this, man?"

"I knew nothing of it."

"And yet the perpetrators were regulars of yours."

"Aye, they were, but if I'd known what they were up to, I'd no' have allowed them to remain."

"Ye harbor thieves and criminals." Brogan glanced at everyone else. "Which else of ye belong to this lot?"

Several shook their heads, hands held up in surrender.

"Ye willingly allowed these men to stay with potential victims." Brogan moved slowly toward the tavern owner until he stood right in front of the man. He held out his palm. "I'll be taking back the coin we gave ye for our stay, since your friends, and likely ye, thought it fine to rob us."

———

Fiona stood at the base of the stairs watching the exchange. The air in the tavern had shifted from one menacing feeling to another, and still she felt danger tingling at the base of her spine. Was the innkeeper going to whip out a pistol and shoot Brogan for demanding the return of his coin? Given what happened, it seemed like a valid request.

Would that give the rest of the criminals a reason to act? Every scenario played out in her head, and the one that seemed best was the one in which they packed up and left now, no matter that it was the middle of the night, no matter her exhaustion. There were several hours until dawn and anything could happen during that time. An urgent need to escape filled her. If she'd been alone, she'd already have left. This was the problem with a larger group, having to harangue them all.

She stared at Brogan, feeling the itch to take flight warring with the desire to stay right where she was. It was this self-preservation that had gotten her as far as she'd come, wasn't it? But the thought of leaving alone, abandoning them all, started a crater in her chest, forcing her feet to remain still.

"Aye, sir," the innkeeper finally said, reaching into the front of his apron and producing several coins.

He passed them to Brogan, who did not bother to count them but instead tucked them into his boot without taking his eyes off the man as he did it.

Brogan flicked his gaze for a fraction of a second to his men. "Stay here with the rest of them while we prepare our departure." Then he returned his harsh regard to the felons on the floor. "If one of ye moves, I'll shoot ye," Brogan warned.

He glanced at her and she nodded, and each of the men with them did in turn.

"I'll stand watch," Dugall volunteered.

"I'll get us some provisions." Fiona didn't wait to see what the rest of the men volunteered to do. She backed toward the kitchen of the tavern, followed by the innkeeper's wife who silently helped her to gather a grain sack full of bread, cheese, and cold chicken, and a fresh jug of ale.

When she came back toward the front of the tavern and headed upstairs to gather her things, she met Brogan at the base.

"I'm sorry we have to leave so quickly," he said. "I know I promised ye another night's good rest. I hate that I'll be dragging ye back out into the rain again."

"I'm no' broken, nor am I weak. A little robbery or a wee bit of rain is no' going to put me down. My clothes are dry now, and might stay that way for a time beneath a blanket. And as for sleep, I got plenty of it the night before."

A prickle of trepidation nudged at the back of her neck. Fiona spun around toward the dining hall, searching out what she felt was missing. And then it struck her. "Where is Milla?"

Concern grew thick in her chest. She'd not seen her hound since this ordeal started.

"Where is Milla?" she asked again, her voice higher pitched with worry.

Everyone ceased their movements, staring at Fiona with questions in their eyes, all except the thieves who kept their gazes on the floor.

Milla had already been through so much with her run-in with Boyd. The hound did not deserve any more torment.

Something had happened to her—on purpose—Fiona was certain.

"What have ye bastards done with our hound?" Brogan growled, stomping into the dining area with murderous rage creasing his features.

But Fiona couldn't waste time waiting for the thieves to find it in their hearts to answer. She had to go now.

"I'll search the stables," Sorley said.

"I'll search the fields, in case she chased after us," volunteered Fin, with Keith going with him.

"I'll go out to the barn," Brogan said. "Dugall, keep watch with James and Charles."

Fiona ran up the stairs as the rest of them took off in various directions looking for Milla. Upstairs in her rented chamber, there was nothing save the rumpled bed and empty wine flagon and cups. No sign of Milla. Worry flooded her veins, making her palms sweat. They wouldn't have hurt the dog, would they? What if Milla had come across them when they were stealing the horses? What if she'd started to bark and they'd silenced her?

From outside came several shouts. Fiona ran to the window, but it was too dark to see anything other than her shadowy reflection in the candlelight. With a whirl on her heels, she ran toward the stairs, leaping down in bounds and crashing into Brogan at the base. He caught her, pulling her up against him, eyes locked on hers. The warmth and solidness of his body lent her some strength she seemed to be missing.

Together, they ran outside toward the yelling. Around the back of the tavern, Fin was kicking at a shed door that had been locked tight with an iron bolt. Fiona nearly collapsed in relief at the sound of growling and barking coming from within.

"Milla!" she cried, and the barking grew louder.

Fin's kicking was deafening but did little to persuade the door lock to crack or the doors to open.

"Stand aside," Brogan said. He lifted an ax he'd found around the side of the shed and brought the blade down in a powerful arc onto the bolt, causing sparks to fly. But the lock did not break open. He swung his arms up, preparing to swing again. Metal crashed against metal in a deafening ping, and this time among the sparks the lock gave way, crashing to the ground.

Fin shoved the door open, and Milla practically flew through the gap, crashing into Fiona as she knelt onto the ground. She wrapped her arms around the hound, allowing herself to fall backward. Milla whimpered and licked Fiona's face in a fury of panicked kisses.

"Ye're safe now," Fiona cooed, stroking the hound and hugging her close. "No one is going to hurt ye."

"That's a good lass," Brogan said, patting the hound on the head, which earned him a hearty lick and a few loving nips from Milla.

Before now, Fiona had not realized how much she'd fallen in love with the dog.

"We would no' let those vile heathens take ye from us," Fiona said against Milla's head. "Ye are far too precious." She hugged the wiggling dog to her and then promised to never let her go again.

"'Tis time for us to go," Brogan said.

Aye, Fiona agreed with a nod, not bothering to add what they were all thinking, which was *before something else terrible happens.* As much as the perpetrators professed their innocence, there was no telling if they had spies sent out to the surrounding area, alerting dragoons of Brogan's group's presence, or alerting other outlaws on the perimeter.

With Milla draped over Fiona's lap, they mounted the horses and headed out in the dark at a gallop. Fiona was glad to leave the tavern behind for the nightmare it had become, but not for the intimacy that she'd shared with Brogan. For a few blissful hours, she'd been in another world. But that heavenly place, shattered by thieves and outlaws, only reminded her what a stark and dangerous world Scotland had become.

It was also a startling reminder not to get too comfortable. That dalliances and, dare she say it, romance were not for her. Fiona had a place in Scotland in the prince's entourage, in the way in which the world should be, and none of it had to do with lying in bed with Brogan.

Still, the thought of ever parting from him, of having to one day say goodbye, even goodbye from the men in this party, made her heart ache.

Fiona studied the motley group surrounding her, realizing they were her family in a way. She cared for them all like brothers, save for Brogan. He brought out feelings in her that were much deeper, more terrifying. Still, it was a comfort to know that she was not all alone in the world, that they had her back. She'd not felt that way in a very long time. Not with Ian off to war and Gus and Leanna gone to America. She'd been very alone, partly by choice and partly by necessity.

By noon the following day, they finally stopped for an extended break to rest the horses and themselves. They'd ridden through the night and most of the next morning, fearing the retaliation of the men at the tavern. There was no telling what they'd do for revenge, and no doubt the dragoons had a bounty on Fiona and Brogan's heads that the thieving bastards would be happy to collect.

Fiona headed toward the brush for some privacy, calling over her shoulder, "I promise no' to be attacked again."

Milla leapt up from the place where she lounged in the field to follow.

"Ah, good, protect your lass," Brogan said.

"Nay, stay," Fiona said with a frown and a wave of her hand at the hound. "Dinna come with me, Milla. I'll take my chances. Last time ye took a boot to the head."

But Milla didn't seem to care and ignored Brogan's whistles to return.

"Fine, come along, but stay out of trouble."

After returning to the fire and warming her hands, Fiona was grateful that the rain had finally let up. The blanket had kept her mostly dry for a time until it had started to soak through.

She wondered how the prince was faring. Did he have a warm, dry bed? Hearty meals? Probably not. Those were the old days. Now he was on the run, his army dwindled, and his coin purse nearly empty. No such luck now, she was certain. The prince would have to rely on the hospitality of his allies, and she prayed they provided him well, keeping him safe and alive. With the dragoons chasing them, and nearly everyone in the country paranoid they were going to be next in Cumberland's slaughter, the danger seemed double what it had been a few weeks before.

There had been some clues along the way that the prince was still out there and that the people were still rallying behind him, but there were signs, too, that the people were starting to lose hope for a future with Prince Charlie as king.

In the end, how were they going to rebuild the army? It'd taken Jenny Mackintosh years to amass hers, as it had everyone else. Years to gather up the coin that didn't end up being enough. They needed the backing of the French if they were going to win this war. They needed the coin, the weapons, and the manpower. Those were the things the prince was supposed to bring with him across the Channel, and yet he'd arrived nearly empty-handed.

With a dawning understanding, Fiona had a feeling that the only way the prince was going to be able to rebuild, to renew this effort, was if he presented himself before the French king and begged for help once more. That required him leaving the country.

If he left, there was no way to predict who would be loyal when he returned. How many Jacobites would be left alive if they were to remain here with the Butcher and his men? Going back to a normal life, without living in fear, seemed a distant dream. She shuddered, and Milla wiggled closer to her feet, sensing her distress. Fiona reached down and stroked her hand over the hound's head, finding comfort in the softness of her fur, the warmth of her body.

Wherever the prince was right then, he must have come to the same conclusion, or at least his advisors would have. Perhaps he'd already sailed for France and they were chasing a ghost. The irony of the Phantom chasing a ghost was not lost on her.

Fiona's thoughts trailed for a moment to her siblings. Ian would not leave the prince's side, of that she was certain. And she could only pray that Gus and Leanna were still far away, across the ocean in America, ignorant of the battles, the wins and the final crushing loss. For if they'd heard, they too would come rushing back to Scotland in hope of helping.

Fortunately, news would take weeks and weeks to arrive across the sea and then to find its way to her siblings' ears. It'd be months before they knew. Still, she prayed they found out before their mission was complete and they landed back on Scottish soil to witness the horror of what had happened to their beloved country. Fiona couldn't imagine what it would be like to come home to a life that was no longer her own. Not the one she'd left behind… After all, she'd been watching every part of her life be ripped away.

Where was Jenny in all of this? She had survived the battle at Culloden, and she and her husband should be in hiding. But knowing Jenny, she'd resumed her midnight rides to gather support for the prince. And Annie… Fiona prayed her friend had made it safely to her family in the east. What Fiona wouldn't give right now to go back and make sure her friend had followed her advice and escaped. There was no telling what could happen to any of them with so much violence that they'd already witnessed and endured.

"What are ye thinking about?"

Brogan's voice broke through her heavy thoughts, and Fiona cocked her head, trying to figure out just how to say what she was thinking.

"Your face is drawn. I can tell 'tis something serious."

He was not wrong.

"I'm thinking of my brothers and my sister, my friends. Thinking about Scotland and what's to become of all of us."

Brogan let out a sympathetic grunt. "I know what that's like." He handed her a flask of whisky. "Here. This will help with the thoughts."

Fiona gently pushed it back. "It might make my mind calm for now, but it will no' answer the questions I seek. For once the whisky clears, we will still be in danger and we will still need to find the prince and figure out a way out of this."

"That is true, lass, but we will rise up against Cumberland. His men will no' defeat us again. Our country has fought too long, too hard for freedom. Did ye stop believing that?" Brogan's brow was furrowed as he studied her, the passion he held for the cause and their country evident in his voice.

"Aye, I do wholeheartedly. I want nothing more than for Scotland to be free, for this war to be over. To no' worry every time I step outside or every time I wake up in a warm bed that something is going be ripped away from me."

Brogan put his arm around her shoulder and tucked her against him. She wanted to resist, but she was weak. The comfort he offered her, though little, seemed to help in a big way.

"We've all lost much, lass. Dinna give up hope. Everyone here is counting on ye. Ye're the reason that we're still fighting. We believe in ye and ye believe in the prince. Ye believe in freedom, just like we do. We'll get through this—together."

"I'm no' going to give up on Scotland," she said, glancing up at him, searching his eyes and finding the confidence she was look-ing for. "That doesna mean I dinna sometimes have doubts about how we will proceed."

Brogan nodded, eyes locked on hers. "Aye, good. Because this is our country, and we need to take it back."

Thirteen

A WEEK AFTER LEAVING THE TAVERN IN THE MIDDLE OF THE night, they arrived at Kyle of Lochalsh. Across the loch, Fiona could make out the rising mountains of the Isle of Skye. The sloping peaks and rolling valleys of green and purple met the white plush clouds of the sky. Peaceful and beautiful. Fiona drew in a deep breath, imagining the scent of heather and sweet grass.

The prince should be there, safe on the island, away from dragoons. Or at least that was what they all hoped. Though Fiona knew Cumberland's men had a far reach, she hoped that the isle was remote enough to harbor more Jacobites than King George loyalists. Likely that line of thinking was only wishful.

"I'll see about a ferry," Brogan said, dismounting and going into the local tavern in the small village.

"I'll come with ye." Fiona passed Milla to Brogan while she climbed off her horse, and he let the little dog down to stretch her legs and sniff about.

The tavern was dimly lit, smelled of stale ale and body odor, and was filled with what looked like daytime regulars. Some were already deep in their cups, and others seemed only to have stopped by for their lunch.

Brogan approached the bar, and Fiona kept to his back like a good wife would, their boots scuffing on the dirty floors. No use drawing attention by pushing her way forward and making demands.

"Afternoon," a barkeep said from behind the counter, wiping his hands on his apron. He had a shock of red hair and ruddy cheeks that made him look a bit too jolly, but his kind eyes belied the flat, defensive line of his lips. "How can I help ye?"

"When does the next ferry go out?" Brogan asked.

"No' until tomorrow, sir. Runs every morning just after dawn and not another minute more." The man pulled down two mugs and set them on the bar. "Ale?"

Brogan shook his head. "Why's that?"

The man shrugged. "Times have changed." The way he said it made it clear he expected no argument over it, and that it should just be accepted as fact.

Fiona found that very irritating. She had a lot of questions and she wanted straight answers. She bit her tongue to keep herself from saying so.

"If that's the case, have ye any rooms to rent?" Brogan asked.

"Aye. How many ye need?" The barkeep looked behind him at Fiona.

"One is enough for the lady. My men and I will sleep down here with the rest."

Fiona worked to hide her disappointment that they wouldn't be sharing a room. Why had he decided that was best?

The barkeep nodded. "'Tis fine, but I'll no' be serving ye ale all night." The man looked behind Brogan at the regulars. "Got enough problems already," he muttered.

Fiona stiffened. Another inn where they might be potential victims. How she longed for just a moment's reprieve from constantly feeling as though she had to fight.

"I've no plans to get sotted, sir, so that's fine by us. And what have ye got to eat?"

"My wife is making supper, but 'twill no' be done for a while now."

"We can wait."

The man nodded again. "I can give ye some nuts to eat while ye wait."

Fiona's stomach growled, and she felt her cheeks heat.

Brogan nodded. "We thank ye for it."

"Gonna cost ye." The way the man said it was as if he wanted to push Brogan off the idea. Since they'd walked in, it seemed he wanted them to turn around and walk out.

Fiona wasn't going to take it personally. The man probably got a lot of trouble being near the ferry to Skye. Better to warn trouble-makers off before they started, she supposed. If only the innkeeper at the last place had been so proactive.

"'Tis fine," Brogan said.

The barkeep nodded. "I'll have the missus take the lady upstairs."

"And ye've a place for our horses?"

"Aye, a stable around back."

Brogan leaned over the bar, his voice low. "Have ye had any problems with thieves?"

The man eyed Brogan as though he'd just said that he himself would be stealing from them all that very day. He reached under the bar, likely for a weapon, and Fiona's stomach did a major flop.

Brogan held out his hands, showing he was unarmed, attempting to de-escalate the situation. "I only ask because we've just come from a tavern several days' ride away where two of our horses were nearly stolen by men who took them in the middle of the night."

The barkeep frowned and took his hand from beneath the counter. "I can assure ye that nothing like that's happened around here for a time. God save the king."

Fiona perked up when the man uttered the words. For they had oft been used to find out if one were a Jacobite or not.

"And his bonnie son," Brogan answered quietly.

The barkeep nodded with the barest hint of a smile, his shoulders relaxing some. "The only exception to that is when the dragoons come 'round. They like to take what they please."

"Aye, we know it."

"This traveling inn is no' a refuge," the barkeep warned. "We take anyone's coin for ale who's willing to pay. Ye can stay for a night but no longer. The only allowances to this rule are for the locals."

"We understand."

Fiona stepped beside Brogan, keeping her eyes downcast and hoping to seem demure, appealing to the barkeep's masculinity even though that grated on her nerves. "Might ye have an idea where the bonnie son is? We heard he was on Skye." She peeked up through her lashes to gauge his reaction.

The barkeep glanced from her to Brogan and back again. "No longer. Gone to South Uist, last I heard. Been there a week or more now."

Fiona nodded. "Our thanks." She flicked her gaze up at Brogan. That meant that once they made it to Skye, somehow, they'd have to convince a ship to take them to South Uist, which seemed like a tall order. Something like that cost money, and none of them were filled with coin. They had enough to get by, and no extra. Not to mention that chartering a boat large enough to fit their horses would raise suspicions.

"What have ye got to do with him?" the barkeep asked.

Fiona smiled and shook her head. "Och, nothing really. We were headed to Skye to stay with family, start over. Heard the prince was headed there too and thought wouldna it be grand if we caught sight of him? But alas, 'tis no' meant to be." She gave a whimsical sigh and patted her chest over her heart, hoping the man fell for her feminine ruse.

Fortunately, he did, passing her a gentle smile before grinning at Brogan with mirth. "Oh, aye, ye'll no' be seeing him there. 'Tis a shame, because I have heard he's quite bonnie and might give this lad a run for his money."

Fiona burst out laughing at that, unable to help herself. There was simply no comparison whatsoever between the two. "Aye, I have no doubt, sir."

The prince was handsome to be sure, but in a soft, pretty way. He was clever, funny, brave even, but he was not a soldier in the true sense of the word. Brogan epitomized everything there was to be seen in a Highland warrior. He was rough, rugged, handsome in a way that made a woman pant rather than sigh, and he was so very large. He too was clever, funny, and brave, but while in the prince it would bring about the fluttering of lashes and girlish laughs, in Brogan it would bring a woman to her knees before she lost her breath altogether.

And having been in his arms, Fiona knew just how well he could take away her breath, take away her sense and her balance. Even thinking about that had a shiver of need coursing through her veins, and she shifted uneasily on her feet, feeling the heat between her thighs go up several degrees. The prince had never been able to do that, not even when he bent over her hand and kissed her knuckles, calling her a clever beauty. She might have been his mistress if she wanted to, but she was more than happy to have that role filled by Lady Clementina. The prince simply wasn't her type. But Brogan, however... *Sigh.*

Aye, there certainly was no comparison whatsoever.

"How many are ye, not including the lady?" asked the barkeep, swiftly changing the subject.

"Seven of us."

"All right. I can tell my missus so she knows how many more to prepare for at supper."

"Our thanks." Brogan placed several coins on the counter, tapping his hands over them.

He turned toward Fiona, lowering his voice. "Alone, ye'll be able to get some rest. And I can stand watch with my men in case we were followed."

Fiona nodded. "Makes the best sense." Which it did, even if she wished it were otherwise.

The man called back to someone behind the counter and had an answering call of denial. He rolled his eyes and called for someone else, and a young lass about age ten or so came from the back, wiping her hands on her apron. She looked just like him, though with a feminine line to her chin.

"Molly, take the lady upstairs to room three. Make sure 'tis suitable."

"Aye." Molly curtsied and then skirted around the counter where her father stood and led the way up the rickety stairs to a room that had a number three carved into the wood of the door. The lass unlocked the door and pushed it open. "Right, there ye are, ma'am."

"Thank ye," Fiona said, taking the proffered key and winking at the wee lass. The room was small, sparse of furniture, and with not a speck of dust in sight, shocking considering the state of the tavern below. The owners took good care of the chambers, at least.

"This will do nicely. Did ye decorate it yourself?" she teased.

"Nay." The lass laughed.

"Your parents have done well with the room then."

"There's no' much to it." The girl shrugged. "Will there be anything else?"

"Nay, thank ye."

But the girl tarried, either really wanting to help or trying to get out of some other chore that awaited her. "Would ye care for a bath?"

"Do ye have one?" A bath would be nice.

"Aye. My da will charge ye extra for it, but my brothers can bring it up, and I can help. I can be your lady's maid."

Fiona smiled and nodded gratefully. "I'm happy to pay for it. I've no' had a good wash in a while. But I'm no' a lady," she lied.

She hadn't been able to bathe since the last tavern they'd stayed at a week ago. Och, but the last sennight had gone by in a blur of racing horses and snoring on the ground, then doing it all over again. It was a wonder she was even still standing.

"That's all right," the lass said. "I can still pretend."

Fiona grinned. "All right." There was a lot of pretending going on lately; what was one more?

The lass disappeared back into the hallway and down the stairs, and Fiona could hear her issuing orders to her brothers. Fiona wondered if the lass was the eldest, the way she bossed them all about. Then again, she herself wasn't the oldest and she still bossed her siblings around when she could. Oh, how she missed them.

Fiona went to the small window and peered outside. The men were no longer in the road, having taken the horses round back to get them settled in the stable, and they too would like to wash up before coming back into the tavern for refreshments.

Movement caught her eye, and she watched Brogan walk shirtless from behind the barn. Water dripped down his abdomen, and he was shaking remnants of his bath from his hair. A slender woman slinked toward him. The coy drop of her shoulder and the way she reached out to touch his arm left no question as to what she wanted of him.

But Brogan shook his head, offered a polite smile, and walked around her.

The woman watched after him longingly, and all Fiona could think was *He's mine.*

The men gathered in the tavern, Sorley and Fin by the bar, James and Charles having engaged in a game of cards with some of the other patrons, while Brogan, Keith, and Dugall sipped their ale, taking it all in.

Fiona had yet to reappear, and Brogan wouldn't be surprised if she decided to take her supper upstairs. Lord knows if he were a woman surrounded by over half a dozen men, he just might. She'd been stuck on the road with them all for days. Not a moment of privacy at all.

At his feet was Milla, who looked up expectantly anytime she heard steps approaching the main tavern hall and then settled down with disappointment when it wasn't Fiona who walked through the door. He reached down and gave her a scratch behind her ears.

The atmosphere inside this tavern was worlds different from the one they'd been in before. There had been something sinister in the air there. They'd all felt it the moment they stepped through the doors. But not here. This place could have been in another time. A time well past men being harassed by dragoons, for all Brogan could tell. The air was charged almost with lightness, happiness. And he knew it couldn't be that they didn't care about the war, but perhaps they'd not been touched as heavily as those near Inverness.

Or it could be that they'd all had plenty of the barkeep's ale and only nuts to soak it up.

He wasn't certain exactly what the difference was, the reason behind it, only that it was so. The men had relaxed, and so did he. A smile had even dared curl his lips when Fin shouted his latest jest. The only thing that would make it more perfect would be Fiona sitting beside him, her warmth seeping into his body.

Brogan shook the thought from his mind. He had to remember that the union they shared would one day be broken. A ruse was all he had, nothing more. Nothing would ever go beyond where they were now. But Lord, did he want to lay her down and kiss her the way he had a week before. To touch her skin, savor her. His body reacted and he shifted uncomfortably, grateful for the table to hide from his men just how affected he was by thoughts of Fiona.

Instead, he picked up another walnut and cracked open the shell, expending a marginal amount of frustration on the nut and forcing thoughts of her out of his mind.

Walnut shells littered the floor of the tavern from the men cracking them open and dumping the meaty contents into their mouths between sips of ale before tossing the shells. A wee lad, who looked an awful lot like the lass who'd taken Fiona upstairs, was going about sweeping up the mess. For his part, Brogan kept the shells on the table and scooped the remnants into the lad's pail when he came by.

He was a lot of things, but lazy and inconsiderate weren't among them.

"Thank ye, sir." The lad beamed up at him gratefully.

Brogan nodded, with a small smile and a wink. He might be a soldier now, but it didn't make him forget where he'd come from or that at one point in his life he'd been just like this lad, walking around sweeping up everyone's rubbish. Having been through so much at a young age made him appreciate others much more. Though he still knew the privilege he'd been afforded as a chief's son, even if he was a bastard, went worlds beyond that given the son of a tavern keeper.

A cheer went up by the bar, and Brogan watch Fin climb onto his stool to stand on the bar. The barkeep handed him up a fiddle and Fin started to play it, tapping his bootheel in time with the chords.

His first song was a lively tune that had the other men tapping their feet, clapping in time, and singing along to the verses during the chorus. They raised their glasses in raucous cheer, even Brogan. The second song was a bit more subdued. Brogan recognized it as "*Siúil a Rún*," an Irish song that was normally sung by a woman lamenting the loss of her lover to the military.

The men started to jeer and toss their walnut shells at Fin, calling him a weak sap. Fin broke down in a fit of laughter, changing his song to something lively again.

Milla jumped up from her place at his feet and trotted toward the door, and Brogan noticed Fiona standing there watching the spectacle. Annoyingly, his belly tightened and he sat up a little straighter, suddenly all of his attention solely on her. She bent to pet and coo at their hound and scratch behind her ears. What he wouldn't give to be in the dog's position! Fiona had a soft smile on her face, and her shoulders were relaxed. He'd not seen her, or any of the men, looking so tranquil in weeks. Perhaps it was that they were nearly there. The end to a long journey, the prince's location.

Of course, they weren't really. But they could see Skye from here, and hadn't that been their destination for weeks?

The men did not yet know about what the barkeep had told them about the prince being on South Uist. Brogan would tell them on the morrow; let them have fun for now, and in the morning they'd be on the ferry, where he'd tell them what to expect next. There was also the chance that the prince would be back on Skye. He had been hopping all over the entire country for weeks, trying to avoid dragoons and keep them off their game.

Fiona joined Brogan at the table, sliding onto the chair beside him and greeting Keith and Dugall. He resisted the urge to reach for her hand.

The first thing he noticed was her warmth beside him and how much he'd missed her. The second was that she smelled clean and sweet and he could have closed his eyes and breathed her in all day.

"Care for some nuts, lass?" Dugall asked, pushing the bowl across the table.

"Aye." She fished one out and cracked it open, dumping the inside into her mouth just as the men had. He didn't know why he would have thought she'd pick at it daintily. The very idea made him want to chuckle, but he held it in.

"Ale?" Keith asked her, beating Brogan to the punch.

"Please."

He poured her a cup and passed it, and Fiona drank heartily.

"Have I missed anything besides the opening of Fin's concert?" she teased.

"Well, in fact, aye. Ye missed Sorley balancing a mug of ale on his forehead while he danced a jig," Brogan said with a chuckle.

She whipped her head toward Sorley, who still had a few droplets on his shoulders as proof.

"The lot of ye have been having a good time then," she said with a smile.

"Aye." Brogan leaned a little closer, wanting to press his lips to her temple, and somehow managing to hold himself back.

"Well deserved." She cracked another walnut.

"Ye're deserving of it too," Brogan said, trailing his fingers over the braid of her hair at her back. "Do ye want to sing and dance?"

She laughed, a little bit of pink coming to her cheeks. "I've got the voice of a rusty portcullis, and I'm afraid my dancing days never did arrive. I'm more liable to elbow someone in the face and trip over my own shoes than make a go of anything remotely close to dancing. But rest assured, husband, I am perfectly content to sit and watch." She ended her speech by leaning affectionately in toward him, a move that seemed so genuine, it shocked him to the core.

Husband... She'd not called him that in public before. And the way she'd done it so naturally made him almost believe that it was so.

A few minutes later, the savory scents that had been teasing them throughout the last hour or so wafted more heartily into the tavern dining hall as the barkeep, his wife, and children began to serve supper.

Steaming bowls of stew were placed before everyone, and platters of freshly baked bread were set in the center of the tables. It was the heartiest stew he'd ever seen in a tavern. Thick with vegetables and meat, and it smelled like heaven. How was it possible? And the bread...soft and light and dripping with butter. Was this a dream?

"She's known for her cooking," Fin said, joining them at the table. "Or so says the bloke over there."

The rest of the men dragged over their stools and bowls to join them as well, which made Brogan and Fiona have to squeeze in closer.

"Oh aye?" Brogan said.

"Aye," Sorley agreed. "Barkeep said men come from miles around just for a taste."

Brogan dipped his spoon into the bowl and brought a bite to his mouth and nearly died of pleasure. "'Tis verra good."

Everyone agreed around mouthfuls of food. Having something good to eat seemed only to brighten everyone's mood, and as they finished their meal, full of delicious food and ale, more jests were bandied about, and Fiona seemed to grow warmer beside him.

He wanted to kiss her. A distraction for himself. For her. He didn't want to ruin everyone's mood by discussing any plans yet. Waiting until they were on the ferry and out of earshot of anyone who just might happen to be lurking was best. Which meant that tonight, maybe he could pull her against him, press his lips to hers…

No one would object. They were supposed to be husband and wife after all. As if reading his thoughts, Fiona glanced up at him with her violet doe eyes and a hint of a smile.

"There's something I was hoping we could discuss," she said. "In private."

Brogan sat up a little taller, and the men started to elbow each other and waggle their brows. He ignored them but not before issuing a few threats.

"Aye, lass. Anything," he said, following her out of the tavern.

Milla, seeming to sense her presence wasn't required, stayed back with Sorley, or maybe it was that the man was feeding her bites of stew and bread.

Brogan followed Fiona up the stairs, unable to take his eyes off the way her hips swayed. The roundness of her bottom that he knew fit so well in his hands. Good God, how he'd like to grip it as he drove inside her…

At the top, she led him down the corridor toward room three and opened the door to the cozy chamber. A fire had been lit in the small hearth. There was a bed big enough for two smaller people, but certainly not for a man his size. How a man could sleep on it without his legs completely off was puzzling. Still, he didn't plan to sleep…at least not for a little while.

Brogan gripped her hand softly to keep her from walking across the chamber. She turned around as he shut the door, putting his back up against it, and pressed against him. Her lush figure collided with his, and he nearly groaned as his mouth sought hers, warm, pliable, salty. They melted together, a perfect fit. Lips sliding over lips. His tongue sought hers, and she kissed him boldly back, her palms sliding over his chest to his shoulders.

Hands on her waist, he moved lower, gripping the roundness of her bottom and tugging her closer, his arousal pressing hotly against her. The lass's arse was everything he'd dreamed of. Soft yet firm, round and supple. God, he could massage it all day, every day. Fiona sighed against him, deepening the kiss, tugging at the hair at the nape of his neck.

She felt so good in his arms, to his touch, her body responding to his kiss just as eagerly. Brogan slid his palm over her ribs toward her breast, groaning when his thumb brushed a puckered nipple. Aye, she wanted him as much as he wanted her. Had she sat through their supper thinking of this moment? Had she made up the excuse of needing to talk to bring him up here? A man could hope…

Brogan broke their kiss but only because he wanted to taste her neck, his lips sliding over her skin, breathing in the sweet scent of her skin up to her ear.

"I want ye so bad it aches," he whispered as he nibbled at her earlobe.

Fiona moaned, sliding her hands down his arms, over his chest, touching him, massaging his skin, and then she was tugging his shirt from where it was tucked in his breeches, her fingers dancing over the bare skin of his belly as she pushed his shirt up.

"I want ye too," she said.

Brogan groaned and tore the shirt from his body, tossing it aside, and she pushed him back to the door, her hands exploring and then her mouth as she kissed the place over his heart, his collarbones. Her lips were light as a butterfly and drove him wild. She flicked her tongue over his nipples, and he could take no more. Brogan gripped her rear and lifted her into the air, encouraging her legs to wrap around him. He turned her around and pressed her back to the door, his cock placed at her heat, wishing to strip away the barriers of clothes between them.

He swiveled his hips against her, showing her with his body what he wanted to do as his lips sought hers. "Ye're a fiery temptress," he groaned.

"Nay," she moaned as he tugged at her gown and clamped his mouth on her freed nipple. "'Tis ye that tempt me."

With one hand holding her up, his other slipped beneath her skirts, over her thigh, and back to her arse, seeking out the slit in her drawers to touch that warm heat. And there it was, slick and on fire as he brushed over the silken folds.

"Oh," Fiona cried out.

Oh, indeed… He stroked against her folds, dipping a finger inside as he ground his hips against her, imagining it was his cock and not his finger wrapped in her heat. And he kissed her with the heat of a thousand suns, until they were both panting, until she was writhing against him, crying out her pleasure.

Forget their pact. Forget rules. He wanted to sink inside her.

Brogan turned them around, his lips on hers, and blindly led them to the bed, trying to remember exactly where it was. When he laid her down, the bed crinkled as if he'd laid her on papers.

Wait…he had laid her on papers. He pulled away for just the barest moment to see that there were scraps of paper littering the coverlet. Letters.

"Ye might put these away." He picked one up, seeing first the signature at the bottom.

Aes.

The lad she'd wanted to marry but he had married someone else.

Here they were running around the country in a deceptive marriage, and she was reading old letters from someone else? Not just someone else—another man. Brogan had been about to make love to her…on top of her letters from another lover.

He stood and handed her back Aes's letter where she lay.

That was the thing, though, wasn't it? Their marriage was a ruse. Not real. Seeing that name should not have sent a lance of jealousy burning through his chest. Thinking of her with another man made him want to bellow at the sky. He wanted to find this Aes and demand to know how he would make up for causing her unhappiness.

"Oh," Fiona said breathlessly, taking the letter and sitting up. She gathered up the rest quickly, shuffling them away from his view. "Sorry."

Sorry… Why did that simple word and her flustered appearance dig in so much?

Brogan forced a laugh. "Sorry about what? We all like to reminisce sometimes." He hated that she was reminiscing about another man. The very one whom she'd told him she'd thought of marrying.

She cocked her head, staring at him strangely before giving a short nod.

Brogan crossed the room and poured two glasses of wine, gulping the contents of one as he tried to act completely natural. All the desire that had been pounding through his skin leached out, replaced with the burn of an emotion he didn't want to identify.

"This is true," she said, taking up her glass of wine as well.

"What did ye want to speak to me about?" he said, changing the subject.

Her cheeks colored and she looked away. "Ah, aye, 'tis about tomorrow. I have a plan."

Fourteen

FIONA'S PLAN TOOK THEM ACROSS THE LOCH ON A FERRY TO Skye just after dawn. There were a few others who loaded their horses and wagons, mostly farmers and merchants trying to sell their wares. No one paid them much attention, and their small band of eight kept quiet, even Milla who trotted around investigating those onboard and making friends with the ferry captain's own hound.

Once they disembarked from the ferry, they made their way north toward Dunvegan Castle where Sorley resided with his wife Kenna, niece of Chief MacLeod.

The massive stone fortress was built on solid rock and overlooked a loch and the mountains beyond. As they'd approached, they'd seen the towers jutting powerfully into the sky. When they arrived, the gates were opened automatically. Kenna and the chief waited for them in the bailey as though they'd been expecting them, which they probably were.

Kenna threw herself into her husband's arms, and the way they embraced left a solid ache in Fiona's chest. She tried not to look at Brogan, not wanting him or anyone else to see how very much she wanted the same thing, for surely it had to be written all over her face.

Brogan approached Chief MacLeod and introduced himself along with the rest of them. When he named her his wife and no one blinked an eye, her belly fluttered. They'd not yet found a priest but that didn't seem to matter. She liked the way his eyes softened when he said *wife*. It'd been days since she'd pressed her body to his, felt his mouth on hers. And she found herself longing for his touch.

Finally, Kenna and Sorley broke apart long enough for Sorley to beam at his newfound family and say, "I'd like to introduce ye to my wife." He led her forward. "Kenna, these are the brave souls who've been keeping me alive these past months."

Kenna greeted Fiona first, gripping her hands and then tugging her in for a hug. "I know who ye are," she whispered. "And I'm most pleased to meet ye."

Fiona suspected the messenger announcing their arrival was the one to explain who she was, but it didn't matter. She felt herself growing heated in the cheeks. "Ye're wed to a wonderful man and a brave soldier."

Kenna peeked over Fiona's shoulder toward Sorley. "Aye. He is a keeper." She giggled as though she'd not been wed to him for over two years, and then her face turned more serious. "Come inside. We've got a hot meal prepared for ye, and we want to hear all of the news."

The rest of the day flew by as they each relayed stories of what had happened on Culloden battlefield and in the weeks following. Kenna insisted on sitting beside Fiona, and for once Fiona felt as though she'd made a fast friend, not something that was easy for her. Kenna didn't care that she'd been traipsing about Scotland, that she'd been instrumental in the rebel cause, or any of that. And Fiona shouldn't have been surprised. But she was. For it was not often that a woman other than Jenny and Annie accepted her for who she was.

Kenna leaned in closed and whispered, "When this is over, we'll have to catch up and share stories. I've no' met another woman with a rebel heart as fierce as my own until now."

Fiona beamed at Kenna. Another rebel heart? Fascinating. "Indeed, we shall."

The night swiftly came, and Fiona found herself trying not to fall asleep where she stood watching the men dance. She quietly excused herself and with Milla in tow found the bedchamber that had been given to her and Brogan for their stay.

He was not far behind her, slipping under the covers, the warmth of his body reaching out to hers, wakening her briefly. Though they'd barely spoken, the comfort of having him beside her was a balm. Fiona rolled over to face him, seeing the light of the moon shine through the slim window in a shaft of silver over his face.

"Hello," she whispered sleepily.

Brogan leaned in, his forehead pressed to hers. "I'm sorry I woke ye. Go back to sleep, angel." His lips brushed her forehead, and she closed her eyes, savoring the feel of his breath on her skin.

Fiona wanted to talk to him about what had happened with the letters and opened her mouth to do so, but then Brogan let out a soft snore, already having fallen into a deep sleep.

When she woke in the morning, he was gone but the warmth of him lingered. She dressed quickly and made her way downstairs.

Brogan was in the great hall with the other men, finishing their porridge. Fiona joined them all, savoring the warm breakfast.

"Are ye ready?" he asked when they'd finished.

"More than ready." Today their plan would go into full effect, and hopefully they would soon be in the prince's contingency.

Using Dunvegan as a base, and knowing each day they set out that they might not return, they began several weeks of reconnaissance. Riding out to the various points in the isle each day, they made friends with those at every port and traced the prince's contacts throughout Skye.

Fiona sent messages to the Outer Hebrides through her connections in hopes they would reach the prince and orders could be delivered back to her.

All the while, she attempted to talk to Brogan about Aes, a topic they'd yet to broach and which still seemed to be a barrier between them. However, he brushed her off each time she started. Neither did they have any more heated sensual moments together. But that didn't mean that Fiona didn't think of Brogan every night when she laid her head to rest beside his. That didn't mean she didn't think about reaching out.

Didn't mean she didn't think about kissing him. Tugging him against her and telling him this was all nonsense.

She knew why he was pushing her away, and it was totally her fault. When she'd been reading her letters from Aes, Jenny, and Annie, she'd been living in the past when things seemed brighter, and with every day that passed now she wondered more and more why she was chasing a prince who didn't seem to have the backbone to take charge. Brogan had seen a happier letter from Aes, one filled with compliments, and she could see where he might think she was pining for another man.

When she'd gone down to dinner that night at the tavern, she should have put the letters away but she'd been too tired—lazy, really—and then she'd forgotten about them until she'd felt them crinkle beneath her back. Seeing Brogan's face when he'd read Aes's name was enough to make her heart break. He'd looked devastated. Embarrassed almost. And then he'd been nothing but business ever since, save for a few tender moments in which he'd seemed to forget.

He still slept beside her each night, the heat of his body filling the mattress and cocooning her in a cloud of safety. But he didn't try to hold her, kiss her.

In front of the men, he kept up a good ruse, but even they could tell something had changed between him and Fiona. She could see it in the way the men eyed them. They knew things were different. But they were all too polite to say anything and it wasn't as if she was going to bring it up, and Brogan had gone back to mostly grunting, so it definitely wasn't going to come out of him.

"My lady." Fiona looked up from scrubbing mud from her boots beside the loch where she'd been walking Milla alone after returning to Dunvegan.

Sorley stood there, hands behind his back, looking serious. It was getting harder and harder to look at him and not be jealous of what he had with Kenna. Why hadn't Brogan come to get her?

"Aye, Sorley?"

"We've had some news."

"All right." Fiona put her boots back on and followed him inside.

A messenger waited in the great hall, his cap in his hands. A day's worth of dust covered his clothes, and his boots were as muddy as hers had been moments before.

"My lady, ye're the prince's messenger," he said.

Fiona nodded, glancing at Sorley and the others. Brogan stood by the hearth, his elbow on the mantel as he stared into the flames.

"I've a message for ye from Prince Charles."

Fiona held out her hand and took the folded paper, breaking the prince's seal and reading the contents. It wasn't from the prince per se.

Dear F.,

We're pleased to announce the impending arrival of our sweet bonnie lad. All of Waternish is planning a celebration for the birth tomorrow. Your presence is requested, for this is a celebration of a new life. New beginnings. Will you not attend your sweet charge?

Your devoted friend,
A.M.

So, at last the prince and his entourage were coming back to Skye. Fiona's heart lurched at the news. They needed to prepare. She glanced up quickly at Brogan, who'd turned back around to face her, his eyes concerned.

"What is it?" Brogan asked.

Fiona swallowed, not wanting to pass him the letter with the initials on it that would only remind him of what he'd seen before. When she hesitated, he came forward, and everyone else leaned in close, waiting for her to say something.

"'Tis good news," she finally said.

"May I?" he asked.

This time, without hesitation for she truly had nothing to hide, she handed him the missive and thanked the lad who'd brought it. Brogan scanned the contents with narrowed eyes and then nodded, having deciphered the meaning. She expected him to say something about the initials, to ask her if Aes was her lover so she could vehemently deny it, which she'd been trying to tell him for days. But he did nothing of the sort and didn't appear to be affected either. She narrowed her eyes. Had he thrust her so very far out of his heart that nothing could touch him anymore? Or had she imagined his sentiments, amplifying them in her head when in fact what had been happening between them was nothing more than contractual?

"We need to get to Waternish," he said to those in attendance. "A special, bonnie prize will be arriving soon."

"Is that so?" Chief MacLeod said, his eyes twinkling.

"Aye," Fiona said.

"Then tonight we shall feast, for on the morrow the lot of ye will be off again on another journey to save Scotland."

———

The journey to Waternish only took a matter of a few hours, and they arrived just before sunset—only to stop dead in their tracks, keeping far enough back not to be noticed.

Cumberland's troops waited on the shore. The red of their coats blinded Fiona and the men from the pink and purple horizon, making the setting sun seem more like it was bleeding out the bastards than saying good night to all. How had they beat her here?

Why was she even going to bother pondering? Cumberland's army had a far reach. Everywhere they went, they found those who did not side with the rebels. Secrets had a way of slipping out. There were so many possibilities to that question that it was almost pointless to try to answer. It would do none of them any good at this juncture.

"Ballocks," Brogan growled under his breath.

Had the prince already made his attempt to land? If he hadn't, how would they be able to warn him that the shores were filled with troops? By the time the prince's entourage reached the shore, it would be too dark to see the enemy waiting unless they were lucky enough for a bright moon to blink off the buttons on the dragoons' coats.

Fiona stared out at the sea beyond the dragoons, squinting and willing the prince and his escort to be there. A tiny dot appeared on the horizon. The barest hint of a blip on top of the sea. A boat? She wasn't sure. But what worried her more were the dragoons waiting.

Her heart leapt into her chest, and she was suddenly grateful for the quickly fading sun, when she'd been irritated moments before because it didn't allow them to see as much out at sea and she didn't want to miss the arrival of the prince. Now she realized it would be harder for the dragoons to spot him too. That meant he had a chance, if they could only find a way to signal and warn him.

"Back away," Brogan warned in a whisper to her and his men. "Before we're seen."

As quietly and stealthily as they could, their party backed away, picking their way along the shoreline until the terrain dropped below where the dragoons stood and they were out of sight. They found their way to a smaller inlet, a creek really, that was concealed from the dragoons on shore but still had a good view of the sea. If the prince could somehow make his way into the nook, he would be able to hide from the troops.

On the right side of the creek were slippery rocks. If Fiona were able to climb up to the top, she could see the troops down the shore.

"Those bastards," Fiona seethed, and Milla nudged her calf as if to say she understood and felt for them in this predicament.

"We'll no' let them take the prince," Brogan said.

"There's two dozen of them and only eight of us," pointed out Keith.

"Aye, plus those on the boat," Dugall said.

"True, but Keith has a point," Brogan conceded. "They may not be prepared if coming to shore in the dark. Cumberland's men could fire upon the prince's boat before they see the dragoons lying in wait."

"We need to signal them to come over this way," Fiona said. "We could make sure they avoided the dragoons altogether."

"Any signal we give would likely also signal the dragoons," Brogan mused.

"No' necessarily," Fiona said. "Unless we climb up on those rocks, we're concealed from the troops, but we have a good view of the sea. Have any of ye got a candle?"

"Aye," Charles said, though he sounded skeptical.

"If we light the candle," Fiona said in a rush, "we can cover the flame and lift the cover over and over again in a sign to come this way."

"That is a great idea," Brogan said.

Charles passed them the candle.

"Have ye a flint box?" Fiona asked him.

"That I dinna have," Charles said. "I usually lit it from the fire."

"And who lights the fire?" Fiona asked, growing only mildly frustrated.

"That'd be me," James said, pressing the flint box toward her.

The night grew darker as Fiona tried to light the stubby candle with the flint box, but every spark was unsuccessful. Frustration mounted as the last of the sun finally disappeared. Damn her fingers for not working! She cursed under her breath, gritting her teeth as she made one attempt after another. Of course, of all nights this would be the night that she wasn't able to get it done.

"Let me try." Brogan gently took the flint from her and tried his own hand at it, finally striking a good enough spark to light the crumbling wick of the candle. All of them let out a collective breath of relief.

"Oh, thank heavens," she murmured, taking the candle Brogan held out.

Fiona held the base of the candle in one hand and placed her other hand in front of the flame, blocking the light from those at sea. Then she withdrew, revealing the light. This she did over and over, praying that the men on the boat saw it as they pushed the prince through the water.

Though the moon shone in a half sliver above, it didn't illuminate the sea enough for them to get a good look at anyone approaching. The prince's boat would be quiet and unlit. She prayed they caught sight of her signal before the candle burned out. Already hot wax dripped over her fingers and down the back of her hand. Saving the prince was worth the pain.

The quiet of their concentration and silent entreaties was shattered when shots rang out from down the shore.

"No!" Fiona hissed. The dragoons must have spotted the prince's boat and thought him close enough to shoot.

The men cursed, several scrambling up the rock to get a view of what was happening.

Fiona's heart plummeted into her stomach. She crossed herself and the men followed, each of them mumbling prayers. Dear God, they'd not been fast enough.

"Dinna stop," Brogan whispered. "If they did see ye, they'll need to steer themselves this way. We canna abandon them now."

He was right, and Fiona kept up the signal, praying the whole of the king's navy wasn't off the shore, seeing the signal, too, and coming toward them. She closed her eyes, breathed in deep, making the motions in front of the flame, and prayed that it would work.

Shots continued to crack the silence and shouts of anger too. It was hard to tell if all the noise was one-sided or if the prince's boat had also engaged in the fight.

Please dinna let this all be over… We need our prince… Our country canna survive without him.

What felt like an interminable time later, the shots faded and so did the shouting. There came and went the sound of hoofbeats, and Fiona and the men all hunkered against the rocks, trying to keep themselves and their horses hidden from view. Fortunately, there was an overhang that hid them well. And the dragoons were not looking for anyone on shore but instead coming from the sea.

All the while, Fiona kept up her pace, even as the candle burned nearly down. At last there came the sound of splashing in the water some distance off.

"They come," Brogan said.

Fiona moved her hands faster as if that would make their oars dip any more speedily. The sounds drew closer, and in the dark, the looming oblong shape of a boat and several passengers came into view. They made their way into the narrow creek, and everyone stilled, waiting.

"Who's there?" came a woman's voice filled with trepidation that Fiona did not recognize.

And Fiona couldn't blame her. This, too, could be a trap for all they knew. "Fiona MacBean and seven men of Clan Grant."

"Lady Fiona!" This time, she did recognize the voice as that of the prince. "You have saved us."

Oh, thank God!

"Not yet," Fiona said, relief flooding her and causing her knees nearly to buckle.

Brogan slipped his arm around her waist to hold her up, not saying a word about her sudden weakness, and she thanked him silently for it.

"We must get ye out of here. The troops are patrolling the shoreline, and 'tis only a matter of moments before they see ye here."

They drew closer and in the dimness of the tiny candle, she could make out two women and five men. None of whom were the prince. She'd sworn she'd heard the prince. How was it possible she didn't *see* him?

"Get in the boat, the lot of you. There is room. We will leave when the dragoons have cleared out." There was Prince Charles's voice again, yet it was coming from one of the…women?

Fiona leaned closer, holding out the stub of the candle and squinting her eyes as if that were somehow going to help her see that the prince was dressed in disguise.

"Are ye…?" Fiona started.

The woman waved her hand and nodded. "I am Betty Burke," said the prince. "A maid traveling with my lady Flora MacDonald. I've taken a note from your book, Lady Fiona, and put on my best disguise."

Fiona would have laughed, she would have doubled over and let all of her frustration and relief out at once in a hearty guffaw, but that would no doubt have alerted the dragoons to their presence.

The candle let out a sizzle and pop as the last of the wick burned out.

Fiona let out the breath she'd been holding and picked away at the wax that had hardened on her skin.

"Did the dragoons see ye row this way?" Brogan was tense beside her, finding no humor in the situation, which was probably how she should also be.

Sometimes in stressful situations, however, humor was a good escape.

"Aye, likely they spotted us," the other woman replied. "They've been shooting at us since we arrived."

"Were ye hit?" Brogan asked.

"No' our bodies," she said, "but it did skim the rail of our vessel. Nothing to sink us, though."

A cold sweat broke out on Fiona's back. How close the prince had come to an execution! If he'd been killed, the whole of their operation would have been turned on its head. The country would be in mourning, and everything she'd lived for her entire life would have died with him.

"My men and I will distract the dragoons, allowing ye to get away," Brogan said, his voice calm and authoritative. Then he turned to Fiona. "Get in the boat with the prince."

Before Fiona could protest, Lady MacDonald spoke again. "We'll meet ye at Kilbride. I've a friend there at Mongstat House who can help."

"We will be there," Brogan agreed.

"Wait," Fiona said, gripping his arm, feeling panic rise in her heart. What was he thinking? Did he want to die? "This is madness. Ye'll get yourselves killed. Dinna go. Come with us on the boat."

"We need to distract the dragoons from the prince. Trust me. We'll no' be caught. We've no' been caught yet, and 'tis our duty to protect the prince. This is why we've come."

Everything he said made perfect sense. Except that Fiona didn't *want* it to make sense. She wanted him to get in the damn boat with her. Separating their party now was only going to end in disaster.

"Then I will come with ye," Fiona said in a rush.

"Nay, lass." Brogan's voice was the sound of reason and it made her angry. "Ye need to stay with the prince. We will meet ye at

Kilbride. We're familiar with it, we've ridden this entire island over the last few weeks."

This was true, but that didn't make her panic any less. They'd ridden the island without a bunch of firing dragoons chasing them. They'd ridden the island knowing they could go back to Dunvegan and sleep well behind the fortified walls.

"We have friends at Dunvegan," Fiona said to Lady MacDonald. "Let us go there instead."

Lady MacDonald's refusal was swift. "Kilbride is closer to the mainland, and that is where His Highness needs to go."

Flora MacDonald was not wrong. It would be safer for the prince to get off the island from there with the dragoons now hunting him down. And she should get into the boat with the prince. She should let the men go and be the distraction. All of the *shoulds* made her want to scream because they were not what she wanted. And yet in times like this one could not be selfish. She had to do what was best for the prince, for Scotland. All of them did.

Fiona closed her eyes, tried to swallow down the rising panic, the fear. Without thinking, she tossed herself into Brogan's arms in full view of everyone, not caring at all who saw or who was scandalized. Or that he might push her away.

Their own men would think nothing of it since they were supposed to be married, but the prince would likely be a wee bit shocked. And she didn't care. All she knew was that she needed to kiss Brogan, feel him hold her. Too long they'd let their differences come between them. Weeks now, and she couldn't take it. Not anymore. Not if he was going to go away and possibly never meet her as promised.

So she wrapped her arms around his shoulders, lifted herself on tiptoe and kissed him for all she was worth. At first he stiffened, not kissing her back, but it only took the span of half a breath before he too was kissing her, tugging her into his arms and melting his mouth with hers. Their kiss was intense, frantic even, and she feared its ending. Because when it did finally cease, they would part. Brogan would be on his way, the dragoons chasing him down, and she'd have no idea what happened to him. No idea if he was safe. No idea about anything until he arrived at Kilbride.

"I'm scared," she whispered against his mouth. "I dinna want to lose ye."

She cared about him deeply. Not something she'd ever thought would happen. But somewhere along this wild journey, she'd grown feelings for Brogan. Feelings she didn't want to put a name to. The only thing she would admit was "If something were to happen to ye, I'd...I'd be verra angry."

Brogan chuckled and gave her one more quick kiss. "Nothing will happen to me, other than getting a bit of exercise and having a bit of fun at those bastards' expense. I will see ye soon, Fiona."

That sounded like a promise, and she'd have to believe that he would hold true to it.

"I say, why do you keep pawing my messenger?" came the bristling voice of the prince.

"They've wed," Sorley offered.

"Wed?" The prince sounded shocked, then said, "Oh, I see. Congratulations are in order, then."

"I trust my wife is in good hands with ye, Your Highness," Brogan said, pushing her gently away now as he took steps backward and didn't deny their union.

"Indeed, very good hands," the prince replied.

"Go now, Fiona," Brogan urged softly. "We must make haste else the bastards find us standing here."

Knowing he was right didn't make walking away any easier.

Lifting her skirts as high as she dared, she walked into the creek, cold water filling her boots and soaking the hem of her gown. Well, she'd been wet most of the last couple of months. A bit more wasn't going to do her any harm now, was it? Milla splashed after her, always eager for a swim. At the boat, Fiona and her hound were hauled over the side by the boatmen.

"Your Highness," she said, bowing her head as she sat.

"Well met, my lady," the prince replied.

"Lady MacDonald," Fiona said in acknowledgment of the prince's companion. "A pleasure to meet ye, and may I say how verra brave ye are."

Lady MacDonald grinned. "Oh, this?" She waved her hand. "Just out for an evening sail, that's all." As if she were saving princes every day.

Fiona liked the lady immediately.

They pushed off the shore, and Fiona watched the shadows of her seven warriors melt into the night as they rode away. There was no doubt she was ecstatic to see the prince was still alive, that he was still in good spirits, but watching Brogan and the men she'd come to know as family ride away caused an ache in her heart that she feared would not go away until she saw them once more.

Fiona crossed herself, murmuring a soft prayer as she swiped her hand over Milla's head and settled into the boat for the ride to Kilbride. She was glad not to hear or see the dragoons chase after Brogan, though her imagination at what was happening was not exactly kind.

Perhaps an hour or two later, she wasn't certain of the passage of time in the dark with her mind firing one terrible thought after another, the boatmen pulled the vessel up onto a shore, and the lot of them climbed out, stretching the kinks from their bodies.

In the black of night with only a sliver of moon for light, Fiona could see that Brogan was not yet on shore. But neither were there any dragoons.

Though her men had not yet come to meet them, this didn't mean they'd been killed by dragoons. However, her brain didn't take that logical line of thought and instead flashed horrible images in her mind, causing her to fear they most certainly must have been murdered.

Fending off dragoons on an island those bastards weren't familiar with was a little harder than Brogan anticipated. The arseholes
were fast. A lot faster than they should have been. Inhumanly fast,
like demons.

He and his men considered splitting up, but determined if
they were finally caught, seven against two dozen was better odds
than a few of them. They'd been riding their horses hard for two
hours now and hid in the craggy rocks on the eastern coast to give
them all a rest. Old Man Storr was what the villagers had called
this place when they'd come weeks before. They were nowhere
near Kilbride, which was on the southern part of the isle. And they
didn't want to try to find refuge at Dunvegan, drawing wrathful
attention to the MacLeods.

Brogan cursed for the thousandth time, wishing he could send
up a message that would somehow magically find its way to Fiona
to let her know they were all right but were going to be later than
expected.

As it turned out, they were much *much* later.

By the time they made it to Kilbride, the passengers on the
prince's boat had departed. Brogan and his men followed Milla's
footprints in the sand above the tide and into the marshy ground,
and then made their way toward Mongstat House where Lady
Margaret MacDonald greeted them. She told them she'd offered
the prince and his entourage refreshment the day before but that
they'd all departed for Kingsburgh House near Portree—and
closer to Old Man Storr—for the night.

Brogan grimaced, frustrated at being behind.

"Can I offer ye some refreshment before ye go?" Lady Margaret
said. "I know your wife was verra eager to see ye, and I'm sure ye're
verra eager to see her in turn."

"Aye, I am. Perhaps some refreshment for the road?"

"And a change of horses?"

"Aye, please."

The men were exhausted, but at least their horses didn't have to be.

By the time he and his men made it to Kingsburgh House, once more they'd missed the party who had apparently headed out for Portree with the prince now changed from his women's garb into male clothes. What he would have given to see the man crossing Skye on foot in a dress. A sight to bring back in memory when this horrible nightmare was over, one at which they could laugh.

When they got to Portree, they were able to trace the prince to a tavern where he and Fiona and the rest of the entourage had an ale and a meal, but missed them once more. Brogan slammed his hand down on the bar, feeling anger and frustration burning their way through him. They were always one step behind, and it was starting to remind him mightily of the time on the road when he felt like he'd been chasing the Phantom Fiona was meant to be.

Was she doing this on purpose? Had she decided to be rid of him and so kept them moving one step ahead?

Of course he knew this was not true. The prince was in danger, and they were running from the dragoons as much as he and his men had been the days preceding, but that didn't make her absence hurt any less.

"Did they say where they were headed?" Brogan asked.

The barkeep narrowed his eyes but answered anyway. "The ferry to Raasay Isle."

"How many ferries a day?"

"Two. One in the morn and one in the evening."

"Damn," Brogan growled. "We've missed them for the night."

"I'm afraid so."

He slammed his hand down again.

The barkeep frowned at Brogan's fist, then asked, "Can I get ye a drink?"

Brogan grunted the affirmative. "Whisky."

Just as he was tossing back his spirits, a prickle raised the hair on the back of his neck. He turned quickly, fearing the barrel of a dragoon's pistol, but his gaze alighted on Fiona.

His mouth fell open at the sight of her grinning at him like she'd just caught him at something naughty. Never had he seen a more beautiful sight. Her face was fresh washed, and the freckles on the bridge of her nose and cheeks were more prominent than ever. There was a curve to her pink lips that was teasing, and a delicately arched red brow above a violet eye challenged him. He wanted to wrap her in his arms and never let go.

"Well, if it is no' my wayward husband," she said with clear mocking in her tone.

A slow grin curled his lips. "And my temptress of a wife."

Fiona let out a light laugh and patted him over the heart. "In the flesh."

Then Brogan frowned, realizing that if she was there in front of him, she wasn't where she was supposed to be. "Why did ye no' go with the prince on the ferry? I told ye to stay with him."

"Oh hush, sir. Dinna get all grouchy with me. I had a few messages to deliver and a missing husband to find. Besides, we shall meet them in the morning."

"Ye never stopped moving. I've been chasing ye for days."

She shook her head, leaning next to him at the bar. "There was no other way. He canna stay in one place more than a few hours. A night is pushing it."

"Too many dragoons?"

"Aye. And enough starving people willing to take some coin to point in the right direction." She side-eyed the patrons of the tavern.

"People are losing hope." The words were grim but necessary.

"Aye."

Brogan passed her his refilled dram, and she sipped, wrinkling her nose.

"Have I ever told ye how adorable ye are?" he asked.

She raised a brow at him. "Are ye calling me a bairn, Grant?"

Brogan chuckled. "I'd no' want to kiss a bairn. I can promise ye that."

She grinned, her eyes sparking mischief. "So ye want to kiss me."

"Every day since the moment I met ye." The confession had his chest squeezing. Too long he'd held a grudge about those damn letters on her bed. An hour, a minute was too long; why had he let it go on for weeks?

"Even this past month?"

He frowned slightly, knowing he deserved to be chastened. "Aye. Even this past month."

"Do ye want to talk about it?"

"No' really."

"We probably should." Her fingers danced over his knuckles, then threaded between his. "Ye grew distant the moment ye saw my letter from Aes. But ye didna notice that the other letters were from Annie, Jenny, my siblings. Even one from my mother. I was rereading letters from those I care about, no' those I pine for."

Brogan's gut clenched. What an arse he'd been to make such a stupid assumption. "I'm sorry."

"So am I. We wasted so many days where I could have had ye naked," she teased.

But this was where he got serious. "We canna," he said, regret filling his voice. "As much as I want to, we have to hold back, else the promises we made to each other about parting when this is over will be voided."

A flicker of disappointment skittered over her features. Her eyes shuttered, lashes touching her cheeks, before she glanced back up at him with a new, distant expression he didn't like. A sour taste formed on his tongue, and he wanted to take back his words and instead pull her into his arms. To say *Never mind*. To say what he really felt.

"Och, well," she said with a smile he knew wasn't genuine. Her fingers disappeared from his to wave nonchalantly in the air as though he'd told her there was only porridge for supper instead of stew. "Ye know I was just teasing. Besides, kissing would distract from the mission." She dismissed the ideas of kissing and being naked, of pleasure, as easily as one might swat away an annoying fly.

"The men will be eager to see ye," Brogan said, not addressing the situation at all, because if he didn't then he wouldn't have to lie and say he didn't want her. For a major lie it was, and probably one he'd regret even insinuating for the rest of his days.

"And I am eager to see them."

"Where is Milla?"

"She took a liking to the prince and he asked for her to remain with him."

Brogan frowned. She'd just abandoned the dog—*again*?

"I jest." She laughed. "She's out back eating scraps the cook has given her. She's quite a little hussy, that Milla, worming her way into every man's heart."

"She takes after her mistress, then," Brogan said.

Fiona pressed her hand to her heart, fluttering her lashes. "Ye canna mean me."

"Och, look around ye. Everyone hangs on your words as though honey dripped from your lips." Why did he have to say that, for it made him think of licking sticky, sweet fluid from her lips, and that only made him want to drip it all over her body and lick every inch of her, savor every nook and cranny.

"Ye're wicked, Brogan. Dinna think I canna see what is going on in your mind. I know ye well." Though she teased, he didn't miss the fleeting hurt look in her eyes.

He grinned and winked, trying to make light of the situation, but before he could reply, Sorley was pounding him on the back. "Ye're no' going to hog our sister all to yourself, are ye? The rest of us would like to hear of her adventures too."

"I can promise my adventures were no' as exciting as some might think," Fiona said with a laugh.

"Then those people should stop thinking and start listening." Sorley tapped Brogan's temple. "Is that no' right, oh fearless leader?"

"Aye." He was spot-on.

They really were a family. How could he ever think of breaking them all apart? And yet he would.

Fifteen

AT NIGHT SHE DREAMED OF HIM. AND DURING THE DAY WHEN they followed in the prince's wake, she wished they were back in that tiny tavern room where the world had melted away and it was just the two of them. Before the letters. Before the separation. Before he'd felt compelled to tell her they would not be together in the future.

Hours melted into days, and days melted into weeks. They barely slept as they followed the prince from one hideout to the next. Learning sometimes too late that the dragoons were on their heels and then having to fend them off as the prince escaped. This existence was not sustainable. She knew that. She'd been trained to run as she delivered messages, but while there had always been a threat of running into the enemy, she had never known the enemy was specifically chasing her, trying to rid the country of her existence.

Flora MacDonald and a few of her entourage had parted ways with the prince on Skye a fortnight prior, and finally now the prince and his men and Fiona made their way back to the mainland to Mallaig, but there they were met with more of the same. Running, hiding.

At one point in the night, Fiona and the prince's men were able to sneak past the dragoons in a glen, and once they made it past, the prince took off at a gallop on his mount, narrowly missing the precipice of a cliff and diving head over heels. Fiona woke every morning thanking the heavens they were still alive, and went to bed each night wishing she were curled in Brogan's embrace.

Rather than pushing her away with his words, he'd seemed to awaken something inside her that needed him more than ever.

Each morning over whatever meal they were able to scrounge, the prince talked of his French ships and how there would be one waiting for him in Poolewe, if they could only just get there. However, they were informed by their host in Glenshiel that the ship was no longer there. By now, Fiona had lost track of how many stops they'd made or even what day it was.

"How in the hell am I going to get away from these godforsaken dragoons without my ship?" the prince bellowed. "We cannot continue to go on this way. I'm a prince of the blood. I am not a criminal. Scotland was meant to be mine!"

He was right; it'd been three weeks since they'd signaled to him on his little boat to come into the creek and hide from the dragoons. Every man in the party, and Fiona, too, had blisters on their feet the size of coins. Some of their blisters had blisters, and even Milla, who loved a good run, was more often than not panting and lying about with exhaustion.

It was all too much. If they kept at this pace, they would all collapse and the entire rebellion would be shattered.

"We'll go to my caves," Brogan said calmly, the voice of reason. "There ye can rest in peace with a stream running by, and we'll make the cave fit as a royal palace for ye." This last part he said partly jesting, Fiona could tell, but it helped to perk up the prince a bit from his despair. "While there, we'll try to find out what has happened to your ship."

And so at last with a safe destination in mind where they might be able to rest for several days, they trekked their way to Glenmoriston and the caves where Fiona had first kissed Brogan.

True to his word, Brogan had supplies gathered, pillows, blankets, and even a feast, so that the prince could feel his royal blood pumping. But Fiona knew that it was about more than that. Brogan did it for his men, and for the prince's few men too. A little bit of revelry in a time when they all felt the noose tightening around their necks.

And so she imbibed the cider and ate the cheese, the cold chicken, and berry tarts.

Sorley, Fin, and one of the prince's men volunteered to go scouting for the prince's ship while the rest of them remained with Prince Charles, entertaining him with cards and conversation, even a hunt.

But rather than feel relaxed, Fiona was starting to grow irritated. They'd been running for far too long. Why didn't the people of Scotland try harder to protect their prince? The more time that passed, the more it felt like the few in their party were the only ones.

Almost as if the rest of Scotland did not value the man who should be their rightful king.

What was it about the prince that did not endear him enough to those who would turn their backs on him?

She found him to be charming, witty, intelligent. Perhaps the people just didn't know him well enough. There had hardly been a chance to do so, given he'd been running and fighting from the moment he set foot in Scotland.

For the briefest of moments it made her question if he would be a good leader after all. The people had not rallied for him. And for all his traipsing about the country, when it came down to a crisis they had not joined him. In the beginning, even, it had been hard for rebels to be recruited. And they were always seen as that—rebels. Not true freedom fighters.

When the battles began to be won and it looked as though the prince might have a victory, more had started to come to his side. But since the cataclysmic loss at Culloden, those supporters had scattered.

When his life was at stake, when the country was in turmoil, they would rather hand Prince Charles over to the enemy. It made no sense. For Cumberland and his father, King George, were a brutal lot. The country would not be better off with them.

What was the issue with Charles as the rightful heir in place of the alternative? Though she racked her brain for an answer, she came up profoundly lacking.

Two days of lounging brought Sorley, Fin, and the prince's man back to the camp. When everyone's eyes were on the prince, Fin and Sorley caught Fiona and Brogan's attention. The expression on the two men's faces was one of caution.

Brogan leapt to his feet and Fiona followed, drawing closer to speak with them about why they should look so worried. But Sorley stopped them with a shake of his head and spread out his arms wide in the prince's direction, a smile splitting his face that looked forced.

"We've brought good news," Sorley said. "We have found your ship, Your Highness."

As Sorley spoke to the prince, making the announcements, Fin quietly walked behind Brogan and Fiona and whispered, "There's a traitor in our midst. The prince's ship had no' gone from Poolewe when we were told it had days ago. He could have made it. Been gone already. Someone lied. Now the ship is sailing about and plans to return to try again at some point, but every time it gets close to shore, Cumberland's ships come in to attack."

"Who do ye think it is?" Brogan asked quietly.

"I'm no' certain, but one of the wharf rats on the dock at Poolewe said he was given a message to give to a man he could trust, and he gave it to me. He said that the ship's captain would be at Borrodale in a month's time if they were no' able to make it back to Poolewe. After we trap the traitor, I think we ought to attempt to make our way back to the western coast, given Poolewe has already been compromised."

"Aye, 'tis a good plan," Brogan said. "But we need to find out who the traitor is first, else we'll be caught at every stop."

"Aye."

"And ye're certain 'twas no' the man ye had with ye?"

"I'm no' thinking 'tis him, but who's to say? I canna be certain."

Fiona watched the few men the prince had with him. Their own party made up more than those who traveled with the prince. There was a man from the boat when they'd found him in Skye, and then a couple more they'd gathered along the way. It could be any of them. If they were going to take that route, it could be any of the seven of those who were with her, too, but she doubted that very seriously. Her men had done and risked too much. And so had the man from the boat.

If she were to hazard a guess, it would be one of the other two men, and one of them had gone with Fin and Sorley.

"We really only have to try and decide between those two," Fiona said.

"I was thinking the same thing," Brogan replied.

The prince lounged on a tartan blanket surrounded by pillows, and for once during this dreaded year of rain and cold, the sun had chosen to shine. It did so now in all its end-of-July glory, through the trees surrounding the cave, alighting on the prince's light hair, his tender-looking skin. Even spending months in hiding had not ruined the bonniness of him, though it had made his cheekbones more pronounced, his body a bit gaunt.

He looked untouchable just now, as though he were a gift from the heavens. Nearly all of her life, Fiona had worshiped him as her prince, her future king. A god. She was old enough now to see that he was just a man, but that didn't make the way the sun shone on him any less ethereal.

Her gaze scanned the two men they'd gathered along the way. A MacDonald and a Cameron. They looked harmless enough. Both dressed in Highland dress like the prince, showing their solidarity, while the rest of them wore plain clothes. That was a nice touch. But if they were traitors, they'd want to blend in, wouldn't they?

MacDonald laughed at something the prince was saying and sipped from a flask that she'd assumed all this time to be whisky.

But it could be water in there, keeping his mind fresh to pass on any and all messages to the enemy. A sharp mind was necessary when memorizing messages and facts; she ought to know.

Cameron was lounging, too, eating an apple down to the core and spitting out the seeds. She almost had a mind not to trust him for eating so far into the fruit, but these were hungry times and she'd likely do the same, probably had and not thought a thing of it.

MacDonald and Cameron spoke so easily to the prince, to the rest of them, causing Fiona to question why they would turn their backs now. Why would they lie? They weren't only betraying their country and those in the camp, but risking their own lives and their families'. And for what? The Butcher and his horde weren't going to protect them.

Feeling her gaze, Cameron looked at her as he tossed the remainder of his apple to the ground and Milla pounced on it. He raised a brow as if to ask why the hell Fiona was looking at him. There was no smile.

It was Cameron.

He was suspicious, perhaps suspected that she knew, or else he would have smiled, would he not? The challenging look he tossed her was not a friendly one, and it sent a chill racing up her spine as she tried to remember every interaction, every syllable uttered in his presence. Tried to recall when he'd come and gone and what advice he'd given the prince.

MacDonald had gone with Fin and Sorley, which meant somehow Cameron had been able to get his messages out without anyone knowing. Was their camp compromised?

Fiona smiled and said, "Now that ye've given Milla one treat, she'll be back for more." Trying to play off that she'd been studying him.

"'Tis no' the first time," Cameron said with a smirk, making Fiona wonder if he'd paid off her dog in the middle of the night with treats as he snuck away, bribing Milla to stay quiet.

Fiona merely smiled and patted her leg for Milla to come to her, which her dog did obediently. Thank goodness. If the hound had turned traitor, Fiona might have lost her mind.

"'Tis nearing evening," the prince was saying to Sorley and the rest. "Shall we leave at first light then and make our way to Poolewe?"

"Aye," Sorley said, misleading whoever was a traitor in their midst.

Out of the side of her eye, Fiona watched Cameron, who perked up at that. She kept her gaze on MacDonald, too, because although she was fairly certain it was Cameron, she wasn't all the way certain and that meant MacDonald could also be in on it.

Bastards.

She wanted to march right over to both of them and box their ears. To demand right then and there why they would do such a thing. They were putting the prince's life at risk and the safety of the country. All for a pouch of coins? What more could they have been offered? There was no telling if they'd even get their prize. The dragoons could not be trusted, and neither could anyone working in their midst.

With their plan in place, Fiona clucked her tongue to Milla and made her way toward the curling stream. She dipped her hand in the chilly water and splashed it on her face, then sipped.

Brogan followed her, doing the same.

"I think 'tis Cameron," she said. "There's something about the way he was watching everyone, the way he interacted with Milla."

"I agree." Brogan sounded as grim as she felt. "I'll warn the men. He'll act soon and we must be prepared, make certain he doesna leave the group."

Fiona saw movement out of the corner of her eye, but when she jerked her head to see, there was no one there. She had a good idea of who had been there—the traitor in their midst.

Fiona woke in the middle of the night with her back cold. She felt around behind her in the dark, trying to connect with warm, soft fur, but Milla was not beside her. Sitting up, she blinked away the sleep in her eyes. The moon was hidden by clouds, making what should have been a silver-black night nearly pitch-dark.

"Milla," she whispered.

There was no sound in answer from the hound.

She patted on the other side of her where Brogan slept, but did not feel Milla there either.

Brogan rolled over, his arm flopping over her thighs. They slept beside each other outside the cave, the prince and his men inside. The other Grant warriors were scattered about, with two on watch. Brogan had taken first watch and now finally slept.

Fiona didn't want to disturb him, but she hated the idea of Milla running off and getting into it with a wild cat or boar. Though Milla was scrappy enough to take care of herself, Fiona had made a promise to protect her. And though she was a feisty hound, Milla was quite small compared to potential threats.

The hair on the nape of Fiona's neck stood on end, and she had the feeling that something wasn't right. Immediately, her mind went to Cameron. She swiveled her head around toward the mouth of the cave, half expecting to see a looming shadow there, waiting to eat her up. But there was only blackness.

Gingerly, she removed Brogan's arm from her lap and stood, stretching out the kinks in her body and listening keenly for any sound at all. The night air was still, not even the night birds or insects making a sound. That was a bad sign.

Slipping toward the cave, she peered inside, seeing both Cameron and MacDonald asleep beside the prince. She frowned, not feeling entirely reassured, but there they were, neither of them going to cause her any trouble right now.

Exiting the cave, she headed toward the water to see if Milla had simply gone for a sip. She could use a sip herself. Fiona brushed the hair away from her face, tightening the knot on the ribbon that held it back at the base of her neck. Then she rubbed her arms. It was colder tonight than usual. The sound of water trickling grew louder. Nearly there, she quickened her pace, but her foot caught on something soft. With a startled gasp she tripped, pitching forward.

Fiona whipped around, ignoring the sting of her fall and scrambled away from the soft mound.

"What the bloo—" But her words were cut off by what she saw from the light of the moon—a body.

Fiona opened her mouth to scream, but a filthy, clammy hand came out of the darkness and pressed around her face, closing over her cry, her very breath.

"Dinna say a word, *bitch*." The voice was low and unrecognizable.

She fumbled for her belt, for the knife inside, but the man wrapped his free arm around hers, blocking her movements. She kicked at his shins, and he trapped her legs between his strong thighs.

Who was on the ground? It had been a person, she was sure. One of Brogan's men.

And the voice of the man who held her…she didn't recognize. Not Cameron. Not MacDonald. Not any of the men in their camp. Who was he?

A scrape of fabric on her lips, and then a vile rag was shoved deep into her mouth causing her to gag and cough.

"Ye'll shut the hell up if ye know what's good for ye," he warned.

Well, she did know what was good for her, and it wasn't doing as he instructed. Fiona tried to scream around the gag, which earned her a painful yank of her hair, leaving her breathless. He wrapped something tight around her head and in her mouth, gagging her even more.

With an arm braced around her ribs as though she were nothing more than a package to be carted, her assailant started to drag her away, across the water, the cold stream soaking the hem of her gown. Fiona struggled. She was not going to be taken; she was not going to let another man hurt her. She bowed her back, thrust herself forward. Kicked and writhed, and on the other side of the water, he tossed her to the ground and slammed a boot in her belly.

All the air left her lungs and she curled inward. But there was no time to recover from the blow. He picked her up and tossed her over his shoulder, running. She bounced painfully in this position, tears stinging her eyes. How had this stranger been able to infiltrate their camp? There'd been no warning. Milla was missing.

Was he in league with Cameron or MacDonald?

Oh God…the two men on watch. She'd tripped over one, though she couldn't be sure if it had been Dugall or James. She didn't remember. She'd been so tired when she finally went to sleep that she'd not listened to who was on watch and when.

Fiona tried to scream through the gag, the sound muffled. The man stopped short and tossed her to the ground, and then he pounced on her. She scratched and fought, but he pinned her tight.

If only she could see who he was.

"I told ye to shut the hell up," he growled. And then he hit her hard on the side of the head, and everything went dark.

"Where the hell is she?" Brogan paced the camp, hands on his hips, feeling an odd sense of déjà vu. The sun had not yet risen when he'd leapt to his feet, woken suddenly but unsure of why or how, but he'd been on high alert. Something was wrong. And then he'd noticed Fiona missing.

The men about camp stirred, sitting up at his call of alarm.

Brogan lurched forward, practically running into Dugall and James, who rubbed at their heads and groaned.

"She hit us," Dugall said.

"What do ye mean she hit ye?" Brogan growled.

"Snuck up behind us and whacked us with something, a thick stick maybe."

"What the bloody hell are ye talking about?" Brogan grabbed both men by the shoulders and hauled them closer as he felt their scalps. They were not wet with blood, which was good. But Dugall and James both had large knots on their heads where they'd been thumped.

"Did ye see who did it? How can ye be sure it was her?" Brogan asked.

"Nay, neither of us did see her coming," Dugall said.

"Nor did we see anyone else sneaking about camp."

Brogan slid his gaze toward the mouth of the cave, counting the shadowed heads. The prince and the three men with him. All of his men were here too. The only one missing was Fiona.

And Milla.

Brogan blew a whistle, listening for the sounds of the wee hound running. And there it was some distance away, a rushing of four paws on the forest floor. Milla appeared a moment later with something large, long, and terrible-smelling in her mouth.

"What the devil?" Brogan groaned, and the rest of the men, too, pinched their noses.

Milla pranced with her prize, making a circle in the center of camp before settling down, happy as could be, to gnaw on a massive, rotting bone that looked to be something she'd dug up in the forest. A deer perhaps.

"That's disgusting," Fin groaned. "Good God, get it away from her."

Brogan swallowed back his frustration, the smell of a rotting carcass the least of his worries. How had Milla gotten it, and where the hell was Fiona?

"Ye canna believe that she did this," Sorley said, sounding completely skeptical.

Dugall and James frowned and shrugged. Brogan's gut churned, rebelling against the very idea.

"She's run away from us before and never hurt anyone for doing it," Fin pointed out. "Why would she do it now?"

Doubt plagued him. Even though she claimed to be a Jacobite through and through, she was also a government postmistress. That meant she spent a good amount of her time working for the enemy. Though she'd claimed it was to keep tabs on the redcoats and their armies, what if that were a lie?

"Lady Fiona would not," the prince announced, sounding peeved. "To say so, or even think it, is a betrayal of all that is good. She has been nothing but a loyal and faithful servant of mine for many years. You should be ashamed for even imagining that the lady has an indecent bone in her body."

Brogan's head ached with anguish, remorse. The prince was right, and he was damned ashamed for letting the thoughts cross his mind. But bloody hell, she'd put them all through the wringer before. He wouldn't be human if he didn't have an inkling of doubt every once in a while, would he?

There were so many thoughts going through his mind right now. Had she run away? Was she the traitor in their midst? It would not have been the first time he'd thought so, except the prince was genuinely upset that she'd left, and Brogan... His heart shredded with every traitorous thought rolling through his mind.

He'd trusted her...*loved* her.

Good God, how he loved her... The notion had been there sitting on his heart for weeks now, maybe even months, and yet it wasn't until now that he fully felt the impact of those sentiments.

Fiona would not have left them. Betrayed them. She would not have attacked his men, not after all they'd been through. Even she had said more than once that the men of his camp were like her brothers. She'd risked her life for the prince on so many occasions that she deserved a medal of high honor and all the riches in the world. She'd not have turned tail for the dreaded dragoons and Cumberland's faction. Not even if it meant her death.

There was no way she would have simply run away, and he'd be willing to bet his life on that. So what in the bloody hell had happened? Milla had not made a sound. He stared at the large bone the dog all too happily gnawed. Somehow she'd been lured deeper into the forest away from the camp to make this discovery. To keep her occupied while Fiona was stolen away.

But who could have stolen her? They were all present. Not even the men they suspected of being traitors were gone, and both of them seemed genuinely concerned—or at least were making a good show of it. Could they have done something to her in the middle of the night, then come back? He supposed it was possible.

Nay, it couldn't be. Because Brogan did not feel like she'd been gone all that long. He could still smell her scent on the wind.

"How long do ye think ye were knocked out for?" he asked Dugall and James.

"No' long. A quarter hour maybe?"

"I think we should consider that she was taken," Brogan said. "And we've failed her. I've failed her."

From the very beginning, he'd wanted her to go home, to be protected, and more than once now she'd been in perilous danger. The other times at least he'd been there to help. Something had happened in the night and he was going to find out exactly what it was.

Brogan racked his brain. If she'd been taken, she would have been lured to simply walk away from their makeshift bed. Otherwise, he was damned certain he would have noticed someone coming into camp and stealing her from her bed.

They couldn't have. He would have noticed… Brogan was certain of it.

"We need to start searching now."

"I'll help," said the prince.

"Nay, this could be a ploy to get ye out alone in the woods. Ye must remain behind with several men."

"MacEachain, ye, Fin, and Keith remain behind. The rest of ye, let's search." If Cameron or even MacDonald had something to do with this, they might give something away in the search. Brogan turned to Sorley. "Retriever," he said, using Sorley's nickname. "Help me."

"I will."

They fanned out, searching for clues, which was difficult in the dark. By the creek, however, where Dugall had been stationed on watch, they found signs of a struggle. Dirt and grass and leaves were all kicked up and askew. A lance of fear pierced Brogan because it was clear now that she had been taken. In the back of his mind, he'd been hoping to find her in the woods needing a bit of privacy, that somehow the two men had come by their injuries by accident.

"Here," Sorley said. "This is where she was overcome."

"And I laid right there," Dugall choked. "I could have helped her."

"Dinna blame yourself," Brogan said. "Ye couldna have helped her. Ye were out cold."

"They went across," Sorley said.

Brogan surreptitiously eyed Cameron, who made no comments nor any moves. In fact, he seemed to only be following the other men. What did he know that he didn't want them to figure out?

"Let's get the horses." Mounted up, they crossed the water. Whoever had taken Fiona was not going to get away with it, of that he was certain.

Theirs might be a fake marriage, and he might have reinforced their future parting, but he loved her so damn much, and there was no way in hell that some phantom melting from the dark was going to take her away from him. The only phantom in their lives was Fiona.

Brogan followed Sorley, who spotted another area of struggle. Fury, red and molten, filled Brogan.

"She struggled." Sorley watched Brogan. "She's a fighter. The lass willna give up."

"Aye." Brogan swiped a hand over his face. "She's strong." *Stay strong, lass, stay bloody strong.*

At the last sign of a struggle there were also hoofprints scattered on the ground.

"How many men?" Brogan asked.

"I'd say three."

"Then all three of them will suffer," Brogan declared. And the pain he would inflict would be worse for every blow and ache Fiona had to endure. His gaze slipped to Cameron, who was avoiding eye contact. One sign from the bastards when they met that they knew Cameron and he was going down too.

Brogan had been mad before, filled with hate and the need for retribution, but never had those feelings been as strong as they were now. He wanted to burn the men to the ground, make them suffer. Make them scream and beg for mercy. And then deny them the mercy they'd not shown Fiona. Deny them everything they wanted, including breath.

In fact, he might just let Fiona help. Aye, he would follow her lead for she would deserve to see their end. And then he would wrap her up in his arms and tell her how much he loved her.

Those bastards better keep her alive or they would pray for the death he had planned for them.

Sixteen

FIONA WOKE TO ACHES AND PAINS, BUT NOTHING SHE couldn't push herself through. What scared her the most was the unknowing.

Who had taken her? Why? What were they going to do with her? She wasn't dead yet, which meant they needed her alive for some reason... What?

Blinking away the blurriness of a headache, she assessed where she was exactly. Sitting on the ground, tied to a tree, her hands at her waist. The wetness of morning dew soaked through her gown at her rear. Thick rope wrapped around her upper arms down to her elbows and her chest, leaving her hands free. But her ankles were also tied.

Panic rose sharp and sour in her throat, but she tamped it down. Now was not the time for emotions to take away her wits. Fear had no place. She closed her eyes a moment, breathing in deeply. *One, two, three, four...* And out, *one, two, three, four...* Over and over she used the breathing technique that had helped her throughout the years until she'd calmed the storm brewing inside her.

Fiona opened her eyes once more into the grayness of pre-dawn, assessing. Shapes of men and horses, three of each, were a couple dozen or so feet away. The men talked in low voices and she couldn't really make out what they were saying. Something about the prince. Something about her.

Did they know she was the prince's messenger? She closed her eyes and tried to envision the ring on the chain around her neck to see if she could feel it there against her skin. A hard object was pressed between her breasts, and she guessed that must be it.

Relieved that they'd yet to find her ring, she listened carefully for sounds of anyone else from camp that she might recognize. Oh God, she prayed no one else had been hurt. Worry filled her for Dugall and James. She imagined a massacre back at camp with Brogan, the prince, and her new brothers all slaughtered, Cameron and MacDonald standing over their bodies.

A glance around showed her to be the only one in the vicinity. So, there were no other prisoners. Or had they put them farther away so they couldn't see each other? She wouldn't put something like that past these men. They were clearly vile and clever.

She shifted ever so slightly, so as not to draw attention, in order to test the ropes. Saints, but they were very tight. She was lucky to be able to breathe the way they had her in there. Even though her lower arms and hands were free, being able to move them was difficult, especially since her elbows were tied.

But she was going to damn well try.

In her belt was a knife, and if she could just flip open that one little tab, she could pull out the blade and start cutting these ropes.

As long as her abductors didn't look. As long as they thought her asleep.

As long as it was still mostly dark.

Fiona worked her hand to the place on her belt, her thumb-nail catching the small button. Concentrating, she flicked it open. Stage one, complete. She sighed in relief, studied the shadows in the distance to see if they'd noticed her moving. If they figured out what she was up to, they'd pounce.

But their conversations didn't stop. No one called out that they'd seen her, so she slowly worked to edge the blade out. With the handle pinched between her thumb and forefinger, she slid it out a fraction of an inch, then pinched it lower down the handle and slid. Because she didn't have range of motion with her arms and elbow, this was the only way she could slowly get it out, and she prayed she didn't drop it. There would be no getting it then.

Oh, God… Come on!

Down the handle she went until her fingers were on the blade and she held tight to it, concentrating so hard that sweat started to bead on her upper lip and beneath her arms. She could do this. She *had* to do this.

Inch by excruciating inch. At last the blade was free.

With both hands, she creeped the point of the blade beneath the ropes, wincing when she pressed the tip a little too hard against her own body. But she'd endured worse pain, and she'd endure more if she didn't get out of these ropes.

When she was finally free, she'd run, just like Ian had told her when they were children. The rest she'd figure out later, but for right now she had to try to get free. Not trying wasn't an option.

She sawed slowly and methodically, feeling as if she was getting nowhere. Watching the men with nearly closed eyes so they would think her asleep, and stilling when they quieted or she thought they were looking her way. But none of them seemed interested in her at the moment. Laughing among themselves between deeper conversations.

Something gave way, the first twine of twisted rope, and a surge of hope ricocheted inside her. There might be dozens more fibers to go, but that one had cut. She was on her way to being free soon.

Another fiber snapped, the sound echoed in her body, and then another. Could they hear it, the tiny snaps that edged her closer and closer to freedom?

But only laughter and snorts came from her abductors. The dark gray of predawn was lightening, and soon she would be fully exposed to daylight. As if fate were on her side, one of their horses strolled into the space between them, munching on grass, and seeing the move, the other two followed suit, their legs blinding the men more to her position.

She used the opportunity, for she wasn't certain how brief it would be, to saw harder, fibers snapping quicker and quicker. Two lines of rope had been sawed through, her elbows gained range of motion, and she was able to move more quickly, up and up, cutting, sweat pouring down her back, until she reached the very top.

Aye! She wanted to shout with joy—she was free!

Her lungs expanded, and she'd barely noticed before that she couldn't breathe. How tight the ropes had been. But there was no time to think about it, no time to revel in breath; she had to cut the rope at her ankles before the horses moved.

Fiona bent over her legs, cutting as fast as she could, fear making her fingers tremble, the blade unsteady. Her palms were sweaty, making the blade slippery. She was so close to being free. She strained to hear the men talking as she worked, their voices a steady, low murmur. Hopefully that meant they were not aware of her movements and preparing to come at her.

She tried to peer at them through the horses' legs, tried to make out their shadows beyond, but she couldn't.

Saw, saw, saw. Dinna stop. Dinna give up.

The rope around her ankles collapsed, and rather than wait to see that she wasn't being watched, she leapt to her feet and started to run, the blade still clutched in her fingers.

She had no idea where she was going. If she was running farther from Prince Charles's camp or toward it, it didn't matter, she just had to get away from them. With her sole objective to be free of her captors, she ran blindly into the forest. All the memories of her past melted into this present moment as the three men shouted behind her. Their feet pounding into the earth, their breathing heavy.

Dinna stop. Dinna give up.

Fiona tripped over something, her body flying forward, but she managed to right herself before she fell, before she stabbed herself. They were gaining on her, and she ran harder. Feet flying out in front of her, legs long and reaching. Strides far apart as she fairly sailed over the ground. She'd not run this hard, this fast in so long. Muscles screamed, but her head screamed louder. Heart pounding a drumbeat of encouragement as she kept going, the monsters crashing through the forest behind her.

The sky was getting lighter, enough that she could make out shapes on the ground to avoid and not trip again. Still she stumbled, as if at the last minute some invisible enemy were thrusting things in front of her feet.

A root caught her foot, sending her flying forward. She landed on all fours, her knife slicing into her palm, but thankfully not through it. She grabbed for the blade with her other hand and shoved herself to her feet. Darting to the left now. Why had she been so dumb running in a straight line? She knew better than that. Knew that she had to confuse her tormenters. Run in a zigzag, keep them guessing. Wasn't that what Gus had said when they were younger? Aye, something like that.

Ignoring the pain in her hand, she ran at a zigzag, feeling at any moment that a meaty paw would grip her by the hair and yank her to a stop. That someone would tackle her from behind, knocking her to the ground before he pounced on her and tore at her clothes.

And she'd stab him. She would. She'd stab him until he stopped.

Fiona shuddered at the thought. Wished she'd never left Brogan's warm side. But Milla... Where was her dog?

Tears streamed down her face, blinding her momentarily as she ran in the quickly lightening forest.

"Get back here, ye bitch!" they yelled behind her.

They were Scots. The thought hadn't truly dawned on her yet. But these were not dragoons. Fellow Scots.

Nay, not fellow. A fellow Scot would not have done this to her. These were traitors.

Fiona veered to the left again, her boots sludging into mud and then water from what looked like a shallow burn. She barreled into it, not caring for the wet, for the cold, only to cross, and when she got to the other side, her lungs burning, she heard them behind her, crashing into the water.

They were closer now.

She sensed they would reach her soon. Could feel their breath heavy on her neck. Feel their painful hands on her body. Felt the ropes squeeze tighter.

———————

"They were just here," Sorley said.

Brogan heard him through the rage of blood pummeling his ears. In his hands he held thick ropes, frayed at the edges, cut with a knife. Three horses nibbled at the forest floor.

"They ran quickly," Brogan said. "She escaped."

"Let's no' tarry."

"Split up," Brogan said. "There are only three of them, and they left their horses. We dinna know which direction she ran."

"Aye, we do, look." Sorley pointed at the ground, and Brogan could just barely make out a footprint.

"Ye're damn good at your job," Brogan said.

Sorley winked. "I know."

They took off following Sorley as he went first in a straight line and then veered back and forth until they reached a shallow burn. Crossing over, they were no longer quiet, no longer caring if the men could hear them because they wanted to be heard. They wanted the bastards to feel the fear of being chased down just as they were instilling that fear in Fiona.

Ahead there was a bloodcurdling scream, the grunts of men. They'd caught her.

"Fiona!" bellowed Brogan, urging his horse faster in the woods.

And then they were upon them. A man on top of Fiona, two others turned to face them, swords drawn.

Brogan stared only for half a breath, dumbfounded—Scots. At the same moment he noticed that, Cameron joined the bastards they'd been chasing, turning his fury on Brogan.

This entire time, he'd been mostly certain he'd been chasing dragoons. He'd had his suspicions about Cameron, but given the man hadn't run, it made him wonder. Well, now he needn't wonder at all because the man had just proven which side he was on. *Traitorous bastards.*

Knowing they were his own people made Brogan all the angrier. He threw himself from the horse, sword drawn, and crashed against Cameron, his blade cutting through sinew and bone.

Then he turned on another man with a pistol and shot him through the heart. The two of them fell where they stood. Another man was taken quickly by Sorley. But the final traitor on Fiona didn't move.

She was shoving at him, grunting with the effort. He wasn't exactly resisting, but he wasn't... Wait. He wasn't moving.

"Get him off me," she cried.

Brogan grabbed the man by the shoulders and tore him off, prepared to kill him. But it was hard to kill a man who was already dead. Fiona's blade was deep in his neck, the whoreson's blood on her face and chest.

An expletive burst from Brogan's lips as he tossed the man aside and reached for her, pulling her into his arms, holding her close. She was sobbing as hard as she had the day they'd seen the crofters executed, trembling in his arms. He wrapped her in his embrace, hoping to still her, settle her, calm her. But he felt himself shaking and the burn of tears in the backs of his eyes.

He'd not cried since he was a lad. Brogan was not a crier. He was a man. A warrior. A fierce Highland soldier. A Jacobite. Fighting for his prince and country. And right now he was also a man deeply in love, who had nearly just lost his beloved. God, he never wanted to let her go.

Never.

And the sting of tears, tears of relief, of love, pricked the backs of his eyes.

"Are ye hurt?" he asked.

She shook her head, then nodded, giving him no definitive answer.

"Where?" he asked. She held up her hand, showing him a long slice against her palm. "Anywhere else?"

She shook her head, and then she nodded, her knees buckling slightly. "My ankle," she said, her voice weak and breathless. "I tripped so many times, and this last time, a hole, I…"

"Shh," he crooned, lifting her into his arms. "Ye're safe now. I know I've said before I'd no' let any harm come to ye. I've failed ye, lass, but I swear with every fiber of my being I will no' fail again. I will no' let anyone hurt ye."

Fiona wrapped her arms around his neck, burying her face in his shoulder, hugging him so tight he could barely breathe, and he didn't care.

"I love ye," he whispered against her ear, pressing his lips to her cheek. "I love ye so much, and I canna lose ye."

She lifted her head from his shoulder, staring into his eyes with those beautiful wide violets. "How can ye love a mess like me?"

"How could I no'?"

Fiona burst into tears again and tucked her face into the crook of space between his neck and shoulder. "Dinna love me, Brogan Grant. Dinna say it ever again."

The vehemence in her demand shook him to the core. The lass had been through so much. "Ye survived, Fiona. Ye're a fighter."

———————————————

Brogan carried Fiona to the small burn, while his men took care of the bodies. She couldn't even look at them; her eyes squeezed shut. He knelt with her by the water, tore off a piece of his shirt and dipped it into the water, then started to clean her face.

All the while he whispered words of how strong she was, how much he admired her, that she was a treasure for Scotland.

And all the while he did that, she sobbed like a wailing bairn, not feeling at all like any of the things he'd said.

"I'm a walking disaster," she said, closing her eyes as he pressed the cool fabric to her skin, washing away the blood of the man who would have hurt her worse.

He cleaned her hand, wrapped a fresh strip of his torn shirt around her wound, brought her fingers to his lips and pressed a kiss to her knuckles.

"Ye're my disaster," he said with a teasing note, which she couldn't help but laugh at a little even through the tears. "Tell me what happened."

She shook her head, but spoke anyway. "I woke, I dinna know why, but I noticed Milla was gone. So I went to the creek to see if she'd gone for a drink, but I fell over someone. I think it was Dugall. Oh God," she cried. "Is he… Is he…?"

"He's fine, lass. Back at the camp nursing a headache with the prince."

"Everyone is all right?"

"Ye were the only one taken. Do ye know why?"

"They knew I was Prince Charlie's messenger. I think that had something to do with it. I'm so thirsty." She leaned forward, dipping her hands in the cool water and bringing it to her lips, drinking scoop after scoop.

When her thirst was satisfied, she continued. "I tried to fight them off, but they knocked me out. When I woke, I fought some more, but they hit me harder. The next time I woke, I was tied to a tree."

"But ye escaped, how?"

"The knife in my belt."

"I really need a belt like that."

Fiona grinned. "Ye do."

She took another sip of water and looked down at her gown, seeing her chest soaked bright red with blood. Her assailant's blood. When he'd tackled her to the ground, she'd thought nothing of shoving her blade into him. Just like she'd done to Boyd what felt like years before. When her captor had fallen on her, he *was* Boyd, transformed in his violent actions. He was everything wrong with men trying to overpower women. She felt no regrets about ridding the world of another man who would hurt her, hurt others.

He was evil, vile, heinous.

Fiona started to cry all over again. For the first time in many months, years, she wanted to go home. But home was so very far away.

"I, um, Brogan—" But she cut herself off, trying to draw in breath. "I feel a coward for saying this, but I want to go home. Not to stay, but…I canna walk. 'Twill be hard to ride. I am useless."

"Ye're no' useless."

"I will slow the prince down. Right now he needs to run, and I canna."

Brogan nodded slowly, and she expected to see disappointment in his eyes, or triumph since she was saying the one thing she'd denied since the moment they met.

"Are ye certain, lass?"

"Are ye no' happy?" Her tone was biting.

"Happy?" He looked taken aback. "Och, love, do ye no' know? I want for ye only what ye want."

His words stunned her, for she didn't know that. Wouldn't have ever guessed. And yet when he said it, his words made sense. He made sense. And she wanted to cry all over again.

"'Tis no' forever. I'm just so tired. Only until I'm healed, and then I will rejoin the cause."

Brogan nodded. "I will come with ye."

"Nay, ye must remain with your men." She dried her hands on her skirts, trying not to look at the blood on her gown.

"I will leave the men in Sorley's capable hands."

"'Haps he wants to go home to his woman." If she were he, she would.

"Then Fin's."

Fiona swiped at her eyes. "Only for a little while. And then I will come back."

"All right." Brogan rubbed his thumb over her chin.

"Ye need no' stay with me."

"I'm never leaving ye again."

"Aye, but ye will. This is no' a real marriage, Brogan. Ye said so yourself."

The smile faded from his face, and he took on a fierce seriousness. "But what if I want it to be real? I told ye I love ye, and I didna lie."

She frowned, his words lodging in her chest and surprisingly warming her, but she tried to put a box around them. Ice, something to keep them from overheating her insides. "And I told ye that ye canna love me."

"Ye canna tell me what to do," he teased, poking the tip of her nose.

Fiona bit her lip, denying the emotion welling in her chest, for she was fairly certain what she'd been feeling for weeks now was love, too, but she just couldn't come out and say it. Didn't want him to feel trapped.

"I want for ye only what ye want," she whispered, repeating his words.

"Then ye must want for me to want ye, because, sweet love, I do." He leaned forward, his lips pressing to hers, soft, gentle, warm.

Brogan's scent, his strength, surrounded her, and she sank into him, the fear and anxiety of the past hours dissipating some and easing into a few moments of peace.

He loved her. And she loved him. They were both alive.

What more could she ask for?

Seventeen

FIONA WAS CURLED INTO BROGAN'S LAP ATOP HIS MOUNT AS they made their way back toward Dòchas Keep. Milla trotted at their side. It'd be several days before they arrived, and for the better part of a few hours now, he'd kept his eyes peeled for a tavern that wasn't teeming with dragoons or enough Scots to question their arrival and intentions.

After the prince found out about Cameron, everyone at camp was thoroughly vetted, themselves included, to find that no one else had traitorous thoughts on their minds. Even MacDonald. Sorley had indeed returned to Dunvegan for a short sojourn with his wife, while the rest of their men had remained with the prince and would go on to the find the ship with Fin in charge.

Eventually they would all meet up again, but right now Fiona was Brogan's priority.

"Did the men make mention of who they were or why they would try to take ye?" he asked.

She shook her head, snuggling close. "No' a word."

Brogan frowned and pressed his lips to the top of her head. He'd not recognized any of the men, not that he'd expected to, but they were on Grant lands, and being they were Scots he half expected them to be part of his clan gone rogue or in league with his father.

With the prince lying only a few feet away in a cave, it was surprising they'd gone after Fiona.

Smoke curled from the trees perhaps a mile or so away, and he headed in that direction, hoping it was a tavern and not a burned-out croft.

The road curved into a small village, and they approached the inn, watching the town with cautious eyes. Like some other towns they'd passed, it was quiet, eerily so, most people keeping indoors and away from the eyes of any passing redcoats.

"We'll see if they have a room to let and at the verra least grab a bite to eat."

Fiona nodded, and he dismounted, reaching up to assist her down. She winced when he set her on her feet, and he wanted to pick her right back up again. He started to do just that, but she stopped him.

"I can manage, if ye let me hold your arm."

"Of course, but if it becomes too much, ye need only tell me and I'll carry ye."

"Thank ye." She smiled shyly and ducked her head.

The tavern was mostly empty save for a few locals, and the proprietor was more than happy to have someone rent the room upstairs since they'd not had many people coming and going of late.

"I can have your meal brought up and then your lady willna have to sit with the animals," the man said with a little laugh.

"We'd like that, thank ye," Brogan said with a nod.

"How many horses?"

"Two. And a hound."

Though Fiona had not ridden her own, they'd taken it all the same for when she was able to ride.

"We've got plenty of room for them too. Will cost ye a wee bit extra though for my groom to take care of them."

"'Tis fine," Brogan agreed.

The man showed them to a chamber abovestairs that had seen better days, and apologized for that while they profusely told him it was fine. For it was. A roof over their heads, a door to lock, a warm meal coming.

They were grateful, relieved. Milla snuck up the stairs behind them and slipped into the room before the innkeeper could complain.

Fiona sagged back on the bed, her skirt up a little, revealing her boots but not her ankle.

"Can I look?"

"Are ye a doctor now, sir?" she teased.

Brogan approached the foot of the bed, kneeling before her. "No' a doctor, but I've seen plenty of men injured."

"Have your fill." Her gaze was on him as he unlaced her boot and carefully pulled it off, then rolled down her hose, his fingers brushing over silky skin.

Brogan sucked in a breath at the sight of her purple and swollen ankle.

"Looks worse than it feels," she offered, gazing down at the puffy appendage.

He doubted that. "Looks awful."

With gentle fingers, he probed the wound, and she winced, hissing a breath. Milla approached, giving Fiona's leg a little lick before sitting to watch him examine her mistress.

"Doesna feel broken though, which I feared."

"Aye."

He glanced up at Fiona, who looked to be trying hard to mask her pain. "Should be better in a fortnight."

"Let's pray."

Brogan bent down without thinking and pressed his lips to the purple of her ankle.

"I'm no' sure ye want to do that, no' with me having been wearing my boots all day. I'm bound to smell."

"I dinna mind your smell," he said with a grin, and meant it. "Covered in barn muck, I'd still find ye beautiful."

"Ye're mad."

He shrugged, shooed Milla to lie down by the hearth, and then gingerly crawled over her, careful not to disturb her ankle, his thighs on the outside of hers, his hands pressed into the mattress beside her shoulders.

"I am mad for ye, Fiona MacBean. When I thought I might have lost ye…" He choked on the last of the words. "I never want to wake to find ye missing. I never want ye to be in danger again, and I know that is unrealistic in the world we live in, but I'd have gone to the edge of the earth to find ye. So, nay, a wee bit of boot smell is no' going to push me away. And if I dinna kiss ye right now, I'll regret not having tried for the rest of my days."

Brogan leaned lower now, his lips brushing hers, and she tilted her face up to meet him. Saints, how he loved kissing her. Delicate fingers brushed his ribs as she wrapped her arms around his middle, tugging him closer.

"Kiss me until I forget," she murmured.

"I'll kiss ye until ye only remember the feel of my lips on ye," he replied.

"Aye. Lips…" She slid her tongue slowly over his lower lip.

Brogan growled and kissed her deeper, claiming her, showing her just how much he wanted her, and forcing them both to forget the precarious moments of the past twenty-four hours.

"I want ye to make love to me," Fiona said. "But only if ye want to."

Brogan pulled away, staring into her violet eyes. "Ye know what that will mean."

"Aye. And I can understand if ye dinna want to."

"I do," he said. He wanted badly to make her his forever. "I told ye I love ye, and I meant it. I want ye to be mine forever."

"Forever," she mused, her arms tightening around him. "I like the sound of that." She smiled up at him, that same shy smile he'd seen earlier, only this time instead of ducking her head away, she met his gaze full on. "I love ye too, Brogan."

The words melted right into him and lodged in the center of his chest. For a moment, he couldn't draw a breath. Since when had words had the power to undo him?

But those words, coming from her… She loved him.

Brogan kissed her, all the emotion he felt welling in his chest coming through his lips as he claimed her, loved her.

"I could die a happy man right now for having heard ye say the words." Brogan wasn't a romantic, nor was he sentimental, and yet in this moment, with his heart pounding and Fiona in his arms, there was no stopping the words tumbling from his mouth.

They'd lain in bed together before. This wasn't something new. And yet it was.

Fiona stared up into Brogan's eyes, filled with love and desire, melting into a powerful haze of what felt like hope. As though they'd wake tomorrow and all the pain and torment of days past would fade away.

She knew that was silly, unrealistic, and yet Fiona couldn't help but see a light of hope in Brogan's gaze. With her arms around him, she hugged him closer, kissed him harder. Wanted to give him all of herself. Wanted him forever.

"Dinna die, Brogan," she said. "I'm no' certain I can live without ye." She shook her head, curled her fingers through his hair. "I dinna even know how it happened, but somewhere along the way, ye burrowed yourself into my heart."

He nibbled at her lower lip and gave her a roguish wink. "As long as I live, I swear I willna die."

Fiona laughed. "Make love to me, ye fool."

"I plan on it."

Brogan kissed her again, harder, more demanding, more filled with primal need, and her body answered the call as she tugged at his shirt, and Brogan finished the job, yanking it over his head. He rolled them to the side and undid the buttons on the back of her gown with nimble fingers that skimmed her warm, smooth flesh.

Brogan kissed her neck and slid his lips over her shoulders as he bared her skin. Inch by inch, his lips traversed the length of her arm as he peeled away the gown. Shimmied the fabric over her hips and down her legs, and tossed the whole contraption somewhere on the floor.

Fiona tugged at her stays, reaching behind for the ties and failing. Brogan rolled her onto her belly, straddling her thighs with his strong legs, and kissed her back while slowly unlacing her stays. But even as the tightness ebbed, she found it harder and harder to breathe. Gasps and pants and moans were the only thing leaving her lips as Brogan kissed every inch of exposed skin.

He slid her stays from beneath her, tossing them to the floor, and then slid the chemise up her back, running his finger along her spine. And then his lips. His tongue. He traced every vertebra until she could scream from the pleasurable torment.

He paused, drawing in a deep breath, his fingers tracing over the bruises from the ropes. "I would kill them all over again if I could for doing this to ye."

"It doesna hurt, I swear."

"Tell me if it does." Brogan kissed the places that had once ached.

Then came her drawers, his fingers dancing over her hips as he slid them down, revealing her buttocks to his view. Lips touched her bare bum, and then a little nip at the cheek. He slid the drawers to her knees, and she wriggled to get them off as he peeled them the rest of the way.

She tried to roll over, wanting to feel the hard length of his body on hers. To feel her breasts rub over his chest, but he held her in place, pinning her gently with his warm weight. She felt the scrape of his breeches on her bare buttocks as he pressed her into the bed, the hardness of his arousal, the brush of his lips on her shoulder, her ear.

"Ye're so lovely," he murmured.

He spread her legs with his, and she gasped as he rocked his hips against her rear. Palms danced over her hips, then her behind as he slid his fingers over the dampness between her thighs, finding the nub of her pleasure.

"Ye're already so wet," he groaned, a finger slipping inside. "I want to feel your pleasure."

Fiona could barely breathe, tried to answer but all that came out was a moan as he stroked her with his fingers, pressed his arousal against her, rocking back and forth, his mouth at her ear, her neck, running his tongue over her back. Her climax was swift and powerful, and she arched her back, pushing her buttocks against him, her channel tightening around his fingers in trembling pulses.

"That's a good lass," he crooned. And then he was flipping her over, and she grabbed for the ties of his breeches.

"I want ye," she said. "Inside me."

Brogan groaned and kicked off his breeches, revealing the long, hard length of his cock. She gripped him, sliding her hand up and down his velvet shaft.

"I want to be inside ye so damn bad."

He collapsed on top of her, and she lifted her legs around his hips. With one swift thrust he was inside her, filling her, and Fiona cried out from pleasure and relief and bliss.

Arms wrapped around his shoulders, legs around his hips, she leaned up to kiss him, and their tongues danced a wild rhythm as their bodies collided. She lifted her hips to meet each rapid plunge, their bodies moving in frantic, passionate rhythm. There was a desperation in their coupling, a deep and frenzied need. As though they'd both been waiting so long for this to happen, and now that it finally had, they were racing to the finish.

Brogan drove deep, his hips surging into hers, pleasure thrumming with every plunge. There was something so primal about their coming together, and she loved the raw passion of it. The pleasure that threatened to uproot everything in her entire world.

"Fiona," he groaned, "God, I love ye."

"I love ye too," she gasped.

Pleasure whipped through her, spiraling up into a crescendo, and she cried out, thighs quivering as she clung tighter to him. Brogan thrust hard and swift, until he too was crying out and shuddering against her, inside her.

Slick with sweat and sated from passion, he collapsed beside her, tugging her into his arms. Fiona curled up into the safety of his embrace, the power of his lovemaking still causing her body to tremble. He skated his fingers down her arms and she shivered.

"Perhaps we should stay here until my ankle is better," she said with a mischievous grin. "We can have them serve us all of our meals in bed."

"No' a bad idea at all." Brogan chuckled, leaned in, and kissed her languidly. "We can stay here forever where no one knows who we are and make love until neither of us can walk another step."

"I'm all in." She brushed her fingers over his cheek, feeling complete bliss for once in her life.

Eighteen

WHILE FIONA AND BROGAN DID SPEND THE NEXT TWO DAYS being languid in bed, they did not spend the fortnight both of them would have preferred, for three reasons.

One—it was expensive, and they were both running low on coin.

Two—the inn was becoming more crowded, and just that morning they'd had to hole up and pay the innkeeper an extra three coins to take care of Milla when several redcoats decided to have their supper and after-supper ales at the establishment, and they couldn't risk letting the dog outside.

And three—given the men all believed them to be headed to Dòchas Keep, rather than a tavern inn located in whatever town they'd happened to stop through, they found the need to be on their way most pressing.

Two days after peeling themselves out of bed, they were riding through the gates of Dòchas.

A mile away from the castle, Fiona had insisted Brogan let her onto her own horse. She couldn't have her people see her riding in on his horse and immediately suspect that she was hurt or that they were lovers. Even though both of these things were true, and in fact she was now—

Married.

Oh, goodness, married in truth now.

A smile curled her lips. Well, she supposed she wasn't going to hide the fact, but she at least needed to tell them first to lessen the shock.

Brogan helped her down from her horse as Uncle Tam came rushing out of the castle and grabbed her up in his arms.

"We feared ye dead," he said, his chest shaking from nerves, his words broken with emotion.

"I'm alive and well." Fiona squeezed him back and then pulled away, but kept hold of her uncle's hands. "Ye remember Brogan Grant, aye, Uncle?"

"Aye." Her uncle let go of her hands to shake Brogan's.

"He is my husband," she blurted out. "We wed on the road."

"Ye wed on the road?" her uncle repeated, looking at her with an expression that was both shocked and confused.

"Informally," Brogan added.

That one word had the power to shake her, and Fiona tried hard not to whip herself in Brogan's direction and demand an explanation.

To that, her uncle raised his brows so high they nearly touched his hairline. "What the hell does that mean?"

Looked like she didn't need to.

"How about we discuss it over a cool drink?" Fiona said with a bright smile that felt like it might crack. If Brogan backed down now after what they'd shared, after the promises they'd made to each other... She hobbled forward to take Brogan's arm, raising a brow when she did, but he only winked in return, and in that one simple dip of his eyelid, she felt everything righted with the world.

"So ye wed her and then made her lame?" Despite her best attempt to walk, her uncle appeared to miss nothing. "There's no other reason for Fiona to come back to Dòchas when there's a prince to chase about and messages to be delivered."

"Uncle," she said, a wee bit hurt at his words. "Brogan would never hurt me."

"While I did no' cause her the injury, the fault is entirely my own," Brogan said.

"What?" Fiona pinched her lips together and shook her head fiercely.

Her uncle frowned. "Come inside."

In the great hall, Uncle Tam ordered food brought out for them, and cool mugs of ale were filled.

"Explain her injury to me," Uncle Tam demanded of Brogan.

But Fiona was no weak lass, so she interrupted. "I'll explain it myself, Uncle Tam. I'm no' a bairn, and I never have and never will need to have a man speak for me."

"Well, then." He grinned at Brogan. "How do ye like that?"

"I love it." Brogan chuckled.

"Then this may be a perfect match. Now tell me, my dear." Uncle Tam leaned forward and squeezed her shoulder. "Leave no detail out."

Fiona obliged, knowing her uncle dearly missed being out in the field, being in battle. He'd been right by her father's side throughout the rebellions and had continued with Gus, but age had made moving about harder. An affliction in his hands made it difficult to grip his weapons. As they feasted on broiled fish and bread, she left out no details—well, some details; her uncle didn't need to know about how much she kissed Brogan. She told him of their travels across Skye, the prince's arrival by boat, and how they'd spent weeks running from dragoons, until she finally came to the part where she'd been abducted, and how Brogan had saved her from her abductors.

"An amazing bit of adventure ye've had. What I wouldn't give to be young again." Uncle Tam took a long sip of his ale, gaze pinned on Brogan. "The truth of the matter is that if Gus were here, or Ian, they'd likely take ye to task for no' asking permission to wed their sister. My brother would have pulled his sword on ye." Uncle Tam frowned into his cup. "Ye're a Grant. And a rebel at that. 'Tis dangerous for us all to be acquainted, let alone joined in matrimony."

"I'm a bastard, too," Brogan added, and Fiona had to hold in her groan.

Why was Brogan trying to bait her uncle further?

"Even better," Uncle Tam ground out.

"In this case, it likely is," Brogan said, his face calm, serious. "I have no claims on the Grant clan, and my father has disowned me for no' following him to King George's side." He glanced at Fiona, and she felt her insides warm. "And I love Fiona. My loyalty is with her. I swear to protect her, fight for her, and cherish her for all the rest of my days."

Uncle Tam grunted, but the frown creases between his brows started to dissipate. "Good. I hope that conviction gets ye through the night."

"Uncle," Fiona said, "I am happy. I love Brogan, and I would be happiest if my family loved him too."

Uncle Tam pursed his lips as though he'd eaten something sour, then let out a long sigh. "I promised your da I would protect the lot of ye children. And when Gus left, and then Ian, each of them made me promise the same. And now we sit here with ye having wed the bastard son of the enemy."

"All of that may be true, but I recall ye found respect for this same man the last time we were here." Fiona put her cup down onto the table a little too forcefully, some of the ale sloshing over the side. "I am happy. I am safe. Forgive me, Uncle, but do ye know how many times I could have died on the road? This man saved me. I'll no' have ye disparage him. Brogan is a man of honor, and ye tarnish him with your distaste."

Uncle Tam watched her through eyes hooded with age. "Well, now, lass," he said softly. "If that is the truth of it."

"It is."

"Then I suppose I owe the two of ye an apology."

"None is necessary," Brogan broke in. "Ye were only trying to protect Fiona."

"I love her as though she were my own daughter," Uncle Tam said. Was that wetness gathering in his eyes?

"I love her too," Brogan proclaimed, the strength in his voice, in his words, making her chest swell with pride.

She had the love of this amazing man. What more did she need to conquer the world?

Uncle Tam held up his cup. "To the two of ye, may ye live a long life full of happiness."

"Thank ye, Uncle." Fiona swallowed the emotion welling in her throat.

Her uncle reached forward, taking her hand in his, and squeezed. "And when this is all over and your brothers are back, we shall hold a feast and gain the blessing of our priest to celebrate your union."

"Aye, Uncle, we would love that."

"For now, get some rest, and in the morning ye can greet the clan as a wedded woman," Uncle Tam said.

Fiona led Brogan upstairs to her chamber, surprising Beitris inside.

Her maid blushed and held her hands folded in front of her. "I hope 'tis all right," she said.

Fiona looked toward the bed, which had been littered with flower petals of pink and white. A bath with the water still steaming from the surface was in the center of the room, also sprinkled with flower petals.

On the small table there were a crystal decanter filled with red wine and two crystal glasses. A platter filled with berry scones and a thick ball of butter graced its side.

"Those were your mother's," Beitris said, pointing to the crystal. "I know 'tis no' your wedding night, but I thought to make it special anyhow."

Tears sprang into Fiona's eyes at the thoughtfulness, and she launched herself into Beitris's arms. "Thank ye so much, 'tis beautiful. I love it."

"Thank ye, Beitris," Brogan said.

"Will ye be requiring anything else?" Beitris asked.

Fiona shook her head, swiping at the tears gathering in her

eyes. Coming home for a respite had been the right decision for so many reasons. "Nay, thank ye, this is wonderful as it is."

"Just call out when ye wish for the bath to be removed." Beitris ducked her head and left the chamber.

Fiona turned to look at Brogan, who was eyeing the smaller bed she'd slept in since she was a lass. The room looked much like it had her entire life.

A tapestried rug depicting a unicorn escaping those who sought to capture him covered the wood-planked floor, a well-worn path in its center denoting the traveling path of her pacing. Similar unicorn tapestries covered the walls, and even the canopy over her four-poster bed was yet another scene.

"Are ye the unicorn?" he asked, coming closer to her and pulling her into his arms.

Fiona laughed. "No' nearly magical enough."

"Ye're magical to me."

She leaned up and pressed her lips to his. "I am a patriot, and given that the unicorn is the animal of our people, it seems only appropriate to have it all over my chamber."

"I would never expect anything less."

"The only thing I might have added is perhaps the unicorn spearing a dragoon. What do ye think of that?" she teased.

"I will commission it tomorrow."

They had a good laugh at that, which turned quickly into a passionate kiss, each of them fumbling to undress the quickest.

Beitris had been very thoughtful in making the bath. She'd chosen the largest tub in the castle—one that would fit two, and Fiona was eager to climb inside the warm depths of the water with Brogan.

They sank in together, with her straddling his lap. She attempted to run soap over his skin, but he only teased her by flicking his tongue at her nipple before taking it into his mouth. All thoughts of getting clean were quickly removed from their minds as his cock grew hard against her. A subtle shift of her hips and she was sinking down onto his length, taking him inside.

They both groaned, then she pressed her hand over his mouth. "We must be quiet. They know I am married, but they need no' know I'm a wanton."

"Och, lass," Brogan said against her palm, "trust me, no one would think ye wanton for taking your pleasure. A man is supposed to pleasure his woman."

"I love being your woman." She smiled down at him and then gently nipped his lower lip.

"And I love pleasuring ye." He captured her mouth for a searing kiss, his fingers gripping her buttocks and guiding her to move.

Pleasure saturated her insides, made her frantic with need. But every time she tried to move faster, he slowed her down, until she was biting his shoulder with the need for release. Finally, lost in the sea of his own pleasure, Brogan pumped hard and fast, and she took the reins, riding him until her body broke apart. They swallowed each other's moans with a heated kiss, but the water sloshing over the sides and soaking the floorboards was evidence enough of how much they'd enjoyed the bath.

"Your secret is out," Brogan teased. "Everyone will know now."

"What secret?"

"That ye're a minx." He gently bit the fleshy top of her breast. "And that I love ye for it."

"'Tis just over here." Fiona jogged through the forest for the first time since injuring her ankle.

They'd been at Dòchas for two weeks, and she'd been waited on hand and foot by not only Beitris and Brogan but by her uncle Tam too.

Her uncle had also apologized for what he'd said about Brogan, and the two actually began to genuinely get along.

Nothing could have made Fiona happier than to see the two men tease each other over supper. She couldn't wait for her entire family to come together again and meet Brogan, though that seemed a far way off.

Brogan grabbed her from behind, pulling her back against his chest, and he kissed her behind the ear. "But ye're right here…"

She knew that tone in his voice, and it sent a shiver of desire coursing through her. Whirling in his arms, she kissed him thoroughly. "More of that later. For now, the box."

Brogan gave a petulant groan, but followed when she tugged him by the hand.

At last they came to the spot she'd been to a thousand times or more over the course of the years.

"My tree," Fiona announced, beaming up at Brogan. "I've never showed it to anyone save for…my friend." She flicked her gaze back at the little nook that held the box, not wanting to say Aes's name after what had happened with the letters.

"Your friend?"

"Aye. Another messenger like me. The letters are placed in the box, and that is how I receive orders from the prince when I'm no' in his company."

"And what if ye're no' close enough to the box to receive orders?" A gentle breeze wafted, splaying his hair onto his forehead, and she pushed it back.

Fiona shrugged. "There is always word of mouth. Secret messages have a way of being passed."

"That is how some secrets get out."

"Ye're no' wrong. 'Tis why I have such trouble with trust." Her gaze locked on his. "But, Brogan, ye know I trust ye."

"Then why no' give me the name of your friend." By the soft expression on his face, the way his fingers brushed her hand, she had an idea that he already knew the answer, but that he was waiting for her to just tell him outright.

"'Tis Aes."

She waited for anger to cloud his features. For him to pull away. Maybe even for him to turn his back on her and walk away.

But Brogan didn't. He only smiled and brushed his lips over hers.

In that moment of acceptance, Fiona's heart lurched behind her ribs, and if possible, her love for him grew tenfold.

"I thought so," he said. "I only wanted to hear ye say it. To know that ye trusted me with that. After what happened last time... I never should have—"

"I do trust ye, Brogan, else I'd no' have brought ye here. No one else knows who Aes is, that he's—"

Brogan pressed his fingers to her lips. "Ye dinna have to tell me all your secrets, Fiona. After all, ye're in the prince's confidence."

"Aye, but..." She bit the tip of his finger teasingly, trying to figure out just what she could say and what should be left a secret. If she couldn't trust Brogan, the man who'd become her partner, her lifesaver, her lover, then what was the purpose of living? He also had made a vow to protect the prince. Knowing Aes's identity as A.M. wasn't going to break the operation. "Let's see if he's left me a letter."

She pulled a key from the chain around her neck and reached inside the hollow for the box. Relief flooded her to feel the packet inside. She'd worried that there would be nothing, and that after all this time away from the prince's entourage, he wouldn't have need of her anymore. Or worse still that he'd been caught, and she and Brogan hadn't been there to protect him.

They'd still not figured out why she'd been taken at the caves, but Brogan had suspected it had something to do with his clan, given it was on Grant lands. The Glenmoriston Grants were supposed to be on his side. But he said he wouldn't put it past bribery from his father. Honorable men couldn't be bribed, and honorable men also didn't abduct women in the middle of the night, injuring her guards in the process. With Cameron on the inside, no one had suspected the Grants would be ambushing them from behind.

"Incredible," Brogan murmured. "I didna think there would be anything there."

"Why?"

He shrugged. "I canna say. I'm no' certain."

She smiled. "I was worried about the same." Fiona broke the seal on the packet, about to break her own rule of reading by the box. "Actually, I never read here. Let us go."

She closed the box and tucked the packet into her bodice with the key. Taking Brogan's hand, she led him to one of her favorite reading spots and tugged him down to the ground with her. The sun shone through the trees, a rare break from the rain. The sweet scent of forest fauna blew on the breeze, and her fingers danced over the little white snowdrop petals. She plucked one and brought it to Brogan's nose, then slid it over his lips and down his neck.

"Ah, so ye finally have come around to my plan," he teased, pushing her gently back and coming over her with his body.

Fiona laughed as they fell backward, the snowdrop forgotten as he nuzzled her neck, and her entire body felt as though it were coming alive. Perhaps the letter could wait just a few more minutes...

Brogan wanted to make love to his wife. Mostly because every time he looked at her, potent desire ran rampant in his veins. Mostly because he loved the sounds of her soft moans of pleasure, the way she broke apart in his arms. But also partly because he didn't want her to open the letter.

The last few weeks alone with her had been a blissful escape from what was happening in the world, and he didn't want it to end.

As soon as she opened the letter and received news or orders regarding the prince and the rebellion, they would both be compelled to leave. It wasn't that he no longer wanted to do his duty by the prince; it was that he didn't want to leave the cocoon of love they'd wrapped around themselves. For the first time in his entire life, he finally felt at home.

Fiona was his home.

Wherever she was, he felt settled and at peace. Despite the war waging all around the country. Despite death looming in every shadow.

There was peace with her.

And the letter was going to shatter that peace.

"I love your plan," Fiona crooned back, pushing on his chest until he lay down on his back and she crawled over him, straddling his hips with her own. She kissed him on the mouth, then sat up, her hand on his chest, and reached into her bodice to pull out the letter. "But first, we must see what news."

Brogan groaned, his cock aching as it pressed to the heat of her through the fabric of her drawers, her skirts bunched up around her thighs and his hands on her rounded hips.

"Ye torment me," he said with a roguish grin.

"Well, good," she said with a waggle of her brows. "For that is certainly my aim."

Fiona broke the seal on the letter and unfolded it. She scanned the contents while he waited—not so patiently—to find out what it said.

"So, are ye curious?" she asked.

"Aye. But I'd never ask ye to divulge if ye didna feel it right." He'd just grin and bear it, because he loved her so damn much. Maybe *too* much.

"I want to share." Fiona scanned the woods, as if waiting for someone to pounce, and given all that had happened, he too was waiting for just that.

"I believe we are quite alone," he said.

"Me too." She cleared her throat and began to read.

Dear F.,

Have you heard about the festival at Borro to celebrate Dale's 19th? I hear it's going to be a real treat. Perhaps they will have all the sweets we could ever dream about, though not many things are being shipped in these days. Everyone is going to be at the fete! Even our bonnie friend who's been entertained these last few days with the most unlikely of hosts! Wee L, you know A's younger brother, called upon our friend in need and housed him in what some would call a cage, but really, some people need to be more generous. We can't all live in a castle.

I do hope to see you there. It's been so long since we've had a rendezvous.

Your devoted friend,
A.M.

"That makes no sense." Brogan frowned.

"This is verra true." Fiona giggled, her cheeks flushed with excitement. "If ye were to come across the box and find the letter, then ye'd see it is all just silly nonsense. But in fact, it is a coded message. Care to take a guess?" She raised her brow in challenge.

"How could I no'?"

She turned the letter around, and he scanned the contents. "Verra clever," he said, wrinkling his forehead. "I see that perhaps ye're wanted in Borrodale on the nineteenth of the month. That the prince has been housed with a friend of yours, though I dinna know the reference to a cage, and a French ship is coming to collect him?"

Fiona beamed down at him, then flopped forward, pressing a

hard kiss to his mouth. Brogan's hands slipped around from her hips to her rear, and he pressed upward, wishing to be inside her.

She sat back up with a moan and a wiggle, taunting him. "Ye got it! The friend is Logan, Annie's brother. And I think the cage might reference her uncle Cluny."

"Fantastic." He caressed her ribs and then blatantly put his hands on her breasts, massaging. "All this has made me...want ye."

Fiona laughed and slapped him with the paper. "Ye wanted me before all this."

"True." Brogan flipped her over. He folded the paper and tucked it back down in her bodice, his fingers skimming her breasts. "Will ye let me?" He kissed his way down her body and hooked her knee over his shoulder, pressing his lips to her inner thigh.

"Oh, aye." She smiled on a sigh, looking down at him, anticipation clear on her features. "Dinna make me wait another moment."

"Never."

Nineteen

BORRODALE WAS BUSTLING WITH ACTIVITY, BUT THANKFULLY none of it was red in color. In fact, their travels to the west coast of Scotland, and then their crossing over to Skye, had been surprisingly lacking in redcoats. Fear had Fiona wondering all the while if they would find that the lot of them had swarmed the small village in northwest Skye. But her fear appeared unfounded.

Likely, her friend Jenny was the culprit behind the lack of dragoons in the area. What sort of trouble was Jenny getting up to now to distract the enemy? For that could be the only way a path was cleared.

The fresh salt-sea air was crisp, and Fiona drew in a long, deep breath. She regarded the pier where a few fishing boats appeared dwarfed by a massive ship that flew no flags.

Merchants carried baskets and crates at a hurried rate toward the pier and, in single lines, climbed the gangplanks of what had to be a French vessel, putting as many supplies as they could onboard. Not that it was going to be much.

If the French ship had come to take away the prince, why had it not instead brought more troops to help keep the prince on Scottish soil? There had to be a plan. Perhaps they were going to float at sea for a while until reinforcements came.

Fiona and Brogan had ridden hard the last two days to arrive in time, considering the letter had only been discovered a few days before the nineteenth. Milla sat on her lap as though she were the director of their travel. Uncle Tam had understood their need for a departure and asked that she take several guards with her, but like usual, Fiona had declined.

It was a lot easier for her and Brogan to travel unnoticed

without a guard coming with them. The only ones she felt safe to travel with were the six other warriors in Brogan's company that she trusted, that knew their movements. They were a team and had a way of silently communicating that newer guards just wouldn't have. It wasn't that she didn't trust newer men to learn, but they didn't have the time, not when she was urgently needed.

"There's Sorley," Brogan said with a wide grin.

Everything would happen very quickly before the dragoons caught word of the French ship in port and sent their guns as had happened the last time.

What wasn't certain, however, was how Fiona was going to play into the prince's plans.

She and Brogan approached the dock, where the six men they'd parted with nearly a month ago stood sentry.

They dismounted, and Brogan launched into pounding his men on the back amid masculine hugs, while she nodded and smiled at them all. Happiness bubbled up in her chest, and it was taking everything she had not to burst with it.

"Come now, dinna be shy," Fin said, grabbing her up in a hug. "We're family, remember?"

"Aye, we are." She wrapped her arms around her Irish brother and squeezed.

"How's the ankle?" Sorley asked, pulling her into his embrace.

"Better than before," Fiona answered, backing away and doing a little jig.

"Good, good." Sorley laughed, along with the rest of the men, who she embraced. "The prince has been waiting for ye both."

As if on cue, Bonnie Prince Charlie descended the gangplank to the dock and strode forward in his scuffed boots and with a slight limp. There was an excitement about him that hadn't been there the last time she'd seen him. As a result, no doubt, of the French ship.

"Lady Fiona," the prince said as he approached. Despite being slightly haggard around the edges, he still presented her with a handsome and winning smile. "And so we meet again. We're glad to have you back."

"Your Highness." Fiona curtsied to the prince, and Brogan bowed his head.

"Sir Brogan," the prince greeted.

Sir?

"Just Brogan, Your Highness," her husband corrected.

"Ah, I almost forgot." The prince pulled out his sword, the blade glinting in the sunlight. "Kneel, Brogan Grant."

Fiona's mouth went dry. Brogan, though his face was stoic, had tensed about the shoulders. Was he about to be knighted? Happiness and pride bubbled in her chest.

Brogan knelt on the pier, pressing his hands over his heart. The six of his men stood in a semicircle around them, and everyone on the pier stilled, the silence an echo of respect. The prince couldn't have known how much this would mean to Brogan. Growing up a bastard, never quite fitting in, telling her he wasn't really in charge when he clearly was. This was what he'd worked for, what he'd earned and deserved.

"For your valor and honor, your service to the rightful crown of Scotland and to God, as your prince regent and commander, I hereby bestow upon you the most noble title of Sir Knight of Glenmoriston. Before these witnesses and with God's grace, Brogan Grant, I dub thee Sir Knight. Arise, Sir Brogan."

Brogan stood slowly, his head held high, though he did have to slightly bend it to see the prince's face.

"I am honored to serve my country, and ye, Your Highness," Brogan said, placing his hand over his heart. "I will protect Scotland with my dying breath."

The prince sheathed his sword. "You've earned it, Sir Brogan. 'Tis I who am honored to count you as an ally."

Brogan nodded, his hands clasped behind his back.

"We are going to France," the prince said, eyes squinted as he looked toward the horizon. There were new lines at the corners of his eyes and his brow. His hair was thin, and his clothes hung loosely. There was no doubt that since arriving in Scotland, he'd fared worse than he likely expected. Than all of them expected. "We leave in the next hour. Before Cumberland's men arrive, which they will no doubt do. Half those in the village have already scattered, expecting the impending onslaught." He shook his head in disappointment.

Fiona swallowed hard, fearful for those in the village, but also, had she heard correctly? The prince was going to France? He wasn't going to sail out to sea and wait a time and then come back in when Cumberland's army least expected it? He wasn't simply going to call for reinforcements from abroad? He was *leaving*. He was abandoning Scotland. He was abandoning the cause. He was abandoning *her*.

"Come with us, Lady Fiona," the prince said. "I will need my messenger. There will be much to plan when we land in France."

"I canna leave without my husband." The words were out of her mouth before she realized she'd said them. She flicked her gaze to Brogan. Publicly calling him her husband to their future king, that made it real, didn't it? The prince had been with them before and thought them wed, but she felt the sudden urge to say it louder. To proclaim it to all, needing it to be real when it felt like everything right now was up in the air.

France… She'd never left Scotland. Not even been in England. She'd never even been to all the Scottish isles, save for those they'd visited on the run, and now the prince was asking her to travel across the Channel to France. She didn't speak French very well. How would she get on? How was she to pass messages when she didn't have a good enough grasp of the language?

"Then the both of you must come." The nonchalance in the prince's words lodged in her chest, as if it were that easy. As if uprooting from the country of their birth, the one they were sworn to protect, was not a big deal. As if the both of them should just board and abandon everything they knew.

If she left now, she wouldn't be here when Gus and Leanna returned. They would find her having left the country with no word. It would be the same for the rest of her family. Uncle Tam expected her to return, and Ian... She glanced toward the ship, searching for her brother's figure. He'd been with the prince this entire time and had now disappeared. Was she already on the ship, or had he decided not to attend the prince and gone back to Dòchas?

There was also the matter of her friends, her family by choice, those she'd made oaths to. She couldn't abandon Jenny and Annie. Nor could she abandon the six warriors who'd stood by her and Brogan during the last months through thick and thin.

"Where is Ian?"

The prince nodded as if he'd been expecting that. "He's returned to your lands. His duty is to your clan and castle, and he will help me from here. I informed him I'd be extending the invitation to you, and he gave his blessing."

That easily... Fiona suppressed the urge to shake her head. This was all moving too quickly.

"If I may, Your Highness, ours was no' a formal wedding," Brogan said, shocking Fiona from her thoughts.

The prince just stared at him, waiting for an explanation.

"We didna wed in a church, before God," Brogan said.

"Ah," said the prince. "But you see, God is everywhere, not just the church. In the eyes of God, and his prince, the two of you are wed. But if you wish it upon the ship, I shall have my personal priest bless your union."

Fiona breathed a sigh of relief. That was the thing, wasn't it? Brogan was simply feeling guilty about them not having wed properly. And now the prince was going to see it done.

A commotion sounded from the ship, and the prince turned around as if that were his cue to depart. "I'll see the both of you onboard."

With the prince and his entourage melting down the planks toward the ship, Fiona faced Brogan. There was a dark shadow on his features that she didn't like. A rock settled in her stomach. Sensing a shift in temperature, Brogan's six men turned around to afford them a measure of privacy. Would the six of them come too? She couldn't imagine Sorley leaving Kenna behind.

"What say ye, Sir Brogan, shall we go to France?" She smiled at him, hoping to calm some of the darkness she saw quickly gathering. Hoping to calm her own fears knotting in her belly.

"Ye should go to France." Conviction filled Brogan's voice.

"Aye, *we* should." She reached for his hands, but he backed up a step and the unsettling feeling she'd had within her moments ago grew.

Brogan gave a curt shake of his head. "Nay, lass, just ye."

"What? Alone? Nay." Fiona vehemently shook her head. This was madness. "What are ye talking about? Ye're to come with me."

Brogan's shoulders straightened, and he looked down at her as though they hadn't shared the most intimate secrets, as though they hadn't made love on the forest floor, in taverns, and in her childhood bedchamber. As if they hadn't told each other and the world that they'd wed, that they wanted to spend the rest of their lives *together*.

"My place is here, *in* Scotland, where I can protect the country, where my skills are best put to use. How am I to protect people when I'm no' here?"

"My place is with ye." There, she'd said the words. Abandoning the notion of one of them only boarding that ship. Abandoning the notion she'd had that her place was beside the prince. There had been a major shift in her over the past weeks, a life-changing shift. She could do better with Brogan by her side than she could alone. Look at all they'd accomplished together.

He shook his head. "This is your chance, Fiona. Your chance to be set free. Free of this marriage that was meant to be temporary and free from fear."

This marriage that was meant to be temporary. She swallowed hard. "I didna think our marriage was going to be temporary."

"It has been from the start."

"And I thought we changed that. I just told the prince we were wed, and he acknowledged that."

Brogan grunted, but said nothing. *Nay! Not that again!*

"Brogan," she urged, trying to fight the tears stinging the backs of her eyes. "Dinna close yourself off from me. We are wed."

He shook his head sharply, and she felt his denial like a crushing blow in the chest. To her back was the ship. She could easily board it and stay by the prince's side. Honor the vow she'd made a decade ago to protect Scotland at all costs. Honor the prince who should be sitting on the throne in England and not run from his country.

Or should she stay here in Scotland with Brogan, her husband? Stay with the man who'd made her feel loved and safe. The safest she'd felt in years. The happiest she'd ever been.

A few months ago, she would have gone to France with no question. But not now. Things had changed.

And yet Brogan was denying their happiness. He was pushing her away.

"Ye canna mean it," she said, trying to reach for him.

Brogan backed away another step. "Ye're better off without me, lass."

"Why do ye no' let me be the judge of that?" Her voice shook as she spoke. Her insides felt like they were being sliced in two. "We made a vow, Brogan, to the cause. If ye dinna wish to be with me, if this has all been a ruse, at least honor your vow to the prince."

"I made a vow to see Scotland free from the tyranny of King George's reign, and how am I to do that an ocean away?"

Fiona shook her head. "With the only man, the prince, who can take King George's place."

All emotion had gone from Brogan's face. Stoic and stubborn. She wanted to slap him until he showed her some real emotion.

"My place is here, Fiona. Go with the prince and fulfill your duties the way ye see fit."

Fiona stared down at her chest, certain to see a knife protruding from her heart the way agony ripped through it, but there was nothing. Nothing save the pain of the words he lobbed at her.

Had this all been a ruse for him?

She took a step back, feeling used and humiliated. This made no sense. She was good at reading people, better at it than nearly everyone she knew, and yet she'd somehow missed the signs…

"Go," he said again.

He need not tell her again. Fiona snapped her fingers at Milla and whirled around, practically running toward the ship with her hound at her heels.

Twenty

BROGAN STORMED DOWN THE PIER, ANGRY AND HURT THAT Fiona had turned her back, but mostly furious with himself for having given her the option. But how could he not? She'd told him how much the cause, the prince, meant to her. Confessed her childhood vow. Showed him the box that Aes left her orders in. Messages she'd been receiving from him for a decade.

With every fiber of his being, Brogan loved her, but how could he make her give up everything she'd worked for simply to live a life with him?

The way her eyes had lit up when she'd seen the prince sauntering down the gangplank, and the way she'd beamed a smile at being asked to go to France to continue out her mission abroad had been both eye-opening and a gut punch for Brogan.

It would be selfish of him to keep her here. Fiona was a brilliant messenger and spy. Who was he to hold her back?

The only right thing to do had been to give her a choice. When you loved someone, you had to give them what they wanted most.

But damn, did it hurt to see her turn her back.

She'd begged him to go with her, and he'd not been mistaken in the tears he'd seen gathering in her eyes. But his place was here, and she knew that. And likely he would only get in her way.

"Brogan," Sorley said, his voice stern.

"We're leaving," Brogan said.

"Why are ye no' on that ship?" Fin asked. "Dinna be a fool."

The rest of the men wore similarly confused looks upon their faces as though Brogan might have sprouted goat horns.

"I've been a fool already," he said. And that was partially true. To allow himself to think that he deserved Fiona in his life. That he could ever be happy, fulfilled, was a cruel jest. He was the bastard son of the Chief of Clan Grant—a traitor. Brogan had so much work to do on Scottish soil that it made his head spin.

Work that would certainly never be done. Now that the prince had knighted him, he had more responsibility to see the country put to rights.

He was born into loneliness and he would die there.

"But ye love her," Sorley said, brows pinched.

"What does love have to do with anything?" Brogan snapped.

"Nearly everything," Fin answered as if he were a complete and utter dullard.

"Ye have love of your country, and ye have love of your woman. So why is your woman getting on a ship to go to another country?" Keith asked, just as incredulous.

"She doesna want to stay." Brogan fisted his hands at his sides, trying hard not to start punching people.

The men looked even more confused by his words, exchanging glances that only served to anger Brogan more.

"And I'll no' be talking about it another second," Brogan said. "I'm leaving, and if ye want to come with me, then mount your blasted horses."

No one moved. With a frustrated growl, Brogan marched down the pier toward where they'd tied their horses, ready to get the hell out of there before the dragoons arrived, pistols blazing.

Behind him, he could hear the clomping of the men's boots.

He snapped his fingers, then winced, for he realized Fiona had taken Milla with her. Traitorous dog. Brogan's chest swelled then with emotion, and he tried to bolster himself against it, but it beat at him as though he were being rammed repeatedly by the bow of the ship.

He had to leave everything on this damned pier.

By the time he climbed up on his horse, he needed to be back to the cold, distant man he'd been months ago when he'd first seen

Fiona on the road. She'd changed him. Made him soft. Made him *feel*. And look where that had gotten him.

A goddamned broken heart.

Lord, he was a fool. A simpering, idiotic fool to have let love in. To have believed he was worthy of someone else's desire, love, admiration. To feel for a moment that he could lay his bare chest open.

She might as well have pulled the dagger from her belt and thrust it into his heart. Else he'd have done it himself. He practically had. For he'd pushed her away to begin with. But she'd hardly pushed back. Not the way he'd needed her too.

Aye, on that pier when he'd given her the chance, Brogan had needed her to fight for him the way he'd fought for her.

That was what he desired most, to be worth fighting for.

And she'd just proven he wasn't.

If the woman he loved, who professed love to him, if everything they'd gone through had meant so little, then he was doomed.

For he was certain never to find a love like that again. Never to find a woman who meant so much. Never to allow himself. Staring back at the ship, he pulled out the invisible iron and built a solid wall around his heart.

With a grunt and a grimace, he turned his horse.

"Where are we going?" Sorley asked.

"West coast. We'll join the MacPhersons of Cluny, that's where ye came from, aye?"

"Aye."

"If the prince does come back, then we'll be ready." Every word tasted like gunpowder on his tongue.

"What about Clan Grant?" Keith asked.

Brogan stilled and turned to his cousin, seeing the hope etched on his face.

"After what happened at Culloden, my da is no' likely to turn his tail on King George. He'll only see the loss as bolstering his choice to have turned in the first place."

"But we've allies in the clan at Glenmoriston."

"Ye mean the ones that were so easily swayed to abduct…" Lord, it was hard to say the words. "My wife?" The words stung him to say, and he could see that they stung Keith too. "The ones who attacked James and Dugall?"

"A few bad apples dinna ruin the whole barrel," Keith said.

"And sometimes they do, cousin," Brogan snapped. "Sometimes the rot spreads, and I for one dinna want to be around to see it. But I willna hold ye back from doing so." He glanced at each man. "Any of ye, if ye wish to go back to your clans, ye need no' follow me. Our mission was to find the prince. To see that he was protected, and we have done that. Our mission is complete, our duty done."

"A soldier's duty is never done," James said. "Especially when the enemy has yet to be defeated."

The men all nodded their agreement.

"Well then, I would be honored to ride with all of ye again," Brogan said, holding out his fist.

The men placed their fists against his, the circle of seven.

They pulled apart, turning toward the road that would lead them west. Somewhere behind them a dog barked, and he imagined Milla on the deck of the ship, paws up on the rail, looking back at him.

———

The moment Fiona's foot settled on the ship, she knew she'd made a terrible mistake. How could she have turned her back on Brogan? How could she have walked away so easily?

She should have fought for him. Fought against his judgment.

The way her heart wrenched in her chest felt as though she'd stood with her arms wide and allowed the dragoons she'd been running from for all this time to lodge their bullets in that sensitive beating organ. This was wrong. Being away from Brogan was wrong.

Nay, this wasn't just being away. She'd left him. Again.

And once this ship set sail in a matter of minutes, there was no telling if she'd ever see him again. In fact, there was a good chance she wouldn't. The distance between them would grow physically and metaphorically. The danger the two of them were in would grow decidedly one-sided as he suffered on Scottish soil at the hands of dragoons while she was safely ensconced at the French court, fattened up on savory foods that smelled like heaven and wine that poured from never-ending fountains.

Delivering messages there would become more about intrigue and flattery than what she was used to here, running in the wild, one with the wind and trees.

Slowly, she'd lose who she was. Forget what she'd always wanted.

A life like that would only have been bearable if she at least had the man she loved. But knowing he was over here, surviving on dried meat and stale bannocks, and running from bullets, just soured all of it.

Fiona pulled the emerald ring from the chain around her neck, staring down into the gemstone where it caught the light just right.

When the prince had presented her with this ring what felt like a lifetime ago, she'd been honored and proud to wear it. And she was still proud of what she'd accomplished. Of who she was and what she represented.

But that girl, that honor, belonged on Scottish soil.

How could she honor her vow, her country, if she abandoned it? Aye, she'd made a pledge to put the rightful heir on the throne, and that was not something she was going to give up, but how could she be of use from afar? There were still messages that needed to be delivered on Scottish soil. Messages that would come from France that she could use to spread the word about the next uprising. How was she to make sure they made it to the right people? She had allies here, connections, more so than most.

"Fiona," a familiar male voice said softly from behind.

She dropped the emerald and it bounced against her bodice. Her entire body stiffened as she looked up and stared out toward the pier. Slowly she turned, disbelieving what she'd heard and what she was seeing.

Standing before her, in the flesh, was Aes.

It'd been nearly a decade since she'd last seen him. He'd aged since then, growing into his man's body, his face more sophisticated. His soft brown hair, long and wavy, blowing in the wind. She remembered him as a gangly youth. An adolescent who'd yet to gain control of his limbs, and here he stood, filled out and broad. Handsomer than she remembered. A man who could break hearts.

"Aes?" she murmured.

"In the flesh." He flashed her a grin and held out his arms.

"What are ye doing here?" She frowned, feeling completely out of sorts, her feet rooted to the deck.

"I'm going to France with the prince." His arms dropped to his sides, and the vibrant smile faded.

"What about your wife?"

He looked away a moment. "She's no longer with us."

"Oh," she said, swallowing hard. "I'm so sorry." And she genuinely was. She didn't know what she'd do if Brogan were to… She couldn't even think about it.

"And I heard ye were married. Where is your husband?"

"We were no'… It was no' official." It was an effort to speak smoothly when her throat felt so tight.

There was a spark of interest in Aes's eyes, his chin notching up slightly. Here standing before her was the man she'd craved for years. The man who'd broken her heart when he'd chosen another. This was a chance to try again. The look in his eyes made it clear he was interested. That all she had to do was walk into the arms he'd held open moments ago.

However, the very thought of it had a knot of resistance rising in her throat. Aes had been everything she used to want. But not anymore.

Everything she wanted was not on this ship at all—save Milla, who was barking toward the shore as if to shout out to Brogan that she would try to change Fiona's mind. That Fiona had made a mistake. Every limb felt heavy with remorse and grief.

Aes took a step forward, held out his arms again. "I've missed ye," he said.

"I have missed ye as well, my friend." She stepped into his arms, the weight of his embrace going around her.

There was a measure of comfort in his hug, one she remembered from years ago. He might have aged, even grown an inch or two taller, but he still smelled the same, sounded the same.

Once she would have given anything to have his arms around her, to be in this spot for the rest of her life, but now her heart was pulled in another direction. Dark eyes flashed before her. A roguish glimmer. *Oh, Brogan...*

Fiona stepped back. "When are we setting sail?" she asked dejectedly.

"I presume it to be any moment. Have ye been shown to your cabin yet?"

Fiona shook her head and turned to the rail, sliding her hand over Milla's head and looking back down the pier where Brogan stood with his men in deep conversation.

That knot in her throat rose, nearly choking off her breath.

"Come, Fiona, let me give ye a tour of the ship," Aes said, his fingers dancing over her elbow.

She glanced down at his hand, back up at his handsome face, and all the years since she'd met him flashed before her eyes. There was still a place for Aes in her heart, but in a different corner. A friend. A confidant.

There was only one man now who consumed her love, her life, her future.

And she'd turned her back on him. Her gaze went back toward the pier. Brogan was mounting his horse.

———

"Let's go," Brogan said.

But with the first few steps of his mount, Milla's barking grew louder, until he could have sworn the dog was getting closer.

He stopped his horse and turned around in time to see Milla's wagging tail and flapping tongue as she jumped around his horse's hooves.

"Milla?" He grimaced. So Fiona had decided to abandon the dog after all. God, that hurt more than anything.

Who was the woman he'd loved? For he'd certainly built her up in his mind to be someone she wasn't.

"Brogan." His name was a breathless shout, and he turned to see Fiona running toward him.

He blinked. Disbelieving what he saw. "Fiona?"

A mirage. A trick of the mind.

But she kept coming toward him.

Brogan leapt down from his horse, taking slow, measured steps toward her. Afraid if he moved too fast, she'd disappear. Was this where she was going to tell him she needed him to keep Milla? Wish him well and then break his heart again?

He'd been devastated to let her go once already. He loved her so damn much, though, that he was willing to do it again. Willing to suffer for her happiness. But why did she have to come back and torture him when he'd barely had a moment to heal at her choice?

Fiona pulled up short, two feet away from him, tears dancing in her eyes, her face awash with devastation, the same as he felt inside.

"I wish I could make myself live a life without ye, but I canna. I *need* ye, Brogan."

Brogan swallowed. Opened his mouth to speak, but no sound came out.

"I canna go to France without ye, and if ye willna go to France, then I willna go. I belong here. In Scotland, with ye, fighting for the cause from the ground. Not across the sea." She waved her hand somewhere behind her. "I made a mistake walking away."

"I dinna want ye to go," he said softly, baring his heart to her. "I want ye to stay. I should never have said that I wanted ye to leave. Because it was a lie."

"I'm no' going." She stepped closer. Close enough he could reach for her.

"I'll go with ye if ye want. I just want to be with ye," he said, not having thought about the words coming out of his mouth at all, his heart doing all the talking. "I love ye, Fiona. I want ye to be happy. But I want to be happy *with* ye."

She shook her head. "We will stay here. Our work is better done here, not in some foreign court." Fiona closed the distance between them, wrapping her arms around his neck. "I love ye too much to just walk away."

How could he have ever doubted her love for him?

"I'm sorry," he said, pressing his forehead to hers. Emotion swirled inside him in a torrent so powerful, he thought she might feel the vibrations. "Can ye forgive me?"

"Ye had every right to doubt the moment I turned my back. Dinna blame yourself for that. I've walked away enough times since we met for ye to believe it true. But I swear from this moment forward, I will never walk away again."

With her declaration, Brogan brought his lips to hers in a searing, possessive kiss. The men around them cheered, and bells pealed in the distance as the prince's ship prepared to set sail.

Brogan wrapped her tightly up in his arms, never wanting to let go. When he was a lad, he'd dreamed of the day his mother would come back, and she never did. When he was a grown man, he watched a number of people walk out of his life as if he were nothing, including his own father.

And for the first time, someone he loved, his Fiona, was walking back into his life and telling him she was never going to leave him. She loved him.

He never would have thought it was possible that he would get what he wanted. That he loved and was loved in return.

Brogan murmured against her lips, holding gently to her face, "I love ye so much."

"I love ye more," she said.

Tears wet his thumbs from where he brushed her cheeks. "Why are ye crying?" He pulled back to stared into her watery violet eyes.

"From happiness. Ye, Brogan, make me happy. Ye have somehow become my whole world."

"Och, lass, but ye are mine. From the moment ye stopped me on the road all those months ago, when ye grinned and flipped me a Jacobite coin, ye might as well have hooked my heart and reeled me in. I am yours, now and always."

She kissed him again, and he would have melted onto the pier with her, made love to her until the sun set, save for the people all around them, and the fact that dragoons would soon descend upon Borrodale. But just a moment more he wanted to hold her. Face buried in her neck, he breathed in her scent.

At last he grudgingly pulled away. "Where are we headed?"

"Where were ye going to go before?"

"To the west coast. We were going to join the MacPhersons there and wait for word from France."

"Annie's cousin. He's a good man." She smiled brightly, her fingers entwining with his. "How about we make a stop at Dòchas along the way? I've a feeling with the prince on his way, I might finally be able to see my brother, and I'm certain he would love to know we've wed."

"I'm no' certain 'love' is the correct word."

She nodded seriously, though there was a twinkle in her eye that made him smile.

"'Tis true, Husband, and I promised him a spar when we met again. It may come to that."

"Perhaps we'll take our time getting there," Brogan teased. "Ye forget I've fought beside your brother and I know what he's capable of."

"'Tis a good thing Gus is in America with Leanna, then."

"Why?"

"He trained Ian."

Brogan chuckled and lifted his wife up into the air, twirling her about. Then he kissed her once more and fiddled with the buttons on her belt where she kept her dagger. "How about we have one of these fashioned for me before we arrive?"

Fiona tossed back her head and laughed, the sound drawing attention from everyone within hearing distance.

This was the start of their life together, and Brogan would remember it for the rest of his days, the pure joy of it.

The *hope*.

Don't miss the first book in the Prince Charlie's Angels series

THE *Rebel* WEARS PLAID

Available now from Sourcebooks Casablanca

One

Inverness, Scottish Highlands
Late June, 1745

WIND WHIPPED AT JENNY MACKINTOSH'S HAIR AS SHE RACED for her life to escape from the English. She and her small band of men pushed their mounts to the limit, flying across the moors, the crack of pistols cutting the night air behind them. At any moment, she'd feel the sting of a bullet in her back.

What else should a rebel recruiting an army expect?

Sweat beaded on her brow and dripped down her back, and her hands trembled against the leather straps of the reins.

"To the forest," she called to her five partners in rebellion following behind her, but her words were lost in the noisy thrum of pounding hooves against the earth. Leaning to the right, she urged her horse down a slope, over a boulder, and onto an unmarked path that led toward the forest, hoping they'd lose the redcoats.

The shouts of the dragoons behind them were fainter now, but that didn't mean they were out of danger.

She burst through the trees, and a twig caught in her hair, the wrench stinging her scalp. Still, she didn't cry out.

Once she knew they were out of sight, she reined in her horse, her heart racing. Jenny tugged the twig from her hair and threw it on the ground, wishing it were the bloody English so she could stomp them into dust as easily. She stroked her mount's mane, patting his neck in thanks for the hard gallop, then reached up to rub at the tightness in her own.

They waited in silence, their breaths growing slower as the minutes ticked by. The shots had ceased the moment she and her soldiers had been able to break away from their enemies' sight, but the pounding of the horses' advance still thundered in her ears—or was that her heart?

Jenny focused her gaze through the foliage and waited for the dragoons to catch up. They'd only been caught once, a few months ago. Jenny had escaped with her life that time, but there were several others who hadn't been as lucky. King George, the usurper, had sent his dragoons to apprehend anyone with sympathies to Prince Charles Stuart, the rightful heir to the Kingdom of Great Britain. King George had given Charles the moniker the Young Pretender, and his father, the Old Pretender.

Prince Charlie's father, King James, had named him Regent of Great Britain, and regent was the name under which she and other Jacobite supporters were bent on returning the prince to the throne. King George would be tossed back to Germany where he had been born and raised and should have remained.

Despite the brightness of tonight's moon that allowed them a good view of the road, the brambles and pines were thick, veiling her and her men's massive horses from their enemies. When the first half dozen redcoats rode past, they did not see the Scots hidden just a few feet away. They barely slowed, too busy chasing phantoms.

As soon as they passed, Jenny and her men let out a collective sigh, only to freeze as several more dragoons rounded the bend and headed right for them. Eyes wide as the moon above, she watched them advance. The gold buttons on their muted red coats glinted in the moonlight, as did the muzzles of their muskets, their pistols, and the hilts of the thin swords at their hips.

Their dress was so different from that of the Scots. They wore starched white breeches, where her men were allowed freedom of movement in their plaids. Stiff tricorns covered their heads, while the Scots wore soft woolen caps that were broad and flat on the top. When Scots were feeling particularly rebellious, they pinned white rosette cockades on them in support of the Stuart line.

The redcoat leader issued an unintelligible order, and for a second, she thought the dragoon was staring right at her. Would he order his men into the forest? Her lungs burned for air, but she couldn't risk even the tiniest sound be heard by these bloodthirsty monsters.

She touched her pistol, prepared to shoot if needed, but then he was pointing and shouting for his men to continue down the road. Jenny watched them kick their horses into a gallop, clouds of dust following in their wake.

Only once the dust settled did Jenny allow herself a moment to exhale. Despite the risk she was taking every time she came out here, there was no way she'd stop her nightly missions. The fate of the entire Mackintosh clan was now Jenny's responsibility. She would not let her brother's betrayal destroy her clan.

Which was exactly why, on this night—while her brother was busy with his nose up an Englishman's arse—she found herself a few miles from an English garrison and several hours from home.

For three generations, her people had been trying to reclaim their country. Jenny, along with all the other Jacobites, had a restless need to do something to aid in bringing the rightful heir home to Scotland. Soon there would be a war, and she knew on which side she'd stand—with Bonnie Prince Charlie, the regent of Scotland. She'd made a vow a lifetime ago, it seemed, to support the Stuart line, and she planned to keep it—to follow in her father's and grandfather's footsteps and honor the warriors who had died for the Jacobite cause. Even if it meant going sword to sword with her brother in battle, a notion that made her stomach sour. At least she was faster and more agile than he was and had bested him more than once in the past because of that.

"We should turn back, my lady."

Jenny glowered at the shadowy figure on the mount beside her. Her cousin Dirk was always with her on these nightly raids. "What did I tell ye about calling me my lady when we're out?" She glanced back at the road, her hand on her pistol, ready to strike should a redcoat suddenly leap out in front of her.

"Apologies, Mistress J."

Jenny couldn't help but smile at the affectionate moniker her people had given her. It took away her title of lady and also didn't give away her given name, keeping her identity shrouded in secrecy. It'd only been a few months since she'd taken up her most sacred duty, and in that time, she'd gained a reputation as a leader.

"We canna go back now," Jenny said. "My brother will return any day now, and there is every chance Hamish will allow the English to billet at Cnàmhan Broch. That'll be a death sentence for me, for ye, and for all loyal to the true and rightful Scottish king." Jenny shuddered at the thought of dozens of redcoats flooding her family's castle.

The bastards had already done enough damage.

Dirk shifted uneasily in his seat. "Aye, but—"

"Cousin, ye grew up with me," Jenny interrupted, running her fingertips over the initials carved into the hilt of her broadsword: JM—Jon Mackintosh. Her voice grew hoarse with emotion. "Ye were beside me listening to all the tales of our clansmen fighting for the Jacobites." Both her father and her uncle had joined the rebellion some thirty years before. Labeled traitors, they had been hunted down and eventually executed by English loyalists and their Scottish supporters when she was still a young lass. "We have to honor them."

Dirk sighed, his shoulders slumping slightly. It was the same conversation they'd had many times. "But not by getting yourself killed. Ye ken the danger of being so near the Sassenach garrison." Dirk grumbled something that sounded a lot like he was warding off the devil, a sentiment echoed by the four men grumbling behind him.

Jenny couldn't blame them. The English dragoons were known for their brutality. Raping, pillaging, and destroying anything on a whim. That was precisely why she had to stand against her brother. How could she wait idly by and let him consign his people to a lifetime of terror? He might have pledged his loyalty to the King George loyalists, but that didn't mean the bloody devils would ever treat them as equals.

"If we're caught, Mistress, they'll not hesitate to shoot us."

Jenny inhaled deeply through her nose. The dragoons had been searching for her for going on two years now, and what Dirk said was true. Even still, she put on a confident front. "We'll just pretend we're looking for a wee one gone missing. They canna fault us for being out late in search of a bairn." They'd used that tactic before.

Dirk nodded, but the air was thick with unspoken words. She knew he wanted tonight's recruitment to come to an end, but she was the leader of these warriors, and she would make that call when she was ready. And something in her gut told her it was not yet the right moment.

"One more village." Dirk rubbed his fingers over his jaw. "But if there is any danger…"

"We'll turn back, I promise."

"We trust ye, Jenny. And we believe in the cause as much as ye do," Dirk reassured her.

If her brother had any idea what she was doing, at best she'd be locked in a dungeon, and at worst she'd be hanging from the ramparts for the crows to eat. The soldiers would suffer certain death, and her mother would be devastated. Already her son's betrayal was enough to have her mother take to her bed and rarely come out.

"I'll never be able to thank ye enough." She reached over and patted Dirk on the shoulder and then eyed the men behind them. "And when the regent is on the throne, we'll see that every risk was worth it."

"Ye needna thank us for being loyal Scots," Dirk said.

"Aye," the four men murmured in unison.

Jenny straightened in her saddle, the creak of the leather mingling with the sounds of insects and the distant birds of prey. "All the same, I'm grateful to have ye by my side. The prince regent will land in Scotland in less than a month. The more soldiers we can gather, the more coin and weapons we present him, the better."

She glanced at Dirk and then the men behind him. In addition to the other two Mackintosh warriors, tonight they'd only gathered two new recruits—the lowest number of any night since she'd started a few months before. And the coin they'd gathered was barely enough to buy a meat pie and ale at the local tavern.

The last village she wanted to visit tonight happened to be closest to the English garrison. Most of the men and women who lived there had been treated cruelly by the soldiers. There had to be at least half a dozen men she could sway to the cause, if for no other reason than the fresh rounds of arrests that had taken place just that morning.

Jenny returned her attention to the road. Not a single redcoat had passed in at least a half hour. "Are ye ready?"

"Lead the way, Mistress."

Jenny grinned, excitement thrumming in her veins. She had no doubt she was doing the right thing. Soon she'd be bowing before the regent, a leader who could oust the English from Scotland for good. And then she'd look into her brother's eyes, and instead of executing him for his betrayal, she'd sway him back to the cause. Wishful thinking, aye.

For now, she needed to focus on what lay ahead. The risks she took could get her killed, and yet she seized them boldly. Fear had no place in a rebellion. Well, perhaps that wasn't entirely true. But one had to master their fear. And if there was one thing she'd been good at since she was a bairn, it was taking control over anything that scared her.

"We ride." Jenny took the reins in both hands as she nudged her heel into her mount's flank.

———————

"Bloody hell," Toran Fraser muttered under his breath.

It was nearing midnight as he stood in the center of the English garrison's courtyard, working hard to hide his alarm. His cousin Archie stood among the condemned. The men had been dragged behind horses, hands shackled in front of them, and in the torch-light it was clear they'd been viciously beaten. Each of them was still dressed in his traditional Highland attire—kilts, shirts, waist-coats, boots. But they'd been stripped of their weapons.

And in mere moments, they'd be stripped of their lives. This was not what was supposed to happen. Aye, he'd intended for the rebels to be caught...but executed? He'd been naive to believe Boyd when he'd said he'd use the men to extort information. Served him right for trusting a bloody Englishman.

Of course Archie recognized Toran. The surprise and hope in his gaze quickly turned to outright disgust when he realized that Toran was standing beside the very English Captain Thomas Boyd.

Toran shifted uneasily. He, too, wore a kilt in Fraser colors. Boyd believed him a loyal deserter, taking up the position his father had vacated upon death, but understood Toran had to play the part of a Scotsman to gather information to hand over. Even so, if Archie let slip that he'd just spoken with Toran about Boyd's plan to trap the rebels, then he'd have a lot of explaining to do to the English captain. It was a careful line to walk—having betrayed one allegiance meant that his new one would always be suspicious, and with good reason.

But family was family despite allegiances. Toran followed in his father's footsteps, solidly on the side of King George's government, while some of his family had chosen to support the Young Pretender, Prince Charles.

Toran had cautioned Archie to stay out of the rebels' planned break-in, refusing to relay how he knew of Boyd's plan. His cousin had obviously ignored his warnings. Maybe Archie had not believed him, or maybe he'd warned the men that it was a trap, and they'd devised a new foolish plan. It didn't matter. The English had won this fight.

Bloody hell!

The only reason that his cousin was imprisoned at all was due to the information Toran had seeded for the rebels, who believed him to be one of them, about the garrison's weaknesses.

Archie was knocked to his knees by a boot to the back of the leg. His gaze never left Toran, silently declaring him a traitor to his country and his own family. Could Toran really stand there and watch his cousin be hanged?

Disgust at himself made Toran's insides burn. He cleared his throat. The knot of his neckerchief grew tighter and tighter, cutting off his air supply. Never once since he'd made his choice had Toran regretted dancing on this double-edged sword. His mother had been sacrificed by Jacobite rebels she'd trusted. How could Toran *not* try to seek vengeance in her name?

But now, watching Archie face death at English hands, his choice looked more and more like a foolish one.

Captain Boyd paced in front of the condemned. "You have all

been charged with treason for betraying King George, your rightful monarch. Do you confess?"

Not one man opened his mouth, and a prickle of pride slid along Toran's spine.

Boyd appeared surprised at the silence. "Then you are all sentenced to hang by the neck until dead. The sentence shall be exacted…" He checked his pocket watch as if trying to determine a time and then said, "Why wait? Let's do it right now."

Toran grimaced. Archie's gaze never left his, and if one could be killed by a glower, then Toran would be lying in a bloody heap. Hell, he would deserve it.

Captain Boyd turned his gaze toward Toran and the other men standing beside him—some Scots, some English, but all known supporters of the English throne.

Toran cleared his throat. "Captain, if I may?"

Boyd narrowed his eyes, probably never having been interrupted during one of his sentencings before. Depending on the man's mood, Toran could very well end up on his knees beside his cousin.

"What is it?" Obvious irritation dripped from Boyd's words.

"I recognize that one." He pointed at Archie. "Might I take him inside for questioning?"

Boyd raised a brow. "You think he knows something?"

"Aye." This was a lie, and Toran was acting as fast as he could to save Archie from death. While he wished he could save them all, that was impossible. Even this hasty plan could fall awry. There was a very high probability that they were both going to die tonight, but at least he'd go to his maker knowing he'd done the right thing.

"Fine. But as soon as you get what you need, bring him back out here to be dealt with."

Dealt with, like rubbish in need of disposal. The sour taste in Toran's mouth grew stronger. After what he was about to do, he'd not be safe anywhere near the English. He'd be labeled a traitor, and the bounty on his head would likely be enough for even his own mother to turn him in, God rest her soul. Hell, he'd not be safe near the Scots either.

Boyd flicked his hand, dismissing Toran, who walked over to Archie and yanked him up by his shackled arms.

"Dinna say a word," Toran warned quietly against Archie's ear.

"Where are ye taking me?" Archie shouted, ignoring Toran's request.

"If ye want to live, ye'll shut your trap," Toran warned once more, then nodded to Boyd. He half-dragged, half-carried his cousin back into the garrison, once a well-fortified Scots castle, the tenants long since evicted. Archie had been badly beaten, both lips split, one eye swollen shut, and a cut above his forehead that dripped down his face. An odd bump on his arm hinted at the broken bone beneath. He didn't know if Archie wasn't walking properly because of an injury, obstinacy, or exhaustion. And there was no time to figure it out.

Toran dragged Archie through a musty corridor dimly lit by a few torches. He nodded to the guards they passed, praying that no one asked questions.

"What are ye doing?" Archie asked. "Ye want to kill me yourself?"

"Keep quiet," Toran ordered.

"I'll not."

Toran pushed his cousin against the wall beneath a torch so Archie could see his eyes. Manhandling his cousin appeared to be the only way to get his attention. He gripped the front of Archie's shirt and leaned in close to whisper. "I'm getting ye out of here. A task that will cost us both our lives if ye dinna shut your mouth and listen."

Archie's one working eye widened, and then he nodded in understanding.

Toran dragged him up a set of dark stairs, pausing to listen every half dozen or so, and then hurrying his cousin as much as possible considering the shackles. At the top of the stairs, he tossed his cousin over his shoulder—not an easy feat since Archie was nearly as tall and easily just as full of muscle. He whispered prayers up to a God he wasn't certain would listen, given his many sins.

But at last he found the door he was looking for, one that led to nowhere.

"This will hurt," Toran cautioned. "We're at least fifteen feet in the air, and once we land, they'll be able to smell us for miles."

"What?" Archie didn't sound convinced by his plan.

"There's no time. 'Tis the only way. Are ye ready?"

"Aye."

Toran didn't hesitate but leapt, arms around his cousin, into the rubbish pile below. They landed with a thud and a disturbing squish.

Archie groaned. Toran ignored the jolt of pain in his back from the landing. "Come on, we've not much time before Boyd tries to find out where we've gone. He'll send out every man with a pistol he's got to shoot us on sight."

Archie rose to his knees, gagging at the scent.

"There's no time to retch. We've got to run." His hands under his cousin's arms, Toran hauled him to standing, thanking the heavens the men had not been shackled at the ankles.

"Have ye a key for these?" Archie asked, holding out his hands.

"Nay, and I've had to leave my horse behind. Damned fine horse, too." Thankfully anything incriminating he always kept on his person, sewn into the lining of his waistcoat—close to his heart, rather than with his mount.

"Thank ye, Cousin."

"Thank me later. Now run."

Grabbing hold of Archie's elbow, he dragged him out of the muck. They ran without looking back, keeping to the woods and hiding behind boulders to catch their breath. Toran had learned over his years of espionage that looking back only got a man killed.

They ran for a mile or two following a familiar path, one Toran often took from the garrison to Fraser lands. Any other night he would have been glad for the fullness of the moon to light the way. But tonight he knew it gave them away, two hunched figures running for their lives.

Archie stumbled over pebbles, roots, his own feet, often falling to his knees, and Toran continued to lift him up.

"I canna, Cousin. Go on without me." Archie sank to the ground, defeated.

"I didna save ye from the English only to let ye die on the road." Toran scanned the moors, waiting for the shadows of their pursuers to make themselves known. "We've got to get this muck off us. Boyd's dogs will be following the scent."

Archie lifted his head. "Ye're no' going to leave me?"

"Of course no'. Where's your Fraser ballocks? Come on."

Archie mustered the strength to stand, but they weren't going to be moving very fast. Thankfully, the sound of rushing water filtered from ahead. "Hurry, we're close to the river."

Less than five minutes later, they were at the river's edge. The glossy black depths reflected the moon and a sprinkle of stars. Holding onto Archie's arm, Toran pulled him into the chilly water.

"Ye didna drag me all this way just to see me drown, did ye?" Archie asked.

Toran chuckled, feeling the weight of his kilt increase as water soaked into the wool. The river bottom sucked at his boots, but he waded in until they were waist deep. That was where the river bottom went out beneath them, and he had to swim the rest of the way across with his cousin in his grasp. "I'd not have risked my own arse only to drown ye in a river."

Once on the other side, Toran wrung out their kilts and shirts, dumped the water from their boots, and used the sharp tip of his *sgian dubh* to fiddle with the locks on the shackles, but the small dagger wasn't narrow enough to fit.

He pulled the pin from his neckerchief and despite the dark was able to use it to free his cousin from the chains, which he tossed into the water.

Archie's teeth chattered. "I dinna know how much further I can go."

"Only a little more," Toran said.

He had no idea where to take his cousin, but he did know staying this close to Boyd was a death sentence.

Dressed again, they continued on their way. Though it was summer, the night air was cool, chilling their sodden clothes and shoes. Another thirty minutes or so passed while Archie's gait continued to slow. Toran led his cousin to a good hiding spot behind a thick boulder that shielded them from view.

"We'll rest here a mo—" But he cut himself off at the sound of a stick breaking.

Toran jerked around. Suddenly, figures melted out from the shadows. Scots, but in the dark and dressed as they were, he couldn't make out what clan they hailed from. At the center of the five men stood a lass. Aye, she wore trews and had her hair up under a cap, wisps of golden strands peeking through, but there was no hiding the curves beneath her shirt and waistcoat. In the moonlight filtering through the trees, she looked bonnie—high, arching cheekbones, a mouth that puckered into a frown. But what struck him most was the spark of fire in her gaze. Her eyes reflected the light of the moon, almost making her look like she was glowing.

And the muzzle of her pistol was pointed right at him. Outlaws... Of all the bloody luck. He reached for his own pistol tucked into his belt.

"Dinna move," the lass said. Her voice was throaty, sensual. "Else I put a bullet through your heart."

A slow grin formed on Toran's face. "What's to say I won't put a bullet in yours first?"

The lass looked down at Archie and then flicked her gaze back to his. "Ye're outnumbered. Let's say ye were willing to pull your weapon before I took my shot, and then ye were to waste your bullet, there'd be five more cutting through ye before ye were able to see the result." Again, she looked at Archie. "And your friend doesna seem like he will be much help."

"We're verra close to the English garrison, lass. Any shot ye make will be a beacon to the dragoons lurking about. And trust me, there are hundreds of them headed this way as we speak."

"Is that so?" She glanced at Archie once more. "A prison break? So ye two are rebels, aye?"

Toran didn't answer. Let her come to her own conclusions.

"We have horses." She kept her gaze on his, and he had the intense urge to draw closer. "Ye and your friend can have one when we return to my camp—for a price. Why not donate your coin to the cause and join us? We've a need for more rebels."

Toran did not want to join her. Now, if she'd asked him to join her for some mutual warmth under a plaid, that would be another story. Then again, she had a point about the bullets. And he truly did not want to die.

"I'm guessing from your current circumstances ye are in need of a helping hand, sir." Her voice was smooth, even melodic, but still filled with authority. And considering that she was the one speaking, she certainly gave the impression that she was the one in charge. Fascinating.

A group of men led by a woman? Not a common thing and intensely intriguing. Whoever she was, she had ballocks as full of steel as his own. And if he weren't trapped in the woods with her, a hundred redcoats on his tail, he might have asked her to join him for a dram.

"Who are ye?" Toran asked.

A soft laugh escaped her, and her hand waved dismissively. "Not yet, sir. Ye'll have to prove yourself first."

Prove himself? He gritted his teeth. "All right, we'll join ye." There really was no other choice. He and Archie needed a quick escape, and her horse would provide that. Just because he was taking her up on the offer now didn't mean he had to stick it out. In fact, as soon as he could, he'd steal the horse and somehow get Archie back to Fraser lands where he could make certain the rest of his family was safe from Boyd.

"Good." She nodded to Dirk. "Search them for weapons, and then help the wounded man onto your horse."

Toran stood still for the inspection, gritting his teeth as his weapons were removed. "I've said we'd join ye. Why then are ye treating me like a prisoner?"

The lass cocked her head to the side, a slight grin curling her upper lip. "We must first see that ye are trustworthy." With an added challenge echoing in her words, she said, "Ye can ride with me. And dinna try any tricks, else ye find yourself verra dead."

The lass didn't beat around the bush, and there was no hint of humor in her tone at all. She meant what she said.

Toran climbed onto the back of her horse, his cold, wet body flush to her warmer, dry back. Beneath the icy exterior was a lass full of lush curves. *Mo chreach...* Good heavens, but she felt good. Hesitantly, he placed an arm around her waist.

She shuddered. "Blast, but ye're soaked," she hissed. "Ye should have warned me. And ye smell like the devil's own chamber pot."

Toran chuckled. "A hazard of escape, lass."

Her back straightened, and she leaned forward, away from him. "Ye can call me Mistress J."

Mistress J? Why did that sound familiar?

"And ye are?" she urged.

"I'm called Toran," he said slowly as realization struck him. The night had taken a very interesting turn. For he was holding onto the woman he suspected might be responsible for his mother's death.

Acknowledgments

As always, I must thank my incredible family. They are my rocks! During the writing of this book, we had to endure one of the hardest times of all of our lives, a pandemic that left all three of my children out of school and my amazing husband stuck overseas. But because of their positivity and support, I was able to pour love onto the pages of this book. I am extremely grateful to them for their unwavering support, their love of baking, and endless rounds of Monopoly and charades. Thank you to my agent, Kevan Lyon, for believing in me and being my pillar. Many thanks to the team at Sourcebooks, especially my editor Deb Werksman, for their excitement about the series and continued support. And last but never least, a shoutout to the most incredible writer friends a gal could have who helped me plot, read pages, offered advice, traveled with me for research, and handed me glasses of wine. Listed in no particular order: Andrea Snider, Brenna Ash, Madeline Martin, Lori Ann Bailey, Christi Barth, and my #MorningWriterChicks. Dreams happen when we believe in ourselves and persist no matter what. We are stronger than we think.

About the Author

Eliza Knight is an award-winning and *USA Today* bestselling author of over fifty sizzling historical romances. Under the name E. Knight, she's known for riveting tales that cross landscapes around the world. Her love of history began as a young girl when she traipsed the halls of Versailles and ran through the fields in Southern France. While not reading, writing, or researching her latest book, she chases after her three children. In her spare time (if there is such a thing...) she likes daydreaming, wine tasting, traveling, hiking, staring at the stars, watching movies, shopping, and visiting with family and friends. She lives atop a small mountain with her own knight in shining armor, three princesses, and two very naughty Newfies.

Visit Eliza at elizaknight.com or her historical blog History Undressed: historyundressed.com.